Bleed the Earth

Book 2 of the

Blood Wild Chronicles

Tamara A. Brigham

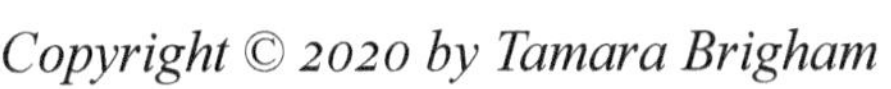

Cover Design by: Tamara Brigham

Published by:
Tamara Brigham
PO Box 151
Clearlake, CA 95422

Printed and bound in the United States of America

First Edition

ISBN # 978-1-7336708-4-5

ര*ര

For Wanda...

...I think you would have enjoyed these.

ര*ര

Prologue

"Jia!"

The leap through the plate glass and the catapult jump from the narrow stone and metal wall ended too near a small ambling herd of grubbers that Kato had not anticipated to find roaming the streets so near the Fortress. Though Fela grace allowed him to twist mid-air, to avoid the reach of their black clawing nails and gnashing, rotted teeth, he lost his grip on the small woman he carried as he did so. Unexpected as the grubbers' presence was, unexpected as the leap and fall were, Jia's effort to roll in a direction away from the unforeseen threat resulted in a startling crash against broken concrete blocks placed for some building project that had yet to begin. Her eyes grew wide for the briefest of moments at the shock of pain, and then her vision went dark.

Kato heard that sound above those of the falling rain and the distant rumble of thunder, above the wailing sirens within the walls of the compound from which they had just escaped, above the moans and growls of the ever-hungry grubbers as they turned to shuffle towards an immobile fresh source of food.

It was the cracking sound when she hit, more than the alarms, which chilled Kato and filled him with panic.

Please don't let her be dead, his frantic thoughts cried to any force in the universe that might hear such pleas.

The grubbers, lured by the tang of new blood, targeted the unmoving woman, provoking a Fela roar. The sound did not distract the putrid things from their pursuit; they did not recognize the sound as a warning, saw no need to turn when there was a meal nearby. None reacted beyond screeches of frustration and a continuing effort to reach the woman as the man-beast ripped through them with great clawed strength, throwing each one aside like weightless dolls.

He was not interested in killing grubbers tonight. If they died, they died. Technically, they were dead already. He was only interested in getting to Jia, making sure she was alive, making sure she stayed that way by getting her away from the increasing number and volume of shouts and thundering boots behind the Fortress wall.

There was no time, however, to check her injuries, to check for sure signs of life. Kato scooped her limp body into his furry arms, leaped over a rusted, twisted length of ancient chain-link fence erected behind the blocks, and disappeared into a structure that might have been under new construction, under renovation, or in the midst of decay like so much else in the world. It was the nearest haven to be had, some place to pause long enough to gain his bearings and make a snap-judgment plan, and the Fela was going to use it, and any other means necessary, to keep Jia safe.

Chapter 1

The disorder in the infirmary was the last thing Lowell noticed when he burst through the door with enough force to make it crash and splinter against the wall behind it. The first thing to catch his eye was Quentin sprawled awkwardly on the floor between the two occupied gurneys, but that detail received no more than a glance before the booted feet visible beneath the toppled cabinet flagged his attention.

"Jonni! Son!"

On the gurney nearest the corridor window, Nik squeezed his eyes closed, his heart hammering, the young man making a resolute effort to normalize his breathing so that no one noticed he was awake.

The man who entered directly behind the Laedan, however, picked up every screaming detail in the room…and many subtler ones that few others would initially notice. Nik's eyes, closed a little too tightly for him to be sleeping, the strained rise and fall of his chest, the rapid quivering of the vein at the side of his neck. The position and angle of the iron mediservice tray in proximity to Thomas Quentin's bleeding skull. Gouges and darkening bruises on Quentin's arms that, from the spacing and depth, suggested an altercation with a Fela…the only Fela known, by the mage at least, to be in the Fortress tonight. The ripple across the man's exposed flesh and the briefest shimmer at his fingertips that suggested a truth Vance had not noted in previous meetings with the Laedan's adjunct. The indentation in the cabinet doors visible only when Lowell pushed the unit upright off Jonni's body that spoke of a shove of great force. The caved-in appearance of Jonni's chest that proved the point of impact…a point that spread across his ribcage in a path the size of a large man's forearm.

He looked again at the bruises spreading across Quentin's arm.

Scents in the air: Jia's, Kato's, Nik's, Jonni's, Quentin's and Roland's. Poison. Death. The window shattered outward that allowed the night air and rain to blow in and left little glass on the floor of the room…but would, he knew, have left plenty on the ground below.

So she had escaped.

That eased the sick sensation burning in the back of Vance's throat, but not enough to erase the desire for a strong, numbing drink.

Roland Marrock again. There was blood around his mouth, trails of it dribbling from the corners down his flushed but slowly greying cheeks into his hair. The distress in the man's open, bloodshot eyes. Eyes that Vance believed had seen what had happened here. Eyes that knew the truth even in death.

Vance edged closer to touch Roland's face, to see what he had seen and felt his foot touch down softly over the unseen, fallen syringe.

Lowell began to wail. On the gurney, Nik forced his eyes open, groggily as if from recent waking, knowing he could not feign sleep through that sound…a sound that could only mean one thing. He pushed up weakly on one elbow to confirm the cause of his father's distress, the rapidness of his breathing cut off by Lowell rocking back and forth with Jonni in his arms.

The door opened again.

Something gripped tight around Vance's ankle.

His hand never made it to Marrock's face.

"Laedan?"

Thank the stars, Vance thought with a groan as he looked at the bleeding man pulling himself up to sitting with the help of the mage's leg. Chief Ernest had arrived.

"Someone killed my son!"

Nik's pasty features grew a horror-stricken, ashen shade of pale.

"Someone?" Ernest began again. He was no mage. There were too many details in this room to take in at a cursory glance. But he was an experienced Protector, and some of the details were difficult to miss.

Vance cleared his throat of the bile and frustration burning the there and murmured, "And Laedan Marrock as well…"

"Fela…" rasped Quentin from the floor, clutching the back of his head where blood came away on his fingers. He raised his face long enough to cast a brief glance at Nik, bitter and threatening, before wiping the blood on the front of his torn shirt. Nik, staring at his brother's limp body, did not notice.

Jonni…the best Channon of them all.

Vance, however, did notice Quentin's glance and the twitching at the corners of Nik's mouth. He wondered, as he offered his hand to assist Quentin to his feet, what Nik knew.

Allowing Jonni's body to drop with a little more callousness then intended, Lowell lurched up to test the veracity of the mage's claim. Disbelieving a mage was often futile, foolish, but Roland had been reported dead once before, only to return to haunt him this very day.

Was it honestly true?

Was Roland dead?

"What do you mean Fela?" asked Ernest.

There were men in uniform now, men with shockers and metal cuffs and what few guns existed legally in LaGuardia, pushing through the doorway behind the chief. Some watched the men in the room, another crossed to the window and stared into the courtyard below. Two women stood in the corridor, gazing through the glass in horror and dismay and curiosity…and one with a heartbroken expression as Lowell's words echoed in her head.

Jonni. Dead.

They could not enter the room past the uniforms and neither of them wanted to. Where they stood was close enough.

The cold, brief look of contempt cast at Vance's offered hand, and Quentin's refusal to accept assistance, were no surprise. If there was any chance that what Vance had witnessed and perceived was correct, it was expected that Quentin would refuse contact to hide his secrets, what he was, what he had witnessed, as long as possible.

Around the sneer, Quentin groaned. "He was here, the stranger who arrived with the Marrocks."

"Arrived with…" started Ernest. "Why would…?"

On his feet now, having used Roland's gurney to pull himself up while resisting touching the dead man's dangling arm, Quentin continued with a moan of distress, "How the shart should I know? But he was here! I tried to stop him…and then Jia…and Jonni…he hit me with the tray…that's the last thing I remember! He must have taken her! Probably killed her too."

His speech was forcibly disjointed, more, Vance heard, from the mental gymnastics of redirecting suspicion than by emotional or physical duress. Again, there was a flash of his gaze towards Nik, again unnoticed by anyone other than the mage. Quentin moved away, beyond Vance's reach, and though Vance contemplated the wisdom of charging at him, making physical contact to get a reading of his thoughts and memories, Ernest stepped between them to get a better look at Roland himself thus cutting Vance off.

The mage would have to get his reading some other way.

Filing the details away for later consideration, Vance squatted, intending to pick up both the metal tray and the syringe still hidden beneath his carefully placed foot. This time, however, despite Ernest's hand that reached to catch and draw him up by the shoulder, Lowell's sharp, anxious voice interrupted his search for evidence.

"Segara, I want the truth of what happened here."

"He's a tracker," protested Quentin, his words underpinning the desperation in his voice as he gawked at Lowell. He touched the back of his head and grimaced as if the pain had worsened. "He should be hunting the murderer! He should be rescuing Jia!"

Nik's countenance twisted with confusion and doubt, a look the middle Channon son…now the oldest Channon son, realized was a mirror of the mage's expression as Vance stood up, seemingly empty-handed though his fist was curled closed. With no love lost between Quentin and Jia, his sudden interest in her welfare was suspect.

Jia killing her beloved father was about as likely as the perpetual clouds suddenly dissipating to reveal whatever lay behind them, about as likely as the world becoming again what it had once been, about as likely as all of the grubbers in the boroughs suddenly dropping dead.

Lowell may have heard that incongruous connection too, but his focus was elsewhere. He scowled, one shaking hand splayed across Roland's chest, and muttered, "Segara is the best mage…"

"Exactly why he should be out there, not in here! If anyone can find them, he can! I'll tell Chief Ernest everything I know, everything I saw, everything I remember…but the mage should be out there."

Ernest and Vance exchanged a look. Ernest suspected that the mage had already made a preliminary evaluation of the crime scene, the room, though he had not, as far as the chief knew, touched anything important within it. Segara was the best chance of learning the truth in this room and the participants in it, but Quentin was right too; he was also the best hope they had for tracking down the Fela and young woman potentially responsible for this dual homicide.

At the very least, Ernest knew the pair were in danger if they were innocent, and Segara finding them might be their only hope of surviving the impending manhunt.

He could read suspicion on his Protector's face, could see that something in this room, in the story told, did not sit easily on the mage's mind. If, by any stroke of luck, the Marrock girl and her Fela friend were innocent, Vance finding them was also the only chance there was of learning their truths…before the Laedan's private forces found her and erased any conflicting stories.

Whatever evidence Ernest and his man gathered from this room…and he intended to be overly thorough in this investigation, he would save it for Vance to read later. He would have the room quarantined too, insist on it, so that Vance could further examine it upon his return.

Ernest could make the order, but it seemed most prudent to leave the call in the Laedan's hands. In those several tense moments, punctuated by the shrieking sirens and the shouts of men in the halls and Fortress courtyards, Lowell's hand fell from Roland's chest so that he could return to Jonni. He sank to the floor, deflated, dejected amidst the rubble of cabinet contents spewed across the room, and cradled his lifeless son against his chest. No one knew if the gesture, and the accompanying tears, were real or part of some elaborate show.

If they were real, Nik thought bitterly, collapsing onto his side on the cot with a shudder and tears of his own, staring at his brother's unmoving face, they were probably the only honest tears Lowell had ever shed for any of his sons since the day each was born.

Eventually, in a voice more broken then commanding, Lowell mumbled, "Find them, Segara. Do whatever you have to. Everything I have is at your disposal. Bring them to me…alive. Ernest, scour this room…find every detail. Every secret. I want the truth. I want to know why. I want whoever did this…" He hesitated long enough to brush Jonni's blonde hair from his forehead. "I want them to suffer. I want them to pay."

Chapter 2

The risk of remaining above ground, holed up in a crumbling ruin anywhere in the streets of the borough immediately surrounding LaGuardia's Fortress far outweighed the risk of entering the water-soaked tunnels that spread beneath the collapsing city. Fela eyes did not require a torch or lantern as soon as any human would in order to find their way into the dim shafts, and it seemed, in his Fela form, that the Unders had little interest in troubling him and no more than a passing interest in the woman he protectively carried. He did not venture far, only deep enough into the first channel to locate an alcove at the fringes of the hooded can fire's glow around which the collection of Unders gathered to roast rats and possums on metal skewers. The alcove he chose was littered with the remains of stained, rotting bedding and discarded food containers. A squatter's shelter, he wagered, near enough to the rusted fire can to enjoy marginal warmth and dim lighting, but distant enough from the entrance that outsiders would not likely pursue anyone daring enough to shelter here, far enough to be out of the immediate reach of wind and rain. It was also distant enough from the fire that the figures with milky pale skin and shimmering eyes were not likely to deem them a threat.

When he ducked into the nook with his precious burden, the Unders who watched went back to feasting and let the pair be.

Kato gambled, as he set Jia gently on the bit of ground he uncluttered with his foot, and then pulled off his now torn, rain-soaked shirt to use as a poor excuse for a covering, that the Laedan's men would not come here, would not challenge the Unders or think he and Jia were desperate enough to do likewise. He gambled that the Unders would not betray their position.

They had no reason to do so.

Only now that he had stopped running, now that the danger was diminished and he had a chance to catch his breath, did he take the opportunity to examine Jia. There was visible damage to her head where it had struck the ground, but the bleeding was slight and her breathing and pulse were slow, steady, normal, the way it always sounded to him except in her moments of exertion. Her left ankle felt swollen, as though she had twisted it during the fall, and though her body reflexively flinched when he touched it, she did not wake.

It was the fact that she did not wake that troubled him.

Given time, he could find his way with her back to the protection of the Pack on the far side of Flushing Wilds. He did not know the path, but he believed her scent, Addi and Deuce's scents, would linger in places where the overgrowth of trees and bushes had protected it from the washing efforts of the rain. But the need to evade their pursuers, whoever they might be, would make the flight difficult, and the odds were, if he carried the wounded Alpha into their midst, the Pack would turn on him, possibly killing him and Vanya. At the very least, they would expel the Fela and his sister from their company. He doubted they would give him the opportunity to explain, and if they did hear him, there was no guarantee they would believe him…or welcome him back.

Besides, Jia's father was still in that vast compound, and despite what she had said, what she believed, Kato had no proof that Roland was dead. There had not been enough time, in those moments of chaos and conflict, for him to assess the truth with his own senses. Perhaps, in her distress, she had overreacted to Roland's condition. Perhaps, once they had escaped, the medistaff arrived and reversed whatever harm had been done to her father.

There was a chance, a hope, however slim, that Roland lived.

Kato did not know the fate of Jonni Channon either. He did not know about the one called Quentin. Nor did he care. He had not killed anyone, carried no blame or guilt for the possibilities of their deaths. Neither man meant anything to him. He only cared about the impact such deaths would have on Jia. Why he and Jia were being pursued, he was not sure, but it did not occur to him that someone would try to pin false accusations on them.

No, Jia would not want to leave. Not until she knew her father's fate. Not until she had the opportunity to get him out from behind those walls alive or dead. As long as she was unconscious, Kato did not feel he should take her further away from her father. It would be best to wait for her eyes to open, wait for her to tell him what she wanted.

But minutes ticked by, cold and damp and silent except for the distant drip of water, muted sounds from the outside world, and the growl and mumble of the Unders as they ate. Hours crept past, dragging the world deeper into night. Hours without the approach of Unders, guards, or far distant grubbers. Hours without food or water. Hours of night that would, he imagined, now be bleeding into dawn. He could not afford to sleep while Gia might need him, and though the tempest in his blood had diminished, allowing him to shift back to the form of a man, without adequate clothing to cover himself for warmth, without the reassurance of their safety, Kato was unable to relax. He needed the rest as surely as Jia did but would take none of it until she opened her eyes. Until he was certain she was alive and safe and could express her wishes about what she wanted him to do next.

Yiva did not have the emotional strength or will to protest Donn's arm about her shoulders as he led her from the infirmary where Jonni's misshapen corpse lay nude, except for a light cloth across his hips, on the gurney Nik had occupied not much earlier. Donn's anger could be felt in the press of his fingers, in the quick short steps they took, and she absently suspected that not even Oasis' hand held in his other hand, on his other side, was going to stay him if he gave in to rage and chose to lash out at one or both of them for an affront, for a situation, that neither had caused or contributed to.

Instead, his fury roiled within him like hot water in a kettle. Yiva feared for the victims of his wrath when it finally did erupt.

She tried hesitantly to make eye contact with the other woman, but Oasis stared straight ahead, her expression unreadable, as if neutrality was her only weapon against Donn's outrage.

At the broken exterior window, where glass inside crunched beneath his feet, and the glass in the courtyard below was being studied by one of Chief Ernest's Protectors, Lowell listened to his wife go, the shattered woman robbed of one son and denied the comfort of a husband whose tumultuous thoughts refused him any comfort to feel or to give. A brief glance over his shoulder connected his gaze with his wife's and afforded him another look at Nik, who had vacated the gurney for the dead and now sat beside it, resting his chin on the edge so that his face was mere inches from his brother's, staring with unnerving focus at Jonni's corpse. There were barrier boards across the door to deter anyone from entering, and as soon as a temporary infirmary was established, the gurneys and their contents would be taken away. Lowell imagined Nik had never seen death so closely before, at least not death like this. Whatever his thoughts and feelings were, Lowell did not expect he would ever know.

Of all of his son's, Nik was the biggest mystery.

"They must be disposed," murmured Quentin, leaning with his buttocks against the broken window frame, his arms crossed to hide the bruises and gashes as best he could, continuing to watch the Chief work his way around the room yet again, now that the medistaff had picked Jonni up from where he had fallen, examined the men on the gurneys, and officially pronounced both dead. Ernest had argued unsuccessfully to leave Jonni where he had fallen to better assess the crime scene, but Lowell would not permit it. His son deserved more respect than to be left on the floor like a discarded, unwanted thing.

He deserved to live. But that was no longer his fate.

"A forepath must be notified first," protested Ernest from near the doorway where he was assessing what anyone coming into the infirmary during the skirmish might have seen. "The causes of death must be determined before…"

"I think the cause is obvious," Quentin snorted with a hint of derision in his voice. "Jonni's ribs were…"

Wondering who that disdain was for, Lowell's hand on his arm prevented him from saying more. Lowell said nothing, only continued to watch the Protectors beneath the window.

"That may be…but we don't know the cause of Marrock's…" started Ernest again.

And again, Quentin interrupted. "He was wounded when they arrived; I'd say he succumbed to his injuries."

"You'd say? Then there was no murder?" Ernest made note of the tick and twitch at the corners of Quentin's mouth and eyes, as if his questions had struck a nerve, an unexpected source of irritation. "Whatever the cause, natural or not, for the record we need to know if there is one murder or two, and if two, how they were accomplished. We will only know that if…"

Quentin interrupted a third time. "We can't risk grubbers in the Fortress!"

Soft and strained, Lowell's offhanded words, spoken as if he had forgotten who else was in the room, dragged a chill like icy fingers up Ernest's spine. "If he's Cana…as you claim…that's not very likely, now is it?"

Quentin growled, huffed, and pursed his lips as if he had eaten something sour and distasteful. Only when it seemed that Ernest had made no obvious notice of the Laedan's statement did Quentin's expression return to something more neutral. "We can't take chances. Believe me…watching someone you love become…" He shuddered and scowled. "You don't want to see that, Lowell. Trust me. You don't want that to be the last memory you have of Jonni…"

A sigh of what sounded like capitulation was swallowed by the wind pushing through the broken exterior window. Thankfully, the sirens no longer blared, else Ernest doubted he would have heard the faint sound the Laedan made. Afraid that the man was going to give in to Quentin's persuasive prompting and deny the Protectorate, deny Segara, the chance to do their jobs, the chief said, "We move them to the basement. Surely you have a room there that can be secured for a short time…something cold…like a liquor storage? We won't need it long…just long enough to do our jobs. I'll put people to guard them, in case they turn before we have a chance to properly…"

"It's too big of a risk!"

"Mr. Quentin." Ernest's voice was terse, annoyed with the ongoing interruptions that felt like a dogged effort to keep him from doing his damn job. "Laedan, I can have my best forepath here in less than an hour. He can be done with his examinations in a day, two at the most, and it takes about three for a change…if there's going to be one. My people are trained to put grubbers down…if necessary. It's what we do. It will be clean and fast if it comes to that. No one in the Fortress will be at risk if they stay out of the way."

He might sound like he was begging, but they needed the truth. They all did. Lowell wanted it. Quentin's apparent rush to dispose of the bodies, of the evidence they might contain, could be out of a legitimate fear of grubbers in the Fortress, but Ernest had never thought Quentin to be a man prone to fear. Two grubbers, if the residents and staff were cautious and alert, would not be much of a threat. If there was some other reason, something else he was trying to hide, no matter how small or insignificant, Ernest wanted to know what it was.

With luck, Vance would return before their time expired to assess the dead for himself.

"Three days. That is all you have, Ernest. You will not defile my son, is that clear? Quentin, arrange a state event, a tribute, for Jonni."

Lowell turned from the window, crossed the room, and stared at Roland silently. Believing the man dead before had been convenient, a truth he had not needed to see, a weight lifted from his shoulders without any need to question blame or guilt or cause. Out of sight, out of mind. Seeing him now, the man he had grown up with, the best friend known all of his life, the reality of his death made Lowell feel sick.

He had not wanted this. Not really. He had just wanted his plans to proceed unimpeded. Wanted them to succeed for LaGuardia's sake.

Now it was too late to go back.

"And for my brother," he mumbled weakly, raking a hand through Roland's hair.

~*~

Having sent the Laedan's men in a variety of directions in pursuit of Jia and Kato, Vance proceeded alone. Too many people around him inhibited his senses, created bedlam in his head, made it difficult, often impossible, to do what he did best. If he worked with anyone, he worked with Sal.

And Sal was dead.

He scowled at the fresh memory set aside in the press of duty and shoved his hands into the pockets of his long, dark blue Protectorate coat. Alone it was.

Within the courtyard created by the Fortress's outer wall, after assessing the spray of shattered glass below the infirmary window, Vance went outside of the Fortress to gauge where the leaping pair could have landed. He made note of the four grubbers, moving still in their unliving state of perpetual hunger but impaled at awkward angles on a nearby fence, a low broken tree branch, a twisted bit of rebar, so that they would never again be ambulatory. There was nothing unusual about such a sight, as people fought with grubbers all the time, whenever they were found. While most fights ended with either the grubbers struck down or the human combatants killed and infected themselves, there were the occasional individuals who could not bring themselves to 'kill' what had once been a living person, who settled for immobilizing the things and leaving them to deteriorate wherever they happened to land.

It was not viewed as cruel. No matter what the grubbers had been in life, it was well-proven that they no longer felt emotion, pain, or anything beyond an all-consuming need to devour.

Vance did not think such mercy had been in play here. These grubbers had been attacked in haste and moved from the way without thought. And when his fingers trailed through traces of blood on the ground that the rain had not yet washed away, he saw Jia in that place, for the briefest of moments before the turmoil of growling grubbers and a burst of excruciating pain gave way to an abrupt lifting from the ground that ended the short vision in blackness.

Crouched in that spot, Vance studied every direction, every path, obvious or less so, that someone could have fled to escape pursuit. The streets, mostly cleared here as most were near the Fortress walls, would have been the most obvious routes. Any Normal would have taken one, left or right, knowing it would be easy for their pursuers to follow. They might have turned into the alleys between buildings, alleys also cleared, in the hopes of losing their hunters. With little time to spare between the moment of escape through that window and the pursuit of the Laedan's guards, taking the time to crawl over rubble, seek shelter in any one of these buildings, many of which were inhabited by Fortress staff, would have slowed them down.

But there, on the wire mesh that had once been a fence protecting a construction site, a site approved for building again according to the sign posted on the lattice, tufts of short, black fur had caught on the rust-red barbs, creating a marker that the guards, it seemed, had failed to notice as they ran further and further from the Fortress in their search. Surely, Vance mused, the Laedan's men were better trained than that, were at least as perceptive as the average Protector. It appeared they were not, however, and since none had commented on that clue to him, nor chose to pursue it, Vance chose to investigate that lead on his own.

It would be better this way.

No one could know, not Quentin, not Lowell, no one in the Laedan's hire, that Vance knew the prey he hunted. So long as no one learned that truth, he would not be required to compromise his position with either his new friend, if that was what Jia was, or his employers.

From the height of the fur tufts, Vance envisioned a third leap, like the one made from the infirmary onto, or over, the Fortress wall. Such leaps could not be made by Normals, not if they wanted to avoid injury. But a Fela and Cana, in their peculiar hybrid beast-animal form or as pure animal, would have found such a leap to be a simple thing.

Those forms increased the probable paths the pair could take.

Such as up and over the fence.

Slowly, touching everything he could reach, Vance picked up traces of their direction, their speed, the fact that there was only a single individual on foot. He retraced his steps twice, seeking an indication where Kato and Jia's paths might have diverged, but when he found none, the mage was left with the conclusion that Kato was carrying Jia. Injured, or perhaps not having had time to shift on her own. But surely not dead. The leap from the window, the wall, should not have killed an anthro, and there had been no traces at the original scene to suggest that the grubbers had killed anyone. Since the crash of glass had come moments before Vance and Lowell reached the infirmary, and there had been no burst of gunfire this evening, she would not have been injured or killed by the Laedan's guards.

But the blood was her blood, and thus she was injured. Injured seriously enough, perhaps, to warrant being carried.

He wondered how long Kato could carry her at a run. The Fela had been injured himself, some wound to his torso from a previous encounter that had been obvious in his movement when Vance met him. And if he ran, in this unfamiliar territory, where would he go? Where would Jia go?

Back to her Pack?

Vance did not believe, after everything she had done in the short time he had known her, that she would choose to leave her father…even if he was dead.

Especially if he was dead.

The rain grew gentler, and behind the veiled clouds, the sun's warmth struggled to push to the earth below, dragging dawn behind it like a reluctant, wounded thing. Flight through daytime streets in any anthrozooidic form was a dangerous undertaking that would make them too noticeable, too easy to find as people could report their movements, and would if anyone in a uniform was following. Daybreak meant the need to seek shelter and there were simply too many abandoned places throughout the borough in which the pair could take refuge.

Stopping on a street corner, having lost the obvious trail more than a block before, Vance noted one pair of Laedan guards in the distance to his right, pausing to converse, possibly trying to decide their course of action since they had not yet had success. Perhaps they had reached the same conclusion, that their quarry had sought shelter for the day. One pointed, and together they stalked into the nearest rubble of a building, weapons at the ready. The mage frowned and listened, fearing gunfire or other evidence of a fight if they had found what they sought. When nothing reached his ears, he relaxed and resumed assessing the area where he stood.

A metal frame arched across a portion of the street not fifty yards away on Vance's left, the sign upon it no longer legible and only hanging there because the wind, age, and scavs had not yet made an effort to pull it down. Only the faded remnant of an arrow was visible on the faded blue-green background. The rest of the text was eroded away. Few paid attention to such ancient relics; whatever information they were meant to convey was no longer relevant to anyone except the Protectorate, scavs, and local residents. Its forgotten directions gave Vance an idea, though it had only a sliver of possible truth to it. After shaking the rain from his hair and coat, he again doubled back to where he had lost Kato's trail.

If he was right, he knew where the two had gone. Following them there, however, might not be easy.

Chapter 3

With the demise of his brother and Roland, Nik and his near-death odose became a thing of memory, a thing of before, a thing that would, in all likelihood, come again sooner rather than later. A thing no one questioned and in the face of the loss of Jonni, a thing that none would feel any current level of remorse or concern about. Not even Donn gave his twin a thought, as he was on the warpath now, setting into play a hunt of known or suspected Fela in every corner of LaGuardia borough, any who might have an inkling of the location of the man believed to have murdered his brother.

The probability that every one of those Fela and other anthro caught in the net, would die in the face of Donn's wrath, regardless of the helpfulness of their testimony, was a detail Nik could not afford to think about.

He was just one lone addict, a voice that no one paid any mind to. What could he possibly do to help?

Sit and watch his brother. That was all. Watch as the early stages of decomposition set in, slowed as it was by the temperature inside the cold storage where the two corpses were held, where the forepath was forced to work. Watch for a sign, a trace, that his brother was becoming a mindless, ravenous thing. Any sign that Roland was not the thing Nik already knew him to be.

His father, his brother, Quentin; they suspected. They questioned. But Nik knew.

No one thought to ask him. If they had, they would never believe him.

His father did not know he was here. After Jonni and Roland were taken from the infirmary, Lowell had marched out of the room without looking back, had gone to check on his wife and to see to the details of whatever great pageant he planned to honor the deceased. He had given the order to Quentin to see to it, but Nik knew he would instead oversee much of the arrangements himself.

Just as he oversaw everything else in LaGuardia.

No, his father did not know he was here…but his father never knew, and right now, Nik knew it was not a far stretch to believe that Lowell cared even less than he normally did.

The last of the night's rain, mixed with the first dabbling of snowflakes of the year, dribbled down the deteriorating steps into the bowels of the city where most scavs dared not go. There had been a time when men and women sought treasures here, goods and materials and trinkets left behind when the world had come undone. But as the Unders numbers grew, and the frequency of those who went Below and never came back rose too, it became the commonly held belief that the risks of Below were not worth whatever might still be down there. Every now and then a brave soul, usually a scav, made the effort, some succeeding, most not, and more than once the Protectorate had found a fugitive attempting to take shelter with the Unders.

The Unders were not a friendly, welcoming lot. Most who tried to integrate with them were recovered, dead or alive, not long after.

It had not immediately crossed Vance's mind that Jia and Kato might seek refuge there. She would know the risks, even if Kato did not. Given what they faced in the streets, however, perhaps coming here was precisely the first place Vance should have looked.

He picked his way around fresh and stagnant pools of water as he descended to the limits of the streetlight, the farthest he dared go without any light source of his own. If he was going to investigate the tunnels properly, if he was going to take that risk on Jia's behalf, he would need a lantern, a shocker, a torch…something to see by and something to fight off the Unders who might come for him…and the grubbers who definitely would. Despite his propensity to drink too much, Vance acknowledged, as he stared deeper into the darkness, he did not actually have a death wish.

At least, he had no desire to die at the hand of Unders or grubbers.

The Unders gathered around the aged fire-can raised their heads and stared, the luminescence of their eyes blinking in a random off and on pattern like some sort of ancient code. When he came no closer to them, however, and instead spread his hand on the corner of the wall to slowly slide down into a squat as he read the details left there, they turned their attention back to their fire and the grooming ritual they were engaged in, picking at one another's bodies through sparse hair and dirty skin in search of fleas, lice, and other vermin nesting there.

Vance shuddered and looked away.

They had passed here. The brush of Jia's dangling hand against the wall as they turned was the only proof of it, beyond Kato's invisible footprints, but it was the only proof Vance needed. Kato had turned right, away from the fire's warmth. He had risked passing the unpredictable Unders for some hidden shelter deeper in darkness, without knowing what he might find.

Or perhaps, following Fela senses and instinct, he had known exactly what was ahead.

Vance scowled, took a breath, and made his choice. If it proved to be the wrong one, he believed he could run back up the steps fast enough to avoid the Unders. With luck, those he sought had not gone far, only far enough for the Unders to serve as a deterrent to anyone following, far enough that the Unders did not consider them a threat.

With any luck, they might hear him now.

"Jia? Kato?"

If he had still been in his Fela form, his feline ears would have flattened against his skull and fangs would have shown beneath snarling lips at the sound of his name, her name, on the mage's lips.

The mage had tracked and betrayed them, surely, had probably led uniformed men and women, Protectors and Laedan's forces, to their shelter here in the darkness. Kato's first thought was to stay silent, say nothing, ignore the tracker until he left.

But a sniff of the fetid underground air told him that the mage was alone. If anyone had followed, they were too far away for Kato to detect. If his tracking skills had brought him this far, then Vance likely knew Kato and Jia were here…somewhere. If Kato let the tracker leave with his suspicion of their presence intact, he could be inclined to return with others to conduct a more thorough search, enough others to overpower him and take Jia away. If Kato took the risk and confronted Vance alone, he could always kill the mage if the man was deemed to be an imminent threat.

And if Kato was somehow killed instead, in his effort to protect her, he clung to the belief that Jia, and Vanya, would be safe. The belief that Vance did not want Jia to suffer any more than Kato did. Whatever the mage's faults, Vance was not going to allow harm to befall the woman, and Jia, likewise, would do her utmost to keep Vanya safe.

If that was true, if Vance was on Jia's side, then Kato decided he was not likely to expose them to outside agents. He most likely had indeed come alone, hoping to protect them. It was on that belief that Kato chose to act.

Crouched low, slinking along the slimy stone wall, he remained out of sight until he knew the shadows would fail to provide cover. At the last moment, he sprang forward to knock the smaller man back onto the steps, straddling him, preventing him from rising or, by the position of his knees and hands holding the mage's wrists, from drawing any weapon he had.

Kato might have chosen to believe the best about the mage's intentions, but he was not taking any chances that he was wrong.

"What do you want, Mage?"

Stunned by the unforeseen attack and by the impact on the floor, for a few moments all Vance did was blink until his vision cleared. The places where the Fela's fingers touched his exposed wrists burned with the clarity of images flooding through the contact. Snippets of so many things, the flight from the Fortress, a woman clutching a discolored yellow bear, grubbers tearing a woman apart before much younger eyes, the impact of two Fela that resulted in an impulsive arm throwing Jonni Channon across the room, a syringe clattering and skittering across a wooden floor, the shattering of glass that left evidence on Kato's arms and face, Jia slipping from his grasp as the launch from Fortress to wall to outside street took them to freedom.

Vance shook his head to clear his vision, to push those images and a host of others into the corners of his mind for assessment later. "Is she alright? Is she alive?"

Unsurprised yet irritated by the expected questions, Kato snarled. Of course, Jia was his primary concern. To be fair, she would have been Kato's too, if his and Vance's situations were reversed. But he did not feel like being fair. He bent his face nearer and snarled again. "What concern is that of yours?"

"I need to know; I need to know what happened." From Kato's touch, Vance knew she was alive, that the Fela's behavior was out of concern for her welfare rather than anger over her death or the situation they were in, but it told Vance little else. When he had time to sort through what he had learned through the silent communication with Kato, he would have a clearer picture of what had happened in the infirmary, know it from the Fela's point of view at least, but he did not have time now to sit quietly and sort through the flotsam and jetsam over a tall stein of hemp ale.

"He killed him, that's what happened! The Fela, Quentin…he injected him with something and then he…" Kato rocked back to his heels, no longer pinning Vance down, his mien morose and colored with regret. "He is dead, isn't he? I want to give her hope but…"

Scooting backward to sit on the step, his gaze left Kato long enough to judge whether their voices, their actions, their previous hostility, had drawn the attention of the Unders. They seemed to be ignoring the two men but Vance did not think that would last. He shook his head, holding on to the claim of 'other Fela' as the important clue he knew it to be. "He's gone, yes," he sighed. While he had not expected a confrontation between Laedans to go smoothly, and had known there was risk involved in Marrock's returning to the Fortress with allegations and questions unlikely to gain him favor with Lowell, Vance had, at worst, imagined arrest, detention, maybe a trial. He had not thought there would be murder.

"She's gonna want his body…gonna want to take him home to Addi. The Pack will demand to see him…demand proof…"

"Of course." Vance would too, after all those people had recently endured. He rubbed his hands to warm them as he contemplated the enormity of such an undertaking. Not only the logistics of carrying the man's body across the borough without being caught, but removing his corpse from the Fortress. "Is she here? Is she…?"

"She hit her head when we…she's sleeping." Kato sighed and looked at the floor. "I think." He had little medical knowledge but he could not believe that being asleep for so long after a head injury could be a good thing. "Will…?"

He glanced into the darkness towards the alcove, considering his options. He needed to get to Roland, but he did not know-how. The mage was their best chance, but Kato did not think he could ask the tracker to take such a risk. It was better, he thought, to do it himself.

"What?"

Pointing towards the alcove, Kato replied, "She's in there. Stay with her while I bring her father back?"

"You're out of your mind."

Kato narrowed his eyes. "You don't think I can…?"

"Maybe you could…but she'd never forgive you…or me…if you fail." Vance considered the possibility of allowing Kato to attempt the impossible, of ridding himself of the Fela competition, for no more than a few moments before shaking his head. Whatever else Vance knew about her, how Jia would feel if she lost Kato now was one fact Vance felt certain of. That knowing left a hollowness in his center, but after so many years of failed and aborted relationships, this was nothing new. Just one more.

He should be used to this feeling now.

Damn, he needed a drink.

"I can get in…out again…find where he is being kept…and I know people." Odds were, Marrock's body had been kept in the Fortress because transporting him through the borough meant the knowledge of his death becoming public prematurely. Whether he was in the infirmary still or had been moved would need to be determined, and Earnest would make damn sure one of the precinct forepaths had at the body before anyone else was allowed to touch it. Vance knew all of the forepaths, just as he knew every sposer in this region of the borough…including the ones most likely to be allowed into the Fortress to retrieve the dead.

If Vance could get to any of them first, he would get to Marrock. That would be the easy part. Getting the man's body out without notice would be less so.

"And I can bring back bandages, smellings…ointment…food and water." Kato could scavenge for those things in the immediate vicinity, but the risk of being seen and followed was not worth it. Finding what he and Jia would need would take much longer for Kato to accomplish then it would take Vance, and there were other things Vance needed to do.

Jia should not be left alone until she woke.

"Stay with her. I'll be back as soon as I'm able."

"Alone?" the Fela growled.

"Alone…or with Marrock's body. I swear." He did not know how he would carry the man if he could get to him, but he would solve that matter after he got inside the Fortress. "If you need to move from here, to hide somewhere else…touch the walls, the grounds…anything as you go…so I can find you again."

Though not entirely trusting the mage to keep his word, feeling that it might be best to flee with Jia as soon as Vance was beyond the range of his senses, Kato did believe that the other man would do his best to bring Roland back to his daughter. That promise, the Fela knew, was sincerely made.

☙*❧

"It is true then?" Geary drained the brown, frothy liquor from his glass as his daughter entered the room, and set it on the table next to his cushioned chair before adding, "Roland Marrock is dead?"

He already knew it to be true, had heard it from his man Fenway whom he had sent into the fray as soon as the sirens began their night-shattering cry. Oasis had left her father's company, fear or curiosity or duty compelling her to seek the truth herself. This was her home now, and Geary felt little concern for her safety; surely the Channons would not be so brazen as to harm her with her father beneath their roof. Whatever the cause of the alarm, Geary had been less certain about his own security outside of this room until the pandemonium subsided, so he remained where he was, away from the windows where someone could have shot at him, one of his guards at the door and his personal weapon on his lap, availing himself of Channon's exquisite collection of alcohol. There had been little he could do except wait, listen to the talk in the hall, in the courtyard outside, and as a man not prone to panic, he had simply kept calm and drank to the warning siren's wail.

No one had come for him.

"And Jonni," Oasis gasped between hurried, gulping breaths. She snatched the glass and poured the rest of the nearly empty bottle into it, downing it in as few swallows as she could manage. "There was a Fela…it's said he killed them both…took Jia Marrock…"

"Murder and abduction?" Geary's tone was thoughtful and perplexed. A logical man, the two things did not add up. "Lowell must be devastated." How lucky they were, he and Oasis, that she had not married that particular Channon. All of their efforts would have been for nothing. "Do they know how? Why?"

She shook her head and sat on the arm of his chair, pushing the empty glass into his hand as he slid his other arm around her waist. "They've not found him yet…but there's a tracker on it. Yiva says he's the best in LaGuardia…and the Protectorate chief is studying the evidence left behind. She thinks we'll have answers soon."

Glancing into his daughter's pensive face, he set the glass down and took her hand, clasping it soothingly. "You don't believe it?"

"I don't know…I…" The truth was, she was afraid of her husband's wrath. The darkness she had witnessed as he commanded every loyal Laedan guard to hunt down Fela, Cana, and Ursa alike and bring them to him, had been a chilling glimpse into something she had not wanted to know about her husband. Yiva was afraid of him too, although she had escaped his company as soon as she was able and had not witnessed that red fury in his eyes as his decree was made.

"We will bleed the earth until I find the beast who killed him," Donn had snarled with ruthless glee. "Every one of them will die."

Oasis' first thought had been, 'and what about the rest of us?'

"This isn't going to end well…for anyone," she finished with a sigh, giving her father some completion to her previously unfinished statement. She could not tell him the truth. The treaty between Kennedy and LaGuardia depended on her strength. She was not ready to risk a war. She was determined to deal with her husband on her own, even if she had to go through Donn's father to do so.

Nor was she going to profess to her father how heartbroken she knew Lowell to be. There had been no chance to talk to Lowell, to offer comfort or condolences, but Oasis intended to do so before the night, or the following day, was over. She would not be able to sleep until she did.

She doubted Lowell would either.

"I suspect not," Geary agreed, "but it doesn't change anything for us, does it?" It erased his hope for working out a peaceful resolution of the Fort Hamilton question via Marrock, filled him with regret that his efforts to keep the dog alive had failed, but he had known such disappointments before. The original plan was still in place. Nothing had changed that. The Channon-Hallister alliance still stood…until Geary had what he needed from Lowell and could be rid of him too.

Oasis shook her head, her hand in her father's pulling away as she stood and moved from the reach of his embrace. "No. It doesn't change anything." The pieces she needed were still in play. Thomas was alive. Lowell could be manipulated. Her plan, like her father's, still stood.

Whether the men knew it or not.

Chapter 4

He was tired, hungry, and the rain that stung his eyes and matted his chestnut brown hair was an inconvenience, but Addison felt compelled to stay on watch tonight. He had chosen to take up this post to escape the raw, unsettling emotions of the Pack, men and women eager to have their Alpha home, now that they knew he was alive, and who wrestled with the young doctor's choice to leave the wounded Alpha and his daughter in LaGuardia.

But what else could he have done? The Pack needed the medicinals and food he had brought back, and they needed to know that Roland was found. He had obeyed his father's wishes by returning to the Pack's library den, but that did not mean that the Pack was happy with his doing so.

Maybe if he waited long enough, he would see his father and sister again and this time, when he went back, they would be with him.

Intending to do this alone, he was surprised to have Deuce join him some forty-five minutes into his watch with a heavy, waxy raincape. Addi had not asked where Deuce found it but accepted it gratefully. The Omega was determined to follow Jia's orders, Roland's orders, in protecting Addison, and though he did not yet fully trust Deuce…indeed he did not know him…Addi felt safer, calmer, with the burly man watching with him.

Addi was no fighter. Perhaps he could defend against a single Normal opponent, so long as that opponent did not have a shocker or gun, but he was not confident of his chances. Deuce, on the other hand, gave the impression that he could survive anything.

With the raincape strung up between the tangled branches of this dense thicket, held in place by hemp string and creativity to serve as a roof rather than a coat around his shoulders, he huddled for several minutes while the Omega continued to keep watch in the downpour where the patter of raindrops mixed with snow on the canvas overhead did not drown out the other night sounds. He felt guilty seeing the other man suffering, cold and wet, while he was relatively dry, so he finally whistled to get the man's attention and motioned for him to join him beneath the makeshift shelter. Deuce hesitated, undoubtedly thinking the request to be some sort of trap and weighing whatever options he imagined he had. The request was not an order, however, and the only hold Addi had was a secure place above him in Pack order. The Omega was free to refuse if he wished.

Several minutes passed before Deuce crabbed closer, his eyes and expression wary, body language tense with the preparation for conflict, but when Addi made no aggressive move and again beckoned him into the narrow shelter with another wave, Deuce accepted the offer and huddled beside him, as far from him as the canvas covering would allow. When Addi handed him a long length of dried meat and then the water flask he had filled in the fountain before coming here, Deuce accepted with far less hesitation.

"What's your name?"

The question brought a pause as the shaved-headed man stared at him. "Deuce," he said around a mouthful of meat, his voice raspy from either exertion or exposure, or perhaps naturally so.

"No…I know…I mean your name."

All of his life, Addi had known the Omega by his rank or by Deuce. Unlike Pain, who had changed the spelling of his name from the original Payne to give himself a more dangerous edge, camp gossip hinted at a different name…an original name…for the pack outcast, a name never spoken. Anyone who knew refused to say. Theba and Maz had prevented Roland from banishing the Omega completely, thus

Roland had endured his lingering at the Pack fringe, but the man's identity had been erased beneath the stain of his status.

If Jia was toying with the option of bringing the Omega back into the pack, if Roland's recent actions were indicative of a possible change in status, Addi thought they should know the man's name.

Deuce scowled and scratched at the side of his neck with dirty, torn nails, staring into the waning night. Though it was difficult to read his expression from his profile, Addi thought he looked pensive, uncomfortable, perhaps ashamed or embarrassed. Or maybe that perception was the effect of the pale light reflecting off his wet skin.

"Seff…Zeller…" The words sounded strained, entangled with memory it seemed he would rather forget, as if the name had not been spoken in so long that he had forgotten what it was. Who he was.

"What sort of name is…?"

Deuce growled with a side-eyed glower and Addi shrugged. "I don't mean insult…just curious." In the aftermath of the Undoing, it had been important to many families to cling to the names, to the legacies, of the ancestors they had lost. That grew harder to do over the decades as survivors intermarried or died or mutated into individuals without any similarity to the heritages they were born with. In a world with few traditions left to bind them, with even the holidays and holy days of old giving way to the inevitable erosion of survival after the Undoing, holding on to names had become one of the few ways left to cement struggling families together.

"I don't know."

Addi opened his mouth but closed it again. There were dozens of reasons one might not know where they came from, might not remember. Not everyone had the illustrious history of the Marrock name to hold on to. Addi, like the majority of the Pack, had no knowledge of Deuce's history, and so his not knowing was acceptable. Unfortunate, but acceptable. It did not really matter where a name originated. Only here and now mattered.

"Why did you come out here…in this?" Deuce stuck his hand out from beneath their shelter, caught the dripping rain in his cupped palm, and drank it.

Less surprised by the question then he was that Deuce had not asked sooner, Addi shrugged. "They think I abandoned Jia and that I should have stayed with them and then Pain would not have found us."

"He would have, in time."

"Maybe." Pain was resilient, persistent, strong. He had been the best scav in the Flushing Pack. If anyone could have tracked the Pack's location, Pain certainly could have. "I just keep hoping…if I wait…they'll catch up."

Not certain what Roland's business in the Fortress would entail, only that it was undoubtedly dangerous for both his sister and his father, Addi hoped that the pair and Fela with them would emerge from the fog and rain and they could return to the Pack together.

An empty-handed return would likely raise eyebrows, from the Pack and from the still-lurking Pain. Addi's wife and the children would welcome him, alone or not, but he was less convinced about his welcome from the others.

"They won't."

Not sure if Deuce meant that Jia, Roland, and Kato would not catch up, or that the Pack would not blame him if he returned alone, Addi side-eyed him. Deuce shrugged.

The Omega only knew what his gut told him, that returning to the Fortress had been a foolish and dangerous thing for the Alpha and his daughter, and that any of the three would be lucky to make it out of that place alive. It grieved him to think he may have allowed them to go to their deaths without staying to assist them, but the request made of him had been incontrovertible. Addi needed protection. The Pack needed protection.

Deuce's sense of duty and loyalty forced him to obey, gut instinct or not.

"She'll make it back," Addi muttered, hearing the unspoken, reluctant acceptance of doom in the older man's voice. "She'll live like she always does. They all will." He would not accept anything less until proof was shoved into his face. The Flushing Pack needed a Marrock to lead it.

Addi was not the Marrock for that job.

"I hope you are right, Addison."

His name sounded strange on the Omega's lips, stilted and tentative.

Addi imagined it was the first time Deuce had ever said it out loud.

In return, he offered a small smile of acceptance of Deuce's effort and his hand. The Omega looked at it, hesitated, and then accepted that handshake as a gesture of camaraderie.

"I am. You'll see her again." He had to be right. The Flushing Pack had no other choice.

⁓*⁓

"How dare you!"

It was not the first time his father had burst into his room, demanding an answer or explanation for something Donn had done or failed to do, but Don wagered, from the look of flushed horror and contempt on his face at the sight of Oasis' red buttocks, her face buried in the pillows in a refusal to look up, her wrists and ankles bound to the bedposts with strips of cloth, and Donn's half undressed state, that Lowell had seen more than he cared to of his son's private activities and would think twice about invading his private rooms again.

The sight, however, was not enough to prevent Lowell from yanking Donn by the arm into the sitting room and shoving him into the first chair they reached. With that chair turned sideways, Donn sprawled over the arm and might have toppled out of it if he had not caught the coffee table with one hand and braced himself.

Doing so wrenched his wrist. He grimaced.

"You have no authority to call for a borough-wide hunt…"

"Someone had to do it," Donn spat, daring to stand, drawing his trousers up in the process, to face his father like a man rather than an unprepared boy, though he expected to be knocked down again for his defiance. "One of those filthy…"

"Until the investigation is complete, we do not know…"

"Investigations are for cowards! We know enough! We know what happened!"

Lowell snarled and caught Donn by the lapels of his shirt. "Are you calling me a coward?"

"We know who did this!" Donn evaded the question, the accusation, because he believed it to be true and was smart enough not to throw it into his father's face a second time. Lowell had heard him. Once was enough.

"We don't…" Lowell began.

"It wasn't Nik! It likely wasn't Jia! She may be a beast but Jonni's her friend…and she would never kill her…"

"The Fella was with…"

"So maybe she did not know who he was…what he was…what he intended to do…but unless it was Quentin…"

The Laedan snorted derisively. "Of course it wasn't Quentin." He had no reason to suspect his aide, but Donn could see in his father's eyes that the doubt was there. There was no way for Lowell not to suspect him, even while defending his adjunct to his son.

Quentin had undertaken the duty to rid him of Marrock the last time, the time that failed. It made sense that Quentin would attempt to rectify his error, although any attempt at doing so inside the Fortress was a stupid one. Even if Quentin had gone after Marrock this time, Lowell knew the blame could not fall there, not if it heightened the possibility that the blame would somehow reflect back on him.

Until he had a plan to shield himself from allegations of conspiracy and duplicity, Lowell could not afford to believe Quentin was to blame.

It was fortunate to have a stranger for that.

A stranger who had to be Jonni's killer too…for surely Quentin would never go that far.

"He knows what will happen if he's responsible for Jonni's…" The thought made Lowell both cold and furious at once. No, Quentin would never betray him that way.

"Then who else do you want to blame? Nik? Jia? The medistaff?"

"Perhaps it was natural, a result of the injuries that brought him…"

"Nothing natural threw Jonni into that cabinet!"

Lowell could not argue that point, even if he wanted to. Perhaps, he mused, he wanted the forepath's proof because he refused to believe that his eldest son was dead. And because such denial seemed like a sign of weakness to him. He growled and snapped, "There shall be no hunt until the forepath's report is…"

"By then he'll have gotten away!"

"This is not up for debate, Donnovan. There shall be no hunt…"

"It is too late for that, Father."

The two glared at one another in the tension-thick room, only the softness of sobbing behind the closed door and the persistent hum of the ventilation system breaking the rhythm of their strained, heavy breathing. Each knew the other's thoughts too well, the unspoken challenges, the unvoiced arguments they did not need to express aloud. The hunt was already underway, men already in the streets seeking any anthrozooids living in the borough. Recalling them would be an embarrassment for Donn, would show a lack of the authority he claimed to have, an inability to stand up and manipulate LaGuardia's only remaining Laedan. Not recalling them, allowing an officially unsanctioned hunt to continue, would show a lack of authority and strength on Lowell's part as well, an inability to control his son.

Neither was acceptable and neither was prepared to surrender.

There was a single choice and they both realized it at almost the same moment. A compromise Lowell was willing to give, a compromise being the only reward Donn's initiative taking could receive. Donn did not appreciate being the one who had to back down, even a little, did not feel that a compromise was sufficient, but he was experienced enough to understand that it was either a compromise or else he withdrew his men from their hunt.

That he would not do.

He would call off the hunt for other anthros but not for that one Fela both father and son wanted to question and see punished for Jonni's death.

And if his men uncovered a handful or so of other anthro in the process to bring in for questioning and detainment…well, who would argue with that?

Donn had HOPE mandates behind him, after all.

Lowell stepped back, confident he had won, equally confident that his son would go behind his back and manipulate the compromise as much as he could. For now, Lowell could live with that. There was one other matter, however, that he was not willing to let rest.

"And if you ever touch her like that again…"

Donn blinked and stared incredulously, trying to determine what his father meant by that threat…and why the man should care.

"She's my wife…"

"She's Normal…a human. She's a Channon now. She's pledged life and loyalty to you…to this family. Respect that…don't abuse it…or you'll live to regret your choices."

Donn wondered if his father was threatening him, and again wondered why Lowell should care what Donn did with his wife beyond the gaze of public perception…or if his father believed Oasis would be the one to turn on him and risk ruining the treaty between LaGuardia and Kennedy if Donn let his tastes go too far. He wiped his face of expression, shrugged with a small twitch of his shoulders, and looked down long enough to straighten his clothes. Pleasures would wait. Summoning his men, giving them new directives, had to be done before his father took more drastic action than a verbal reprimand.

Leaving Oasis unbound would, he hoped, appease his father's sensibilities.

He made it as far as the bedroom door, deciding if he did not untie her, Lowell probably would, and spoke without looking back. "No, Father…I won't."

We'll see about that, Lowell thought bitterly, resisting the impulse to follow, to offer comfort and reassurance to the woman beyond that closed door. He resisted because he did not think he could ignore the temptation she offered…whether Donn was in the room or not.

If she did not demand respect and loyalty from Donnovan, Lowell sure as shart would.

*

"You found them."

Nik, wearing cut-off gray trousers and a worn, faded red tee with some nearly absent logo from before the Undoing, sounded disappointed. He sat on one of the many benches in this vast entrance galley where he was so often found basking in the sunlight, his expression hinting that he had been waiting for someone, something, rather than waiting here randomly as many often did. This room was usually warmer than much of the Fortress, as if the panes of glass that remained drew the heat from the overcast sky and held it within. It was not the first time Vance had found Nik here over the course of his employment with the Protectorate but it was the first time he could recall the middle son not looking thoroughly strung out on some substance. Nik looked less than healthy but not high.

Instead of addressing the question Nik raised, not sure how far he could trust the junkie Channon, the mage approached and asked, "Should you be up already?"

The younger man shrugged and swiped his hand over his scalp, wiping sweat from his brow into his disheveled hair, a symptom, Vance imagined, of either craving or withdrawal as it was not warm enough here for sweating. Symptoms of withdrawal and craving were things Vance understood too well.

It had been too damn long since he had a drink.

"Didn't want to be in there anymore. Too many ghosts." Nik slid sideways on the bench in invitation, his bare feet making a squeak against the recently cleaned floor, and waited for Vance to join him.

"I can understand that." There were ghosts at crime scenes for Vance too. He wondered if there was some trace of mage in Nik's blood. He sat, looked around for anyone within visual or auditory range, and then leaned back against the plaster post behind the bench. It was morning, too early for a significant amount of foot traffic, but that would change as the sun crept higher. The men who normally stood guard at the door were somewhere in the borough or on the Fortress grounds, seeking a killer they would not find.

It looked as if the Laedan was unconcerned for his safety now that his son and Roland were dead.

Nik appeared to want to talk but was reluctant to start, or he was uncertain how to begin, so on the off chance hinted at in his request for company, the off chance that Kato was right, and that Nik had answers, Vance asked, “He didn’t do it, did he?” as he stared at the windows across the room and the door through which he had entered.

Nik shook his head. He knew who the Tracker-Mage meant. He knew what he meant. He was telling the truth.

“Did you see any of it?”

“They didn’t know…they can’t know…” he whispered, casting a furtive glance at the once mobile staircase that led to the offices and dwellings above. “He won’t believe me…and if Thomas finds out…”

But Thomas already knew that Nik had seen, had heard, too much the night before. He knew Nik had struck him with the metal hospital tray, knocking him out…and he knew why.

And he knew that Nik did not have the stomach, or the courage, to risk crossing him. Not when it would be Nik’s words against his…and Nik’s addiction-addled senses would be used to explain away anything he claimed he had seen.

“I don’t want her hurt…this isn’t her fault…” Nik mumbled. “She shouldn’t have come back…”

Vance patted his knee, the last pat allowing for a lingering moment of contact that drew a wash of images and remembrances Nik was unwilling to voice. From the way he stared at the mage at that moment, Vance guessed Nik understood what the Protector had done, that it was what Nik had hoped he would do.

“That’s okay…I understand. You don’t need to talk about it yet.” At some point, the Chief would insist on an interrogation of everyone at the scene, and others who had not been, but Vance did not need to participate in that.

He hoped.

If he was lucky, he would have the answers before such an interrogation became necessary.

A trio of guards entered through the front doors, casting the pair a curious look but continuing on towards their in-Fortress barracks in search of their commanding officer. Two men Vance recognized as cohorts of Laedan Hallister were chatting as they descended the stairs; they too cast Nik and Vance a brief glance, more scathing and judgmental than the others, before going out the main doors.

Vance was running out of time. The day was waning, even though it had just begun. He had come to the Fortress with a purpose and could dally no longer.

"Where's Chief now?" If Nik had been here long enough, had stayed in the infirmary long enough, he might know where Ernest had gone, if he had left the Fortress. "What's been done with the dead?"

No reason to couch the question in euphemisms. Nik seemed the sort to prefer straightforward words.

"In storage…downstairs. Want me to show you?"

Though Vance knew the way, he knew there were many rooms there, storages of all sorts for food, or furniture, for supplies that would later be redistributed to the borough, but mostly they were supplies used by the Laedans and the Fortress staff. It might take him too long to find the room he wanted, mage senses or not.

A few more minutes with Nik might afford additional information, or at least provide a legitimate escort should anyone question his being there. He could pull his credentials, for those who did not recognize his face, his coat, or the insignia on his lapel, but no one was likely to say a word if he was in a Channon's company.

"Thank you. Yes…please."

The stairwell to the lower level was damp and colder than the outside air, feeling more so after the warmth of the lobby. Beyond walls covered with peeling plaster that here and there allowed beads of water to seep through, the pulse of the sea was heard for a time, but eventually, the sound faded, giving way to the silence so typical of subterranean caverns, a silence marked only by the hum of the generators that lit sporadic lights marking one passage from another.

Vance could smell it. Death. Not a grubber smell, but death all the same.

At least neither of the dead had turned yet.

"This way."

Nik seemed impervious to the smell, to the chill, to the puddles on the floor that gathered where the lights pulled condensation from the air and allowed it to accumulate in the lowest points of the corridors. They rounded a corner to find Ernest leaning against the wall near a closed door and the two Protectors nodded at one another.

No one else stood in the hall.

Ernest did not have the stomach, or the need, to watch the forepath at work. He never had. But he did feel the need to stand guard in case anyone came to intrude on the forepath's work, particularly the impatient Laedan or his more impatient right-hand.

He also waited in case the dead within became something other than dead.

"Anything?"

Ernest shook his head. "Not yet. Not that Guire's said."

Cole Guire was the Protectorate's primary forepath, had held that job for some time before Ernest had become chief. Sometimes it seemed surprising that the man continued to surround himself with the dead day after day for so long, that he had not retired to some more pleasant existence.

But like many since the Undoing, Guire had no family and only just eked out a living at the Protectorate. He had nothing to retire to except a life of relative uselessness and the scratching away for survival that left many elderly dead before their time.

Like so many others, Guire would continue doing exactly as he was until some physical incapacity or limitation forced him to stop. There were not many other options.

"How much longer?"

"Laedan's given us three days."

In three days, the bodies would turn. Or they would not.

Vance nodded his head once.

"I need Marrock's body."

The chief pursed his lips, wishing he had something to settle his stomach. It did not matter to him why his tracker wanted the man's corpse. Ernest trusted Segara's judgment even when he did not understand it. But if he released it now, ahead of the deadline, someone was going to ask questions.

He also knew, however, that in an investigation of this nature, timing was everything. If Segara needed the body now, that was enough for Ernest, whatever the reason.

"I should also inspect Jonni…"

Ernest shook his head. "Laedan said no…no one in there…except Guire." It was stupid to the chief; Jonni was not going to hurt anyone in his state. And no one was going to be foolish enough to defile the Channon boy's corpse. But rules were rules, even when they interfered with the Protectorate's duty.

Vance snorted. "Of course he did." Quentin's doing, most likely. Anything to hide the truth longer. "But you can get me Marrock?"

After a quick glance at Nik, whom the mage seemed unconcerned about overhearing their exchange, Ernest asked, "Can it wait until Guire's finished? Maybe then I can get you in to both…"

"Probably for the best, yeah." Lowell was going to want the report, and Guire was already elbow-deep in the dead men's blood.

"What do you…how do you propose to…?"

Nik's face brightened. "I can do it." The older men looked at him skeptically. "No…I can…just tell me where and when and I can do this." He hoped Vance intended to take Roland's body 'home', wherever that was, to his family, to his daughter and son who had risked so much in coming back and now suffered the costs of that risk.

Addi might not have been at the Fortress, but he was undoubtedly suffering too.

Footsteps echoing through the basement interrupted before either Vance or Ernest could speak. The man who came around the corner scowled with narrowed eyes, and Nik, worried that he had been heard, sides stepped so that Vance was between him and his father.

"Well?"

"Fa…" Nik stammered.

"I need to talk with the Chief," interrupted Vance, reading in the direction of Lowell's gaze that the question was aimed at him.

"Did you find them? Any trace?" The Laedan's tone was impatient but he appeared uninterested in his son's presence.

"Found where they landed in the street…traces of blood that suggested their direction. The men are following…"

"Why aren't you?" Lowell did not know how being a mage worked, how their tracking senses and skills functioned or how much time was needed to produce results. Nor was he aware of how little sleep, and food, Segara was functioning on.

In his impatience to see an end to the matter, he did not care.

"They appear to have gone into the tunnels. I need permission to take a team…" started Vance.

Though his expression changed at the mention of those miles of snaking veins beneath the borough's surface, Lowell snorted, "Anything. If they're down there, get in there and find them!"

Ernest's eyes narrowed and he pushed off the wall to defend his favorite tracker. "Without lights and weapons, Laedan, I am not letting him go into that hell. I'm not sending him in alone. We don't have maps. One man going alone is asking for a futile death with no one coming back to report…and no one finding anything. Segara's gonna go to the Protectorate, round up the on-duty roster who are able, get some equipment and…"

"Then get to it!" Every minute of delay meant another minute Jonni's killer got further away. Lowell might not have approved of either Donnovan or Quentin's methods, but he still wanted results. "Don't step foot in the Fortress again until you find them."

After a quick exchange of glances with the chief, Vance nodded and made his retreat. That command was banishment, but it was necessary if Vance was to get back to Jia and Kato with the supplies the Fela needed and it would be a relief not to have to worry about facing the Laedan again. Vance needed to warn the pair that their approximate location had been compromised. Unfortunate, but also necessary. Giving Lowell nothing would steer the situation into more hostile territory and result in an argument Vance could not afford.

Besides, he had no reason to believe that anyone, Protectorate or Laedan guard, would venture into the tunnels very far, and with so many openings into the labyrinth spread throughout the borough, so many within easy running distance of the Fortress, there were many places the Fela and Cana could have sought refuge.

It could also be a dead-end search. Anyone stupid enough to risk the tunnels was probably dead already.

He caught Nik's eye after slinking past the Laedan so that he was behind him, where Lowell could not see, long enough to cock his head in Ernest's direction. Somehow, the three of them would work out when and how to remove Marrock's corpse from the Fortress.

There were ways. The only criterion was the need to be careful. If Nik had an idea, it was worth hearing. His knowledge of hidden exits within the Fortress might prove to be just what was needed.

Lowell missed the short exchange since his attention was on the chief who, in his irritability, seemed to be going out of his way to circumvent every demand Lowell made.

"Where's my men?"

"They'd been here all night," shrugged Ernest as he half-watched Segara escape this unpleasant location. He was less intimidated by the Laedan than Nik was, the young man now having moved closer to Ernest after the mage's departure. "No reason I can't watch while they use the letty and get something to eat. Guire's in there now…"

"Guire?"

"My forepath. Best there is. We should know soon enough what killed Laedan Marrock."

Again Lowell grunted. "And my son?"

"I thought you didn't want him touched?"

They stared at one another, Ernest's expression one of question and challenge, Lowell's one of conflict and pain. Eventually, he groused, "If he's so good, he can tell without dismembering my boy."

Ernest nodded. Limited to the externally visible injuries, he thought it obvious to anyone that head trauma and deflated lungs punctured by fractured ribs had killed Jonni Channon. He knew it. Lowell knew it. If confirmation from the forepath was what the Laedan wanted, he would have it soon enough.

But that would not tell him who had killed his son.

Nik took a few steps after Lowell. "Fa…I need to speak…"

With an annoyed sound that reminded Nik of the noises one made when shooing a fly from a dinner plate, Lowell said, "Not now, Nik. I'm late for a meeting…"

"But Fa, it's important…"

"I said not now."

Nik stopped following. As though an afterthought, Lowell paused and looked back at the defeated, crushed expression on his son's face. He sighed, refusing to roll his eyes despite the impulse.

"Later, Nik," he said contritely. "Come find me later…after lunch. You can tell me…talk to me…then."

"Alright."

It was Ernest's perception as both left him alone with the forepath and the dead, letting his held breath out in a long, slow hiss, that neither Channon was all that interested in speaking to the other.

It was also his perception that, whatever Nik had in mind to get Marrock out of the Fortress unnoticed, it was going to have to be one hell of a plan.

And if the matter Nik wanted to discuss with his father involved the moving of that body, the chief and mage were in for deep, unavoidable, trouble.

By now Liam had lost track of hours, lost track of days, and knew he was gradually losing track of the outside world. How long was he unconscious after Roland knocked him out to make him appear guiltless of the Alpha's escape? How long had he been interrogated by the woman who appeared to be in charge, by another doctor afterward, and by three separate guards with shockers and guns? He knew he had slept twice in between, though he did not know for how long, and had serviced the unfortunate anthros trapped here with him, slowly being bled to death, three times. And though he guessed, by the nature of the questions and their push for answers, that Roland had gotten free of the compound, Liam had no proof that was true, no idea if the man was dead or on his way to rally the Pack and come for him.

He had no idea if the Pack had survived the hunt.

But as he hosed down another bleeder, as the medics called them, cleaning and drying the last withering woman of her own filth and the trickle of red left on her arm by the insertion and removal of the blood-letting needle, Liam had to hope that Roland's efforts were successful. Liam had to believe the Pack would come and would survive whatever effort necessary to rescue him from this place.

He missed Jia. He missed Zen. He missed Addi and the children. He missed Maz and Uncle. He missed them all. He missed the sunlight, meager as it was behind the grey cloud veil. He missed the fresh air, damp and musty though it could often be. He missed the hunt, missed running free through the decaying streets.

As much as he longed to be away from this nightmare, however, to return to the life he had known, it would be better for him to perish here than for any member of the Flushing Pack to die on his behalf.

If any of them died for him, he did not think he would ever forgive himself. It would be Roland's decision, of course, but Liam would still feel responsible. The Alpha had bid him not give up hope, but Liam was not, in his own eyes, that strong of character. He clung to hope now, while the memories were fresh, but how long would it take, he mused, dropping the damp towel into the bin, before all of that left him, memory and hope and the will to go on?

He sighed, expecting it would not be very long at all.

Chapter 5

From the room across the corridor, she had seen the comings and goings of men and women throughout the last hours of night and the early hours of day. Twice he had left the office without seeing her, only to return looking no more settled, no less devastated. There were plans to be made. Arrangements for some manner of public address, something Lowell could not easily foist off onto anyone else…the necessity of letting it be known to the world that both his co-Laedan and his eldest son were dead.

Murdered.

There were arrangements for disposal to be made as well, for a memorial celebration for each or perhaps something conducted together. There was his wife to console and cater to, although to Oasis' eye, Lowell had little patience or endurance for doing that yet. He had matters of government to sort, as Jonni's loss created a power vacuum in District 1 that needed to be resolved. All of this left little time for managing his own grief, which is what he wanted, something she could plainly see when he dragged into his office one more time. He did not close the door before sinking into the chair behind his desk and dropping his head into his hands.

She knew he did not see her. Nor did he seem to hear her, as his head neither lifted nor turned when she entered the room, eased the door closed, and came around the desk. Only when she stopped beside him did he move, turning just enough to wrap his arms around her waist and press his face into her stomach.

If he was grieving, mourning, that gesture, the tightness of his embrace, and his silence were the only indications he gave.

"I'm so sorry…" She ran the fingers of one hand through his short hair and rubbed between his shoulders with the other.

Oasis did not know what else to say. She had not known Jonni and had only met Roland in the series of meetings that had led to the treaty's initial drafting and the eventual marriage between LaGuardia and Kennedy's ruling families. She could not grieve their deaths as Lowell did, but she knew what it was to lose someone close. She could grieve for the pain he suffered.

"Promise me…" he rasped. His hands hovered over her buttocks, and when she winced, a reminder for both of what he earlier witnessed, he brought them back up to a safer, less tender location.

"What?" She reached sideways without pulling away to pour a tumbler of expensive alcohol from the open bottle on his desk and slid it within his easy reach. "How can I help, Lowell? Tell me."

His head shook no, the rubbing of it against her sending pleasant tingles through her body. Lowell was not a man prone to silence; if he wanted or needed something, he would say so, but in his time and in his way. Or maybe this once, she mused while stroking his hair, what he wanted was something he knew he could not have and thus he was uninclined to continue the request. Perhaps he knew it was something she could not give.

Would she leave her new husband for his father, she wondered? Would Lowell leave his steadfast wife for her?

Would Yiva survive such humiliation when she was already teetering on the brink of taking her own life?

Would Oasis be able to live with herself if she drove the older woman to that?

Perhaps it was best if Lowell never voiced his request.

"Do we know anything? Has the killer been found?"

Again Lowell shook his head where it pressed against her. "Not yet…but they are closing in. By the end of the day, surely." He chose to believe that, though neither the chief nor the mage had made that promise. Surely a day was long enough. How far could the pair of fugitives have gone on foot in such a short time?

If Segara failed to bring that Fela in before nightfall, there was going to be hell to pay.

Oasis frowned and pulled him closer with both hands. The gesture seemed to calm him.

"My father has men here. He will help if I ask him to."

Tempted at first to decline, wanting to refuse aid from the other Laedan, wanting to reveal no sign of weakness or failure, Lowell quickly changed his mind. The marriage of their children afforded them certain rights and freedoms. A threat to one Laedan, the murder of another, was surely also a danger to the third. There was no diplomatic reason not to ask…and if Oasis was the one to make the request on his behalf, Lowell could save face.

"Do not let him think I am weak…"

"Weak? Lowell…" she chuckled affectionately before bending to kiss the top of his head, "you're anything but weak. Trust me, he will never know we have talked."

Satisfied with that, and with the kiss, he lifted his face enough to press his lips to her clothed belly and then straightened in his chair. She thought him strong. Unexpectedly, that made him feel so.

She interpreted that as her signal to depart, as the only comfort he was going to allow himself for now, and after sliding her fingers down his temple and over his cheek, she let her hand drop. He caught it before she stepped away, however, and held it tightly.

"Don't let him do that to you again."

Though she forced a chuckle when she realized what he meant, she suspected he heard it as the awkward and uncomfortable thing she felt it to be.

"He's my husband." She smiled a little as she said it, hoping to soothe him.

"All the more reason he should respect you. It's uncalled for…and undignified…disrespectful. He shouldn't…"

"It was my idea."

Lowell's narrowed eyes stared at her, seeking any truth behind those words, any hint of falsehood or proof that they were not a cover for some shame or embarrassment for the abuse. He knew his son had a cruel streak and could be easily angered, though what she might have done to draw Donn's wrath Lowell could not imagine.

Oasis was every bit her name.

What he saw in the young woman's eyes, however, was strength of purpose and determination. Maybe she spoke the truth. Maybe she had, in the short few days of her marriage, learned enough about Donnovan to be able to manipulate him by channeling his brutality and giving it a safer outlet.

A less public one.

Maybe there was more to Oasis than Lowell had yet seen.

He nodded once. "If he ever…if it comes that you do not feel safe…that he…you will tell me?"

Easing her hand from his after a kiss to his knuckles, she murmured, "I promise, Lowell."

That promise would best serve for both their sakes, and she wondered, as she left in search of her father, if that promise could be extended to include the Laedan's wife.

Perhaps it was time for Lowell to know the truth. Or perhaps, until she had all of the threads drawn into play where she needed them to be, she would let Yiva's secret be, and do her best to stand between mother and son.

*

The stop at the Protectorate was only long enough to give the Chief's report and unspecific request for an investigation of the tunnels, for the teams to be on the lookout for a Fela murder suspect. Vance dodged the handful of questions about who had been murdered as he knew those to be details the Laedan did not yet want to be public, only indicating that the dual murder had occurred in the vicinity of the Fortress in order to give his fellow Protectors a place to begin their searches. There were at least two dozen known tunnel openings there, some into train and subway tunnels, some into sewage and drainage channels, probably others buried beneath civilization's collapse, and the eight officers loitering in the Protectorate at this shift change, upon his arrival there, needed a place to start.

They would spread the word to other officers already in the streets, requiring overtime from many of them, and that, suspected Vance, would be the end of it. Standard procedures with the tunnels would mean pairs descending into the Below, moving in each direction only as far as the light from above would reach, shining their torches or lanterns to extend their vision…and then retreating. A few pairs, more adventurous individuals prone to risk-taking, might venture further into the darkness, but as soon as they reached an intersection or turn, they would retreat, not taking the risk of being lost in the black maze.

Then Vance went home. Once any suspicious Protectors who were following him, hoping to ride the tails of what they expected to be another of his successes in the apprehension of a murderer, saw where he was going, they would stop following him and scatter. But his main purpose in coming here was not to lose those tails. His main purpose was a quick washing and a change of clothes, as he had been wearing these for too long, and to stuff his knapsack with a variety of food and all of the mediplies he had on hand. He could replace them later, and if, by some sinking twist of fate, he never made it back…he would not need them anyhow.

That would be a shame, he thought with a glance at his liquor cabinet. He had grown rather attached to this place.

It was not roomy; it was not fancy. Water seeped in around the north windows and the floor sagged in multiple places. But it was home, had been home, for most of his tenure as Protector. He was going to miss it if he never came back.

Trying to resist the lure of the cabinet, he did stuff the largest full bottle of liquor he had into his pack. "Medi purposes," he said to the ghosts in the air of the too cold apartment before fastening the straps, ties, and buttons on the pack to keep its contents in.

He did not think the ghosts believed him. Or cared.

Passing between the long, low table piled with the remnants of the last few meals he had eaten here and the sofa littered with a sweat-stained pillow and the collection of blankets pushed into haphazardly tangled piles, he noted one squat, wide-mouthed liquor bottle still open. Its strong aroma of the potent liquid within was enough, it seemed, to have repelled the flies, or maybe it had been too cold for flies. There was enough, just enough, for a single, large swallow. The bottle had cost him; they all had. Would be a shame, said the little nagging voice in the back of his skull, to let it go to waste.

The internal battle was brief, the brown elixir downed in a single, well-practiced gulp. Vance felt it burn down into his empty belly, into every fiber of his body, bringing immediate relief to nerves and mind that had been deprived for too long.

"What the hell," he muttered with a shrug, grabbing the other smaller bottle sitting on that table and shoving it into one of the deep pockets of his Protectorate coat.

It was time to return to Kato and Jia.

A glance at the sky through the day's accumulation of hearth smoke, fog and snow clouds hinted that it was later than he thought. With so much of his day having been spent trekking to and fro across the borough, the hours had blurred, bringing him to late afternoon and further realization that he had not eaten in more hours than he could recall. A slight detour took him past the home of an older woman who every day served some manner of meal through the open window of her kitchen. From the aroma today, the heaviness of hemp beer and a hint of paprika intermixed with the scent of roasted goat, he was guessing that it was the stew she most often served in exchange for the ingredients of another day's cooking, a handful of credits, or a collection of cleaned serving containers.

"Protector," she waved him over when she saw him, smiling as she filled a small bowl from her ample pot and gave it to a boy who looked no older than ten or twelve. Behind her, her husband could be heard chopping the makings of the next meal she would undertake, or perhaps a meal of their own. "Come by for dinner?"

Hers was often the only decent meal he, and the residents of this stretch of street, ate during a day.

Thinking Jia and Kato would enjoy a hot meal as well, even if it came with the risk of attracting the Unders with its aroma, Vance fished in his pocket for the collection of tin credits he had stuffed there in case he needed them. He neither had ingredients to offer nor containers to spare today, and as usual, he refused to accept a meal from her as charity.

"Guests tonight, Urlina. Think you can spare enough for three?" He set the credits on the lip of the wide sill, nine in all, enough to buy herself a chicken or a large crate of vegetables. It was more than adequate payment for the molded hemplastic tub full of thick, chunky stew she ladled into it or the woven hemp bag she nestled it carefully into after sealing the lid so it would not spill as he carried it. Three sweetbreads, cool now that they had set on the sill for too long, were wrapped in a lightweight cloth and put into the bag as well.

"For you, always Protector."

"It's Vance…not Protector," he chuckled, the sound feeling foreign to him today. He wondered if it sounded foreign to her too. He was not a man prone to humor or amusement, and with the weight of recent events dragging behind him, he imagined that amusement was going to be a long way off.

She clicked her tongue in a scolding sound and handed him the bag. "Of course it is," she teased. No matter how many times he told her his name, she never used it, out of respect, stubbornness, or forgetfulness. The credits were stuffed into one of the floury front pockets of her worn apron as he stepped to one side of the window to allow the customers behind him to approach.

"I'll bring this back," he promised. He always returned her containers when he could, but this time he was less certain he would have that opportunity.

It was a good thing he had given her the extra credits.

Maybe he should give her more, just to be sure she had enough to get by on once he was gone. But she had already waved him goodbye as she served the stooped couple behind him, and the gust of cold wind that slid beneath the hair at the nape of his neck and down the back of his coat reminded him that the day was not getting any younger.

He still needed a way for the Chief, for Nik, to find him…and he was not certain where that should be. He did not even know yet how they could get Marrock's body out before the sposers came for it. He paused at the corner of the building to ponder all of the places he thought both Ernest and Nik might know, all of the places he might wait inconspicuously for them, places that might lend themselves to the exchange of a corpse.

Vance made it as far as the end of the street, the tang of paprika perfuming the air behind him, the line at Urlina's window having grown longer now as the dinner hour drew nearer, before noticing the boy he had seen in line before him perched in the shadow of a rickety wooden staircase that led into a building full of the screams and laughter of children. Perhaps one of many siblings, he mused, or part of a collection of orphans and runaways that congregated inside, either on their own or under the care of a foster. While the boy bore no outward signs of abuse, he was gaunt and wan. But those symptoms were common indicators of poverty, signs seen too often in this world after the Undoing.

Poverty was not a crime.

A word, filtering to him from amidst the shouts and laughter and crying inside sparked an idea, and Vance crossed the street to where the youngster shoveled his bowl of stew into his mouth with his dirty fingers. He did not seem overly wary of the Protector's approach, telling Vance he felt he had nothing to hide.

A good boy then. Well treated, if underfed.

"If I give you a message, could you deliver it for me?"

"Maybe," said the boy, hedging around commitment as he swallowed what he had been chewing. Most in the boroughs knew that doing favors for the Protectors meant getting favors in return, but the return would need to be worth his while before the child agreed.

Squatting, setting the bag of food between his feet and shrugging off his pack, Vance rummaged inside for the items he wanted. The woven bandage he cut from the roll with his knife was not the best substance for a written message, since the dense charcoal stick he wrote with would be illegible if handled too much or subjected to water, but it was all he had. The written message was a backup, in case the words he spoke next were forgotten or jumbled in their repetition.

"Take this to the Fortress. You'll probably have to give it to the guards at the gate. Tell them that Mage Segara needs to meet with the Chief and his friend at the Ivy Leaf Lounge. Tell them I'll stay until they get there…that it's important."

From the way the boy stared at the characters being written on the fabric, it was obvious he could not read. His thin face lit up at hearing the word mage and he stared in awe. "You're a mage? Can you teach me? I want to be a mage too."

"It isn't something you can teach…it's something you're born with," The boy's fingers brushed against his skin when he took the message out of Vance's hand. There was no trace of anything in him that would allow him to be a mage, but it was still possible that, when puberty came, the gift could awaken in him. "But you can be a Protector without being a mage," Vance assured him, reading the real reason why the boy wanted to be a mage in that contact. "All it takes to be a Protector is caring about people. LaGuardia needs good folks like you to protect and care about others."

"I can? It does? It doesn't matter that I'm poor?"

Vance shook his head. "We're all poor. Most of us anyhow. Now, do you remember what I said?"

"Chief and his friend are to meet you at the Ivy Leaf as soon as they can. You'll wait for them. And it's important, right?" the boy repeated with a confident nod.

"Right. Do that for me and…" He drew the three lemon-scented sweetbreads from his sack and offered them. Sweets of any sort were a rare commodity, but he did not think Kato or Jia would miss them.

"Yessa!" the child exclaimed, snatching the wrapped treasures, shoving them into the deep pockets of his flimsy coat, and after gulping the last of the broth in the bowl, allowed it to clatter to the ground in his haste to run off in the direction of the Fortress.

Not knowing how much time he might have before the message reached Ernest and action could be taken, whether his message would be understood and if any of them would have time to formulate any sort of plan in the interim, Vance scooped up the discarded bowl. He had gotten the stew but had not thought about how three were to share it without spoons or bowls.

He was going to have to consider that as he hurried across the borough into the lengthening shadows of evening.

*

For the fourth time since the rain stopped, at what Addi perceived to be regular intervals without any means of reliably gauging the time, Deuce left their makeshift shelter, disappeared into the trees, and from the location of his scent and the faint sounds he made traveling through the brush…sounds that only another anthro, or an animal, might perceive, circled their lookout. Watching for danger, Addi guessed, wondering if the Omega had done this every night of his life, every night since being expelled to the fringes of the Flushing Pack, around the building Roland had made into their home. How much of their security and safety was due to the battle-scarred Omega? How much of his expulsion had been for exactly that purpose, to give the Pack a silent, hidden protector?

Were all Omegas like this? Were they all protectors? Had the expulsion been less due to Roland's obvious dislike of the man and more for the well-being of the Pack?

Had Addi and the others misjudged Deuce?

Why would Roland have allowed that misconception to remain?

Deuce never spoke when he returned, only shook his head to reassure Addi that there were no threats, and then the two resumed their silent vigil, waiting for something that had not yet come to pass.

No one from the Pack came to check on them, not even Trill. No one came to report trouble with Pain, and no one came close enough to the thicket to be detected. The time for Jia and Roland's arrival was running short, however. Pain would demand a confrontation, would demand dominance of the Pack, if the Alpha, one or the other or both of them, did not arrive soon.

Addi was surprised Pain had not already done so, now that he and Deuce were not at the library to protest or fight back.

He hoped Pain was more eager for Roland's return then he was for the leadership of the Pack.

As the scents of the evening settled, they brought a slight shifting of the winds, and this time when Deuce returned from his circling, he did not re-enter the shelter. Instead, he crouched in the open, the darting of his eyes and the constant cocking of his head, along with the tension Addi could see and smell on him, speaking of some potential threat that Addi had not yet sensed.

"We should go back."

Addi frowned. "But Jia…Father…"

Addi knew Jia and Roland were not returning any time soon. Either they were delayed, hopefully with good news brought from LaGuardia, or they would never arrive. Perhaps they were approaching, and drawing danger along behind them, meaning Addi and Deuce had to return to the library, warn the Pack. The dropping temperature threatened a potentially freezing night ahead and building a fire here, where it would expose them to anyone looking for them, was a risk they could not take.

Returning to the Pack meant warmth and security and if there was some threat at hand, would give them the safety of numbers in the event of a fight.

Soon, they could be among family with a fire and a substantial meal. Remaining here was stubborn foolishness.

"They will join us when they can."

This time Addi noticed the use of 'when'. Not 'if'.

He wondered if Deuce said it to reassure himself as well as Addi or if he believed it. If perhaps his guess that his father and sister were coming, but were in danger, was the right one.

The raincape was taken down and wrapped around his shoulders, the most convenient way to carry it, and because of its repellent nature, it would keep some of his body warmth close to his skin. As he picked up the nearly empty pack of supplies he had brought to sustain himself through this extended watch, Addi glanced at the fidgeting Omega. Something was amiss.

"Go."

He took a few steps but noticed that Deuce was not following. "What about you?" Addi was surprised to feel concern for the Omega's welfare, in addition to his concern for his own. Deuce likely wanted him to go because he was no fighter. He wanted Addi amidst the safety of the Pack.

That could not be a good sign.

Head cocked again, lips beginning to curl into a snarl as Cana fur began to sprout across the larger man's bare arms and back, Deuce growled, "I have something to take care of. Go. Run."

Before Addi could ask again, press for an answer, Deuce bounded into the mottled pattern of shadows and light left on the forest floor by the dwindling day, further into the Wilds from the direction Jia and Roland were supposed to come from.

Addi wanted to follow, but by now he could smell it too, the faintest taste of something marginally familiar covered beneath the stench of death…the stench of grubbers. It was not unheard of for grubbers to be found in the Wilds, but why, he thought in a panic as he started east, did that reek carry the faintness of familiarity?

He did not want to stay long enough to find out, nor lead whatever, whoever it was, back to the Pack.

He needed to warn them.

Taking the Omega's advice, he ran.

Chapter 6

The throbbing at the side of her head was not the most peculiar thing Jia noticed as she swam towards consciousness, it was only the first. There was the strong taint of must and mildew and unwashed skin, the sorts of smells that immediately suggested Unders to her pain-fogged brain, a screaming thought that brought her to immediate wakefulness and jarred her upright with one hand against her skull to stop the thundering the movement created in her temple.

Sitting made her realize, before hunching forward against the nausea of movement and hunger pangs in her belly, that her head had previously been cushioned on someone's lap.

Kato's lap, she knew at once, his scent overwhelming as she turned her head in spite of the pain to see him seated with her in this recessed alcove in the dark. Not total darkness, as there was a glow to one side at the periphery of her vision that suggested a light source not far away. There was enough of that light to produce a faint halo around the Fela's tousled hair and illuminate the sparks of concern in his eyes. He caught her arm to steady her as she lurched.

"If you're hungry, I can find something," he began, perturbed that the mage had not yet returned and worried about the roar in Jia's belly and the lump at the side of her head.

"Stay." She tried to shake her head, but it only increased her discomfort. Her free hand clutching his wrist kept him from leaving as she waited for the nausea to pass. Her gesture was unneeded, however. The word itself was enough to keep him there. “What…where are…my father…?”

“The mage says he’s gone…” Couching the unfortunate news, though it was news she was already aware of, in the mage’s words made the telling Vance’s fault, not Kato’s. Part of him hoped that would make it easier for her to hear, make her less inclined to look favorably on the mage, take some of the sting from her loss.

From experience, he knew that not to be true.

Jia twisted her neck from side to side to ease the stiffness, which in turn helped ease the pulsing in her skull. It also meant Kato could not see the hurt in her eyes. She remembered everything that had happened, or as much of it as she had seen in that room where her focus had been entirely on her father. She remembered Quentin. She remembered the needle. She remembered Jonni entering the room and the fight, the hit, that sent him flying. But she could not remember the outcome of that fight. It was a blur to her. And she remembered Kato’s arm around her and the leap through the glass, from window to wall to the street below. She remembered grubbers.

Nothing existed after that.

“Where are we? How long?” Her voice was small, weak, forced, an effort to see to the business of survival rather than focus on painful remembrances.

Kato shrugged. “Below.” He did not know these streets, did not know where they were within the borough. He was unaware of there being any tunnels in the area where he had grown up, so he knew nothing about the refuge he had found. “A day…or most of it. Seemed unlikely they would follow us here. Once it’s night, we can move…”

“I have to go back…my father…”

“Would not want you to risk your life…” It was going to be a losing argument, but it was a reminder he believed Jia needed.

“I’m not leaving him there…”

“And you’re not going back in there.” Not alone, at least. Kato had no idea how he could stop her, but he was determined to try, even if he had to knock her out again.

Before revealing the news that the mage had promised to accomplish the thing Jia wanted most, the retrieval of the dead man from the Fortress, a feat that would undoubtedly set the mage as a hero in her eyes if he was successful, Kato twisted into a crouch, the approaching scent and sound bringing with it just enough of the news Kato had yet to share to spare him the need to speak it. As unwelcome as one of those scents was, the other accompanying it made his mouth water against his wishes."

"Vance."

There was hope and relief in Jia's voice, both of which brought an unexpected, but successfully stifled, growl into Kato's throat, but she was up out of his reach before he could hold her back.

Thankfully, the Unders had shuffled deeper into the tunnels hours before, leaving the fire can's contents to gradually burn itself out. Only the embers lit the tunnel now, giving off very little warmth.

"Jia." Blinking in surprise at her unanticipated embrace, the way she held him with one arm, mindful of the knapsack and bag he carried, her face pressed to the side of his for a few moments longer than the greeting hug he had not expected, Vance soaked in every detail, the feel of her body, the scent of her skin, her breath, her hair, and every frightening image of those last minutes of consciousness in the Fortress infirmary. Each new morsel of insight into those events cemented the picture of what had happened the night before, and that picture was one Vance did not know how he would ever reveal. Not if he was to make it out of the Fortress alive afterward.

Jia, too, noted keenly the scent of him, the masculine fragrance that had struck her so strongly when they first met. She noted the burn of alcohol on his breath, the warmth of fragrant soap that remained despite his time outdoors. But his awkward tension in that hug was what struck her the strongest, something she did not immediately understand but guessed must be rooted in his mage perceptions.

How sad, she mused, that his hyperactive senses must condemn him to a life of solitude and inability to share affection with others.

Overwhelmed, feeling awkward and off-balance, Vance drew back, mumbling, "I brought food," as he held the bag for her to take.

Protectively squatting behind her, Kato snatched the bag as if it might contain a threat, his hunger overriding gratitude or patience, and retreated into the alcove. Jia grasped Vance by the elbow, making certain there was no skin to skin contact, and led him there as well.

Along his journey here he had accumulated another bowl and three mismatched spoons. Kato growled in annoyance that he was expected to share this meal with anyone other than Jia, but he dutifully portioned the contents of the bowls and kept the largest for himself.

Vance, with a smirk, wondered if the Fela had kept the largest portion of stew for himself as well.

"You said you'd bring…" Kato started, handing the first bowl to Jia in the hopes that, if he started an argument about Vance's failure, the mage would leave. Seeing that was not going to happen, however, he reluctantly offered the other bowl to the tracker.

"I'm working on it. I can't just walk in and walk out with hin. Not in daylight at least, not while everyone's awake." He did not think he had the physical strength to carry a corpse either, at least not very far. Drag it, yes, but he would not get far across town without being noticed that way. "I'm supposed to meet Chief before long." It was not the only reason he was eating as fast as he could, as the shuffling of the Unders was beginning to echo through the tunnel, the shadow people drawn by the fragrance of a warm meal. Grubbers would likely be next. Unders would not attack with the same abandon grubbers did, in their hopes for food, but if they sensed a weakness, an opportunity, they would work together to take it.

Grubbers were only out for themselves.

"He'll either bring…" The body? The corpse? Roland? Vance did not know how he should refer to the man in Jia's company. "Or we'll make a plan to get him to you."

"We're going with you."

Vance scowled. "Bad idea. You're both wanted for murder."

"No one would believe I killed my…" Jia began to protest.

"Maybe not…but he wasn't the only…" Vance's palms began to sweat and he wiped them on his trousers.

"Who?" Jia tried to remember who else had been in that room and the sequence of events that precipitated their leap from the window. Jonni had been thrown into the cabinet. Quentin had sustained injuries in the fight with Kato and had then been struck on the head…by who? Nik? He had been unconscious when they entered the room, suffering the effects of his latest odose. How could he have done anything? Had there been anyone else she did not remember? Or had Nik acted, bid them flee, and then succumbed to either the drugs in his system or retaliation from Quentin?

Longer odds lay on her father having lived long enough, despite what she witnessed, to have taken revenge on his killer. Quentin then. Between that blow to the head, injuries in the fight, and potential revenge by a momentarily revived Roland, Quentin seemed the most likely target, and a death Lowell would never let go unpunished.

"Who?" she demanded again when Vance did not reply.

Another moment of silence as the mage lowered his bowl to his lap, clutching it between his hands. "Jonni."

"No."

Her nearly empty bowl dropped from her hands, clattering on the cracked cement floor, splattering what little remained on her clothing.

"No."

She collapsed back against the wall, her heart beating so hard that it stifled the flow of air into her lungs.

"Not…"

Not Jonni. He was the very last Channon she would expect to be the first to die. The kind son. The wise son. The gentle and just and loyal son. Nik was those things too, but his gentler nature was lost beneath his substance abuse, his host of addictions meant that it was only a matter of time, one odose too many, before death claimed him. With the way Donnovan treated others, superiors, equals, and subordinates alike, it had seemed inevitable that someone would make an attempt on his life one day, just as others had done on his father during his years as Laedan. Lowell had enemies too, and the possibility that Quentin would be one of those to make an attempt on his employer's life grew higher with every detail Jia learned about him. Any one of the others, perhaps.

But never Jonni.

"The cabinet shouldn't have…"

Again Vance shook his head without looking at her. "Not the cabinet." It was too lightweight overall, stocked with lighter materials, to have killed anyone in its falling. "His ribs were crushed when he was struck…thrown…"

"Him…" growled Kato.

"Quentin?" asked Jia. He had been the one to deliver that blow, even if it seemed unlikely he would make an attempt on a Channon's life so brazenly.

"I know, but…"

"Arrest him!"

"I can't!"

Jia lurched onto her knees, grabbed the lapels of Vance's coat, and snarled into his face, her eyes yellow with the effort to hold back the wolf beneath her skin. "He killed them both!"

Seizing her wrists, knowing what he risked in doing so…and in letting her anger bleed out unchecked, Vance growled, "I know he did, Jia." Her anger was fueling darker emotions within him, emotions he had to struggle to keep in check. "But right now, it is your word, Kato's word, against his. I need proof!"

"You're a mage! You are proof!"

He sighed heavily, voice strained. "The Chief will accept my report, maybe even the juds will accept it given my history and track record, but Lowell never will without…"

"Nik knows!"

"And won't talk about it, at least not to me. Can you blame him? With the state he was in…odds are no one will believe his story to be anything more than an addict's ramblings…not even Lowell."

Pouting, struggling against a crushing sense of defeat and the feedback loop of draining emotion in his grip on her wrists, Jia shook her head and pulled away. Vance was right. Nik was not the sort of man to stand up to his father. He never had. His form of rebellion came at the end of a needle, the bottom of a liquor glass, the stem of a pipe or a bottle of pills. It was possible, she reluctantly admitted, that Nik remembered very little of what had happened in that room, that he only remembered enough to be a danger to himself…to Quentin. Maybe he did not even remember his own valiant efforts to help.

Both Nik and Jonni had tried to protect her from Quentin. And Jonni had died because of it.

"If I can get your father out of there, I will. I swear it. I have connections…but it will be tricky to do it unnoticed." Especially when he had been forbidden to go back inside until he had Jia and Kato in custody. Mentioning that detail, however, would lead to some silly plan where they would all go in, confront Lowell and Quentin together, and likely die for their efforts. There had to be a better way.

"Let me do this. Stay here, out of sight, and…"

Again Jia repeated, this time with more resolve, "We are going with you." Before Vance could protest, she continued, "No one's going to recognize Kato. As long as I hide my face, no one will know me." Some of the guards at the gates would, thanks to so many days spent in the Fortress over the course of her young life, and a few of the Protectors might recognize her as well after her visit to the Protectorate. But she was less known publically than her father had been; as long as she was careful, she believed she would be safe.

And if it was necessary, she could call out the wolf.

"I need to take my father home to the Pack. By now Addi has reached them. They know he's alive…or that he was…and that he knows where Liam is. If I go back without him…" Her voice cracked and it was Kato's arms that reached and pulled her close for comfort before Vance could do so.

The Fela threw the mage a triumphant look over Jia's head as she wrapped her arms around him.

Vance swallowed his sigh and gathered the bowls, spoons, and container to tuck back into his bag, refusing to be baited by Kato's gloating. The Unders were nearer, approaching with their typical caution. He recalled something his father had once told him after Vance, as a young boy, had pushed a length of wire into the electrical generator the man had fashioned, despite numerous warnings against such an act. When the jolt threw the boy across the rooftop shed where the generator was housed, his father, rather than scold Vance, had said only, "It's human nature to think wisely and act foolishly."

How many times had Vance thought better of an action only to do it anyhow?

He knew he was about to do it now.

"You stay out of sight…do what I tell you…and if I have to go into the Fortress…or anywhere near it…you stay out. Agreed?"

Jia began to protest, despite knowing what foolhardiness would be involved in that sort of risk, but Kato clapped his hand over her mouth and pulled her to his feet as he stood.

From his knapsack, Vance produced clothing that he thrust in Kato's direction. Kato accepted with a hasty, "Agreed."

He would rather not go anywhere near that place again and he would be damned if he would allow Jia to do so.

Chapter 7

Torben Moller had been a sposer nearly all of his life, like his father and grandfather before him and generations of other Mollers according to his father…although before the Undoing the disposal of the deceased had been a much different business. It was not a job for everyone; few had the temperament, the stomach, or the desire to face the dead day after day. Few had the fortitude to endure a life of exclusion, ostracized by the living because of one's occupation. Most sposers, those who did not come to the job via exposure by family members as Torben had, were oddities, anti-social sorts who preferred to distance themselves from the living either by choice or necessity. Many who worked in one of the nine sposer facilities scattered across the borough, called Plants by everyone else, were mutani, men and women who could, at a glance, pass as Normals despite the genetic hand they had been dealt. By living on the fringe as this job demanded, it ensured they would not likely be discovered and banished to the Zone.

Others, like Torben, were anthro, and like their mutani coworkers, they chose an existence that garnered them little notice and allowed anonymity. They lived by the sposer code: do not pry into the business, the lives, of others, do not judge what you do not understand, and never, under any circumstances, share anything you know about another sposer with anyone.

In a job so few wanted, it kept the business alive. Someone had to dispose of the dead and the grubbers. Few wanted to do it. Those who did the job were loyal to one another in a way members of many other professions were not.

Sposers had to protect themselves and each other.

Some sposers had families they needed to protect, families who would perpetuate the business by picking up the responsibility when that one member could no longer continue. Most, however, like Torben, lived a solitary existence. And no one, or almost no one, came to the top level of the remarkably intact brownstone that Torben's family, as far back as there had been Mollers in New York City, had called home. It was the same for the other three families living in the building, each with a level of their own, each taking enough pride in the exterior of their dwelling to maintain it against decay and collapse.

Torben did not know much about the inside of those levels. He had never been in them, not even to claim their dead. Those families did not know what he did to survive and never asked, and he never advertised his business. There were enough dead in the world to collect without soliciting more.

Only once had Torben considered leaving this place, where the insides continued to fade and deteriorate around him. Only once, for a period of months, had he wanted nothing more than to never see those familiar, unchanging rooms again.

But he could not get the grand piano out of the apartment, and of all of the belongings he possessed, that was the one item he could not bear to part with. It had belonged to his father, and his father before him, and if he tried, he could still, at times, hear his wife playing simple tunes on its well-worn keys. As long as the piano played, he would remain here. He would die with that piano.

He would be buried in it, she had said.

Torben would be perfectly fine with that when that day came. There were no sons or daughters to pass it down to.

It was his typical lack of visitors, his reluctance to tell anyone where he lived borne out of an intense desire to be left alone with his memories, that birthed surprise and momentary annoyance in seeing the hunched figure in shabby clothes sitting at the top of the creaky staircase near his door, knees drawn up to chin, knit cap pulled down so far and hands tucked under armpits that it was impossible to tell if the intruder was a man or a woman.

Torben did not care.

"Go away."

When Nik Channon lifted his head, however, face gaunt, eyes sunken into dark circles though clearer than Torben had seen in a long while, his annoyance with the visitor vanished. He should have sniffed the air before snapping. He would have recognized his visitor then.

Presuming to know what Nik wanted, what Nik always wanted, he grunted as he unlocked his door and waved the middle Channon inside.

"What can I get you, Niki?"

Almost no one else called him that.

Despite his sometimes use of the variety of substances he collected from the dead, Torben had never become an addict. He chalked that up to the bear in his blood that afforded him a constitution many would have killed to have. He had never been ill, never made sick by the ailments and toxins his work exposed him to, never truly intoxicated or high. Recreational substances did sometimes produce a buzz of warmth and hazy memory, sometimes heightened his senses or helped clear his head to help him sleep or focus. It had been in using those, on some distant day in the past that he no longer recalled, that he had met Nik in a back alley dive trying to score a hit. At the time, Torben had not known who Nik was, had not cared if he was an addict if it gained Torben the few credits he had been seeking for a glass of hemp ale, had not cared to know him at all.

But that one time, and a brief discussion over drinks about how Torben scored such an unusual assortment of product, had introduced Nik to the world of body disposal and had changed both of their lives, particularly Torben's, for the better.

How many times had Nik come to the Plant, not for product, as he could have, but to watch the dead, to strip them, clean them, learn the multitude of processes by which a body could be disposed of to produce energy or fertilizing nutrients the borough needed, when ground for burial was at a premium and generally conserved for growing things or for use by those who were better off than everyone else? How many times had Nik helped in those processes while waxing philosophical about the meaning of death, about what might come after? About how the dead continued to provide for the living and thus were never truly gone?

That Nik was mulling over his own mortality, the restfulness and peace of death, had been painfully obvious to Torben, and despite the callous walls constructed around himself, he found it sad that one so young should be so focused on death as an escape from whatever torments life had thrust on him.

Nik was the same age as Torben's daughter would have been.

If she had lived to be born…and had not taken her mother with her into that impenetrable void.

If anything came after, if the dead continued to provide for him, Torben could not see it.

And still Nik came.

Sometimes he and Nik partook of some recreation or other together in the hours after Torben's shift, discussing mortality and grief and the things each sought escape from. Torben carefully monitored what he gave Nik, the dosage and purity and addictability of it. He tried often to wean Nik from his need to self-medicate, and when he would find Nik in a stupor in one dive or another, or slouched outside of the Plant door, he would see him back to sobriety with the sort of care that Nik had stopped receiving from his parents years ago. Sometimes he would elicit a promise from the young man that this would be the last time, that it would never happen again.

Of course, it always did, causing Torben to wonder if the path of addiction was Nik's way of reaching out for the familial grounding he did not, it seemed, receive within the Fortress.

Or maybe he was an addict like so many others since the Undoing because there was nothing else to fill his life with meaning.

With the old iron kettle set for the particularly strong hemp and ivy tea he favored, Torben opened the cupboard where he stored his collection. When Nik did not immediately answer his query, when it was noted that he was not hovering anxiously behind the bigger man's shoulder as he usually did when needing a hit, Torben removed the hanker tied around his bald head, wiped the sweat from his scalp and face, and watched the slow circle of the room Nik was making. The younger man stopped at the piano, rubbed his fingers over the polished keys without making a sound, and then stopped at the window which afforded a view across the collapsed rooftops of several buildings not as fortunate in their survival as the brownstone.

"Niki?"

Hat removed from his head, a throwback to polite manners that not many in LaGuardia followed anymore, Nik shook his head. "I didn't come for that." Not because he did not crave it, and shart knew that forgetting everything from the last twenty-four hours would be preferable to remembering. No, he sighed with heavy resolve. This time he had a responsibility, a duty that no one could see to but him. This time he would not run from it as he had before. This time he would stand up and be the man he had avoided being all of his life.

He was a Channon by god. It was time he acted like one.

"I need a favor."

Unable to imagine any sort of favor Nik could ask for that did not involve mind-altering substances, Torben closed the cabinet door, checked the kettle one more time, and then joined him at the window.

Nik waited until Torben stood beside him, until the silence was pregnant to bursting, before speaking. "I know I…you don't owe me anything. Shart…if anything…I owe you…" Torben had been more of a father to him in many ways than his own father had ever been. It was his trust in the Ursa that brought Nik to him now. That and the fact that the big man had the single most important qualification that could get him into the Fortress and out again without anyone asking questions about his right to be there tonight of all nights.

It did not matter who owed who what. Torben did not live his life with a scorecard. He helped when he could without a thought about recompense. "What do you need?"

One breath, inhaled sharply, nervously, and then Nik pushed the words out before he could allow his fears and reluctance to force him into silence.

"I need you to get Roland Marrock's body out of the Fortress."

Torben frowned and rapped his fingers on the sill. Given his usual gruff expression that matched his typical outer demeanor, that frown was only noticeable because Nik knew him better than anyone else.

"Marrock is…?"

"Murdered."

Side-eying the young man, dismissing the fleeting question of whether Nik had been the one to kill his father's best friend, Torben grunted. He knew nothing of politics; he resisted involvement in most things that might draw attention to himself and kept his focus entirely on his work and his own meager existence. But like so many in the borough, he knew that Marrock was a champion for the rights of anthro and mutani, and Torben respected him for that. Few outside the Fortress had known Marrock was missing, so the intrigue behind the man's death was a mystery.

But everyone knew the co-Laedans had grown up together and were as much friends as they were working partners in the endeavor of keeping peace, stability, and prosperity in LaGuardia. If Marrock had been murdered, with no public announcement having yet been made, it seemed likely it had just occurred and that removing him under the cover of darkness was an effort to cover up his death…

…or at least to cover up it being a murder.

"Doing this for your father?" If so, it was an unusual thing. Nik loved his father, yes, despite the man's failings. Most sons did. But never had Nik performed any favors for his father, and to Torben's knowledge, the Laedan was unaware of any connection between his son and the sposer.

So why was Nik here with this request?

"No…my father can't know of this." He twisted his knit cap in his trembling hands, the shaking born both of nerves and the onset of withdrawal symptoms as his body struggled to find a new balance. "It's taken care of…I mean…someone will be summoned in a day or two anyhow…to give him a proper burial when the forepath is done with him…but whatever my father has in mind…he wouldn't want that. He would want to go back home…to his family…to his pack…" Nik met Torben's gaze. "I want to give him that."

If the sposer was surprised, it did not show. Maybe he had already known the truth about Marrock. Maybe a lifetime of keeping the secrets of others had schooled him in the ability of keeping his expression neutral and unsurprised, unconcerned.

"They don't know," Nik continued. "None of them do. They suspect…my father and Quentin and the rest…but they don't know. Not for sure. But if we don't take him out tonight…"

"How many days?"

"Last night…after dinner."

Torben nodded with a grunt. If another few days passed and Marrock did not change into a grubber, the world would know he was anthro. Anthro never became grubbers. Of course, not all Normals became grubbers either. No one understood why, despite speculation that it was due to some latent anthro gene, but the change, or resistance to it, could have had any number of other causes left by the Undoing. No one really knew. Not changing was not proof that someone was anthro, but if the suspicion was already there, it could serve as proof enough to condemn his memory and his entire family.

"If I do this…"

"No one will suspect anything. They don't know you…and we've already arranged the story." It seemed odd to be in secretive league with the Protectorate Chief, the Protectorate's leading forepath, and their number one mage, but it also felt good…right.

It might be the first good and right thing he had ever done. Nik felt as if he had finally found a purpose. For however long it lasted, Nik felt good.

"Where would I…?"

Anticipating words as he often did, particularly in lucid moments, Nik replied, "The Plant. They'll meet you there, to take him."

By they, Torben assumed Nik meant Marrock's pack.

An eruption of loud shouts from a nearby street, an argument between at least three individuals indecipherable beyond the swearing, drew Torben's attention to the view from the window. He did not have to agree to this. No one would pay him, and it could blow trouble his way that he did not need. But the sposer code, the need to protect the secrets of others, weighed on his conscience. Marrock had been no sposer, but he had been a good man, an honorable and decent man. An anthro. For those reasons, and for Nik, it was a risk Torben would undertake, and a secret he would carry until the end of his days.

"Will you be safe? If I do this?" He assumed no one would make a connection between them, but he wanted to be certain.

Nik shrugged. "No one will suspect me. Hell, no one even believes what I say anymore. Shart…I've been a user for so long, I can play one without anyone knowing the difference." He tried to grin, but the light in his eyes was more serious than Torben had seen before.

For however long sobriety lasted, however long Nik could maintain the fight against withdrawal and relapse, he was strong.

"Now?"

Nik studied the faint light behind the clouds that revealed the moon's position. "By the time we get to the Fortress, most will be turning in. We can't go in together, of course…but I'll make sure the way is clear for you…tell you where you'll find him as we go…"

Torben nodded his agreement and left the window.

"Then you had better take this." From the drawer of the desk that made up one of the few furnishings in the room, the surface on which Torben normally ate and worked, he removed a bag of pale apple-green powder. A pinch of it was mixed with a cup of the not yet boiling tea he poured into one of the two mugs set on the counter.

He only owned two. One of them was his favorite. Nik was the only one to use the other since Torben's wife had died.

Seeing the question in Nik's eyes, the Ursa said, "Not addictive." At least it was not as far as Torben knew. "It'll help with the shakes."

That reassurance was good enough for Nik. Normally he would have devoured such an offering without question or thought about the consequences. Tonight, and for the foreseeable future, Nik needed to keep a clear head.

If he did not, he knew, as he downed the bittersweet brew without a grimace or a breath, he might be on a table next to his brother.

Donnovan, and Thomas Quentin, would have everything they wanted.

He handed the empty mug back to Torben, stretched his cap back over his head, realizing only then that Torben had not removed his heavy coat, and grunted, "Let's go."

☙*❧

Addi could, and did, hunt with the Pack for their occasional rituals, unless he was the one selected to remain with those pups still too young to participate. Such hunts rarely involved extended periods of top speed sprinting in the form of a Normal. Even without Cana senses, he knew he was not running in a straight line, knew he was likely traveling in circles, doubling back on himself, but maybe that would throw off any pursuers.

Or, if they waited, it might bring him running right back to them.

He had not seen or detected them yet, beyond that previous smell on the air, but he knew they were there. If they were not, Deuce would have rejoined him by now.

By the time Addi forced himself to stop running, breathless and shaky from thirst and exhaustion, he felt as if he was going to die.

It had been running from, as much as running to, but whatever was behind, whatever Deuce felt compelled to confront or draw away, never caught up to Addi. He could not say how much of that was due to his running and how much was due to the stubborn bravery of the Omega, but he had little doubt he might be dead already without the man's protection.

He heard no sounds of combat or confrontation, no sounds of a kill, but that did not mean there had not been one. He was about to return home again without his father, without his sister, and this time without the Omega too.

But at least he was alive. He could warn the others of danger.

His run brought him upwind of the Pack, where he could scent them as he regained his breath and composure and assessed the situation. There were no sounds of pups playing, but at this hour they would already have settled to sleep. He could not see the front door of their library haven, but the familiar voices heard within were engaged in friendly conversation. Eventually, a few figures came from the other side of the building, shuffling north in the direction of the mutani encampment and the Zone. They were nothing but shadows at this distance in the unlit hour of night, traveling as they were without torches or lanterns, but he gauged them to be their new mutani allies.

Who else, except those who loved them, would willingly consign themselves to live as outcasts in the Zone.

The voices inside, quieter though still mixed with the unfamiliar, seemed at ease. At peace.

It thankfully appeared that no tragedies had befallen the Pack during Addi's second absence.

"Gonna hide there all night?"

Maz's voice would have startled him if not for the warning given by his upwind position. The older Cana emerged from the shadows and offered his hand in welcome. "You're alone."

Addi shrugged. What else would he be, he thought miserably.

"Pain?"

"Nothing so far," Maz said with a miserable frown of his own. "You shouldn't have left them."

"You try talking my father out of anything he has set his mind on," grunted Addi, knowing that Maz had tried on many occasions to do just that. Roland was stubborn in his opinions, steadfast and unshakable in his choices.

His daughter was the same way.

The two combined were like an immovable, indestructible wall that Addi had been helpless to overcome.

"I thought if I stayed out long enough they would…" He shrugged and looked back, hoping again to see those he had left behind.

A snapping of twigs drew both men's attention, but after several moments, when nothing emerged from the trees, Addi sighed and let his shoulders slump.

"What?"

"We might have been followed; Deuce went back."

"Maybe it's Roland." Maz's words were more hopeful than his voice. He knew what Addi meant, however, trusted his instincts, and because he was not willing to shrug off a premonition of danger, he added, "I'll get others to extend the watch…push out further. If anyone's there…if he's…out there…" He being Pain, the one man Maz did not want to confront but who was their most pressing potential source of danger, "we'll take care of it." Addi looked exhausted, too tired for a fight, and he was a healer, not a killer. If there was a fight tonight, it would be with those capable of winning.

Addi's skills would be needed after.

He needed his rest, just in case.

Sometimes, Maz thought as he escorted Addi to the library door, this Marrock sibling seemed more Normal than Cana. But he was one of them, Roland's son. Not one member of the Flushing Pack had ever doubted that.

He would always be welcome here.

Chapter 8

"Don't get comfortable."

Looking up at the owner of the sneering voice as the other man entered the lounge where Quentin sprawled in a cushioned chair sipping dusky brandy and awaiting whatever came next, he refused to move despite the obvious warning. Nothing was going to happen until the forepath finished his assessment, until Jia and her Fela companion…abductor…were found and returned to the Fortress in chains, and Quentin had no reason to worry until one or both of those things came to pass.

He was not afraid of this voice.

Jia and the Fela could make claims against him, but who would believe such accusations from those already accused of murder?

The only other witness to those events was written off as living in a perpetual haze of addiction, and what had he really seen? Quentin had retained enough control of himself to prevent a change and no one else, besides the accused, knew the truth.

No one except perhaps Oasis, and she would never turn on him. He had done his best to keep the truth from her during their acquaintance, but it was possible that she knew. Somehow. She loved him and would want to retain the favor and good graces of HOPE. If she revealed anything she knew, or thought she knew, she could be expelled from the pedestal Francis Lord and her father had placed her on by virtue of the fact that she had slept with him. A Fela.

HOPE would never forgive such a betrayal of their beliefs, not unless she could prove that she had no foreknowledge of the fact, or could prove that what they had shared had been rape rather than a consensual relationship. Nor would her father. Nor the smug younger man whom fate had tricked her into marrying.

Lowell trusted Thomas. Trusted his opinions, his choices, his words. He would believe Thomas before he believed a naïve girl. Quentin's greatest obstacle was not Lowell or Oasis but rather Donnovan. Quentin felt assured that was an obstacle easily overcome.

"Comfortable?" He looked lazily around the dim room, at the drink in his hand, and then at his feet propped next to the plate of uneaten dinner he felt no desire to touch on the short table in front of him. He doubted anyone in the Fortress had eaten much since last evening. Anyone except Geary Hallister and his entourage, and the HOPE delegation that had arrived just in time to witness the aftermath of the chaos.

Pretending that Donn referred to his feet on the table, though he knew the truth, Quentin set them on the floor and put the half-full glass beside the plate. Donn rolled his eyes. Quentin stared at him blankly.

"You won't get District 1. The borough will be re-sectioned between Nik and me…"

"Nik can't manage what he's mayor of now. You do all the work for him. He only shows up for the kudos and the parties."

Though the assertion was largely true, Donn easily denied it in a sincere tone that would have swayed almost anyone in the Fortress or LaGuardia who did not already know the truth. "You'd be surprised how much Nik does. Sure, I offer advice, help, but that's what brothers are for."

Deciding not to open the liquor cabinet, he took the bottle from which Quentin had been serving himself, picked up Quentin's glass, and after topping off the contents, drank the entire thing, finishing the bottle by filling the glass again.

He did not set it on the table but chose to nurse it between his hands. "Or Father will govern District 1 himself the way he used to."

"The way he used to…when he had Marrock to assist him. With Marrock gone, who do you think'll assist now?" asked Quentin with a smirk that barely covered his annoyance with Donn's impudence.

A flicker of something shadowed across Donn's face, annoyance for the reminder, annoyance that he had not considered that possibility, or perhaps annoyance at Quentin's arrogant belief in his own indispensableness.

"It will never happen." If his father wanted to keep Quentin as his adjunct, there was little Donnovan could do about that. But he would do anything in his power, and beyond, to prevent Quentin from standing on equal footing with the Channon brothers…now one short but still strong by blood and birth.

"It will never happen."

Both heads turned with surprise to find Nik standing there, dressed as if he had come in from slumming the streets for a fix, the exact thing everyone in the Fortress, his family and those who served them, expected Nik to do. He had lost a brother. Nik could barely cope with normal life. How would he ever cope with the loss of Jonni without some substance or other burning through his veins?

Nik felt the testosterone-fueled tension the moment he reached the open door though he had heard it in the dialogue as he came down the hall. They had no way of knowing how long he had stood there, as they had been too focused on one another in their macho posturing to notice anything but one another. Letting them worry and wonder was more gratifying than calling them out on their argument. He kept his erratic, wandering gaze off of Quentin's face, hoping to hide the truths he knew, and as he swayed where he leaned against the doorframe, he doubted Quentin would see him as a threat at that moment.

In the future, however, was different.

Regardless of the love shared between twins, Nik doubted Donn would believe the truth of the previous night's events. Donn might pretend to in order to use the information against Quentin, and maybe pretending would be enough to get something done, bring Quentin to justice. But for the time being, Nik was not ready to take that chance.

Not tonight while there was clandestine business afoot that he needed to oversee. Nik could keep his brother busy easily enough. If he could think fast on his feet, he might keep Quentin busy too.

"I'm mayor…I can do this," he slurred, furthering their perception that he was high again. "Donn and I can do this together. We're Channons. We can do anything. We don't need you."

With a triumphant, affectionate expression, Donn emptied the glass, set it down, and joined Nik in the doorway, his arm around his twin's shoulders in a fraternal fashion, conveying a united front not often presented by the Channon sons.

There were only two now. They had to stand together like never before.

"You're right, brother." Feeling Nik sway against him and lean against his side, Donn added, "You need a good night's sleep. Come on…let me take you…"

It was the best way to get out of Quentin's company.

"Yeah…sleep…"

Intoxicated, high, or wasted. They were the only ways Nik slept.

Quentin scowled.

"Oh…" Nik looked back over his shoulder as though to look at Quentin though his focus was intentionally kept off-center of the man's face, "Da is looking for you…"

It was Donn's turn to scowl, and Quentin's turn to gloat as he got to his feet, the meal forgotten, straighten his clothes, and say politely, "Thank you, Nik."

Maybe Donn was right about Quentin's place in the Fortress. But the Laedan was not through with him yet.

By the time Quentin found Lowell and learned the truth, Nik hoped what needed to be done would be. He was not worried about servants or staff or soldiers. They were not the ones who would ask questions. Only these two men and his father could be a problem. But Nik had occupied them both, clearing the way for Torben as promised. Quentin, Donn, and soon Lowell, would all be occupied for however long that might last. Unless his efforts failed, for tonight, Nik's part in this charade was complete.

☙*❧

It was the diplomatically courteous thing to do; Lowell understood that. But he wished Francis Lord had chosen a better time, a better day, a better lifetime, to offer his condolences. He wished the man had not come at all, and was admittedly suspicious about the timing of the visit. He wished that some twisted arm of fortune had not seen fit to thrust the Grand Mas of HOPE into his home on the night after his eldest son and co-Laedan were both taken from him.

Alternatively, he wished there were some means, rather than by playing the grief and exhaustion card, or simply being rude, that he could get out of seeing the man.

His sense of debt to duty and desire to remain in good standing with HOPE, however, would not allow it as it had allowed him to avoid Geary Hallister all day.

"Unfortunate turn of events," the older man muttered, smoothing his hair with a sweep of his hand. "By a Fela, here, in your halls…"

"I know what happened. I don't need a reminder."

"Of course. Apologies. I only meant…"

"You only meant to imply that my security could not catch one lone Fela to prevent this…"

"Lowell…"

"We don't even know how they died yet…"

"Donnovan said…"

"Donnovan speculates and runs with his gut rather than his head… the impetuousness of youth," Lowell reminded Francis sternly. "He's heard rumors and believes them without proof."

To be fair, he admitted grimly, he had believed them too…the rumors about his best friend. Damn Quentin for feeding those to him.

"Until the forepath finishes his examination and Mage Segara…"

Francis's face lit. "You have a mage on this? Good. Good. I'm sure he will find the suspects and get to the truth so you can be done with this."

"We'll see. He hasn't found anything yet."

Francis nodded sympathetically. “Can’t rush these things, Laedan. You don’t want speculation or rumor, correct?” He used Lowell’s words against him in an effort to twist the conversation back in his favor, reshaping it into a dialogue rather than the attacking argument it was about to become. “If you want justice for Jonni, you need…”

“I want justice for both of them.”

A dismissive wave brushed aside the notion of justice for Roland. “A deceiver does not deserve justice.”

If that was true, Lowell sighed as he looked across the sea through the large pane of glass at the back of the room, then no one in the room, the Fortress, deserved justice…except Jonni.

Lowell certainly did not, and with the mountain of secrets and deceits he knew came with Francis’ position, the Grand Mas did not deserve it either.

“There is no proof of murder, of a murderer, of Roland being Cana. You know it as well as I do. Speculation is not proof and privacy is not deception.” Where his breath misted on the glass, he wiped it away with the side of his hand. “Did you know he was abducted…held against his will? He was trying to tell me about it…but he was so weary and…” He shrugged. “He escaped though, injured as he was, and made it back to me. To me, Francis. That means something.

His friend had beaten the odds and made it back to the Fortress. Whatever complicated feelings Lowell had, Roland had come back. That touched Lowell more deeply than he could express.

“Maybe the wounds of his escape killed him. Maybe whoever abducted him did it…or had it done to keep him quiet.”

“So you do not know who?”

The words dropped away as if the floor had collapsed beneath the Grand Mas and Lowell sighed eyed him, wondering what, if anything, Francis knew about Marrock’s abduction.

Had HOPE done these things, based on that same, as yet unfounded, accusation of anthrozooidism? Had HOPE done this at Quentin’s request? If not HOPE, did Francis know who had? Or why?

He was beginning to believe the man knew something, though he doubted he could ever prove it.

"I mean…he did not tell you anything you could use?" Francis tried to correct himself.

There was a knock, the firm sound of a man who felt no regret for his intrusion on a private conversation. But the door to Lowell's office was open so that anyone passing could hear them and enter, and so it was the Laedan's fault if he had wanted privacy and was denied it.

Or rather, it was Francis' fault as the man had not closed the door behind him when he entered.

"Excuse me, sir…you wanted to see me?"

Lowell scowled. "I did?"

"Nik said…" Quentin shrugged. In his altered state, it was impossible to know if Nik had heard those words from his father or if the request had been a product of Nik's impaired mind. Perhaps Lowell, in his grief, had forgotten the summons. No one could blame Nik for that. It was just the way he was. And after the last twenty-four hours Lowell had lived through, no one could blame him either.

Seeing the out he had been seeking to escape a conversation that had not gone as planned, Francis stepped forward and offered his hand. "Mr. Quentin, thank you for coming. Actually, I was the one who sent for you. Laedan…if you will excuse us?"

Lowell had no idea why the Grand Mas would want to speak to his assistant. Tonight, he did not care. He was tired and wanted sleep.

What he wanted was to have his son, and Roland, alive again.

Oasis' company would have been a suitable substitute.

He would not have any of those things.

If the two men had business to conduct elsewhere, at least they would leave him alone.

Lowell waved them away with one hand and sank into his chair.

This time when he passed through it, Francis Lord closed the door behind him.

Several long strides down the corridor away from the Laedan's door removed them from easy earshot, but Francis was confident that Lowell was not eavesdropping. From what he had witnessed during the last several minutes together, and from what he had seen across rooms and corridors and lobbies over the course of the day, Francis doubted Lowell had the head for skulking or suspicions. He wanted answers and he wanted to be left in peace to grieve.

Some of the answers Francis sought might reside in the man who had been present at the moment the others had died. How fortuitous that Quentin had come to him instead of having to be tracked down.

"Is it true then? There was a Fela…?"

"Yes."

"How do you know? Did he change? Here? In the Fortress?"

"Enough for me to be sure." Yellow eyes and fangs could just as easily have indicated Cana or Ursa, and he was no expert in either eyes or fangs, but it was either stand by that claim or indicate that he could feel the cat in the other man's presence, smell him.

That would expose his own dual nature, and Quentin would never do that. "With that strength…when he threw Jonni…what else could he be? How else could he make the jump from the window to the other wall, and then down again, without killing himself?"

"Indeed…indeed," Francis murmured with a nod. "How did he get in…a stranger…a Fela? One of the staff?"

"He came with Roland and Jia; they seemed to know him."

"Do you think he ingratiated himself with them to kill Marrock? Or do you think they brought him here to kill Lowell?"

Quentin had not considered why the Marrocks had brought the stranger with them, beyond the obvious assistance Jia would have needed to get her injured father to help. He had the impression the Fela was close to Jia somehow, or pretending to be, but if she was Cana it made little sense for her to befriend a typically solitary Fela.

Maybe getting to Lowell had been the intention all along. Or else the stranger had been brought in to confront and kill Quentin.

Particularly if Marrock had known the truth.

Decision made, Quentin shook his head. "Not Lowell. I think Marrock…" He paused in spite of himself. "I think it was me the Fela was here for."

"To expose you to Lowell?"

Not to expose his nature, something Lord knew nothing about, but to expose a secret just as dangerous. "Maybe…to get rid of me. Marrock's wanted to do that since I got here."

"True." Francis did not know what Quentin had planned, what his intentions were beyond the growth of power at the Laedan's side, perhaps even the position of co-Laedan. But he did know that Quentin carried no love for anthro and carried a deep desire to destroy them all…starting with the traitorous Marrocks.

That would be reason enough for a Cana and Fela to conspire to be rid of Thomas Quentin.

"If we could plant conspiracy charges as well as murder…"

With a little effort and some cooperation from the Fela, perhaps they could spin the case to read that Lowell and Quentin had been the targets, that the Fela had a change of heart and fought with Roland over the plan. Perhaps he had killed Roland so as not to kill the other two men? Jonni had been an unfortunate innocent bystander, killed only because he had been in the wrong place at the wrong time. It would not remove the stain of murder from the Fela, but protecting two men ought to buy him leniency with the juds, might condemn him to a work camp instead of an immediate death sentence.

He could claim to have removed a thorny problem in HOPE's side. Such an act would be rewarded in some way, even if he was Fela.

And for many, a work camp was a worse penalty than death.

"Have to find him first."

"You've got the borough's best mage on it, I hear. He'll find them." Francis felt confident about that. He detested mages, truth be told; they were not natural and most were barely tolerable as people. But they had uses, and honesty was often their motto. And their downfall.

"Maybe," countered Quentin with a shrug. "I hope so." He had little faith in the mage. And when it came down to the truth, he would much rather see the mage fail. Too much else was at stake.

Chapter 9

It was not uncommon for people to lurk in the shadowed alleyways around dives throughout the borough, men and women looking to score drugs or sex, spoiling for a fight or an easy mark to rob who was too intoxicated to defend themselves. Most brave enough to go out after dark knew to pass alleys with caution and resist entering them even if they were the shortest route to wherever they intended to go. To enter an alley, one had better mean business, and had better come prepared for it. Even the Protectors most often ignored and avoided alleys; they might pause long enough to judge the shadow peoples' intentions, but so long as they did not seem intent on theft or violence, they were left alone.

There were no laws against trading sex for favors, credits, food or drugs. No laws against the buying or selling of intoxicants. Basic survival was a more important matter to regulate. What people did in their private lives was too difficult to monitor. Remain unnoticed, don't hurt or steal from others, don't become a public nuisance, and the Protectorate left you alone.

Tonight, however, was not normal, particularly in the streets nearest the Fortress. Tonight the Laedan Guard and a good portion of the Protectorate were looking for a pair of anthro murderers.

Curious, Vance thought, how the story had gotten so twisted.

That rumor confined Jia and Kato to the shadows, to an alley that Vance had cleared nearly an hour earlier. Every Guard and Protector was combing the shadows in their search, depriving the dives of some of their normal clientele, but until the killers, or killer, was found, it could not be helped. That clearing, however, also meant that no one expected the pair to be hiding there with a direct line of sight to the door of the Ivy Leaf. The mage who leaned against the wall to the left of the door, one leg bent to plant his foot against the old brick stained with piss and vomit and the dregs left by one too many broken bottles, looked no more suspicious with his coat collar turned up than any other patron waiting for a friend or date who had yet to arrive.

Those passing in and out who recognized him as a Protector ignored him.

His willingness to loiter in the open, in sight of Guards and other Protectors, concerned Jia and she, like Kato, was ill-content to wait through each agonizingly endless minute for a meeting that never seemed to come. Vance promised he would be fine, that there was no need to worry, but with each uniformed individual that paused to speak to him, or side-eyed him as they passed, Jia felt her pulse quicken a little more, felt the beast beneath her skin itching to be free as it often did in moments of high stress.

With each encounter or near encounter Vance faced, Kato growled or hissed, sounds audible only to the woman hunkered next to him.

Her hand in his, however, kept him from action as surely as it grounded her and kept her from doing something impulsive.

She had to trust that the mage would not betray them. During the last thirty minutes, he had been given every opportunity to do so and had not. For whatever reason, Vance was on her side. Had been since they met. She should believe that, and fought to do so, despite the sporadic creeping flashes of doubt.

She heard him each time, the excuses that were, in their way, both lies and truths at the same time. He had cause to believe the hunted pair would come here. He was waiting for a contact who would provide information. He was waiting for his night's drinking companion so that he could drink and then head home. The first two reasons were acceptable enough to the Guards and Protectors with whom he spoke, who left to continue their search without feeling the need to stay with him, and the last excuse satisfied everyone else.

Very few, she knew, desired to spend any more time than necessary in the company of a mage. Not when that mage could glean details about them that they would rather not share.

There was no mistaking the chief's shuffling ambling when he approached the dive from the direction of the Fortress, out of uniform though he was, his hands shoved into his pockets against the cold. Jia's grip on Kato's hand tightened, drawing the Fela's attention away from a boisterous collection of young men and women coming from the opposite direction and turning it back onto the mage he had little desire to watch.

But the chief's arrival was worth noting, particularly when he stopped in front of the other man at the dive door.

Jia released Kato's hand to inch forward to hear the conversation.

"You got a reef?"

Vance nodded and dug out the hemp cigarette he had bummed off of a patron on their way out of the dive earlier. Neither man had a way to light it, but the Chief put the reef between his lips anyhow, seemed to be tasting the end with his tongue, and then withdrew it to hold it in his hand.

"Any luck?"

Vance shrugged as the loud group of dive clients pushed their way inside. He was not about to say anything incriminating while others were near enough to overhear.

"Nik's done it," Ernest continued. "He's got an in…who should be there be by now I'm sure."

"Who?"

"Moller."

The tracker nodded with unexpected relief. While having no idea how Nik knew Moller well enough to prompt the sposer to undertake this risk, Moller was certainly the one Vance would have approached for this job if it had been up to him.

He was impressed that Nik had devised what seemed, on the surface, like a workable plan.

In a world where people were known to stage fights with one another for credits as much as for the sport of the fight, Vance had been known, when his credits were low, to place bets on the occasional match. There was nothing illegal in the sport, as it was deemed an acceptable outlet for people's natural aggression, an acceptable channeling of it. Nor was betting on the outcome of fights an illegal use of one's credits. So long as the combatants were not obviously enhanced by some drug or substance, and they were not using any sort of weapon beyond hands, feet, and head, it was an 'everything goes' sort of affair.

Many fighters were assumed to be anthro or mutani, but unless one of them exhibited an obvious indication of it, fangs, claws, or some other physical alteration deemed unnatural by the general population, that they were not Normal seemed not to matter.

It was the one profession where those particular individuals could survive without the public turning against them. It was more lucrative for the public to protect their favorite fighters and earn a few credits for their wins then it was to turn them over to the law.

It was a sport Torben Moller engaged in from time to time as well.

It had been after one such fight, with a handful of unexpected credits made off the win he had bet on, that Vance turned up in the dive where that very man, bloody and bruised but remarkably steady on his feet after the fight he had just engaged in, was propped on his elbows at the bar. The place had been crowded, the only empty stools being on either side of the beastly-built man no one else was willing to approach, and so Vance had taken one of them without hesitation.

It was his lack of reluctance and fear that attracted Moller's marginal interest in him, and the brief, awkward conversation that followed, in which they bought one another drinks to celebrate the win, had been the start of a long, reliable acquaintance. Moller would alert him to upcoming fights he was participating in and Vance would make modest bets on the Ursa he was sure would win. It kept his pockets lined during lean times, kept his liquor cabinet full, and it felt nice to have a 'friend' he felt he could go to if he ever needed him. If either of them ever needed anything.

Later, when Ernest introduced them during the line of duty, when Moller came as part of a team to dispose of a grubber nest the Protectors had put down, the relationship was further strengthened. Professional colleagues as well as off-duty friends…of a sort.

They did not socialize, as neither was the sort, beyond an occasional shared drink. Moller was even more private than the tracker, but they knew each other's secrets by now, and neither was inclined to talk more about them. They had each other's back. That was enough.

How the Chief knew Moller, whether through the job, as both had been in the same businesses all of their adult lives and were no more than ten years apart in age, or if they had encountered one another outside the job, Vance did not know. He never asked and had never probed the thoughts of either man to learn. That detail did not matter.

"They'll be at the Plant in an hour…maybe two," Ernest said as he stuffed the reef into his breast pocket, perhaps to give away to an informant later, perhaps for personal use when he was not on the job.

Again Vance nodded. It would take Moller time to get in, get the body, and get out again, even if he was unhindered by Guards or Fortress staff. It was a long trek from the Fortress to the Plant where Moller worked, and even for a man of Moller's strength and constitution, carrying a body or dragging a sposer's cart as would likely be the case, would be no easy feat.

"You going to meet him there?"

Vance scowled, any quick reply he might have made cut off by three men pushing and jostling each other through the dive door to stumble and fall in the street. As there was no hostility between them, only the laughter of friends in a hurry to stagger drunkenly to whatever destination they intended next, Vance and Ernest helped them to their feet and silently watched the trio weave their way towards the nearest southbound street where they turned and disappeared from view.

It took longer for their loud laughter to fade.

They appeared sober enough to know where they were going.

Considering his option, Vance finally answered the question. "Yeah…we will." He could send Jia and Kato on alone, letting them take her father's body and be done with it, bow out of this mess that had deprived him of sleep for too many hours. But Moller did not know them, at least Vance doubted he did, and might not be willing to relinquish the corpse to strangers. And it would be just like Kato to push the Ursa into a fight if he felt slighted. Despite his personal feelings about Kato, Vance did not want Moller to kill him.

Jia was going to need the Fela to get her father across the Wilds.

No, he decided, the handoff would run smoother if Vance was there as an intermediary.

Ernest did not question whether the mage already knew where the Marrock girl was, whether the Fela was with her, did not ask what his tracker knew about guilt or innocence of murder. He did not ask why Vance wanted to be there, although he assumed the mage wanted to inspect Marrock himself. The less he knew, the better.

"Watch your back," was all he muttered as he pushed into the dive for a much-deserved drink. There were no more words to exchange and he did not want to see which way the mage went next.

Again, the less he knew, the better.

Vance made a show of adjusting the collar of his coat with a tilt of his head, the turn of his body indicating the direction he intended to travel, hoping as he did so that Jia was watching, that she would read his intent and travel through the shadows to join him somewhere away from the Ivy Leaf. If she had been listening, if she had been able to hear the exchange with the chief, she already knew their destination was a Plant. She would discover which one soon enough.

It was good to be home, to be warm with Trill curled beside him, the pups in a tangled pile for warmth and security, others in the pack gathered in their own slumber, each there for the safety of the others. With Maz, Helena, and Wist on watch at points near their library sanctuary, watching for the Omega's return, it was not likely the Pack would be caught unawares by any manner of threat, but Addi admitted, as he sat up from his restless failed effort to sleep, that he would feel better if Jia was here, if Roland was here, if he knew that Deuce was safe. Though he had never given the Omega's watchful presence a thought in the past, the last few days had given him a different, more appreciative view of the man and a respect that he believed was well-deserved and long overdue.

"Addi?"

Though he patted her arm reassuringly without looking at her, his gaze fixed on the library door, Trill knew her mate too well. She knew he was eager for his sister and father's return, worrying about their welfare, worrying about whatever he believed had followed him home from his watch. More than an hour had passed since his return with no sign of that threat, but that did not mean it did not exist.

Addi could be a worrier, often about things that never came to be, but this time, Trill believed his premonition. The Omega had not returned. If Addi thought that someone, something, had followed him, it likely had.

She sat to wrap her arms around his shoulders but he sprang to his feet as the door flung open and Wist stumbled backward through it, his posture that of one under threat, the scent of his blood on the air though none was immediately visible. His hands were raised as if in surrender to the man with a long knife who dragged the staggering Deuce through the door, a blade dripping with blood. The same blood spreading from the gash in Deuce's side. The sound of the intrusion, the unexpected scents, brought the adults and children alike awake, and when Reif got off a quick howl of warning to those adults outside the library, the blade was pressed to the Omega's throat, a threat that did not need to be given in words.

Reif fell silent and skittered back behind Trill, using her body to shield the frightened pups. The sound had been enough, however, for those on watch, and the rest of the Queen's College Pack to have heard her, and soon they would come to add strength to the Flushing Pack.

Pain knew there would be others to contend with, but his hesitation was brief. He took a step forward, dragging Deuce, enough threat in his movement to force Wist back to the security of the others.

"Let him go, Pain," growled Addi, body low as he crept forward, hands upturned in submission. Pain knew him; surely he knew the medic, who had just been asleep with the rest of the Pack…or had been trying to sleep…would be unarmed. The others too, likewise awakened, were also unarmed. "He's bleeding. Let me…"

"He's Omega." That was Zen's voice, spat from behind Pain as she emerged into the room from the cold. Her gaze swept the group, again seeking her brother's face, and when she did not see him, her expression grew darker. The others followed, Ilba, Xan and Uncle. They looked little worse for wear after their expulsion from the Pack, but to Addi's eyes, few of them seemed content with their choice to leave, particularly after Pain's last attempt to claim the Pack.

Addi had no doubt Pain was here to try again, that it had been Pain and the others that Deuce had sensed. Maybe the others, and even Pain, had come to request remittance into the Pack, but that was a decision only Roland or Jia could approve.

Maz, having entered via a broken window on the second floor that was easily accessed for a Cana or Fela from the roof of the nearest building, perched at the top of the stairs that led to the upper floors. He must have shared Addi's thoughts, for when he crouched, not in submission but in preparation to leap, he asked, "Have you come home?" with a note of longing in his voice that made the knife at Deuce's throat shake with the emotional trembling of Pain's hand.

Deuce did not move.

Rather than answer, Pain countered, "She's not here."

Though it was impossible to prove that merely by Jia's absence from the room, none of them could deny the assertion and none chose to try. Instead, Addi repeated, "Let him go. He's going to die…"

Deuce was strong, stronger than nearly anyone Addi knew, and the wound did not look fatal, but Addi could not be sure without closer examination. From the pasty look of his skin, the crimson stain down his side, his stomach, his trousers, and the groggy expression on his face, however, the Omega had lost a lot of blood.

"He's…"

"You've got our attention," Maz interrupted. "You don't need him."

The two men locked gazes across the room, across the levels, and soon, with a growl and a huff, Pain shoved the injured man forward. Addi caught Deuce as he stumbled, before he fell, and with Candace's help, dragged him back into the midst of the pack.

"I gave you time; I claim Flushing Pack as mine."

The words were enough to rouse Deuce from his painful stupor, enough to force him to sit with a warning growl only to have Candace push him back down as Addi exclaimed, "There hasn't been enough time! You have no right!"

"You have no Alpha. I have every right…unless you wish to challenge me, Marrock."

"I swear to you; Roland is coming home!"

Those behind Pain looked at one another and back at Addi and Maz, who had spoken near-identical words simultaneously. Pain asserted otherwise, but the doctor and Maz both sounded certain of their claim. They did not speak the words merely to buy time.

They spoke the truth as they believed it.

If what they said was still true, if it turned out those behind Pain had abandoned the Pack in its darkest hour over differences with the Alpha Roland appointed to be his successor, what chance would they have of being forgiven if they continued in their obstinacy? The bloody clothing Addi provided before had been the only proof to support his claim, and they had stubbornly clung to the possibility that it was not proof enough.

But maybe it should have been.

"I don't see…"

"I told you, his injury was bad, enough to keep him from traveling. That's why I came ahead. They may be traveling slow, but they will come. They will be here as soon as…"

Pain snarled, cutting Addi off. He did not look up but continued to concentrate on Deuce's injury. The doctor stitched the wound closed when he was confident there was no internal mutilation or bleeding. Deuce hissed and grunted but never pulled away from the needle's pinch.

"You have not told us where you found him."

Where should not matter, would not give any more proof then Addi's assertion had. Maz, assessing that the initial danger had passed and that perhaps Pain was looking for an excuse not to act, stood up and began to descend the stairs. If he could keep Pain talking, he hoped he could diffuse the situation, convince Pain of the folly of his actions. There had been a time when Pain listened to him, heeded his advice…and surely he understood that he had no claim here so long as Roland lived, so long as Roland's appointed successor, lived.

Maybe the foul weather and not having a proper den or enough food and supplies was pushing Pain to act in order to provide for those following him, but it was not enough.

He could challenge Jia again for the right to be Alpha, challenge her the right way, if she returned without her father, but Maz knew Pain would never challenge Roland. Pain owed the Alpha his life many times over.

He seemed to feel he owed no such debt to Jia, even though she had allowed him to live after his illegal challenge.

If they fought again and Pain lost, Maz did not think Jia would be as lenient as she had been the first time.

"He does not owe you an explanation. Where does not matter. Roland and Jia will return. That is all you need to know."

"When?"

The ultimatum in that question was impossible to miss.

"It does not…" Maz began again.

"It does! Leaving the Pack leaderless is…"

"How many times did Roland entrust the Pack to me? You doubt my leadership?" It was a painful question to repeat, made even more so by the scorn in the lift and tilt of Pain's chin.

Maz growled.

"When?" Pain repeated.

"A few more days…a week if the weather holds…I don't know!" Addi could not be certain of a timeline as he could neither judge the weather, the injury he had treated but could not monitor across the Wilds, or the nature of the political dance his father and sister had intended to engage in. But if he had to return to deal with the threat Pain represented to their leadership, he would do it. Or he would send someone who could.

Pain grunted. "One more week. A week…then the Pack is mine unless," he stared defiantly at Maz, "Someone wants to challenge me."

Glances were exchanged between members of the Pack, again worried and fearful. They had just begun to settle after Pain's last threat. His efforts to keep them off-balance and uncomfortable would wear some of them down until eventually they relented just to have peace. Of all of those here, only Maz or Deuce stood a chance against Pain. Or perhaps Orliss, if the leader of the Queen's College Pack was inclined to fight for them. With Deuce now injured, it left Maz, and not one member of the Flushing Pack believed Maz had the will or desire to stand against the man he loved. Unless he did, unless Orliss could be persuaded to take the risk, take the Pack, or unless Roland and Jia came home, they would belong to Pain's leadership within a week, and those who supported the Marrocks' right to the Pack would be beaten into submission or killed.

Addison Marrock, valuable doctor or not, included.

Chapter 10

"You haven't done this before, have you?"

There was panic in Liam's eyes when the doctor, the stately woman he had heard called Torrance by other staff members, stopped behind him to monitor the way he bathed the body of the young woman who had begun to seize in the pod that had kept her alive for however many days she had been in this place. She had been here when Roland left. How long before that, how long it had been since, Liam did not know.

She had been transferred to a gurney for treatment in a vain effort to keep her alive, but whatever the cause of her convulsions, her body rejected treatment, and its contents, through her bowels and throat, leaving her motionless in the stench of her waste. She was cold now, the blood that sustained her hastily drained as the last of her life left, but she was still a person, still deserved his respect, all the more so because of the undignified way in which she had passed.

So he bathed her with all of the tenderness he would have bathed an infant.

"I've cleaned up children," he mumbled, hoping that was what Torrance was asking. "I've cleaned my share of dead."

"But you're no medic."

Swallowing hard, his hands trembling though he refused to acknowledge it or to look at her as he continued his efforts to clean the dead woman's flesh, he shrugged. Her claws and fangs were beginning to emerge on their own now, as so often happened with anthro corpses, and though it would not yet be noticeable to Torrance or her staff, it would, within less than a day, reveal the dead's true Cana nature.

She had been barely older than a pup. It made him think about Reif and the Flushing pups, wonder how they were fairing in the chaos of that forced uprooting.

He wondered if they were still alive.

"Medic assistant. My friend's a medic…I've helped enough to know what I'm doing."

Doctor Torrance grunted, a sound that expressed neither belief nor disbelief. "Do you know what killed her?"

Liam shook his head. His first response would have been that the constant bloodletting had killed her, but he was smart enough to keep those words to himself. Yet he had never seen the loss of blood result in seizures, in the relaxing of muscles that allowed the body to expel everything it contained. Such expulsion usually came after death, not before. She might have been ill before her capture, in which case she had contaminated everyone in the facility, or Torrance and her staff had injected the unfortunate woman with any number of toxins to hasten her end or to study her reaction.

"Could have been something wrong before she came here," he offered, expecting that an 'I don't know' response would work against him. "Without knowing more about her, I couldn't say."

"We could study her in the lab."

"I've never been in a lab." He looked at Torrance then, not surprised by her expression of mild triumph, and hastily added, "We didn't have access to one at the medishelter…"

Torrance toed the pile of dirty towels further away from where she stood, the disgust for the smell and the waste and the annoyance of possibly staining her shoes evident on her face. "Of course not," she said in a condescending tone. "There isn't one like this in LaGuardia."

Liam thought her admission should tell him more. Did she mean this was the best-equipped lab in the boroughs, and if so, then Liam thought he must surely know where that was. Or did she mean they were not in LaGuardia…and if not in LaGuardia, then where? Kennedy? The Zone?

Or had he been taken into HOPE's well-guarded territory?

None of the possibilities was reassuring, but it was more information than he had possessed minutes before.

She knew he had come here from LaGuardia. He wondered what, if anything else, she knew about him.

He bent to pick up the dirty towels but Torrance said, "Leave those. Bring her. Follow me."

Having seen other bodies wheeled out of the room when they ceased to provide the usable commodity they were brought to give, Liam believed he knew what came next. Autopsy and testing, surely. He pushed the gurney through the lab door into the dimly lit nighttime corridor and followed the clacking of the doctor's shoes without watching her. The sound was enough to direct him while his eyes took the opportunity to memorize every detail along their route. Every door they passed, every change in the air that hinted at what might lay behind them, every shift from warm to cold and back that revealed which areas were inhabited and in use and which were used less frequently or not at all. He would never make it out of the compound the way Roland had. The air duct above his cot was welded shut now so it would never open again. If there was a way out along this path, he would hate to miss it by being distracted by the annoyance of those hard-soled shoes on the tile.

The room they finally entered was spared being the coldest in the building, a storage for the dead until they could be processed, by the glowing red of a great furnace at one end, in which all waste…food, medical and dead combined…ended up in order to produce power for the rest of the facility. Two individuals in suits meant to protect them from the heat and stench of burning bodies, chemicals, and hemp plastic, operated the furnace door and the gauges used to monitor the power output and the fullness or emptiness of the space behind the door. They paid Torrance no attention, beyond a glance at the body on the gurney, before returning to their efforts to shove corpses and other debris, all in various stages of decomposition, into the fiery maw.

So many corpses suggested other captive victims elsewhere unless this place served as a Plant for the streets around it.

To the right side of the vast room full of bins, crates, and barrels of various waste material, a pair of wide corrugated metal doors were sliding shut, to be held with a manner of lock Liam had never seen elsewhere. The sound of clattering wheels beyond it supported the brief glimpse he had seen of some sort of delivery wagon, the sound growing fainter as the wagon moved away to retrieve more refuse from the region this facility served.

Liam hid the frown that threatened to cross his face with a more appropriate cough and grimace, things not faked due to the collection of strong, foul odors in the room, smells which became stronger and more noticeable as the last of the fresh air allowed in by the open doors was sucked out of the room and into the furnace to aid in the combustion process. He imagined some of the generated heat was distributed throughout the complex by the continual whirring of fans he could hear, but how the rest of the heat was turned into power to run lights and other equipment, he would never understand.

There was not a mechanical bone in his body, and no knowledge of engineering or the physics of power generation. To Liam, things either worked or they did not. The how of it was left to other, smarter people to understand.

There were things he did understand, however, as he gazed about the room. The double doors would be the easiest escape route if he could find a way past the workers and break that lock. Come morning, others would arrive to replace these two at their furnace duties, sorting through the mountain of waste the wagon deposited not far inside the doorway. Likely, the room was busier during the day, and so any effort to escape would have to come in the night, after Torrance and most others were asleep. After the doctor motioned for him to put the poor girl's corpse onto the heap of perhaps a dozen other recently deceased and a few immobile grubbers as well, he realized she was permitting him to see this because she intended for him to die here too. She wanted him to know where his journey would end.

Or she was trying to frighten him into never attempting anything as brazen as what Roland had done.

"I didn't think there would be a lab at a Plant," he murmured as he lay the body gently with the others. There was no sentimentality to it, as everyone knew that what was left after life departed was merely a lump of organic matter meant to service man or nature just as the living did. But Liam did feel remorse over the death she had suffered, and so acted as much to appease his own feelings of his part in it as he did out of any respect for who she might have been.

His attempt to fish for information went unheeded. Torrance beckoned him to follow her back to the room that had been his home for however many days he had been here. Someone, a member of the night crew Liam had not seen the doctor summon, had taken away the towels and left a clean mop and fresh towels in their place.

"You may sleep after you finish. We will be late tomorrow."

Liam cocked one eyebrow but did not ask why as the woman left him alone at last. He hoped lateness might permit him a little more sleep but he could not count on that.

The souls he tended could not be left waiting for care for too long. Delays in feeding, in cleaning, in checking that their tubes were attached and clean and functioning, that their straps were not too tight or too loose, that their oxygen was still flowing, meant death.

Not just for them, but for Liam as well, He had avoided death tonight, despite her apparent belief in his incompetence, but how much longer she might afford him the chance to continue breathing was not something he wished to explore.

"Here for the dead."

As had happened at the Fortress gates on his arrival, the men standing watch at the cold storage room door where Nik had said the dead were kept did not ask questions of the big man in the dark gray coveralls with the sposer insignia on both shoulders of his winter coat, his head covered in a dirty red bandana and faded black woolen cap.

Over the years, so many had died within the Fortress walls, employees and prisoners and family alike, that all except the newest guards recognized the man and the cart he drew behind him. If not his face, they knew the insignia, and after more than a day on an active hunt for murder suspects, they all knew that someone in the Fortress was dead.

Those who stood watch at this interior door knew who they guarded, though very few others did.

It was inevitable that sooner or later a sposer would come to carry out whatever manner of processing had been requested for the dead.

Because there were numerous possible ends for the deceased, and because it would be no surprise that the Laedan would keep his son close as long as he was able, once the truth was made public, there were no questions when only one body was placed on the cart to be taken away. No one came to pay final respects or say goodbye as the wrapped corpse on the cart was covered with another, heavier tarp to block the moisture in the night air, but Torben mused, why should they? The dead did not care for goodbyes, or for any degree of respect. Only the living cared about those things, and at this late hour, there were few of the living awake to express their grief.

Those things would resume with the dawn.

From his bedroom window, Nik watched the little wagon, with its single canvas-wrapped body, pull into the nighttime street, relieved that the retrieval had gone without incident. No one was likely to ask questions or raise a fuss about the potential oddity of the transfer at this too late hour; no one was likely to speak of it until breakfast the following morning. By then, Roland would be far away from the place he had lived and served most of his life…where he had done what was best for LaGuardia and where he had ultimately become a sacrifice to subterfuge Nik had yet to uncover and expose.

But he would. By the stars, he would, even if it killed him too.

To any suspicious eyes that might have followed him, there were no unusual deviations to the sposer's route between the Fortress and the Plant that helped feed the borough the power it needed to survive.

Left along the stone hedge, along the misty boulevard where the icy sea kissed the crumbling pavement behind the wall as its high-tide surf beat at the edges of civilization. Right for the two long blocks necessary to avoid the devastated collection of buildings gradually transforming into a mossy wooded hill as dirt and dust accumulated around fallen wood and brick, filling the crevices and erasing any sign that it was a remnant of human inhabitation. Then left again, back towards the sea wall, until the outer stone barrier of the North Plant came into view. The salty fog rolling in over the water was thicker here than further inland, meaning the gray walls of the plant were almost invisible, but Torben knew they were there, ahead of him.

He had walked this path more times than he could tell.

Just as he knew the mage and two others waited out of sight as well, hidden between a cement brick outbuilding used by some of the Plant employees for housing and recreation and a similar cement building that housed sposcr wagons, big and small, in need of repair. Both buildings were dark, locked for the night, just as they had been when Torben departed earlier. No one was likely to see them or notice the clatter of the cart as it was a familiar sound here, passing in and out day and night since the dead did not always wait for daylight to accumulate. If anyone was following Torben, as the fog swallowed him, they would not likely notice any discussion that took place, so long as they spoke quietly and the exchange was brief.

"Mage."

His soft voice, gruff as it was, carried through the mist and brought the hidden individuals into view. Torben did not know the longhaired Fela, only sensed the cat by his movement and the scent of his nervous energy. But he knew Vance after so many years of acquaintance, though the mage's hair had grown out enough since their last meeting to require being tucked back behind his ears. The few times he had seen this young woman in the Fortress halls at her father's side were enough to identify the Cana as Marrock's daughter. Odd that he had never considered her to be grown up.

Just a little older than his daughter should have been.

"That him?" she asked, referring to the contents of the cart, her quavering voice and the aversion of her eyes away from the canvas-covered lump revealing that she was not yet resigned to her father's death. How could she be? She had likely just learned of an event that had happened little more than a day ago. At her side, the Fela growled softly, the yellow of his eyes suggesting an anthro on the verge of change, one who could be easily provoked into doing so by the Ursa whose size alone could seem threatening.

Torben could not fault her uneasiness with the dead when he had yet to resign himself to the deaths of his wife and daughter even after so many years. Nor could he fault the Fela for his anxiety, as this situation was hardly normal.

He nodded as he looked the strangers over, gauging their strengths and weaknesses the way he judged his opponents when he fought. Tonight he had no desire for a fight, no wish to provoke the Fela. He wanted only to keep his promise to Nik, hold to a bargain struck.

"How far?"

Though neither Jia nor Kato understood the question or its reference, Vance was accustomed to the Ursa's abrupt, short manner of speech and his reliance on as few words as possible to convey anything. Torben did not like to talk, did not want unnecessary details. He wanted simple answers as succinctly as possible.

"Across the Wilds."

The downturn of Torben's lips mirrored the concerns Vance had harbored since his meeting with Ernest, concerns he had not shared with Jia out of fear of starting an argument they could not afford to have in the open street…or while hiding here in the fog waiting for Torben's arrival. Vance had no doubt that the anthro were physically stronger than he was, but both were recently injured and functioning on inadequate food and sleep…just as he was. The distance was not long, but at the speed they would need to travel to reach the Wilds by sun up, to reach a place where they could rest without fear of detection by Laedan Guards or the Protectorate, they would collapse and be useless to travel for too many hours afterward.

There had to be a better way. Perhaps if he asked politely and promised to return it, claiming Protectorate business as the excuse for confiscating private property, Torben and the Plant staff would permit Vance to use the cart on which Roland already lay. It would slow them, make them too easy to hear, would be difficult to manipulate through the Wilds, but it might be easier than hauling a corpse on their back. Maybe they only needed to take the cart to the edge of the Wilds and carry Roland from there.

Torben, however, had another idea, one that came to him as the cart jostled across LaGuardia's stony streets.

"I will carry him."

"You sure?" started Vance as Kato growled, "Not necessary," and Jia started, "I cannot ask you to…"

"No one is asking." Torben parked the cart near the repair building door. Someone would notice its absence from the primary shed; someone would find it here come morning, and assume it needed repair and then be confused to discover nothing was wrong with it, but it was the best he could arrange.

There was not enough time to put it back. Taking time to do so came with too high a risk of detection.

"It's too dangerous…" Jia whispered.

"For you, or for us?" That was Vance's question, one that drew Jia's puzzled gaze to his face.

"We're the ones accused of murder…" Kato reminded him with a perturbed snort. "Not you."

Vance nodded. "And I'm the one told not to return to the Fortress until I found you both, brought you in. Look at us. Little sleep, little food…that nasty bump on your head." He looked at the rough bandaging he had tried to do in the dark that was now sliding free and unraveling to reveal the bruised protrusion at Jia's temple. "And you…" He did not know the nature of the injury to Kato's side, but he knew it was there, and it still troubled Kato despite the Fela's efforts to pretend otherwise. "None of us are up to the task of carrying…"

"He's my father."

"Too heavy for you to carry far," interrupted Kato, for once agreeing with Vance's assessment. Roland had not been a big man, but surely he was too much for his daughter to carry across the Wilds.

"And too much for me," Vance agreed. "But not for Torben." He offered the Ursa his hand. "You understand the risk."

It was not a question.

He shook the tracker's hand. "He'd want it." Looks passed between the others, none having known that Roland had known the sposer, or how deep that knowledge might have been. Given Roland's position as Laedan, his interaction with the community and the likelihood that he had been on hand to facilitate the removal of deceased family and coworkers inside the fortress, it made sense the men had crossed paths. Torben shrugged to their unspoken questions and let go of Vance's hand. "Never been to the Wilds."

That was difficult for Jia to believe, as almost every anthro in LaGuardia, as far as she knew, took advantage of the Wilds. It was not necessary, of course, as the ruined city streets provided enough shelter and wildlife for an anthro to hunt if they chose, with little risk of being exposed. For many, that was risk enough, and some chose never to hunt at all but rather to suppress the beast that was their nature. There were other, smaller patches of wildland scattered about the borough where some liked to hunt. As often as she had hunted with her father and mother, it had been Jia's perception that the Flushing Wilds was the preferred stretch of earth to be free in for everyone.

Roland had always made it seem that way.

She inhaled once, long and slow, considering their options. If the Ursa accompanied them as far into the Wilds where they could find shelter for the daylight hours, she believed she and Kato could make the rest of the journey with her father. The Pack would react anxiously to another unfamiliar Ursa, if he insisted on making the entire trip, but Vance's presence would make them even more so.

A tracker in their midst could be a dangerous thing.

"Halfway then…if you would…and thank you." She shot Vance a look of gratitude for helping bring Roland this far.

The mage nodded once.

“Halfway,” Torben agreed, swinging the body over his broad shoulder with an ease that no one except Vance expected.

Maybe, thought Jia, having Torben’s strength along would be a good thing.

At least when it came time to rest, if he would agree to stay a little while longer, she would feel more at ease with him there.

Chapter 11

"How does a body go missing?" Lowell cried with exhausted alarm, erupting from his chair beneath the onslaught of fear that there was now a grubber, in the shape of his best friend, loose in the Fortress' underbelly. Grubbers were not good with stairs, only found open doors by the trial and error of bumping about until they passed through one, unless some potent smell or loud sound drew them to and through it, so the chances were high that none of the staff was in danger. But the thought that his co-Laedan was a mindless, flesh-devouring thing, after so many months of suspicion fueled by the man's detractors, burned in Lowell's belly like too much strong alcohol before breakfast.

It was before breakfast, but he had not yet had a drink. Hearing this report, as the morning meal trays were brought into the room, made him desperately wish he had.

Ernest shook his head and considered reaching for the Laedan's arm to calm him but decided against it. He would likely lose that hand if Lowell lashed out with any sort of weapon he might have on him. Or at least Ernest risked it being broken for any attempt to be kind.

"Didn't say missing; I said he's gone," Ernest clarified after clearing his throat. The story devised the night before between him and Nik was given an unexpected enhancement, one he believed would work in Jia Marrock's favor, if not in Roland's. "There was something strange when Guire was finishing the exam; it seemed better to send him off last night than keep him here and risk…"

"You mean he was turning?" Lowell's wan features grew more ashen. The faces of the men nearby, Quentin and Donnovan, looked less ill but equally troubled…though not to the degree the Laedan did.

Nik looked as though he was high or nearly asleep in his slouched posture in his chair.

Nodding, hands clutched behind him to suppress the urge to fidget, Ernest continued, "It appeared so. Of course, we couldn't be certain, without waiting another hour or two, but there were enough signs that we thought it best not to wait. I summoned the sposers for first thing this morning but those on watch said they came last night." The chief shrugged. "Maybe Guire thought it shouldn't wait until morning…or the sposers did at any rate."

It was the sposers' job, or part of it, to control the grubber population. If they thought retrieval was best not put off, no one, not even the Laedan, was likely to argue with them.

"So he wasn't…" Lowell could not say it. Saying the words would be an admission that he had been swayed by rumors to turn against his best friend and believe the worst. Politically, it was best he never voice that doubt. "And Jonni?"

"No change yet. Sposers did inquire what's to be done with…"

"He will be buried in the garden, of course. Roland too."

Every other Channon, even those who had been inflicted and turned, had been interred in the open Fortress garden, the only private area of open ground in the borough that had neither reverted to its wild natural state nor been cultivated for farming. Flowers and fruit trees were grown there, groomed and manicured, and berry shrubs and decorative grass, all of it fertilized by the Channon dead buried vertically with nothing between the body and the earth and no chemical embalming to beautify or preserve their corpses.

The earth needed the dead, just as the living needed the earth. And while the majority of the dead were fed to the Plant, providing power or fertilizing nutrients for light, heat, and growing things, those select few who belonged to families of import were not sent there. They, like Jonni, had the privilege of returning straight to the earth.

There would be no stone, no stone with a name to mark his end, but those who remembered him would know.

Roland, by virtue of Marrock prominence, should have had that same honor. But no Marrock had ever been buried in the Fortress garden. What had been done with them was a private matter known only to their families, and with no Marrocks to claim Roland, once he was processed, there was no telling what would become of him.

"I want him brought back."

"Sir?" asked Ernest.

"If he was turning…" started Quentin, ignoring Earnest's query.

"By now they'll have processed him, stopped that from happening." Lowell did not know how that was done, what the process entailed, but he had heard tales. Beheading, disembowelment, grinding up, liquification, incineration…each option more abhorrent than the next. "Whatever is left of him, I want him back here. To be buried in the…"

Donnovan rolled his eyes with a snort. "Fa…he's not a Channon. He doesn't deserve to be…"

His statement was aborted by one swing, his father's fist connecting with the side of his face with enough force to knock him from the chair, enough impact to be heard by everyone in the room not looking at him, enough to jar Nik out of his stupor to stare at his brother and father with almost sober clarity.

"Lowell…" started Quentin, thankful he was out of the Laedan's reach as he began to speak.

Donn, on his feet now, glared at his father, both men aware that Quentin was debating whether to intervene or take a side. Nik was smart enough, or wasted enough, to stay quiet and out of the drama.

"He deserves what I say he deserves." Unlike their previous dispute, there would be no compromise this time and Donn chose not to push the matter. This was not an argument he needed to win. He stalked from the room as Lowell barked, "Ernest…do it. Get him back here…before the ceremony begins."

The chief nodded, murmured, "At once," and gratefully retreated before further violence erupted.

*

The well-worn trail, a track oft traveled by the Flushing Pack and others on hunts in the Wilds because it crisscrossed the paths of so many animals, brought the group to a copse thick with Addison's scent, bringing Jia up short when she realized it. He had been here long enough to leave more than a passing impression, enough to reassure her that he had made it safely this far. But he was not here now and the traces were beginning to fade as the moisture in the air soaked it into droplets that slid from the leaves and dripped onto the forest floor. The thought of seeing him, of bringing back her father's body rather than the living man her brother had tried to save in their last minutes together brought tears to her eyes as she squatted to press her fingers to the damp earth where he had waited.

The awareness of what lay ahead ate at her resolve to continue.

While Kato leaned against a tree, a hand clutching his bandaged side though he otherwise fought not to reveal either pain, weariness, or weakness, and Torben remained alert to the possibility of danger, Vance crouched beside Jia, his hand on her back to steady himself, the other pressed into the leaves she was touching, eliminating the need to ask what she saw, what she sensed, what she knew.

There was no need to ask how she felt or to read it through contact. It was etched into every line on her face.

"We rest here." He took the choice from her hands, making it for her as he straightened and helped lower Roland's wrapped body gently to the ground. He could not read details of the man's death through the heavy covering and he was not sure, to be honest, if this was the time or the place to attempt to do so.

There had been little talking during the hours they had walked. Twice their combined efforts allowed them to avoid the Laedan Guard, and Vance's quick thinking helped them elude a lone Protector on patrol making one last pass through his own neighborhood on his way home. The group made it to the fringes of the Wilds as the first warmth of dawn touched the air, as the first wailing calls of mourning punctured the borough's tranquility. Though for a moment Jia had hesitated, listening to the call meant for her father and for Jonni, she swallowed the bitter pill of grief and pushed on, deeper into the wilderness. It allowed them, when they felt safe enough to do so, a short respite of water and the sharing of a still-warm loaf of bread Kato snatched from someone's open window cooling rack beneath Vance's disapproving eye.

Vance had noted the location of the home, however. He would make sure the residents were compensated for the theft. His disapproval of the method of procurement did not lessen his appreciation of much-needed nourishment.

The quick, sparse meal bolstered the group in body and in spirit, allowing further slow travel, but by now they were all being dragged down by a lack of sleep and, for one of them at least, the dogged heaviness of heartache.

Vance wished he knew the words to say to take away Jia's grief. He had lost his father too, as had Torben, and, he guessed, Kato as well, but not one of those men, to the mage's knowledge, had been poisoned by someone they worked with and trusted. A man drinking himself to death or succumbing to age was hardly the same as murder. And on top of that, Vance knew he had failed her.

He had helped her find Roland, it was true. If not for him, she might never have seen her father again. But he had not kept the man alive as he had promised he would do if he could. He had known, as had Jia and Roland, that the odds were against them if they went back into the Fortress, and Vance had tried, along with Addison and Deuce, to talk them out of going, but Roland's determination had been too strong. What use were mage skills, Vance thought bitterly, if he could not prevent tragedies such as this?

Kato sat next to Jia, determined to be strong for her as she wilted against his shoulder rather than against the tracker's. He also had no words to say, his experience at offering comfort limited to Vanya who most often only wanted a hug, a bit of sweets, and Peppermint the bear to make everything right. He did not think any of those things were adequate substitutes for a father's love, but he offered an arm around her when she chose to lean against him.

His desire to throw the mage another triumphant look was lost beneath the burden of overwhelming weariness.

"He was a good man."

Jia opened her drooping lids to look at the Ursa who sat before her, his broad torso blocking the entrance to the thicket they had crowded into. The position left him exposed, vulnerable should someone overtake them, but when she reached to draw him further into their tight-quartered shelter, he clasped her hand between his, refusing the request with a rarely given gesture of kindness.

"You knew him?"

It felt strange to speak after so many hours of silence, her parched throat and her grief creating a cracking to her words that prompted Vance to pull out his water flask and offer it to her.

She accepted with a weary smile.

"Not well…but what he was…what I am…" Torben shrugged, a struggle creeping over his face. "We met. He wanted good things, right things, for all of us in the borough. He will be missed."

Wondering if he meant they had met because both were anthro, if they had met during the course of official business because one was Laedan and the other a sposer, or if Torben meant something else and expected Jia to know what that was, she decided against asking. The memories seemed as painful to him as hers were to her, and pain was not something she wanted to indulge in.

She would rather howl her outrage and sorrow at the midday sun.

The Pack would hear her if she did, however; the sound would carry and they would come seeking her. It would also summon anyone who might be following them, anyone in the Wilds who might wish them harm.

Silent suffering, for now, was her only recourse.

From his brief statement, Jia understood something else. Without her father's voice in the Fortress halls, the rights of men and women in LaGuardia Borough, Normal, anthro, and mutani alike, would no longer have a voice. There would be none from the Channons without even Jonni there to make a championing effort, and certainly none from Thomas Quentin. It was almost as if her father was demanding for her to go back, to take up where he had left off, but it was a ludicrous notion that she could not consider now. The Pack needed her. Liam needed her…if her dear best friend still lived.

LaGuardia was going to have to survive without her, no matter what duty Torben's words prompted.

As if understanding her unspoken thoughts, as if he too were a mage, Torben muttered with a sigh, "We'll go on soon." He released her hand with a grim reluctant expression.

Next to him, propped against a tangle of young trees, knees drawn up to his chin, Vance wiped his arm across his face while he fiddled with the edge of Roland's protective canvas, wrestling with himself rather than look at her.

"Sleep," he mumbled. "A few hours will do us good. We're safe here." If Torben was traveling the rest of the way across the Wilds, committing himself to a journey he was not required to make, then Vance was going too. There was nothing back in the borough that could not wait another day or two. That time might give him some direction about what the shart he was supposed to do next.

And if she slept, it might give him the opportunity to do what he was dreading doing.

Skies knew, he thought only after Jia's eyes closed and Kato, eyes also shut, laid his cheek against the top of her head on his shoulder, we have to rest. The odds were against any of them being safe much longer, no matter what direction their lives took next.

He waited as long as he dared, until he was certain Jia and Kato were asleep. He knew Roland's eyes, like Sal's, would have been closed by the attending medistaff, and thus he would be unable to see anything in them. But that was also a fortunate thing, as it meant he did not have to expose any more of Roland's corpse then was necessary to place his hand against the man's icy, clay-like skin. Unzipping the protective tarp sack covering he was carried in gave Vance the chance to press his hand against the man's head, his forehead, without looking at him, thus enabling him to keep his focus on whatever his inner sight would show him.

But Roland had been asleep at that moment, the prick of the needle rousing him to a shadow standing over him, silhouetted by the infirmary lights, and before Vance read anything more, Torben's hand closed around his wrist.

"Don't," mumbled the Ursa. "Don't invade his privacy here."

Vance hissed. "If I don't, I'll never..."

"You know. You know enough."

The mage looked at the hand holding his arm, the hand that had pulled his away from the dead man and broke the vision that had begun to pull him in. Did he know enough? Did he have enough clues to divine the truth?

Was he simply too afraid to make those connections, afraid of what he was going to find?

What he was going to be required to do to make all of this right?

Torben nodded.

Vance scowled again and wrapped his arms around his knees while the Ursa closed the corpse bag.

If Torben was right, Vance did not look forward to admitting it. Not one damned bit.

*

Dawn had not yet come when the criers' calls split the silence of the sleeping streets, the somber "oy ay" punctuated by the clacking of wooden claves and strikers or the shrill dual-note shriek of carved wooden pipes following the spidering trail of human voice that took the news of death to the far reaches of LaGuardia Borough. The sound bleeding through the fog lent an eeriness to the darkness that kept many from sleep once it was heard, and instead beckoned them to don their warmest clothing and gather in the paved promenade outside of the Fortress where others had also gathered to hear the unfortunate proclamation the Laedans were to make.

But this would be no decree of law or celebration. That sing-song change and the instruments that accompanied it meant only one thing.

A Laedan, or someone in their family, had died.

Odd that no one had known one of them was ill.

Some throughout the borough remembered that summons from times long past when first Brunis Channon had died and then Tyle Marrock within less than a year of one another, when the coughing sickness swept through the land, decimating the already struggling population. Power in LaGuardia had already been relegated into the hands of Lowell and Roland, so the borough did not suffer a loss of leadership, but those alive and capable during that time remembered the haunting sounds the claves and pipes and criers had made throughout the long, sorrowful night. They, as their elders before them, gathered at the Fortress wall, whether an expected tradition or an impulsive act of respect and communal grief, compelling this generation of borough residents to do the same. They came with the rising of the sun through every passable street, trickling in response to the fading 'oy ay' that would continue until the farthest borders of LaGuardia were reached, until the promenade was packed and the stragglers forced to congregate in the streets and in the doorways and windows of every nearby structure.

They gathered, Nik mused, but what was there to see? What was there to hear besides the somber clack, clack, clack of claves and the periodic bleating of polished goat horns made by the six men who stood atop the wall at the gate in the immaculate ceremonial uniforms of the Laedan Guard? There were no windows in the walls to allow witness of the family gathered in the Fortress garden, no way to see beyond the closed wooden gates that only opened some time after mid-day to allow the returning criers to come back inside.

If it was anything like the fading, blurred memory of his grandfather's service, Nik knew these people would remain throughout the day and far into the night until their perceived period of public mourning was appeased by the last blast of the horn, the silence that came after, and the rekindling of the torches along the wall with the rising of the sun the following day.

Why the need for ritual darkness, he wondered? What did the dead care whether the living continued to see? Who benefitted from the twenty-four hours of pretend darkness? What did it mean to anyone?

Not even Torben had been able to give a sensible explanation the time Nik had asked him about such things. After the Undoing, it had become a common practice to mourn a family's dead by a twenty-four-hour time of darkness in a home, almost as if the family was venerating the time when the Undoing had plunged all of humanity into physical, intellectual, emotional, and spiritual blackness.

As if the death of a loved one was the same thing.

Maybe that was reason enough, as each new death reminded each of them of a time when the world had lost so much more.

Since the revelation of the preemptive disposal of Roland's body, as the Channon men had awaited their morning meal, Nik had seen no one else from the family. As if abandoned behind the Fortress walls, he took his own private watch on a garden bench that allowed him to be the single witness to the digging of two vertical pits where the dead would be put to rest. A pair of green apple trees, Jonni's favorites, waited nearby in biodegradable hemp pots. They and the earth taken from those holes would be left as cushions and markers for the dead.

Digging done, the gardeners had left him alone some time ago. The sun crawled across the sky behind the clouds, leaving hunger and thirst in their wake and the strengthening tremors and nausea of withdrawal followed, but Nik stubbornly refused to end his vigil. Someone needed to be here. Someone needed to bear witness to Jonni's final moments from beginning to end. Someone needed to listen to the 'oy ay' chant now softly taken up by the grieving throng of people he could not see.

They did not even know who had died. It seemed a pathetic waste to mourn the unknown. But who, he wondered, would tell them?

He had seen Chief Ernest's return, a hemplastic box under his arm, the man's weary face determined despite his desire to be anywhere else today. Lowell's order notwithstanding, there was no way that box contained any part of Roland. Judging by the size of the box, the ashes of some incinerated soul had been collected and brought here and left beside one of the holes for burial.

No other Marrock was buried here. The Marrocks always tended their dead elsewhere. The irony of an outsider, a random grubber perhaps, an anthro or mutani or lowly scav, being interred in the 'sacred' Channon plot at Lowell's insistence, in an effort to assuage whatever guilt he felt over his friend's death, was not lost on Nik.

It would almost be worth it, someday, to tell his father the truth, if Nik was ever able to learn who was sent for burial in Roland's place.

Next time he saw Torben, perhaps he would ask.

Ernest had gone inside, Nik presumed to give word to Lowell of his successful efforts in retrieving Roland's remains, but if he found the grieving Laedan, Lowell did not come to the garden to see the box of cremains himself.

The box could contain a collection of dead rodents for all of the interest Lowell had in it.

As sunset approached, bringing with it an offshore wind that emptied the borough of the day's tenacious fog and threatened to extinguish the single torch lit on a pole between the burial holes that was there only to keep the body-bearers, familial guests, and Fortress staff from falling into them. Family and staff came gradually at first, and then more swiftly once the goat horn blatted an extended note as long as the horn blower was able to sustain his breath. Quentin came first, his expression distant and disdainful as he circled the box near the gravesite as if expecting it to provide answers about the man believed to be inside. Then Donn and Oasis, neither looking comfortable, and shortly thereafter, Lowell and Yiva. There was little affectionate contact, few gestures of remorse or comfort passing between either couple, the physical and emotional reserve between them something Nik noticed though it seemed no one else did, or cared. Lowell stood apart, kept his distance from everyone, alone and aloof, his hands clasped behind his back, his face set with the sternness of a man determined not to show his grief as he watched Francis Lord ascend the steps that would take him to the top of the outer Fortress wall where only the claves continued to clap their call. The Channon women gradually gravitated towards one another, Oasis standing between her father and Yiva. Though they did not look at one another, did not touch the other, they at least exhibited more familial solidarity than the Channon men did.

Donn sprawled on the bench at Nik's side as soon as he left his wife in the good hands of the older adults. His legs were outstretched casually, the red of his cheeks and nose and the swelling of his lips suggesting that he had consumed more than his share of alcohol today. Funny that should be so, when Nik, for once, had not touched any foreign substance, not even food.

Nik side-eyed him for his brother's seemingly disrespectful posture but said nothing of it. He was not his twin's keeper.

Three rapid successive claps of the claves brought most of those in the garden to respectful attention, brought Nik to his feet as a hush descended over the crowd in the promenade outside. Donn did not move. The silence announced the approach of the dead, the methodical military steps of the four who carried Jonni strapped on a woven pallet between them. Clap, clap, clap…four silent beets as two steps closer were taken. Three more claps, four more silent beats, the cycle repeated until the men reached the holes with their precious burden.

Donn ignored Lowell's harsh scowl, refused to stand, until Nik elbowed him once in the head. The twins glowered at one another. Finally, Donn capitulated with an eye roll and audible sigh that turned heads. Most looks were met with a cool, drunken smirk; only Oasis' sad expression melted his countenance enough that he appeared, at last, to be mournful of his older brother's death.

Nik knew he was. He also knew that Donn had trouble showing that grief, just as their father did. But he was thankful that between he and Oasis, Donn was at least prompted to put on a show of it, even if his expression and posture did not adequately express what he was feeling inside.

"Lost is the son, the brother, taken in his prime, too soon from his family's loving embrace. Jonatan was a good man, an honest man, a man of principles…"

Tuning out the droning list of accomplishments, admirable qualities, and less than heartfelt platitudes, Nik watched the tension ripple across Lowell's shoulders, watched his jaw tighten, as the Grand Mas' words were intoned over the heads of the house, of LaGuardia's citizens gathered today. It should have been his place to speak the benediction to the lives lost, his place to send them to whatever eternity awaited their souls, but he had failed to set down any words worth saying and had been unwilling to face the adoration and grief the masses carried for both his son and for his co-Laedan.

Perhaps the two most honorable men in the Fortress.

And they were both taken from him at once.

"We mourn Jonatan's loss and await the Rejoining in the time that comes after."

The Grand Mas' presence in the Fortress was fortuitous for that reason, but hearing the man speak of things he knew nothing about, and of Time After that Lowell did not believe in, felt like a serrated blade twisting between his ribs.

It did not matter what HOPE touted as truth. This life was all there was. And now Jonni was robbed of it. Lowell felt as guilty over his son's death as he felt over Roland's.

The reaction of the crowd for the loss of the District 1 mayor was impossible to know for those within the courtyard. Nik, however, imagined he could hear their breathing stopped, their feet shuffle, their groans and moans.

The claves and the Grand Mas' voice were silent for the span of time it took the young man's body to be lowered into the hole, pallet and all. Jonni Channon disappeared from view, never to be seen again.

When the bearers stepped away, the wooden clicking continued.

"Lost too, by a twice murderous hand, we mourn co-Laedan Marrock, taken by those whose cause he championed in life, taken by one who has abducted his heir to leave LaGuardia without the dual leadership that has blessed this borough since the days after the Undoing. Until she is found, keep faith in your Laedan as Roland Marrock did, and remember his generosity, steadfastness, and courage throughout the trying days ahead. LaGuardia will rise above its suffering. LaGuardia shall triumph."

Nik scowled. Claims of murder were unnecessary at this solemn event. Did the public need to know the cause of his death? Perhaps. But Lord's words were meant to inflame the masses, meant to lend support to Lowell's claim to sole leadership not venerate the dead. Of that Nik was certain.

Though unseen, this time the crowd's reaction was unmistakable, the murmurs, the gasps, the sobs, punctuated by a few wails at the abrupt loss of their beloved champion a telling testimony that Lowell did not want to hear. Roland might have been no statesman, no speaker of rousing words, but he had walked among them, worked with them, fought for them, been accessible in ways that they had never perceived Lowell to be. Lowell was not despised or feared, not in the way Donn was, but nor was he adored the way Roland had been.

Getting Jia back alive, clearing her name of these events or proving duplicitous involvement in them was all the more imperative now. The people would side with her, clamor for her to take her place. Until his grip on solitary power could be secured, the Marrock name assured stability in LaGuardia. Lowell understood that he needed her here until Fort Hamilton was found.

After that, whatever stance she took, none of this mattered.

His straight-ahead gaze did not waver as the smaller box was dropped into the second hole, just as it had not wavered when his son had gone to earth. Lowell could not look at what little remained of his son, his friend. It did not seem real. Only the final bleating of the goat horn, which signified the end of the ceremony, seemed real to him, and he was the first one to leave when the sound died away, refusing to watch the filling of the graves, the planting of the trees, the erasing from his life two of those who had been most important to it.

Donn strode away as well, leaving his wife in her father's care. Quentin took a step as if to join Oasis and Geary at their graveside post, appeared to reconsider, and instead joined Grand Mas Lord at the bottom of the Fortress gate stairs. Left alone by husband and son, appearing unaware that Nik was still there, Yiva gave a grateful yet melancholy gaze of longing and remorse at Chief Ernest when he took her elbow and escorted her inside.

There would be no feasting tonight, not in the gloom of LaGuardia's Fortress, nor in any home across the borough. The night would pass in silence, the world would remain black and still. Come dawn, the mundanity of life would be resumed as nearly unchanged as it could be after the loss of those they had buried.

Only Nik remained, ignoring Donn's departing, cynical look as his twin bent to dirty his hands by aiding the gardeners with their work, kneeling between the shoulder tall saplings that he intended to see grow into flourishing adulthood.

In a year's time, he wondered if anyone would remember which tree, which grave, was which.

In a year's time, he wondered if Jia would return to the Fortress long enough to share the remembrance of this day with him…even if Roland was buried somewhere else.

Wherever that was, Nik hoped the man's daughter and son were safe.

Chapter 12

Nose wrinkling in distaste and instinctual agitated alertness, the bad news she bore and the company she kept became less important than the intrusion on Pack territory she sensed at the outer border of the campus. If the intrusion marker had only been there, she might have let the matter slide. But as it crossed the edge of their claimed land, an outcast's challenge, Jia pushed forward at a more determined pace that compelled those with her to hasten as well. The scents of mutani, of Ursa, of the newly familiar Cana who lived nearby, were there as well, but were of minimal concern.

It was the outcast she did not want here. It was the outcast who no longer belonged. If he had harmed anyone in the Pack, or any ally they had made, or had tried again to take the Pack, blood would be spilled.

Vance read the bloodlust's burn without seeing the golden-red tint in her eyes, read the uneasiness in Kato as the Fela moved closer to her, and felt a more anxious alertness in Torben then he had expressed during their entire journey. Their shift in mood made the tracker more alert as well, but with no visible hint of danger, as the sprawling compound of similarly constructed buildings came in to view, his senses focused more there, on the unfamiliar, on the efforts made to manicure the shrubbery and the gurgle of a fountain…the likes of which he had never seen working before. While his eyes read those details, his ears picked up the audible clues of children, of family, and his nose twitched at the familiar scent of wood fires and cooking meals through the doorway they were approaching. It was his internal mage senses that revealed a threat in the shadows as Jia snarled and froze in a stance both defensive and antagonistic.

In the same instant, the door of that building flung open, spilling a more pervasive aroma of fire and food across their path and stretching the glow of firelight caught in the adversarial Cana's eyes.

"Kato!"

Vanya squealed with glee and raced to throw her arms around her brother, nearly knocking him off his feet. Other's came behind her, to stop her perhaps, or to protect her from the loitering threat to the Pack that Pain had become, expressing their surprise and relief to find Jia and her companions there.

"Go," Jia growled, positioning herself between the whole of the Flushing Pack and Pain and his followers who emerged from the darkness. They may not have been anticipating her arrival tonight, but they were watching for her, waiting, and they were there to support her against the threat they had known was beyond their door. Near from the library entrance, the scatter of the debris of living surrounded the smoldering remnants of a nearly extinguished fire, telling her everything she needed to know about Pain and his intentions. He had come to claim the Pack, had been here, too close, threatening them with his aggressive proximity, waiting for a moment of weakness when he could make his move.

If he had come to beg for clemency, to beg for remittance into the Pack, his posture as he emerged from the dark and the hostility that forced the growth of dark fur across his arms, hands, cheek, and neck would have been kept in check.

"You have no right…"

"I don't see him." His words, made guttural by the eruption of fangs, felt both hot and cold to her. "Where is Roland?"

Torben, having battled his share of men like Pain, exhibited no fear as he swung his wrapped burden from his shoulder and lay it tenderly on the ground. "Here."

On the opposite side of the group of Cana, QiangXu paced the edges of the gathered cluster, eyes on the unfamiliar Ursa. Notoriously solitary, it was rare for Ursa to remain in close proximity with others of their kind without conflict. Even mates rarely lived together, though parents would live near enough to each other to share the raising of cubs until the young came of age. Only the newcomer's focus on Pain and not QiangXu, and the fact that he had born Roland's body home, kept the smaller man from any aggressive action.

Pain was the bigger threat.

QiangXu's stare, however, was enough to prompt Vance to shuffle into a position that placed him between the two Ursa and closer to Jia. The Pack's grief and shock at Torben's words, at the sight of the Alpha's face when Addi opened the fasteners that kept the canvas closed so that he could see the proof for himself, hit Vance's mage senses like a board against his head. He winced and rubbed the back of his skull, and then the bridge of his nose, in an effort to reduce the throbbing that threatened to rob him of his vision.

"What…?" Addi began in shock before snapping his mouth closed. This was not the time for questions or answers, even if a dialogue might have diffused the brewing conflict. After Pain's insistence in sitting near the library door as if holding the Flushing Pack at siege, the medic knew that nothing but blood was going to erase the anger from the air.

Pain only glanced at the corpse, taking no time to express respect or remorse. "Then the Flushing Pack is mine."

Dropping the jacket she had been wearing, Jia growled through erupting fangs. "Only if you take it." Anticipating his move, the shift from human to half-form Cana was swift, both shifting and leaping as one to crash into a grabbling embrace of claws and fangs.

Combat was not what she wanted. Jia wanted those familiar faces, men and women she had grown up with, to come back to the Pack, to make it strong and stable and whole again so that she felt safe in the attempt she must make to bring Liam home. But Pain was not willing to allow that, not without force, and now that there was irrefutable proof of their Alpha's fate, there would be no holding back in a fight for dominance and supremacy. She did not know what compelled Pain's motives, but she knew without question what compelled hers.

Rage. Remorse. Regret. Resolve. And above all, the conviction that, regardless of her misgivings about her readiness to be the Alpha of Flushing Pack, it was what her father wanted. She had failed him by being unable to bring him home alive. She would not fail him again.

The fierceness of the battle brought those on both sides of the fight, even some of the older pups, to various degrees of hostile displays, leaving Vance surrounded by Cana. Though the yellow-eyed Ursa both appeared prepared to enter the fray if it became necessary, their Ursa forms were held at bay, and Kato, arms wrapped around Vanya, poised to protect her, also resisted the lure of change. His posture and the movements of his body suggested a struggle against the need to charge to Jia's aid, but whatever the woman Vanya was to him...daughter or sister or otherwise kin, his primary motivation for the moment was to keep her safe.

It seemed unlikely, Vance mused as he fingered the gun at his hip beneath his coat, taken from the Protectorate office with the chief's blessing, that the Fela was willingly abiding by Cana law and ritual, resisting interference so long as Jia's life, and the woman he was protecting, were not at stake.

He had not wanted to carry that damned gun.

Ernest had insisted he should.

He pushed the coat back and unsnapped the flap that kept the gun in place when Pain threw Jia's slighter weight off. She flew through the air and landed painfully at the feet of the fully shifted Pack Omega.

One of the other males in the Pack snarled at Vance in warning, and he reluctantly dropped his hand. He did not want to use the weapon anyhow; he never wanted to use it. But surrounded by those who could shred him before he could escape, the gun might be, if this situation disintegrated into chaos, the only thing to keep him alive.

"Get up!"

Jia did not need her brother's pleading to prompt her back into the fight, but his desperation, as he knelt beside their father, reminded her what she was fighting for. With Pain's size, strength, and experience, with the shame and resentment he felt after his previous loss to her, she knew she might be at a disadvantage she had not had the first time.

She did, however, remember the lessons learned in that fight, tells to his actions, his favored moves, the choices he seemed most likely to make in combat. Both were bruised and cut, bleeding where fangs and claws had raked long incisions through the remnants of torn cloth and thick fur, but there was no guarantee, if she re-engaged, that she would survive. Yet his body was trembling with uncontrollable fury meaning he might be prone to mistakes. There was no guarantee he would survive either.

Wolves in the wild did not always kill another over a challenge for leadership. Cana, as much human as wolf, were driven by different impulses, needs, desires…instincts that demanded such a threat be put down, particularly if that threat would not listen to reason.

Jia had not done so before. She might not have the same choice this time.

Fueled by the insult to her leadership, to her father's choices and wishes, and the encouraging, supportive nudge of Deuce's nose against her hip, Jia charged, ignoring the ripping pain in the muscles along her other side.

Too late she saw it, some brief flash in Pain's eyes that expressed a moment of fear before her righteous fury, a realization that prompted an unexpected action she could not thwart. Though she spun sideways to get free of his fist, he caught her instead with his forearm and flung her into the nearest tangle of bushes to hit the wall behind it. She howled, flailing to free herself from the thorny branches.

In those few moments, Pain snatched Vanya out of Kato's arms.

Warning or not, the gun was drawn. This was no longer a fight between Cana alphas. This was a man threatening an innocent, a Normal, and Vance, as a Protector, was sworn to act.

The Cana who had threatened him before did not do so again.

One arm around her body, the other around her neck, claws against her skin, fangs inches away from the side of her throat, he barked in that awkward Cana speech, "Stand down. Release the Pack to me or she dies."

Kato's charge forward, his body now metamorphosed into his Fela half form, ended abruptly as those claws, drawing his sister's blood, ripped the Fela to the surface at last.

Vanya screamed and fainted.

The Fela growled deep and crouched to spring. If he possessed a tail in this hybrid form, it would have been wildly swishing from side to side. Instead, he waited with feline patience for the smallest hint that Pain's guard was compromised.

Vance had no doubt he would pounce.

The youngest pups at the rear of the gathering cried out too and huddled more tightly together as the older ones, Rief and the Arden boys, snapped and snarled in protective indignation that one of their own was being used as leverage. Taking his cue from the only adult Fela in the group, Eddie shifted too, his smaller full Fela form hissing and spitting in warning. At his side, Petr, Reif, and Wist likewise shifted, all to hybrid; they were more capable of fighting, of defending themselves and the younger pups, in their hybrid form than in the form of Normal children.

Pain barely noticed them.

The adults who had not already shifted were compelled to do likewise, though more adept at controlling their fear and outrage then the children were. Pain had overstepped the boundaries of Cana law. Only an enemy of the Pack would dare attack a pup. Despite her physical age, Vanya was accepted as a Pack pup, as one of their own. She was not Cana, but the Flushing Pack accepted that too, a choice supported by the Alpha they had elected to follow regardless of her still unofficial status.

The Cana behind Pain withdrew several steps, their whining and posture expressing shock and dismay, as well as their uncertainty about the man they had chosen to follow. Their experience with Vanya was limited, but they understood her to be childlike in manner, a non-Cana, an innocent, and such a threat to her spoke of darkness beneath Pain's quest for leadership that none of them expected. Even if his choice was a desperate act borne of fear of defeat, it was unacceptable.

Particularly since it appeared that Pain had the upper hand.

Maz snatched the gun out of Vance's grip and aimed it with trembling hands at Pain's head. Free of the brush now, though in obvious agony as she struggled to her feet, Jia's recovery was unexpected, as was her choosing to face him again, and Pain had to stretch his focus to monitor all three threats.

"Let her go, Pain," begged Maz in a voice close to breaking.

Still crouched, Addi too began to creep closer, hoping his movement would distract Pain long enough for his sister, or Kato, to act. He did not want Maz to shoot the man. He only wanted Vanya to be freed and for the fight to end. Pain noted his movement out of the corner of his eye, but rather than relent, his arm tightened around Vanya's neck. The unconscious girl began to choke in her fight for air.

Addi stopped moving.

"Just do it, Pain," Uncle pleaded behind him. "Let her go." If Pain pushed too far, if he killed the woman he held and the Flushing Pack chose to kill him, those who had followed him stood less of a chance of survival, of being welcomed back into the Pack. Any good Alpha would consider the needs of the Pack. Pain, as alpha of their outcast family, should consider them now.

Jia, young and inexperienced though she was, had again proven her willingness to fight for the Flushing Pack's leadership, fighting with courage, tactical skill, instinct, and intelligence. She was proving, so far, to be the leader Roland wanted her to be.

Uncle knew he had misjudged her, had been wrong to make a rash, emotional, impulsive action in leaving the Pack. He hoped, by encouraging Pain to do the right thing, to prove renewed fealty to Flushing Pack's new Alpha.

"Release her," Uncle repeated. The others with him offered their own words and sounds of encouragement for him to do the same.

"Please…Pain…" Maz cocked the hammer and waited. No one knew if he had experience with guns, if he could make the shot without killing Vanya. Vance lifted his hand to retake the weapon, afraid the man's shaky stance would result in exactly that tragedy. Maz growled again, although there was a whining note beneath the sound that begged to be spared the responsibility of this course of action without his needing to relinquish the gun.

Vance swallowed hard and allowed his gaze to circle the group. What the shart was he supposed to do?

Jia could have crouched to plead as well, but she no longer carried any desire to express submission or forgiveness. In those moments of quiet tension, she could see the bone in his forearm protruding through the skin, the blood streaming from a gash on his head into his dilated eyes, and a palm-sized length of glass dug deep into his thigh. She had not noticed any broken glass on the ground but there was no time to examine the area for more. Each of his injuries was potentially debilitating, each likely to throw off his focus, his balance, his effectiveness, which could give her an advantage, perhaps, if they engaged in combat again. Perhaps he felt he needed Vanya as leverage in order to have enough time to rest, to re-orient himself, to regain some chance of winning.

"Don't make me kill you." Jia was not going to wait long enough for that to happen.

Killing him was not her preference. She respected Pain's unique and useful set of skills, the strength he brought to the Pack. She respected her father's opinion of the bristly man that most of the pups and younger members had never gotten close enough to, to know. If she made any attack now, he would likely kill Vanya, either accidentally or deliberately, and Kato was in no position to reach her without causing the same result. It was not fair to expect Maz, in the best position to act, to be the one to end this fight, but her only other option was surrender.

She could not do that either.

Neither Kato nor Maz would forgive her if she left the choice to them, or if her actions, or lack of them, resulted in Pain or Vanya's death. Whatever happened next had to be her choice, had to be on her shoulders. If she was to be the Alpha, it was the only way.

"Step down, and she and the others," Pain's gaze swept from Kato to Eddie and Petr, "will live and be free to leave…"

"You can't make us kill them," cried Trill, voicing the Pack's defiance.

"You won't need to. I will."

Vanya's face was beginning to discolor and she was limp in Pain's grasp. Kato growled again as little by little he inched closer.

Pain's claws dug a little deeper, drawing more blood.

"Your fight is with me; let her go," demanded Jia, struggling against physical injuries that threatened to pull her feet out from under her and give Pain the victory despite her intentions.

Maz hissed, "Pain, please; come back to me. I forgive you; just…"

The moment of connection between the two men who had once pledged their lives to the other, the moment when their eyes met and the corners of Pain's mouth and eyes twitched, caused the gun to slowly lower.

It was all that was needed.

Vance's hand closed around the barrel.

Jia lunged.

But it was the pale wolf at the far side of the group whose leap broadsided Pain with enough force to knock the unsteady man off his feet. Jia's dive wrenched Vanya away, bringing all three crashing to the ground, a painful fall cushioned only by the black Fela whose body was suddenly beneath them in an attempt to catch Vanya.

Jia rolled one way; Kato rolled the other, shifting back to man to clutch Vanya to his chest and pull her out of harm's way. The gun went off in Vance's attempt to retrieve it, eliciting a scream; he jerked back, clutching his hand as the gun fell. Helena, the closest to them, dove, covering the weapon with her body so that the second discharge sent the bullet's trajectory raking across Deuce's side before he and Pain ended in a pile. His jaws were clenched around Pain's throat, pinning him to the ground. Pain fought to reach the glass shard in his leg, intending to use it against the impudent Omega, but Jia stepped on his wrist, preventing further injury to the wolf who had tried to spare them all some uncomfortable choices.

The blood visible around Deuce's fangs hinted at imminent death if she did not intervene. Without paying attention to where she placed her hand on his side, she stopped when he winced. Her fingers left a red smear across his fur when she slid them away from where the bullet had penetrated.

"Release him, Deuce," she murmured. "Let him be."

The wolf shifted back to human but he refused to leave his crouched position over Pain's body. The trapped man tried once to wiggle his broken arm free of the bare foot that held him, hoping again to reach the shard, but Jia increased the pressure of her weight there, making him wince and snarl and give up the attempt.

"Deuce."

Though clearly unhappy about the command, the Omega retreated as ordered, obeying only because Jia asked it. He crouched nearby, awaiting further commands.

"Let him kill me, Alpha!" Pain spat, laying where he had fallen as Jia too took a step away, releasing his arm, giving him his freedom. Her stance was unsteady, her step uneven, despite her posture of victory. His use of title acknowledged his surrender to a claim on the Pack, acknowledged her leadership of it, but his demand also proved that he was not prepared to submit to her rule.

Maz scowled at the other man's audacity, his heart sinking. Any hope of making Pain see reason, of coaxing Pain to come back, was boiling away with the intensity of the man's nervous resentment.

Wiping her bloody arm across her eyes, creating a blood-red mask, Jia said in a tone of quiet defiance. "I will not…Omega."

It was an insult worse than exile to a man of Pain's strength and pride, that single word releasing Deuce from his history as the Pack's outcast and condemning Pain to it. Pain shot up, enraged, aiming for Jia's throat with the glass shard. She stumbled away before the cut was made, with the cry of "Daughter!" echoing in the air in the wake of the blurring impact that knocked Pain away from her seconds before her head struck the ground and the night enveloped her.

Chapter 13

"Fa?"

Nik had waited in the conference room across the corridor from his father's office since coming inside, his hands and face smudged with the rich, damp soil of the garden in which his brother and Roland were buried. There had been voices behind the closed office door, a man and a woman's, but their words were not easily heard and Nik made no effort to spy. Assuming it to be a female staff member, or hoping that his father and mother were involved in an all too rare conversation, Nik accepted the need to wait, made the choice to do so in the dark, and instead watched what he could see of the gradually thinning promenade crowd through the window. Most of those there would wait until the torches were lit again at daybreak, until the gates were opened, but with no need or reason to remain exposed to the bitter wind, he was not surprised that the very young and very old were taken back indoors.

Nor was he surprised that the bored and apathetic departed as well.

With no idea of the passage of time and no lights to announce his presence in that room to anyone else, he did not know how much time passed before that door opened and Oasis slid into the corridor, closing the door behind her to slink off down the hall without knowing Nik was there. He frowned at the stealth of her movement, as if she were hiding something, or hiding from someone, but he pushed any pondering of his father's reason for privacy with her out of his head.

Discussion about her father, perhaps, about Roland's death. Some talk about Donn. Hells, even wanting Donn to not get the wrong idea about any meeting they might have…innocent though it was…would be reason enough for privacy and secrecy.

After today, just about anything would send Donn into a fury.

All of those thoughts were too unsettling for his stomach tonight, and he would prefer not to know the truth. For now, it was none of Nik's business.

There was something else he needed to accomplish while his courage held. He waited for several minutes, for what seemed like a prudent amount of time to pass after her departure, took a deep breath, and then knocked on his father's door.

No voice bid him enter, no one spoke, but after a series of dragging steps the door opened and Lowell, his shirt unbuttoned, a drink in his hand, his usually tidy hair disheveled, paused, surprised to see Nik there, surprised to see the young man looking clear-eyed on this rare occasion. There had been a time, in Nik's childhood, before the drugs, that the boy had been awake for hours on end, plagued by insomnia that no one was able to treat, when his eyes had looked like this.

They had not, to Lowell's memory, looked this way in a long time.

If he was not high now, it was no surprise that Nik was awake at this ungodly hour, only a surprise that he sought out his father's company as it was also something he rarely did. Even more so than Jonni or Donn, Lowell had never known what to say to Nik since he had stopped coming to his father for answers as a little boy.

The impediments to communication between them were mutual.

"Can I…there's something I need to tell you…"

Lowell waved him into the dark room, paused to refill his glass without closing the door, and then sank into a defeated posture in the chair behind his desk. Traces of Oasis' perfume lingered, but other than a second glass, empty with lip rouge smudges along the rim, there was no hint of what she had been doing here.

Again Nik pushed the host of possibilities out of his mind. Glad that his father did not offer him a drink he would have felt tempted and obligated to accept, he sat in the empty chair on the nearest side of the desk, one leg bouncing nervously, damp palms rubbing back and forth over his soil-stained knees.

Neither of them had changed out of their formal, graveside attire.

"You were helping…filling the…"

"Planting the trees, yeah." It felt less painful to say then to admit to words Lowell was unable to say. "Needed to do something, to help.

Lowell nodded as if he understood, but he did not. Few things Nik did made sense to him. This was no different. There were people for things like that, people for planting trees and filling holes. The Channons did not need to do those things.

Yet Nik often did them anyhow.

Thinking Nik was anxious about the distribution of duties that would arise as the governing of District 1 was re-allocated, Lowell emptied the drink down a throat that no longer felt the alcohol burn and refilled his glass. "Don't fret about District 1. I'll handle it."

He knew that his middle son, despite the addictions that kept him from consistently performing his mayoral duties, did try to do what was right, what was good, what was best for his District, that he did worry about the people under his care and protection. If not for those addictions, Lowell often thought that Nik had the head and heart of a damn fine politician.

Too bad he could not be trusted to stay clean to do the job.

"It's not that…it's…" Nik wiped his hands on the front of his shirt, exposing the tremors, and heard his father's swallowed sigh of disappointment, as if he expected Nik to ask permission to go out on a night when it was expected for the family of the dead to stay together.

Not that the Channons did anything together outside of the public eye. Not anymore. Nothing except dine…and often not even then.

Nik scowled at his father's well-deserved lack of faith, If Nik wanted to go out for a score, he was sure as shart not going to ask for permission.

"The other night…when it happened…when Jonni and Roland…" His gaze dropped and he cocked his head as if listening for someone approaching in the hall beyond the open door. Voice softer, he continued, "It wasn't the Fela who…it wasn't…"

His scowl was mirrored by his father's. "You mean Jia did this?"

Head shaking, Nik croaked, "You must be mad!" He stood unexpectedly, crossed the room to the liquor cabinet, and though he opened it as if to give in to the temptation of inebriation, he closed it again without removing anything from it and stared at his hand on the latch. "No…it wasn't her. They didn't come in until after…"

"After what? You were awake?" Given his son's condition after his odose, Lowell had not considered that Nik might have been conscious, might have been a witness to his brother's murder.

"Since the morning, in and out." No one, not a member of the family nor the medistaff, had come to examine him after Donn's initial departure that morning, leaving Nik to awaken…or die…on his own. "I heard the footsteps…just one man. I thought it was Donni come back to check on me, or one of the medics, but it wasn't. I didn't see his face at first but I know that suit. I know the scent."

"Scent?" Lowell tried to think of any one man in the Fortress with a recognizable suit or one who bore any particular smell about them. Some had a fondness for hemp cigs, and Donn often carried the strong tang of bitter ale…particularly late in the day when his duties were behind him. But no one else, in particular, came to mind.

"You're not…Donn killed Roland?"

Such an act was a strong possibility. The youngest Channon had a violent streak, and a temper, and was the one most convinced that the Marrocks were Cana. But while Lowell knew Donn could be cruel and sadistic and had no compunction about ordering death when it suited him, Lowell never imagined that Donn possessed the capacity to murder with his own hands.

And he certainly would not kill his own brother.

"Not Donn…the Fela…"

"The Fela…but you said…" The glass was set heavily onto the desk, its weight creating a loud echo. "You're not making sense. Speak plainly, Nik, or go to bed. It's too late for puzzles."

Frustrated, Nik clutched at his hair with one hand, struggling against mounting nervousness. His father seemed determined to place blame everywhere except where it should be, and as Lowell's agitation spiked, so too did Nik's reluctance to speak the truth.

But his determination to do right by Jia, by Addi, by Roland and by Jonni, made him swallow that anxiety and start again.

"Not that Fela…not the one with Jia. They came in after…after the contents of the needle were…"

"There was no needle." Someone, one of the Protectors, the Chief, the mage…someone would have found a needle if there had been one. They would have shown him, the Laedan, would they not?

If Nik was imagining needles, this whole tale was likely a fever dream born from the odose that had nearly killed him.

"It fell to the floor when he turned to face them. I saw his eyes; they were yellow as they fought…while Jia tried to save Roland." He faced his father, gravity in his eyes. "Jonni came in, tried to break up the fight…and when Thomas threw him into the cabinet…"

"Thomas?"

"I hit him in the head with the tray so he couldn't hurt anyone else."

By now Lowell was on his feet, stalking across the room towards Nik, who backed away seeking an escape but finding none as his father was between him and the doorway.

"Quentin did this?"

It was impossible. While a ruthless politician, Quentin did not have a violent bone in his body. And while he too staunchly believed that the Marrocks were Cana, had been the one to plant the seeds of doubt in Donn and in Lowell…a claim now proven incorrect by Ernest's leading forepath, Lowell trusted him.

Or wanted to.

"You're wrong."

But it had been Quentin's belief in the Marrocks anthro nature that had pushed for the union between Channon and Hallister rather than Channon and Marrock as Jonni had wanted, not the long-held tradition that had kept the co-Laedan families from intermarrying since the Undoing. It was Quentin who supported every idea Lowell had for consolidation of ruling power in LaGuardia under one family name, who had offered a few ideas about how to accomplish that as well. Yes, he had supported the prospect of ousting the Marrocks from power, but he had also argued repeatedly for putting the Marrock matter into HOPE's hands. Quentin would never murder Roland, surely…and he certainly would never have the nerve to kill one of the Laedan's sons.

"You're mad…it's the shart…what have you been…?"

"Nothing. Not since waking. I swear it…"

Lowell's scoff of disbelief was not surprising nor was his disbelieving Nik's account of murder. Nik had been an addict nearly half as long as he had been alive. Why would anyone believe him?

Nik had not expected it, but he had hoped.

"So help me, if you did this…"

Slipping around his father's grasp and the incredulous claim of his accusatory hands, Nik made it to the door, disappointed to now be a suspect in his father's eyes. How could Lowell believe that one son had killed another, had killed Roland…and for what? Neither man had held anything Nik wanted. He was the person with the least amount of motive for murder of anyone.

There was no logic behind such an accusation.

"Think about it," Nik murmured. "You'll know I'm right. Ask the chief…ask the mage."

He made it easily away from the lunging reach of his father's grasp and into the corridor, passing the figure in the adjacent doorway without realizing anyone was there.

His father might not believe him, but Nik had done what he intended to do. And if he had to find some proof against Quentin to support his claims, he would. All it would take was that damn needle. That needle and the return of the Tracker Mage to the Fortress.

*

She remembered little things as consciousness brought her into the warmth of daylight and out of it again. The taste of blood in her mouth. Arguments and words spoken over her as her brother tended her injuries and stabilized her condition so that she would be whole and well again. She remembered Vanya crying, clinging to Kato with a strength that would not allow him to remain at Jia's bedside, her hand clutching her neck. She remembered the heat of the fire, Vance sitting between it and her, his bloody, gauze-wrapped hand awkwardly holding hers as Deuce limped in furious determined circles around her, growling a threat to anyone who tried to come near. The smell of chicken, the hushed sing-song of Reif offering comforting distraction to the younger children in tandem with Wist's uncertain baritone.

And always the echoes of Cana in combat, and the single word chipping at the inside of her skull to expose a lifetime of uncertainties she had carried but never dared look at too closely.

Daughter.

If only Addison's eyes did not burn with those same questions and with nervous accusation every time he looked at her. Every time that cry echoed in her pain-stuffed ears.

Daughter.

But what did it mean?

Chapter 14

"Your hand?"

Lost in his thoughts, or rather trying to avoid thinking by shutting out external stimuli and letting his mind go blank, and the throbbing in the hand of which she spoke, as he stared into the dying remains of the morning's cook fire, Vance had not sensed the waking of the woman next to him. Trill and Helena had just taken the pups to one of the library's upper floors to show them a collection of maps discovered some days earlier, using their schooling to distract them from the events of the night before. Already exposed to violence, fear and death, this world and the ways of Pack robbing them of any sort of sheltered upbringing, none seemed traumatized by the fight, the blood, or its aftermath, except for Vanya. Though she had finally been lulled to sleep by her brother's soft, rough singing, she had awakened quieter than usual. She followed the children, interacted with them as she had before, but her hand periodically came to her throat, where the evidence of blood drawn remained, and her gaze would dart around the room as though she was seeking the source of a pain she felt but could not quite recall receiving.

But her eyes would eventually settle on her brother's face and she would smile and be calm again.

Vance wondered what the world was like inside her head. How nice it must be…or terrifying…to forget so easily.

Throughout breakfast Kato had hovered near his sister, anticipating her needs and accommodating her desire for reassurance. But once the children gathered for schooling, Vanya willingly going with them so as not to be left out, the Fela eagerly accepted the opportunity to join several of the Cana adults in a patrol of their new territory. It was an act intended to reassure the Pack, as well as to offer a show of strength and solidarity, to remind Pain of his new status and keep him in his place. Addi had tended the new Omega's injuries, setting broken bones, stitching the worst of his gashes, ensuring he would not bleed to death. But as a common Pack practice Vance had seen before, when supplies were lean and difficult to come by, no cleansing alcohol, no bandages, and no pain relief were offered to the outcast. The bare minimum was spared to give him the hope of survival, but their meager resources were reserved for the core of its members. In time, perhaps, if Pain opted to remain on the Pack's fringes after his wounds healed enough to enable him to leave if he wished, he might win small favors, morsels of food, and better medical care. His future was for him to decide.

Jia had given him that much.

It was more, Vance mused, then he felt the man deserved.

"It's nothing." There had been no opportunity or need even to berate himself for the carelessness of his action, for grasping the barrel of the pistol that, when it discharged the first time, had damaged the ring finger of his left hand so severely that the decision had been made to remove it from the middle knuckle up rather than risk the onset of some life-threatening infection. Infection was always a risk, and he saw no use in complicating his health with a bit of bone and flesh that would never again be useful.

His actions, combined with Jia's effort and Deuce's attack, had saved Vanya's life, had possibly also saved Jia's and Pain's, maybe even Deuce's, and so Vance felt no regret for what he had done. There had been a brief self-scolding for grabbing the gun rather than Maz's wrist, and then the inevitableness of the injury was discarded along with the end of his finger.

Torben had taken it with him when he set off for LaGuardia during the night. Vance had not asked why.

Jia lay her hand on his wrist and he winced, not in pain but in response to the sympathy and gratitude that bled through her touch. He was not used to feeling either from anyone, not so directly at least, and the tightening in his chest in response to those emotions briefly cut off the flow of air into his lungs. His mouth opened to speak, to breathe, but no sound came forth and then her hand slid away as if the effort to keep it there was too difficult.

"Where are the others?" From where she lay near the fire, facing the library door, she could hear the children's voices above them but could see no one in the room. Memories of the fight for dominance began to slowly settle into place, bringing with it the creeping fear for the safety of the rest of the Pack.

"Everyone's fine," Vance assured her, following the path her gaze had taken. "Addi took care of everyone who was injured; no one was lost." He lay his good hand on her shoulder. Vanya's wounds had been superficial, the bullet had been drawn from Deuce's shoulder and his wounds cleaned and stitched, and Jia's injuries had been likewise cleaned, stitched, and bandaged where needed. She was a sorry sight, but she was alive and talking and not seemingly suffering any major effects from her head injuries.

"Those who were with Pain have been detained until you tell them what you want to do…and Pain's somewhere nearby…recovering. Several mutani arrived at dawn and went out with the others to make sure last night's ruckus didn't attract unwanted visitors."

Jia nodded, though the effort hurt her neck and made her vision blur. The noise of the fight, the howling, hissing, and shouting, in addition to the pair of gunshots, was likely to draw grubbers at least, and possibly scavs who hoped to pilfer the dead. Those things would have to be dealt with before the pups were allowed to play outdoors again. There was a chance that other Cana had been drawn to the area in the hopes of either shelter or an opportunity to lay claim to a weak pack or discarded members. After seeing to the welfare of their own, securing their territory was a wise thing to do. It was what Jia would have directed, had she been conscious and able to do so.

She wondered who had given the order in her stead.

Her eyes drooped closed, but as he was not looking at her, Vance did not see it. "Is it always like that…like last night?" He had never made a study of Cana behavior, had never concerned himself with the societal or familial organization of anthro…or anyone else. His focus had always been on individuals, the men and women he investigated or sought, their immediate relationships that might influence their actions or result in their deaths. For those he tracked, he was less concerned with the why than he was with the finding, the solving.

Last night had been his first immersion into Cana pack structure and he wanted to understand what he had witnessed.

He wanted to understand how much danger Jia would be in once he left her here alone.

"No, it's pretty rare actually. Real wolves congregate by families, led by the primary breeding pair; they don't let strangers in often. We…" Her eyes opened again and she looked around as much as she could without moving her head. "We have the entirety of human history at play too…plus the need for survival. I know people think there are a lot of us…but there really aren't…and with low birthrates and child survivability…it complicates things. It's human nature to socialize…to band together for self-preservation, I think…so we look for those like us and make alliances to take advantage of the skills and strengths of others…for companionship…to protect the children."

She sighed and achingly rubbed the tender side of her head. "Inevitably, human nature produces conflict and demands resolution. If we can't talk or argue our way out of disagreement or confrontation, the result is a fight. When pushed that far, the wolf comes out. It's inevitable…and unfortunate."

"He wanted to die."

Jia shrugged one shoulder. "He wanted not to be humiliated for failure. He fought twice, lost twice. But he was one of my father's friends…a supporter and ally. He and Maz were…I can't just kill him because he doesn't agree with me. My father wasn't like that; I won't be like that. I've given him two chances, but if he tries again…if he harms anyone else…I may be forced into it. But I don't want to. He is an asset I would rather live peacefully with…but I wonder if that is too much to ask."

Grunting with a scowl, Vance muttered, "Not so sure people know how to live peacefully…Normals or not." The inability to do so had contributed to the Undoing, had resulted in the rise of HOPE, the segregation of the mutani from the rest of the population…and even the mutani bickered and fought and challenged one another for dominance. Vance had seen it time and again. The inability to live peacefully had spawned hunts for anthro, their abduction and slaughter, the willingness to use them as slave labor or unwilling blood donors for a dangerous drug that flowed through LaGuardia's streets. It had contributed to the murders of Roland and Jonni.

In turn, it had led to some anthro striking out against their oppressors, or anyone deemed to be a threat, killing first before they could be killed instead.

Given what he knew of LaGuardia's history since the Undoing, it was surprising that the Marrocks had survived and flourished.

It was surprising anyone had.

"We try. We just want to live…like everyone else." Eyes closing wearily, her breathing softened and he thought she was drifting back to sleep. Two head injuries so near to one another in time were worrisome, which was why Addison had insisted that someone stayed at Jia's side, to make sure she would wake up, until he deemed her out of imminent danger.

Instead of sleeping, however, she mumbled, "Torben? Is he with them? My father…?"

"Roland's over there." When she looked at him again, he indicated the collection of potted plants the Pack had hauled here with them, their mobile garden, and though the still wrapped corpse could not be seen, Jia trusted it was there, as Vance said, amidst the strong odors of garlic, onion, and other plants that would mask the scent of gradual decay. They could not wait to bury him much longer.

"Torben's gone back…he's concerned about Nik."

"Nik? Channon?" Grimacing as she tried to roll to her side to face him, but finding the position too uncomfortable with the gashes Pain's claws had left, she forced herself to sit up, grateful for Vance's assistance until she was able to find balance in a less painful position. She could see his concern about letting her sit, but she was tired of that horizontal view of her world. She needed to be up and a part of it.

"He brought Torben in…helped us get Roland out of the Fortress. He would not tell me much when I spoke to him, but he knows. Everything. What happened…" He met her gaze as he cradled his injured hand to his chest. "Who's to blame. Don't know what he told Torben…or how they know each other…but Torben doesn't think he should be alone back there right now…"

"Yeah." Alone, whether he knew the truth or not, after the death of his older brother, was the last thing Nik needed to be.

"So…what's next? Will they let you…?"

She looked up from her hands, curled on her lap, in an effort to interpret the question he did not finish. Again she shrugged, although this time she appeared uncertain, afraid, prompting him to gently brush the hair from her face and tuck it behind her ear in an attempt to offer kindness and compassion and support without too much intimacy.

"We're not led by the strongest…or the oldest. Flushing Pack has always been led by a Marrock."

That should mean, by order of birth, that Addi became the Alpha after their father's death. But Addi did not want to lead, felt he had no qualities suitable for that position. Out of respect for his son's calling, and his daughter's strengths, Roland had chosen her. Her, by default, rather than force Addi into a place he did not fit. But if Deuce's words were true, if Jia was not a Marrock…then neither was Addison, and what then became of the Flushing Pack? The only kin with Marrock blood was Reif, who was neither old enough nor experienced enough to be Alpha. The girl was protective of others, stubborn and determined, but Jia did not know if Reif was alpha material. Although it had been Roland's choice for Jia to replace him, it would fall to the Pack to decide whether they wished to honor that appointment now that they were presented with an alternative truth, and though she had won the right of Alpha from Pain, twice, her father's wishes were no longer guaranteed.

Because she could not tell him what he wanted to know, she instead said, "Once it is decided, he will be buried in the Wilds." She was not even certain about that, as the Pack's ritual burial ground was now too far south to be within easy reach. Relocation had changed many things for them. Here, in this library, they were starting again, a new home, a new alpha…whoever that turned out to be…new members and a collection of allies they had never had before. A breaking of ties, perhaps, with the Channons, although that relationship was still in flux. A severing, it appeared, from the history the Marrocks had built for the Pack in LaGuardia after the Undoing and the dawn of the Pack's creation.

"There will be a hunt in his honor...a feast…an initiation."

"I'd like to see it." It was unusual for him to feel any interest in the lives and customs of others, for him to care about others outside of work. Caring for others created too much chaos for his mage senses. This time he wanted to follow this new interest, to embrace the experience as long as it lasted. But duty and the reality of their clashing worlds demanded something else. "But I should go back…"

He hoped Jia would try to talk him out of it, to talk him into staying. Though her eyes expressed that hope, and regret at the thought of his departure, she nodded in resolute acceptance of his choice.

Feeling compelled to offer an explanation, though she did not ask for one, he hurriedly added, "I need to know the forepath's report…on both of them. I need to know what the Chief's found. I need to know what was in that needle. And someone needs to keep an eye on the Channons and Quentin."

"Liam?" It was the only protest she made about him leaving. "You promised."

Vance rubbed the back of his neck with his good hand and looked away. Yes, he had promised. He had made that promise before their lives had become immensely more complicated and hazardous. But without Roland to show her the way, without Vance's limited knowledge of the elder Marrock's escape path found in that carefully guarded keycard, Jia might never locate her friend.

And if she did find him, given his likely condition, Vance doubted either would survive the attempt to bring Liam home.

Decision made, his expression steeled. "You're going to be laid up for a few days…and you've got matters to settle. A burial, a hunt, an initiation…"

"Liam might not be able to wait that long…"

"If he's out there, he'll have to. I know you don't want me doing this alone and you're in no condition to help. And they need you."

As if in response to his words, the library door opened and Addison entered, his nose and cheeks red from prolonged exposure to the cold, light snow accumulated on his hair and lashes. He saw that his sister was awake, almost smiled, but he did not approach to intrude on the conversation between her and the mage.

He carried an armload of kindling that he needed to deposit, but it was Jia's impression that he was avoiding her, and that made her shiver with remorse. Or maybe it was Vance's presence rather than some change in their twin status that Addi was reacting to.

Vance was not truly welcome, but he had been instrumental in returning Roland to the Pack, and in saving Vanya's life. The Pack elected to tolerate his presence until Jia was able to vouch for him, decide his future, but that did not mean they liked having him here.

And Vance knew it.

Clasping her shoulder, he stood, body stiff with cold and the lack of alcohol to bolster him, and added, "That'll give me time. Do what you need to do…and I'll be back as soon as I can. We'll find Liam."

After another side glance at her brother, Jia caught his good hand and squeezed. "You're leaving now?"

"Best I take advantage of the daylight." He forced a chuckle in the hopes of overriding the emotions that bled through her touch. "I might have other senses to use…but I don't have your eyes or ears."

Not caring what he might learn in that contact, she gave his hand another squeeze and let him go. "Take whatever you need…bandages, food, water…do what you need to do…and come back to me. If you don't…I will find you."

In the word find, Vance heard the word 'hunt', and as he was not certain that hunting would be a good thing, he nodded.

There was always a chance, when the truth came out and the Pack's decision was made, that she would no longer be welcome here. What her brother would do then, what Kato would do, her future was as uncertain as Vance's. If she was lucky enough to find Liam alive, to rescue him, even that was no guarantee that she would not end up alone, ostracized, with the mage being the only friend she had left.

He was her friend. Of that much, they were both certain.

Chapter 15

Fingers tracing the forming bruises around his wife's wrists where the tight fabric looped to bind her hands to the metal headboard, Donn relished the sounds of her labored breathing and the furious flutter of her pulse on the inside of her wrists beneath the pink skin there. How easy it would be…one little cut…to watch her lifeblood stain the sheets of their marriage bed.

Donn often entertained such ideas about others, what it would be like to watch their lives leave them. Nik's fascination was with the dead, what came after. Donn's was with the act of dying. But he had never actively taken the opportunity to harm anyone or anything with the intent of watching them die, nor taken the opportunity to seek out the dying in order to watch it happen beyond the very rare public executions his father sometimes called for.

And despite the flash of fantasy now, he had no desire for Oasis to die. She had too many uses, including the one they had just finished engaging in, the one intended to provide further Channon heirs.

Such games as this were never the same with his mother. That was something else entirely.

"I think," he purred, a sticky, sickening sound that made her shudder, although he attributed the shiver to the coolness of the room and the raking of his nails across her wrist, "it is time for you to prove your loyalty."

"I'm your wife. This isn't loyal enough?" There was a warmth to her chuckle, just enough of a challenge to keep him interested and aroused without being enough to elicit some form of punishment.

"This is duty…pleasurable and desirable as it is…but its duty nonetheless."

Oasis, wondering if he meant that he would have no interest in bedding her if not for the responsibility of producing Channon children, turned her face to look at him. The veins at the side of his neck still pulsed with the dwindling of passion, and his pale skin, pink with exertion, was sweat-puckered in the chill of the air. Though she preferred men with less pallid complexions, men like Thom and Lowell, Donn's pale features were gradually growing on her.

"What do you have in mind?"

"Quentin's hiding something. I need to know what it is."

Her neutral expression did not change. "Aren't we all?"

Holding her face still with a tight grip on her chin, Donn bent closer, narrowed his eyes, and growled, "You'd better not be hiding anything from me."

She smiled, an awkward expression due to that grip. "I only mean that we don't know each other very well yet…there hasn't been time for all our intimate secrets to come out. Same with Quentin. Besides…isn't it the nature of politics to keep things close to the breast until it is expedient to share them?"

"I don't like secrets," he snarled, releasing her, knowing she had valid points while also knowing perfectly well that he had secrets of his own to keep, some from her, some from his father, some from the Grand Mas, his brother, his mother. People passed through life accumulating secrets. Most of those were taken to the grave. That only fueled Donn's determination to uncover them.

He wanted no secrets that might, in some way, turn on him.

Stretching her neck as best she could to enable a kiss to his bare shoulder, she added, "Neither do I. What do you want to know? What do you think he's hiding?"

"Something Nik said…about the night Jonni was killed." Not died. His brother did not 'just die'. His brother was taken, and Donn wanted the truth. As expedient as blaming Jia's Fela friend might be, it might be just that, a convenient cover. "He believes Quentin is Fela."

Eyes wide, Oasis stared at him. "How…he can't be. That's not…"

"Possible? It's as possible as it was for the Marrocks to be Cana, maybe even more so if he wanted to avoid detection by misdirection. He's the one that planted that seed in the fertile garden of Fa's imagination…and now it's been proven otherwise." Not definitively proven, because no one had seen Roland turn. It was possible his body had been sposed to hide the truth. But Donn knew of no reason for there to be a conspiracy between the forepath and Chief Ernest, knew of no reason for either man to lie. They had nothing to gain in doing so and everything to lose if such lies were discovered.

Quentin, on the other hand, had a lot to gain by lying.

"Maybe he said it to misdirect attention away from himself."

"And maybe," Oasis said sympathetically, "whatever Nik thinks he saw was due to his odose, drugs still in his system."

Though Donn growled a warning, he did not argue the point. Her conjecture was not only possible. It was likely.

But Quentin's involvement was likely too.

"If there's the slightest chance…any possibility that Nik saw what he says he saw…we need to know." It was knowledge Donn could hold over Quentin's head, knowledge he could use to manipulate the man or oust him from his position of influence in Lowell's life if he did not capitulate to Donn's wishes.

It might even be enough to warrant Quentin's death if his hands were stained with Jonni's blood.

Without accusing Quentin of murder, for that was a card he was not ready to play, Donn continued, "An anthro advisor to the Laedan? That's dangerous. Whether it's a Marrock, or someone else, we can't have an anthro in a position of power. Grand Mas Lord will never stand for it…and neither should we."

Bringing HOPE into the equation made Oasis nod grimly. Keeping the influence of HOPE on one's side was best for anyone who wanted public power. And Donn was right, an anthro should never stand in a position of governance over the Normals in any borough.

Geary Hallister would never stand for it either.

"If he is…as you say…he'll never admit…"

Donn's laughter was dark. "Oh, I think he will. Have faith in yourself; have you seen the way he looks at you?" At her suddenly stricken expression, he laughed again. "I'm certain you can convince him to tell you anything you want to know. But do not," he growled, grabbing her chin again to force her to look at him, "bed him. If you ever…if I find you in bed with anyone…or suspect it…"

The threat remained intentionally incomplete, leaving the consequences of such an act to her imagination. Though she said in an even, contrite and sincere tone, "I will do my best, learn what I can," she wondered what Donn would do if he discovered that such an act of disloyalty had already been committed with his very own father.

He untied her wrists and slapped her buttocks hard enough to leave a stinging handprint. "Go on then…you've got work to do."

Donn, however, showed no intention of rising from their bed or doing anything other than watch her dress and leave the room.

*

Her day was spent in and out of slumber, each period interrupted by the comings and goings of pack members and her brother's occasional efforts to assess her condition. Though her head and body ached from the fight she had won, and she felt weak from the exertion and blood loss, Jia had suffered no injuries that would keep her down for long. Once the lingering dizziness created by the head injuries was passed, she would be on her feet and ready to face whatever future the Pack would lay out for her.

Kato, however, avoided her.

By unspoken consensus, with the mutani and QiangXu agreeing to stand watch, the Pack gathered for the evening meal to face their future rather than avoid it for some indefinite amount of time. They needed reassurance, stability, guidance, now that Roland's body had returned and awaited attendance, and whether Jia was ready for their judgment, or Deuce was ready to reveal hidden Pack secrets, the rest deserved answers.

The Pack deserved an Alpha.

With Deuce reluctantly welcome at the fire for the first time in Jia's memory, she felt she and Addi deserved those answers too.

"Is the perimeter…?"

"Secure," replied Orliss. Jia assumed, because of his established relationship with the neighboring out-of-zone mutani, that he had arranged for them to take the watch while the Cana deliberated their future. She also assumed, because he and his own small pack were gathered here, that they had chosen to link their future with the Flushing Pack…pending the outcome of the discussion at hand.

Maybe Orliss hoped he would be the new joint pack Alpha.

The last one to join the group, Addi sat next to his wife so that he could see both his sister and the one man they all waited to hear, but before he could demand answers, after waiting several moments for Jia to be the one to ask, Deuce scratched his chin, cleared his throat, and lowered his gaze to begin.

"We were a small pack…in the Zone. Two families. Theba's and my own, plus two sisters from the east…"

"There are Cana in the Zone?" asked Candace in surprise. The Zone was known to house mutani, everyone along the eastern fringe of LaGuardia knew that. But few were aware of anthro residing there.

"What better place to be?" Maz murmured without looking up from the pot he stirred over the night's fire. "No one hunts us there."

Contemplating if taking the Flushing Pack into the Zone might have been safer than their new library home, Jia nodded for Deuce to continue.

Deuce bobbed his head once in acknowledgment. "Her father was gone…there was me and mine…the only males. We protected them, with the intent that together we would grow strong, thrive…but the other women…my mother, were older, veterans, survivors who did not conceive despite my father's efforts. We were doomed, we knew…the Zone was our only hope for survival. Theba and I were young…too young then though we didn't know it…but we understood survival, responsibility, and took it on ourselves to do what the elders were failing to do…"

"Breed."

There was no need for Addi to point out the obvious, but he felt compelled to say the word aloud as if challenging Deuce to deny it. The thought of their mother with anyone other than Roland was a foreign one.

Not doing so, but not confirming it either, Deuce continued, his voice melancholy with remembrance. "She was my best friend. I loved her more than anything…anyone." He hesitated to steady his voice, making Jia feel bad for him. All of those years…on the outside…so close to her and yet so far away.

"We crossed paths with Roland and the Flushing Pack during a Wilds hunt, and over the course of three years, our packs grew closer, relying on each other for supplies and support. There were talks of combining the Packs…our females, Flushing's abundance of males…it would have been the best for both packs. Roland was not yet Laedan then…but he was the newly appointed Flushing Alpha…young and vital…as were Theba…and I…

"But then the coughing sickness struck for the first time. So many died, so many Normals, mutani, and anthro alike. My father thought the Wilds would be the safest place for us to go, so we left the Zone and isolated ourselves, always on the move. We did not see Roland or the Flushing Pack for nearly a year in my father's fear that outside exposure would kill us. Perhaps he was right..." Deuce groaned, "but it did not matter. Only she and I survived…"

No one spoke for many minutes as they digested what had been said and noted the exchange of glances between Maz and Deuce. Of the original Flushing Pack, from the days before many of those here were born, Maz and Uncle had been there. Both had been young, barely more than pups, but they had been there during the coughing time and they knew the truths of which Deuce spoke.

They had known these truths for years.

If Uncle had been welcomed to speak during this conclave, from where he and the other rebels were held, he could have supported the story. Maz's shared glances with Deuce were enough.

"We needed to scav. Winter was coming and we needed bedding, clothing, or the means to repair what we had. We took the risk of entering the unfamiliar LaGuardia streets…and fell into a HOPE sweep. I was taken, but Theba made it away…into the security of the Flushing Pack. To guarantee her safety, she agreed to marry Roland."

"That doesn't explain…" began Jia. She knew that she and her brother had been born less than a year after their parent's marriage, but if Deuce had been a HOPE captive during those early months of Roland and Theba's union, it seemed unlikely he could be…

Unless.

"Unless Mother was already with child." Addi scowled. "That means I am also…"

"No…it does not."

That scowl deepened as brother stared at sister, and she at him, trying to make sense of the timing, of the story they were being told. It was possible, though rare, for a woman to carry conceived children of separate fathers, a peculiarity more common amongst anthro than amongst Normals, but still rare enough to go unnoticed in most cases unless the children showed some sort of remarkable differences, such as variances in skin color or a differing anthro subspecies. Even then, with the newness of anthro genetics in the human gene pool, it was not always possible to know.

Addison and Jia showed no visible distinctions beyond gender. There were few reasons for anyone to suspect they could be biologically born of separate fathers.

"Did he…did Father…know…?" Jia whispered.

"I do not know about at first…I was not there. I do not think he gave the possibility any thought. When I escaped HOPE, when I found the Pack almost two years later, I came for her. She was married then, of course…to a man she had been drawn to even when she and I…and a mother. I tried to change her mind…woo her back…" His voice caught, the roughness of it a product of both emotion and of speaking more in one sitting than he had in many years. "There, in that room…the three of us…with you and Addison…we all knew."

Trill entwined her fingers with Addi's as she nodded and murmured, "The scents." Pups of the same parents typically carried an underlying scent marker, a combination of both parents. Siblings that shared only one biological parent were marked by the genetics of that one, but differed in scent slightly due to the genes of the other. The differences were often subtle enough that no one questioned it, and with no reason to believe the twins should be different, any differences they shared had been ignored.

Until that night.

Theba had likely known the difference from the moment of their birth. Roland accepted both as his, nurtured them equally in that belief, until Deuce's return forced the truth into the open.

"There was no anger…no blame…no infidelity. It had been before...there was no fault to be had or made. But he was angry that he had not known before. He did not want me there, did not want the truth to be known by anyone else, did not want me in Theba's life…or yours…" He looked at Jia but was unable to hold her gaze, as if he was ashamed that he had been unable to do more to be part of her life.

"So you became Omega."

Roland's dislike and intolerance of the other man made sense. The reason Deuce had never been welcome, had endured years of solitude and rejection made sense. The reason he showed so much devotion and protectiveness of Jia made sense.

What did not make sense to Jia, was Roland's other choice.

"If he knew, then why did he choose me to be…?"

It was Uncle who answered, despite the directive he and those with him had been given to remain quiet. "Because of your aptitude for it, because Addison did not want to follow that path, and…"

"And because he loved you," Maz said, completing Uncle's words. "You are Theba's daughter…and that makes you his. He might not have been your biological parent, but he raised you, taught you, loved you as his own. That never changed, because in his heart you were as much his as hers."

"But she is no Marrock," muttered Trill's brother Xan from where he glowered at Uncle's side.

"She is…by name and upbringing," Addi said, his expression finally settling into the familiar one of affection he shared with his sister. Maz was right. She was Theba's child, just as he was. Regardless of the paternal genetics involved in their DNA, they had shared a womb, and the love and guidance of the same set of parents. Learning this particular detail now made no difference in who they were as people. Roland had always treated them the same.

As his children.

In some ways, Roland had favored Jia because of their shared interests, outlooks, aptitudes, and similar stubborn demeanor, in spite of who her biological father was. That spoke highly of his opinion of her as an individual. She was a Marrock, not the outcast's child.

"He chose her to be his heir. He believed in her, and so do I."

Unable to hold her brother's gaze without shedding overwhelmed tears, Jia instead looked at the unexpected ally who spoke next.

"As do I." Kato had no say in the matter of Pack politics, in the succession of Alpha as he was not officially one of them, but his expressed belief in her, after a day spent avoiding her and, she believed, blaming her for what had happened, and almost happened, to Vanya, hit close to home.

"And I." Deuce's opinion, however, after this revelation and her having broken the noose of Omega from around his neck, was expected and carried less weight than even Kato or Addi's opinions. But it was important to her nonetheless.

"I…" she began, voice cracking as she sought words to say, despite her determination to be strong and stoic. "Father's decision, his preference, only matters if it is accepted by each of you. I know I have made what seem to be rash decisions, have left the Pack alone when I should have…"

Maz gave a snort, the closest sound to amusement he could make given the uncomfortable position thrust on him now that his partner was the Pack Omega. "You left us in capable hands. Roland would have done the same thing…"

"And often did," pointed out Reif. She might not have been initiated as an adult yet, but she was old enough to have an opinion and old enough for the adults to take her seriously. She was also old enough to vividly remember all of the times Roland had been away from the Pack, whether it was to perform duties as co-Laedan in the Fortress or to travel here to the library that had been a sanctuary and source of inspiration , knowledge, and escape.

"You brought Roland back…as you promised," Zen whispered. She had distanced herself from those with whom she had previously defected just enough to draw attention to herself. "Addi says you can find Liam…that you know where he is. You can bring him home?" The three looked at one another as Liam's only living relative sought confirmation of Addi's claim.

"With Van…with Mage Segara's help, if Liam is alive, I will find him," Jia promised. "And when I do I will bring him home too. Getting them back…it's all I wanted. I never expected Father would be…"

"That is on the other Fela," Kato growled, "not you."

QiangXu, who had been leaning against the door frame listening to the story that he might, or might not, have already known, listening but not participating in Pack politics that were not his concern, straightened at Kato's words. "A Fela? In the Fortress?"

"Thomas Quentin," confirmed Jia with a gruff, choking sound.

"That explains why he always rubbed me the wrong way," Addi muttered. "No offense to present company," he added with a side glance at Kato.

Not knowing if Addi was claiming to find his company irritating, Kato shrugged. "None taken. He rubbed me the wrong way too."

His snort and eye-rolling expression made Eddie giggle and say, "I bet he did." As Fela himself, he was just beginning to understand that the proximity of other Fela made him uncomfortable. Except for Kato. Kato made him feel safe.

"Jia fought for Alpha twice," Trill reminded them. "And won. She Called new blood." Though she looked at Helena, Candace, Brie, and their pups, she intentionally avoided the members of the Queen's College Pack. They might be seated with the Flushing Pack this night, listening to the deliberations, but the packs had not merged and it was not up to any of them to assume that discussion was in the offing. "Do we honor that, honor Roland's wishes, or choose another Alpha?"

The last words were added to make the question a choice rather than a yes or no query.

Maz, his voice strained tighter than before, was the first to reply. "As Roland's second, if there is any dissension…any who wish to put forth a viable alternative Alpha…this is the time to speak it."

Pain was no longer a viable choice, and those who stood apart knew it as well as the others did. Any other adult in the room, male or female, even a member of the Queen's College Pack, could be. But the Flushing packmates, most of whom had known the others all or most of their lives, knew what their best option was.

If Roland had trusted Jia to lead the pack, they should too.

Even Uncle, Zen, Ilba and Xan accepted it now.

It was unfortunate, many felt, that Pain did not and had pushed the matter to the point of being exiled from his family and had laid sanctions on the shoulders of all who had followed him.

There was no spoken answer to the question. One by one, adults and pups alike got up from where they sat and knelt before their chosen Alpha, rubbing their faces against the sides of hers to express submission, affection, and acceptance. Those previously banished waited for her hands on their heads, followed by an embrace that welcomed them back into the family before offering that same sign of fealty. When the gruff, surly Ele did likewise without prompting, a supplication to submit to the larger, stronger pack, abandoning the small Queen's Pack to be quickly followed by Wist in doing so…the younger man flashing Reif a bright smile as if to win her approval of his choice, Orliss and Ayla looked at each other, a new decision now left to be made. There had been no poaching, the choice to merge with the stronger pack was one of self-preservation and solidarity and not a choice to be taken lightly. Jia would not lay claim to what was not hers unless the smaller pack's Alpha agreed.

Only when Orliss and Ayla came to her too, in a pledge of unity and support, did Jia welcome all four of them.

The rest of the Flushing Pack likewise accepted them.

Not wanting to be left out when every pup who was capable of doing so, including two of the Arden brothers, made the same show of submission, Vanya rushed to Jia, threw her arms around the woman, and imitated the actions of everyone else, rubbing her face enthusiastically against Jia's. Kato bristled when Jia's gaze met his over Vanya's shoulder. He made no effort to stop his sister but he made no effort to move either.

He would support Jia, would follow and protect her anywhere. But submit to her?

He was not about to submit to anyone.

Maybe Jia was disappointed by his choice, but she only nodded in acceptance.

He was Fela. There was no reason he had to join the Pack.

But to Jia, he was welcome here. Member or not. Just as young Neel was.

"Tomorrow we bury him…here…near the fountain." She spoke to distract the others from Kato and Neel's choice, from raising questions or argument she was too weary to tolerate. The fountain seemed the best place for Roland, not in the Wilds near their old home, where his father and theirs before had been buried but here, near their new home, the sanctuary he had found for them. "Then tomorrow night…we hunt."

"And as soon as your mage returns," Zen reminded her, "we go after Liam."

After a short visual exchange with Kato, Jia nodded her promise. "As soon as he returns."

Whatever Kato's feelings about Vance, without the tracker-mage, they had no hope of finding where Liam had been taken.

No hope of proving any connection, if there was one, between Roland's abduction and murder, the blood drug, and whatever plans Lowell Channon was making for LaGuardia's future.

Chapter 16

"It's Segara, isn't it? Mage Segara?"

Having worn the hood of his coat up with the intention of avoiding recognition, even though the coat itself and the insignia on it marked him as a Protector, Vance was surprised that someone picked him out of the evening street crowd and called him by name. He was even more surprised to turn and find himself face to face with Francis Lord, a man he had never personally met, had taken great pains to avoid, whom he had seen often enough over the years in the halls of the Fortress at some function or other. In the Fortress, but never on the street. His steps faltered, the only visible indication he gave that this was a conversation, a meeting, he would rather not have. The hesitation allowed the Grand Mas to retrace his steps and come back to where Vance was, making the hesitation not appear suspicious.

"It is, sir…yes."

A mage rarely offered his hand, as most learned early that other people interpreted the request for physical contact not as one of greeting or respect but rather as a request for information, for the opportunity to read thoughts and impressions and emotions from the other. Francis, however, showed no fear of such things as he grabbed Vance's hand before Vance could retreat from the contact.

"I did not see you at the interment."

"No, sir; I've been searching for the murderer." The rush and swirl of thoughts and images were too convoluted for Vance to untangle quickly, not when Francis continued to talk, thus distracting the mage from the reading process within his head.

"Or murderers? I've heard there were two?"

"Don't know where you heard that, sir. I was told to track a Fela."

"And the Marrock girl?"

"Only because it appears he has taken her against her will," Vance corrected.

"Oh…my mistake then."

Vance thought it was hardly a mistake, that it was the Grand Mas' way of probing for details he should not have.

Lord continued, "I've heard no talk of abduction…but I suppose the focus is on the dead rather than the living."

Unable to comment on either that remark or the information Lord was clearly looking for, Vance said nothing. Lord studied the shorter man's face, seeking some clue of his own; finding nothing, he released the mage's hand and asked, "Did you find him? Any evidence?"

In that last moment of physical touch, something forced its way into Vance's mind's eye, a sprawling building, mostly a single, but tall, level, burdened with the stench of chemical death and blood. The smell of it reawakened the lingering traces of the substance that had tainted his own blood not so many days ago, and it was all Vance could do not to wince dizzily at the recollection and vomit the bile in his empty stomach.

"Are you well, Mage?"

Vance nodded. "I'm fine. Haven't slept or eaten in a few days…"

"And that hand looks bad." The Grand Mas made a small gesture and brief glance at the bandaged hand where it appeared the blood had begun to flow again.

"An accident."

Lord motioned to one of his men to join them; the fellow stepped forward with a battered leather case of the sort Vance knew men had once taken to business meetings. "Allow my man to…"

Not trusting Lord or his man or the contents of that case, Vance shook his head. "That's not necessary. On my way to tend to it…"

"Nonsense. It won't be so easy with one hand…"

"I'll be fine," Vance reiterated, his refusal of help just as forceful as Lord's offer of it. "I've found a connection between the murderer, a new drug fabricated from anthro blood, and a medifac across the border. Laedan Channon is expecting a report and I'm going to be late as it is. Please…my apologies…but I must take my leave…"

The Grand Mas' man lowered the case after another gesture from Lord, whose face, despite his effort to remain neutral and cordial, took on a mask-like expression meant to cover an emotional reaction to those words that could not be hidden from any skilled mage.

It was bait enough, whether true or assumed. HOPE's Grand Mas knew something, perhaps about the murders, perhaps about the drug and its production, perhaps about the facility Vance assumed was run by HOPE…because no one else was likely to possess the resources to amass equipment, manpower, and expertise to run such a place…even though, as Vance recalled, the pull of the drug in his veins was more southerly than southeasterly. HOPE territory or Kennedy Borough.

He did not know which end of the path he would find.

"Yes…well…go then. And please…relay my regrets again to Lowell for my untimely departure. Duty and all of that…but I will return as soon as I am able to discuss LaGuardia's future."

"Of course."

Doubting that Lowell would care to hear such words, that beneath the grief over the loss of his son he probably cared little about Lord and his departure from the Fortress. Vance's promise to relay those sentiments to the Laedan was an empty one, as empty as his intent to meet with Channon. He had his hand to tend, the Chief to talk to, and Torben Moeller to find. There was business to conduct, and none of it involved Lowell…not when the Laedan had threatened his life, or at least his livelihood, if he returned to the Fortress empty-handed.

"You know they suspect you, don't you?"

The question came out more bluntly than Oasis intended, but despite Donn's ultimatum that she learn the truth of Quentin's genetic heritage, she did not believe Thom would easily reveal what she already suspected. Not to her…not when this was a secret that, if true, he had kept through all of the years they had known one another.

She had never pried, never pushed to know before.

But things were different now. She hoped, as she joined him at the conference room window staring at the sea in the light of mid-morning, that her question came out more concerned than accusatory.

"Suspect me of what?" His voice and posture were relaxed, almost bored, but Oasis recognized the tick at the corner of his eye that revealed tension he would rather no one know was there. He was not looking at her, but the fingers of his nearest hand were rubbing against the back of hers. In this public room, where they could be interrupted at any time, it was the only intimacy he would allow, despite the long unfed longing he nursed.

"Killing Marrock…Jonni…Nik saw it all…"

Thom snorted. His posture did not change. "It was the Fela."

"I know," she murmured. "But not the one they are hunting."

This time he did turn to stare at her, hearing something that cut cold to the pit of his stomach, a note in her voice more dangerous than the words she spoke.

"How long…?'

Though she knew what he was asking, she countered, "How long what?" as she continued to face the window. Despite his underlying fear and the anger it carried, she did not believe he would hurt her.

Not the way Donnovan would if he learned how much she knew and withheld from him.

"Have you known?"

She considered the question, trying to remember when she first began to suspect his duality. She admitted no such suspicions to Donn, nor to anyone else, because doing so would reveal how long and how well she had known Thom Quentin, a secret never to be shared with any Channon. "Not till now," she admitted, "but I suspected the first time we shared a bed. Your eyes change when you…"

Roughly he grabbed her arm and spun her to face him. "Change how?" he hissed. No other woman he had ever bedded had said such a thing. Most had been hooks, paid in favors or credits for the service of sexual gratification, for who ignoring a client's peculiarities was part of the job…so long as that client did not hurt them or carry any obvious contagious ailments. Even mutani could hire a hook without fear of exposure.

How many had there been? How many knew and could expose him if given the proper incentive? If they could be found?

"You go gold…your pupils elongate…like a cat." She shrugged. She was either pretending not to care or, he thought with a sneer, maybe she did not.

But she should. She definitely should.

"So what do you want from me?"

"Want? Who said I want…?"

"Why tell me now? What purpose does it serve if you don't want…?"

"I'm worried about you, Thom. Isn't that enough?"

Again he snorted; the sneer not fading. "You want to blackmail me."

Looking more offended by the accusation than she felt, she said, "If I wanted to blackmail you with that, I would have done it years ago."

"Or hold onto it until you want something…need something…or it suits you to…"

"I love you…you know that. There's never been a reason to…"

"Love me? If you…then why did you marry…?"

"You know why. It was your idea…and I agreed. For Kennedy's future. For ours. Once he…I didn't have a choice once the idea got into my father's head. But you have a choice…and I want to help you."

Thom knew Geary. He knew the hold the man had kept, or tried to keep, on his daughter's life. Not as tight a hold as he had believed, but tight enough that, once he saw the value of a Hallister-Channon marriage, the prospect had become unavoidable. And Thomas had done his share of maneuvering within LaGuardia's fortress to make it happen. Though Oasis had been the one to suggest to him the power such a union could reap, once she had done so, there was no going back. That marriage had become unavoidable, even if she had wanted to back out of it.

"Help me how?"

"Keep your secret, redirect Donn's suspicions, in exchange for information."

"Blackmail."

"Not blackmail, just…"

"You tell anyone, and you know what that means for your future?"

She stared at him with a wide-eyed innocence that he took to mean she had no idea what he was suggesting. "One word from you…one rumor…and I'll take you down with me. What do you think your father will do when he learns you've bedded a…?" He could not finish the sentence, could not speak the word he had struggled his entire life to hide and deny. "What will Grand Mas do? What do you think Donn will do? Do you think they will accept and forgive you for knowingly…?"

"I told you, I did not know until now. I love you. I would never…"

"But you suspected…and you stayed anyhow…" Or perhaps she had not, since it had not been so long afterward that the prospect of a Hallister-Channon marriage had come up and Thomas had relocated his political ambitions to LaGuardia. Maybe she had accepted the idea willingly to be rid of him. "And you've threatened…"

He seemed to be the one making threats, and despite her saying the words, not once had he acknowledged them or repeated the sentiment back to her. Not for the first time she wondered if she was merely a means to an end for him.

The way he was increasingly becoming for her.

That suspicion made it easier to continue. "The only information I want is about Fort Hamilton…and how I can help you find it. I want to be included, Thom. From what I've guessed…I don't think it's the kind of place Donn should be allowed to get to first. Trust me…let me help you…and I'll do what I can to help you get there…and to keep the others from uncovering your secret."

The secret being that, though he had not admitted it, he had not denied being Jonni and Roland's killer either. Oasis knew him well enough to know he had a killer's instinct.

Redirecting his talent to LaGuardia, encouraging him to seek power there so they could rise in eminence together away from her father's sway, had been the only way to keep Laedan Hallister alive.

"There's no secret to tell." But he was going to have to make certain, he realized, that Nik never again talked about what he thought he knew. It should not take much effort. Unlike Donn and Jonni, Nik had one easily manipulated interest.

All Thom had to do was turn him back to the shart. Once strung out again, Nik would forget about anything he might have seen, or imagined he had seen. Even if he did not forget, no one was going to believe the words of a junkie. Turn him back to the shart and Thom was safe…and he had multiple ideas of just how to do it.

He stormed from the room without another word, but the emotion left in his wake did not take a mage to decipher. He was lying to her…and somehow she had to find out why.

The Protectorate was closer, and safer he thought, than home, and so that was where Vance stumbled in the aftermath of the head rush worth of information Grand Mas Lord dumped into his skull. He had never come across an individual capable of selectively driving thoughts through his sense shields, had never met anyone willing to risk exposure that way, and he wondered again, as he forced the Protectorate doors open and staggered into the Chief's empty office, what it was about Grand Mas that had made that brief contact so overwhelming. Was he a mutani, perhaps, without knowing it? A mage with only marginal, untapped and untrained potential?

Or was it something else? Did he know what he had done?

Vance grabbed one of Ernest's liquor bottles, popped the top, and guzzled the foul-smelling, bitter-tasting substance so that it burned like molten lead into his belly.

"Eff..." he groaned, clutching the edge of the desk with his injured hand as best he could to avoid collapsing onto the Chief's well-worn chair. The effort shot pain up his arm, but the pain was dulled by the first drink he had enjoyed in days.

Maybe not enjoyed, but it gave him what he needed.

The bottles he had taken from his flat had been left unopened with the Flushing Pack.

He was surprised he had not drunk any of it.

Setting the bottle down, he began to fumble through the deepest desk drawer in search of the medikit he knew the chief kept there.

Not having considered where Ernest was, only grateful that the office was empty, when Vance recognized the approaching footsteps before they crossed the threshold into the room, he muttered under his breath and tried to ignore the sound. But the sound was not going to ignore him. Rather than wait for the expected question or comment about his hand, he groused, "Where's the kit?"

Before Ernest could reply, however, Vance found what he was looking for and dropped it on the desk with a clatter loud enough to startle those in the room beyond the door.

"And before you ask...don't."

Ernest grunted, found a glass, and filled it from the bottle Vance had opened. It was too early to drink, but he had a hunch, judging by the mage's demeanor, that he was going to need that drink before the day was out and so decided to start his day the same way. "Help yourself," he muttered, his tone echoing the exhaustion in his eyes. One swallow of the thicker than normal liquid in his glass made him grimace and croak, "Shart...you could have at least gone for the good stuff." This was good, in that it was probably the strongest alcohol Ernest had on hand, but it tasted like old coffee grounds, hemp bitters, and stale burnt bread on top of the alcohol burn.

Where in the hell had he gotten this stuff, he wondered.

If Vance was looking to wake himself up and jump-start his day, or else knock himself out, this ought to do the trick for both.

Mumbling something unintelligible in response, Vance worked the wrappings off of his injured hand and reached for the bottle again.

"Not that stuff…that'll kill you." It would not, of course, but the thickness of it would not wash away blood as well as something of a more liquid consistency could. It would, however, probably shock Vance's system into collapse. "Here." He pulled Vance's arm to the side so that, when the clear liquid was dribbled over the stump of the man's half finger, it dripped into the waste bin rather than onto the desk or the floor. When Vance barely winced, Ernest guessed the man had already consumed enough alcohol to dull his nerves.

"Looks like the stitches have pulled…not too bad…probably just do with some fresh bandages." The stains on the discarded linens indicated the injury had bled for a while and begun to dry and close up; removing the old dressings had aggravated the wound so that it began to seep again. Having tended enough similar injuries during his tenure on the force, Ernest quickly finished the job and got Vance's hand bound once more.

The mage took the bottle he had opened and drank again before trudging to the sofa. Ernest preferred the less acidic pungency of the clear vintage he had on hand and poured some into his glass.

"You learn anything while I was gone?"

"Take it you didn't find them."

Vance looked at him over the edge of the upturned bottle and shrugged. With the office door open, he sure as shart was not going to say anything incriminating that might find its way back to the Laedan.

Taking the hint, Ernest nodded. "Got a few things in the vault for you to examine…when you're ready." It took no genius to guess that ready was not going to come tonight. Vance was on the verge of collapse as it was. "The kid…it was like every rib was driven back into his lungs. Probably died within moments…drowned in his own blood. Guessing with the impact into that cabinet, he was out…didn't know what was happening."

"Unfortunate." Jonni did not deserve that sort of death. Jonni had been a good kid, kept himself clean, did right by the people in his district, refused to follow in his father's tight-fisted footsteps or his brother's sadistic ones. He should have lived a long life. He should have become Laedan in his father's place. "No clues?"

"Just that it was someone strong. Very strong."

An anthro. That did not narrow the suspect pool, although it did eliminate Nik from the list.

"Tried to get them to hold off on the burial long enough for you to examine him, but his father refused to wait." Some in the office might piece together that they were discussing the recent murders in the Fortress, but the chief still felt it best not to name names.

"And the other? Can I see him?" Vance knew the answer, of course, but for the sake of those eavesdropping in the other room, he had to keep up the charade.

After a quick glance through the door, where he saw that no one was watching or appeared to be actively listening, Ernest shook his head. "Guire said he was turning…so he was sposed and buried next to the kid."

That meant that someone else, or maybe no one, was buried in the Fortress garden alongside Jonni, and that meant that their ruse to remove Roland from the Fortress had gone undetected. To the Laedan and the rest of the Protectorate, it meant that the mage would have no opportunity to examine the dead men for clues, meant a decreased chance of using those clues to catch the killer, but such setbacks were hardly uncommon. Vance Segara was still considered by many to be the best tracker there was, no matter the setbacks.

Few had doubts that the killer would go unpunished for long.

"Guire did say there was bloody fluid in his lungs…that did not appear to be a symptom of any previously acquired injury…and his heart showed no damage that could have contributed to respiratory distress. Something else burst the vessels in his lungs…something else killed him…but we don't have the equipment to determine what that was. A physical defect, perhaps, some previously unrealized weakness unmanifested until now. Hell, even an odose could have done it, but there was no sign he was a user."

"Think if he'd been an addict, everyone would've known." It only took one use, however, not a lifetime of substance abuse, to result in an odose. How many first-timers died because they did not know what they were doing or how to get hold of the good stuff rather than some of that cheap, impure shart floating around the streets. One hit of something strong and pure, or something tainted with poisons, either medicinal or recreational, would have been enough to kill a man.

Another long swallow from the bottle and then he reached sideways without looking to set it on the end table. The bottle teetered on the edge before crashing to the floor and spraying its syrupy contents across the worn tile and the legs of the nearest chair.

Vance did not flinch or react to the sharpness of the sound. Ernest doubted he heard it. “You’ll bring me what you’ve got?” he asked with a sleepy-eyed yawn.

With so much high proof alcohol in his body, the chief was surprised the tracker was talking. “Sure. You wait here. I’ll be back.”

Ernest had not made it to the door before Vance’s eyes were closed and the man, with his head dropped back against the cushioned sofa, began to snore. For however long it lasted Ernest would let him sleep where he was. He was going to go home, where he had intended to be hours ago, and get a little sleep of his own.

Damn inconvenient duty.

Of all of the various substances he had partaken of over the course of his addiction, many of them produced paranoia as one of the possible side effects. There were enough drugs to take for that too, one for nearly every unpleasant ailment or effect a person could experience in their day to day. By now, Nik believed he knew them all, believed he could recommend anything to anyone in an effort to make their lives better…at least for the relatively short duration of that chemical’s presence in the body.

Without resorting to one of those many substances, however, there was not a single thing Nik could think of that could ease the nausea and sweats and cramped muscles that threatened to devour him if he did not feed his neural pathways soon. He was struggling not to retreat back down that familiar hole, wanted to stay strong for Jonni and Jia’s sake, but the paranoia, this time, as much a symptom of withdrawal as it was a symptom of use, felt stronger than ever.

Or maybe, he reminded himself from the darkest corner of his empty room where he drew his knees to his chest and tried to hide behind them, he was not really paranoid.

Perhaps someone had heard his confession to his father. Maybe someone had seen him sneak away to Torben's…or had seen him return…and had connected those things to what had really happened to Roland's body. Maybe one of the whispering shadows knew that it was not Roland buried in the Channon garden and was seeking recompense for that.

Maybe it was Jonni taunting him, demanding justice or else intent on driving Nik mad.

Too late for that, Nik chuckled darkly, wiping the sweat from his forehead before it trickled into his already stinging eyes.

He heard footsteps creaking at the window, not inside the room but rather outside of it, where a shadow drifted across the glass, a shade darker than the overcast, moonlit sky. It paused to tap on the glass, gnarled fingers raking the surface with the gun it held.

A gun pointed at him.

Nik did not know much about guns, but he knew they could kill him. He leaped to his feet and bolted with a shriek as a loud sound cracked the glass behind him.

If it was a bullet, they had missed.

Someone wanted him dead. He might be fascinated with death, but tonight Nik was not ready to die. There was only one place he could think of to go, only one man he could think of, in that panicked state of paranoia, with whom to seek shelter.

The shattered glass of the nearly empty gas lamp, knocked from the desk in his passing, sprayed across the floor. There was not enough fuel in it to catch fire or spread the flame. The struggling orange glow sputtered out, leaving the room dark behind Nik's retreat.

*

It was peaceful in the garden, communing with the dead in the frigid evening air, with no one to disturb her or look at her with curiosity or pity except for the neverending parade of Guards passing in and out of the gates looking for a killer they would not find.

How could they when the killer was inside of her?

Yiva might not have done the deed, but surely there was something she could have done in the years since Jonni's birth that could have saved his life. It was her failure as a mother that had killed him as surely as it had been anyone else.

Silently, her hand on the newly planted tree that marked her son's grave, she begged for forgiveness. If he heard her, he did not reply.

Perhaps that was another of her failings.

Over an hour ago she had witnessed the return of Grand Mas Lord, who had made an elaborate show about his departure earlier that day, bidding the family farewell with flowery speeches of regret for their loss and hollow promises to provide whatever they needed if they would only ask. It was possible he had forgotten something and returned to retrieve it, but if his business elsewhere was as urgent as he had sworn to Lowell it was, Yiva thought it would be more expedient for him to have sent any of the dozen attendants who traveled with him to fetch it and bring it to his destination.

Whatever the purpose of his return, he had entered the courtyard only long enough, on the heels of two of those early-arriving envoys, to conduct a brief conversation with Laedan Hallister. Neither had seen her there, ghost of a person that she was, or perhaps they had not cared. Now Hallister stood in that same place with his daughter's hands in his, his head bent forward to press his forehead to hers in a loving fashion that made Yiva's heart ache.

What she would have given for her only conceived daughter to have lived to be born, to love her the way it appeared Oasis loved her father.

But no, Yiva thought, as Donnovan joined his wife and her father's conversation, an intrusion that did not seem welcome judging by the way Hallister took a retreating step backward. Yiva shook her head, burying her regret too deeply with the hope that it would never again resurface. A daughter would have been vulnerable to Donn's predilections, a thought that horrified, disgusted, and angered Yiva in equal parts. The terrors he inflicted on her were bad enough. She could not imagine what she would have done if he had visited such things upon a sister.

She pitied Oasis for what the young woman surely endured at her husband's hands.

Thus far, however, Oasis bore no scars, nothing physical or visibly mental or emotional, from her relationship with Donn, and the one bright side, if there was one, of her being in LaGuardia…beyond the friendship she sought to give to Yiva…was that it kept her son away from her. Only once, shortly after the marriage had taken place, had he come. She was fortunate to have been left alone since then. It had been long enough, longer than ever before, that Yiva dared to hope her nightmares might be over.

Laedan Hallister and his men, all of them except a thin, grey-haired fellow with icy blue eyes that Yiva had heard called Fenway, followed the Grand Mas' earlier footsteps into the borough streets, the Fortress gates closing behind them. Arm around his wife's shoulders, Donn began to steer her inside though his words, whatever they were, were for Fenway. Across the courtyard's dimming distance, Donn saw her there, Yiva knew he did, and though she could not make out any details of his expression or mood from so far away, that moment was enough to send a violent shudder up and down her spine and bring the revolted bile into the back of her mouth.

Hopes dashed, she realized she had clutched onto the tails of hope too soon.

Her nightmares, inevitably, would soon return.

Chapter 17

Though her bruised muscles still screamed from the recently endured abuse, and turning her head too quickly resulted in intermittent dizziness, Jia would not stay confined to the fireside within the library as a large portion of the pack set off on her father's honor hunt. She should have been there, leading them as they wove through the Wilds in search of the night's memorial feast, but she had, however reluctantly, given that honor to Maz, her father's stalwart Second and the man she felt was most affected by this shift of power. Whether he would choose to remain in the position of Second that put him further above his exiled mate in terms of pack power, for tonight, at least, he retained the honor and led where she could not. Recovering her strength was a more pressing use of her time. She could hear his deep baritone echoing through the trees, directing, leading the others with yips and barks and howls as they split into smaller groups to run down whatever creature they had chosen for their prey.

There was no shame in remaining behind as someone had to stay with those pups too young to join the elders in the Wilds. The oldest pups, Reif, Wist, and the two anthro Arden boys had taken the change, joined the hunt to honor the lost Alpha Cana, monitored by their mother and the Fela Eddie looked up to. It left the younger ones for Jia and Neel to watch. And because he trusted neither her health nor Pain's full submission to the rank of Omega, and was nursing the bullet wound in his shoulder, Deuce stayed behind as well. The youngsters listened to the cries of their parents and guardians, and those who could do so added their youthful voices into the mix.

There was no fear tonight of invasion by Guards or an assault from outside Cana. LaGuardia's guards had no jurisdiction on this side of the Wilds, and any Cana within earshot would recognize the sound of a hunt and know better than to interfere lest they became the hunted.

It had taken more than an hour earlier in the day for the strongest in the Pack, Maz, Uncle, Orliss, and Deuce, to dig the burial site chosen near the Queen's College Fountain, done as it was with Cana paws instead of shovels and picks. As those four worked, others circled around the area, around them, all in their hybrid form, yipping, growling, bodies low, ears flat to their skulls in the Cana posture of mourning. Jia, Addi, and Reif, the accepted kin of the deceased, paced around the body, no longer wrapped in its protective canvas, his skin pale and discolored. The blood had pooled and settled inside and the rigor of death had subsided to leave him limp and pliant. Their mourning postures were the same as the others and they paused now and then to nose and lick the man's face, his hands, to nudge him as if their adoration and attention might restore him.

When the time came, he was lowered, bound in a fetal position with hemp cloth strips, into the deep hole. It had to be deep. No foragers save those in the moist earth could have at his corpse. He was Cana, one with nature, but Roland had also been a man, a leader, and deserved the respect afforded such an individual…afforded to family. No tokens were buried here, no personal items or treasures that someone might later want to dig up. There was only a man and the earth that would reclaim and recycle him.

There was no shame or regret in that. It was as it should be. There was no tree to mark his grave, no sign but the upturned earth that would eventually cover over with grasses to blend seamlessly with the ground around it. No marker, but the Pack would remember. Pack always remembered where their fallen kin were laid to rest. The scent of it, the communal memory, would remain with them until the last member of the Flushing Pack fell.

For those never afforded this honor, Liam and Xen's mother, their aunt, they mourned too, keeping alive in that communal memory what had been taken from them.

A pyre was built, provisions made in the open air for the fragrant feast to follow the hunt. Finding enough fuel to burn had taken the rest of the day, but it was done by the time night fell, a night devoid of fog, rain, snow, though as ever, the clouds persisted.

What an honor it would have been, Jia thought with her muzzle tilted to the sky, if the clouds had parted just this once so that the fabled stars behind them could look down and bless Roland and the Pack with their rumored shimmering light.

A change in the Pack's cries and the echoes of their snarls announced the imminent kill, and in time the Pack regrouped and returned to the fountain and the pyre, dragging a large deer with them, Kato aiding in that dragging. Petr and Eddie, muzzles and fangs red with the kill, had helped until they youthful strength gave out, but from the size and angle of the bite at the deer's throat, Jia knew the ultimate kill had been Maz's.

That was the way it was meant to be too.

The deer was gutted and skinned, the entrails to be cooked and savored along with the rest of the animal, the pelt to be cured and used in whatever way the Pack required. While the meat roasted, a process that would last far into the night and meant they were unlikely to eat before dawn, each member fell into collective grooming…and grieving…long, mournful howls filling the night, sometimes alone, sometimes in unison with others. Though Kato groomed alone, his instinctual Fela nature not yet comfortable in accepting, or giving, that manner of attention or affection to anyone, he sat next to Jia, nuzzling her shoulder, her neck, her cheek whenever she raised her voice in ritualized grief.

He understood the loss of a parent. He understood the need to grieve, even though he had never been allowed that luxury. Here, amongst the Flushing Pack, he was able to feel it, relive what he had previously suppressed, though he did not know how to express those feelings beyond the occasional comforting gestures he offered to the woman at his side.

As if she understood what he had never shared, she paused her own mourning each time to lick his nose, his cheeks, or rest her muzzle against his neck.

It was enough.

And oddly, despite the previous traumatic experience, Vanya showed no fear of any of the strange wolf people, nor of the black cat-person she had long ago accepted as her protector. If she understood that this was her brother, that the wolves were the people she spent every hour of her days with, she seemed to accept it without question or observable fear. She appeared to feel safe, welcome now that she had 'joined' the Pack in her own way, and Kato felt more certain each hour that his choice to accept the Pack's hospitality and protection, to place his trust in them, was the right one. For Vanya, if not for himself.

He might not be prepared to submit to Jia's ruling, but they were home. Whatever lay west in the quest he had initially set for himself could wait. It would still be there if the day came he felt the need to move on. Here Vanya was safe. For tonight, for the foreseeable future, Kato did not intend to go anywhere.

After the exposure to the Plant and the brief glimpse of the world beyond the walls of his prison, Liam grew more cooperative with his captors, more determined to gain their trust…

…and more determined to survive and escape.

By keeping his head down, dropping the timbre of his voice, obeying orders without question, submissive behaviors well-practiced amidst the rules of the pack, he did his best to seem concerned about his survival, to make himself useful, as if he was afraid of prematurely becoming fuel in that vast furnace that powered what he had dubbed, within his head where no one else could hear it, a death factory.

He did not know any better name for it.

He timed the cycles of the light and dark, timed the arrivals of meals and the shifts of lab workers. He counted the number of steps from one side of the storage room to the other, to the lab doors and into the corridor beyond. He counted what had likely once been windows, covered over now with sheets of wood, metal, or hemplastic, where the air ducts were and were not, to gauge which walls of his confinement might be exterior and which were likely not. He made note of what, in times past, had been another set of sliding doors for delivery vehicles but which had been sealed to aid in keeping this room a consistent temperature for the preservation of the bloodstock.

It was sealed, but it was not made of concrete or brick as the rest of the room was, covered over with thermal material that was durable, more easily cleaned than the original materials had been. If he was stronger, if he had others to assist, he might be able to punch through the wall and claw their way to freedom. But with only his own strength to rely on, without knowing what awaited beyond that wall, and knowing how much noise such an effort to break through would create, the likelihood of dying for such efforts was high.

And so, with each sedated subject strapped in for bleeding, with each new death or new victim brought in to replenish the stock, Liam continued to watch…and wait for the day when Roland and others might return for him.

His Alpha would be here.

He had promised.

It seemed more and more of late that the Laedan kept him waiting whenever he came to call, whether he was summoned or not. This time, his arrival was without invitation, and Lowell was smart enough to anticipate the nature of the visit, the subject likely to be discussed. Knowing the whys and hows would not bring back the dead, would only serve as a reminder when Lowell was trying to put these unhappy events behind him. No wonder he put off meeting with his guest.

In the chief's experience, getting over the unexpected death of a loved one was made easier by the knowing. What Lowell chose to do with that information after he learned it was not the chief's concern.

At least Ernest was not forced to wait alone, though Yiva's silent, nervously flitting company could not be called relaxing. He tried small talk when the woman first entered the room where he had been told to wait, but her monosyllabic replies made her seem uncomfortable, on the verge of being frightened, and after his last question of "What's wrong, Yiva?" the silence in the room became suffocating and he chose not to compound it by speaking again.

He wondered if she was put off by the familiar use of her name, or if she simply would rather not discuss whatever was on her mind.

He nursed the drink she poured for him rather than drink it and stared into it as he waited for Lowell's arrival, trying not to watch her, trying not to make it obvious that he was too aware of her movements no matter where she was in the room. Why was he now, after all of these years of crossing paths with her, noticing her this way? Though he tried to attribute it to some protectiveness on his part, to knowing that someone was hurting her and wanting to help, he wagered there was more to it than that.

He decided he was better off not knowing why, or acknowledging those feelings any more than he already had.

"Can you help me?"

Realizing she had been speaking to him and he had not heard her, he turned the glass between his hands, looked at her heart-shaped face, and cleared his throat. "I'm sorry…did you say something?"

She offered a half smile, or less than half, a look that expressed she was accustomed to the men around her being absorbed in their own thoughts and business and ignoring her. She also looked embarrassed and frightened as if it had taken all of her courage to speak the first time, words he had not heard, and the thought of repeating herself was mortifying.

Her request for help filtered into his head as if the words had echoed around the room before coming to him, and though he looked at her empty hands and the vase of flowers she had finished arranging on the table, he saw nothing obvious that she might need his help with.

"Certainly," he replied obligingly, not knowing what he was committing to, his unfamiliar willingness to be helpful feeding the warm pit in his belly. "What can I…?"

She began to lower herself into the nearest chair and took the glass from his hand. "I was hoping…I thought you might…I'm afraid…"

"Afraid?" Lowell's question as he opened the door and stepped into the room did not sound suspicious. It did not seem that he heard the note of fear in his wife's words that Ernest had heard. Or believed he had heard. Ernest's desire to make Yiva safe might have lent itself to reading emotion into the words that was not there.

Yiva laughed, quickly on her feet again with the liquor glass in her hand. "That I didn't know when you would be able to see him," she explained cordially. "You are so busy…"

"Well, I am here now." He stopped beside her, an arm around her with his hand on her waist, and kissed her temple. "Leave us to our…"

"Of course," she agreed before he finished, putting the glass back in front of Ernest in case he wanted more to drink. If she had been going to refill it for herself or take it for cleaning, she seemed to have changed her mind.

Lowell watched her depart, seeking an indication that he might have walked in on proof of an affair but finding none. The chief's expression was blank, though weary, and nothing about his wife seemed any different than usual.

He rubbed the back of his neck and closed the door with his other hand. "I was held up…borough business…"

"I imagine so." Now that District 1 was without its mayor, and LaGuardia was missing its second Laedan, there was bound to be a lot of extra work until those leadership positions were accommodated.

"You've got the forepath's report?"

"I do." Earnest sighed and filled his glass, hoping that, in the stillness, Lowell would change his mind about hearing what the report had to say. When Lowell did not speak, his silence bidding Ernest continue, the chief did so. "Jonni's was as expected…a single blow of someone's forearm broke several ribs, causing punctures and tears in his lungs…so he drowned in his own blood. Fortunately, he was unconscious at the time…he didn't know what was happening."

Not understanding how any man could not know he was dying, conscious or not, Lowell grunted. "Small consolation." Dead was still dead, whether one realized it was happening or not. "And Roland?"

Ernest did not know if he was a good liar. He did not do it often enough, to anyone who might call him out on it, for him to say. Vance did not count; he usually knew when someone was lying, no matter how adept they were at it. But his reply to the Laedan's question was a measure of half-truth and vagueness that he did not believe Lowell would question.

"Inconclusive…without more extensive tests in an equipped lab." There were not many of those in the borough and few people who could staff them. "The bullet wound showed traces of new infection, but that was not likely to have killed him so quickly. He was malnourished and dehydrated…but not to the point of being irreversibly so. There was enough bruising to suggest a recent, but not too recent, beating, and fresh needle tracks on both arms…one fresh enough to have occurred near the time of death. There was a foreign substance in his blood that could have been there from his time as a hostage, or could have been introduced with the final penetration. Guire's reasonably certain that substance, whatever it was, is what killed him…caused a massive bursting of vessels in his lungs…but without knowing what it is…without the opportunity to study it more closely, there is no way to be certain. It could have contributed to that…or contributed to heart failure which is known, on occasion, to rupture blood vessels as the victim fights to breathe. Without a lab…"

"You can't tell…I know." Lowell sighed and scrubbed his face with his hands. How many times had Roland pushed to invest in a laboratory set up in the borough for cases such as this, for research to develop aid for the people in their care? Maybe if Lowell had listened, he would have the full truth now.

"So maybe no one killed him? Or whoever abducted him did…and we have no way of knowing who was responsible…?"

"I would suggest Mage Segara…"

The snort that time was one of irritation. "Where is he anyhow? He was supposed to bring me that Fela's…"

"The Fela crossed into the Wilds…took Miss Marrock with him it appears…"

"He was supposed to tell me…"

"You told him not to return to the Fortress until he had the murderer in custody."

Lowell grunted, remembering saying that and not surprised to have been taken literally when he had not meant that at all. At least, he had not meant it beyond the moment when the words had been spoken. "Then what's he…?"

"Still looking…last I knew…and trying to find that medishipment you sent him after."

"Oh…yes…that." Lowell had forgotten about that matter in the chaos of the past few days. "When you see him next, tell him I want an update." What use was there in finding the Fela now? If the borough's best Tracker had failed to find him, if his skills were inhibited in the Wilds and his safety there uncertain, then the odds of finding Jonni and Roland's killer grew smaller with each passing hour.

Lowell was not giving up. He would never give up. But he was realistic about the chances of success. And the importance of that stolen shipment could not be overlooked.

It was fortunate the tracker had not forgotten, although the problem of explaining whatever truth Vance found still remained.

He wondered if he should share Nik's claim. The chief had mentioned an injection, which implied a needle, a needle that Nik said he had seen even if one had not been found in the room. What if the tale was not a delusion but truth? Though he still found it difficult to believe, and he doubted the Protectorate would find proof for or against Nik's claim without Segara to test its veracity, Lowell was beginning to consider that he should examine the prospect that Nik was telling the truth. Not doing so might mean the murderer slipped through his grasp. Lowell owed Jonni, and Roland, that much.

"You didn't see Nik on your way up, did you?"

"Should I have?"

"No…I just thought…I haven't seen him in a while…and he said some things to me earlier…"

Ernest leaned forward, interested and worried, though he kept that second emotion off his face. The potential for Nik to blow everything they had done together in removing Roland from the Fortress was a risk he and Vance had willingly taken. It was also a risk Ernest knew they had to fear until long after the dust settled around the co-Laedan's death. "What sort of things?"

Again, Lowell shook his head. "I never know when to take him seriously…but you should talk to him…"

"If you know something…"

"I don't…just…talk to Nik." Drawing the subject closed, Lowell got to his feet and gestured for the chief to likewise rise. "Better yet…have Segara talk to him."

If anyone could get to the truth of Nik's claims, it would be the mage.

"And if anyone sees or hears anything about Jia…or that Fela who took her…I want to know. I want her back here…where she belongs."

"Of course." Ernest accepted the offered hand, not needing tracker senses to know that the Laedan was hiding something, or to know that Lowell was not going to tell him anything about what he knew or suspected. There was nothing more to be had here, he decided with a sigh, but wondered, as Lowell escorted him to the top of the staircase, if he might be able to learn anything from Yiva.

Whatever the woman was afraid of, Jonni's killer could certainly be it.

Chapter 18

None of the chief's visits in and out of the office during the day jarred Vance out of the badly needed sleep his body demanded, a sleep that dose of strong liquor had forced on him when the thoughts in his head pressed too loudly for action and answers. It was the eventual throbbing of his injured hand, where it hung over the end of the sofa so that blood accumulated in his fingers, and the pressure in his bladder, that pulled him back to waking, into a dark office that announced that day had passed into night. The skeletal night shift was on call, two desk personnel, the on-duty forepath, and three members of the upkeep crew who came to make repairs and clean when there was the least amount of activity in the building, all gathered around the tea kettle sharing the day's gossip. Any on-duty officers were out patrolling LaGuardia's streets.

Vance saw them there as he jerked awake, and though a few heads turned at the sudden movement in the chief's office, they did not see the dampness he wiped from his chin or his disheveled, bleary-eyed state. Or if they did, they were too far away to address it and knew better than to mention it.

The glass of the broken bottle and the residual spray of the earlier spilled alcohol had been cleaned up, the contents of the chief's desk shifted to indicate the passage of a day's work, and a sandwich on a covered plate was left on the corner of the desk nearest him. Unable to clearly remember the last time he had eaten…had it been with the

Flushing Pack…or before that…how long ago had that been…he grabbed the plate without considering that it might not have been left for him, and devoured the sandwich. He felt better for doing so, the heaviness of bread and roasted pork settling the alcohol queasiness in his stomach enough that when he stood he felt neither weak nor dizzy.

There were things to do. He could not wait for the chief's return. There were clues to find and plans to make if he was going to return to the Flushing Pack to help Jia rescue her friend. The plan was about more than a rescue, however. This was also about a missing shipment of mediplies and a drug potentially potent enough to poison LaGuardia's population.

A trip to the privy allowed him to tend to his bodily functions, wash his face with his good hand, and then rake that hand through his shaggy hair to make himself reasonably presentable. It had been too long between trimmings, but the look was beginning to grow on him, so perhaps he would leave it. He ignored the gazes of others as he went in, and again as he came out, and not one of those watching spoke or interrupted his foray into the basement where the guarded room of evidence was located. Even the young woman there, an unfamiliar face that looked both friendly and dangerous at once, said nothing at his arrival. Her willingness to unlock the door and let him enter suggested she had been told to expect him, and she took him directly to a sealed hemplastic box marked with the date of the murders. She cut the seal with the retractable blade she carried, as only the on-duty attendant was allowed to do, and then left him to his analysis while she filled out the necessary paperwork to indicate the time of his visit.

It would be too easy to steal something, to overpower her and take whatever he wanted if he felt the need. Too easy for anyone to do so. Fortunately, he was not inclined, nor had anyone else ever been to his knowledge. If any Protector had tried such a disgraceful act, a mage could easily track them, and any Protector accused of such a crime would be banned from the force and severely punished in whatever manner the chief and Laedans deemed fit.

Laedan, Vance reminded himself. There was only one now, likely to be only one unless Jia decided to fill her father's shoes in the

Fortress as well as in the Pack. It was an unfortunate turn of events that bode ill, he felt, for the borough.

The box contained a number of items taken from the Fortress infirmary, most of which proved unimportant to Vance's quest for either a killer or the ultimate cause of Roland's death. He wished now that Torben had not prevented him from reading Roland's body when he had the chance. There was the metal tray, badly dented in the middle, the weapon Nik had wielded against Quentin in an effort to save Jia's life, a weapon wielded as much in fear for himself, since his waking made him a witness to the horrifying chaos that had occurred in that room. Nik was, Vance read in the imprints left in the conductive metal, not afraid of his brother, not afraid of Jia, not even afraid of the stranger who had fought beside her…for her. He had been afraid of the only other combatant in the room.

The same combatant who had lashed out at Jonni for his unanticipated interference, who had come into that room alone, in the dark, before anyone else arrived.

Nik had seen the back of that figure clearly. What came after, from the imagery left in the tray, was a blur.

Shaking his head, Vance lay the tray aside to press his hand to the sheet from the bed on which Roland had laid, the only item likely to carry a death imprint since the clothes he had worn in death were absent. Even the clothes he had worn on his return to the Fortress were not there, clothes that Vance had hoped might lead him back along the Alpha Cana's escape route to the place where he had been held, where Liam possibly still was…where the blood drug was manufactured, or at least where the anthro blood necessary to create it was extracted, stored and possibly processed.

The thin hemp fabric, with spots of pale red visible where Roland's head had thrashed from side to side in his final moments of life, gave Vance none of the directional details he desired, but it did release the tell-tale reflections of pain that spread up the mage's arm and took root in his chest, in his lungs, sharing the lingering memories of that agony with him. Sharp, searing claws of pain tearing through the tissues of his lungs, releasing the blood that bubbled to Roland's lips in a pink froth as he struggled for air, a burning that traveled through his bloodstream, into his desperately pumping heart, back along the web of veins and vessels to the faintest sting of a pinprick in his arm, barely felt in the depths of his healing slumber.

Back to where the end had begun.

Eyes closed in his trance, Vance was only marginally aware of the movement of his hand until it closed around the syringe he had noted on the floor, had protected from anyone else's notice until it could be retrieved and placed in the chief's care. He was no expert in science, in drugs, in the ingredients used or in the effects they could have. But he could follow whatever had been in Roland's blood to the traces that remained on the unbroken needle and the glass vial at its base.

Every nerve in his good hand blasted the same image of the wielder of this weapon of death into his mind's eye. A man whose eyes turned unexpected amber-gold in the instant before the syringe dropped, a man whose skin prickled with an instinctual need to shift, to protect himself from the unanticipated presence of another in the doorway, interrupting his efforts. Vance's head turned, lifted, hearing the steps, smelling the masculine scent of sweat and fur he had grown accustomed to during several days in its presence.

He snarled. Growled.

"Easy, Vance."

The chief's voice, incongruous with the vision, forced Vance to hesitate, to refocus his thoughts and re-center his senses before he followed through with the impulse to attack. His hand in the box released the syringe and he stepped away from the table to distance himself from what he had witnessed, what he had felt compelled to do.

"What'd you see?"

"We're looking for the wrong killer." His voice sounded peculiar even to him, not his voice at all though a familiar one he had heard often enough over the last couple of years, and his world swayed as the dizzying effects of the vision rapidly bled away. He winced when he tried to grab the table's edge with his injured hand in an effort not to stumble and fall. Ernest dragged the nearest metal stool towards

Vance, but by the time it was in place, the younger man shook his head and refused to sit.

Ernest snorted. "No normal man did that to the Channon kid. I saw…"

"Anthro, yes…but the wrong one."

"You're not suggesting the Marrock girl…?"

"Thomas Quentin."

If Vance was not going to use that stool, he damned well would. Ernest collapsed onto it, the mention of that name making him realize that moments before, Vance had spoken with Quentin's voice. The revelation was not a particular surprise; very little surprised the chief anymore, and Quentin had been the only other confirmed individual in that room, unconscious though he was at first. He knew just enough of Quentin to know Channon's right-hand was an ambitious fellow with a nose for seeking power. It was the sort of person that often gravitated into Channon's orbit, though in the past, Lowell had been quick to spot the overly ambitious and appoint them in positions that removed potential threats from his immediate vicinity. Whatever the reason the Laedan had made an exception for Quentin, the odds of the younger man making a play for stronger ties and influence were high.

But murder? Not only of the co-Laedan but of Lowell's eldest son? That sounded almost absurd, almost too convenient to be true.

With how often mages were accused of fabricating clues and evidence to protect someone they favored, to harm the innocent for some sort of gain, the thought flitted through the chief's head that this was all a hoax, a ruse, some play on Segara's part to settle a vendetta with Thom Quentin.

Except that Vance was not the sort of man to hold onto a grudge or seek revenge. Of all the trackers Ernest had ever crossed paths with, there was never anything vindictive in Vance. His efforts had never proven false, as far as Ernest knew, and he never wrongly convicted an innocent person, had never proven dishonest, disloyal, or in error.

"Are you sure?

If he was not sure, Vance would not have spoken the name. He would have hedged his bets to await more information. Ernest knew it, even if he found the possibility difficult to believe.

Vance shrugged. "I could be wrong."

Could be, but they both knew his record. Ernest snorted and pinched the bridge of his nose as he squeezed his eyes shut. "Motive?"

"Jonni's death was an accident." Jonni had rushed in to protect the woman he had waited his whole life to marry, regardless of her refusal to accept his proposal. He had not realized, had not known, what he was charging into, the abnormal strength of the man he confronted. Quentin lashed out in self-defense without intending to kill him.

Intention or not, he had done so. He would have to answer for that.

"Marrock?"

Again, Vance shrugged. "I don't know…yet." That detail would have to be learned from Quentin, unless there were others, outsiders, involved in whatever scheme Quentin was plotting. Vance could make any number of calculated, educated, assumptive guesses, but he did not feel he had enough proof to substantiate any of them. Certainly not enough proof to take before the Laedan that would make the charges of murder and treason stick.

"Nik might know." Ernest's hand dropped back into his lap but his eyes remained squinted as though he was facing a too-bright light. "Channon suggested I talk to him…that you talk to him. Didn't' say why…didn't say what to expect…but he seems to think Nik knows something…more than about what we did, of course…"

"He might. He's the one that knocked Quentin out. Odds are he saw…or heard…something he shouldn't have."

"Enough to make him act." Even if his actions had only been to protect Jia, for reasons Ernest could not guess at beyond childhood loyalty, he might have seen enough of a threat in Quentin to warrant it. That clue, in addition to Vance's work, added up to something worth looking into.

"I could arrest…"

"No…not yet. Leave him."

"What if he kills someone else?"

"Long as he thinks he's in the clear, long as he doesn't feel threatened, he won't. If I'm right, he's got too much to gain by keeping his head down. I think he's right where he wants to be and he's not going to risk that while there's another suspect to pursue."

"What about Yiva?" Vance cocked his head curiously and Ernest quickly continued, before the mage could ask potentially embarrassing questions. "She told me she's afraid. Dunno of what. Lowell came in before she could tell me…but I got the feeling she knows something she shouldn't…and she's afraid of someone finding out."

The mage's concerned scowl was a reaction the chief could accept, better than one that would question his personal interest in, or possible involvement with, the Laedan's wife. There was nothing to tell, no involvement, and he knew the mage would not be one to judge or criticize, but it was best for everyone, Ernest believed, if such questions and thoughts were never given voice.

"Maybe Nik confided in her." He did not know the nature of the relationship between the Channon boys and their parents, but from what Vance knew of each individually, it seemed more likely that Nik would confide in his mother rather than his father…if he was going to confide in anyone. Or maybe she had seen or overheard something, that led her to suspect Quentin of some manner of wrongdoing.

It was worth looking into.

"You should talk to her."

Ernest scowled and shook his head. "It should be you."

"I've been told not to…"

"Channon wants an update…says he was overreacting before and didn't mean…"

"You believe that?"

"Why shouldn't I?" The Laedan could be a dangerous man but Ernest did not believe he would stoop to murdering a Protector out of displeasure. The Laedans were a lot of things, but they were not above the law.

Vance snorted. "Doesn't matter. I've got somewhere I need to be."

"Where?"

For a moment he considered not answering that question, but having the chief know what he was up against, if the bottom fell out of his choices, was probably a good contingency plan.

"Got a lead on that medishipment…and a hunch about where the blood drug is coming from." Seeing the chief's peaked interest, Vance held up his good hand to stop him from asking a rush of questions and shook his head. "Something Grand Mas Lord said…"

"You're going up against HOPE?"

"Not if I can help it. I've no proof yet…gonna do some recon…"

"We've no jurisdiction…I can't send backup…"

"Don't need it." If he was honest, backup would be a wise precaution, probably a needed one in his condition, but it was not wanted. Not when he had an entire Cana pack at his back. Hopefully, the Flushing Pack would be all of the support he would need.

"What I do need is a new shocker…another gun if there's one to spare…and another hit if there's one here in lockup."

"Another hit?" It did not take Ernest long to deduce what his tracker was asking for and he vehemently shook his head. "No. Not after the last time. Thought you'd died on me. I'm not putting your neck on the…"

"Neck was on the block soon as Channon dragged me into this shart. Still think his request is a misdirect…that it's not mediplies that were stolen. Hell, maybe nothing was taken…but if following these leads gets that shart of the streets…solves a pair of murders…busts open whatever's going on inside HOPE…"

"It'll get you killed, Vance. Sure shartin'. If that's what this is all leading to…HOPE's involvement…you know that don't you?"

"Maybe. Maybe it'll be worth it." Not that he wanted to die. Maybe his death would matter little outside the Protectorate, but learning the truth was what mages did. He would not be able to live with himself if he stepped away from this now. Finding that facility was part of a promise made, and Vance would never go back on a promise. "You got any here or not?"

"No. And if I did," Ernest reiterated, "I wouldn't give it to you."

“Fair enough.” Vance knew where he could get what he was after, at least a likely connection, and he had already intended to pay the man a visit before heading back into the Wilds. There would be no time wasted by doing both at once. Turning up the collar of the uniform coat he still wore, one he might have to ditch before he undertook his next assignment, he winced again at the pain in his hand and added. “I’ll let you know what I find.”

“At least let me give you something for that.” Ernest gestured at the tracker’s bandaged hand and Vance followed him out of the storage room, past the attendant’s desk, empty at the chief’s direction. If the odds of going up against HOPE meant Segara was not going to make it back, Ernest wanted to be able to say that his last act of kindness was helping the man endure his pain.

He did not envy Vance this task in the slightest, any more than he looked forward to facing Yiva Channon again.

Chapter 19

There was little Torben could do for the young man curled on his side in a ball in the sheltering space beneath the piano, one of the only places to hide in the open arrangement of the Ursa's home. The interior walls were long ago removed from most of the level, save where it was structurally unsafe to do so, to reduce the number of places where someone could hide in ambush. It also allowed heat and air to flow freely throughout the house. The kitchen and bathroom remained, rarely used as intended once the Undoing had led to the collapse of the borough's basic infrastructure, but Nik had not sought refuge in either of those rooms. When he stumbled through Torben's door, chasing away the sleep the Ursa had intended to pursue, he puked on the floor and immediately crawled with agonizing slowness under the piano, out of the light.

It was not the first time Torben had nursed Nik through this. He had not counted the times he found the middle Channon collapsed at his doorstep, seeking an out from the agony of withdrawals. This time, however, Nik did not ask for an out. He refused every elixir, every soothing agent and remedy Torben offered, accepting only water now and then as he fought his way through hell.

Now, surrounded by blankets that were on and then off again as his temperature fluctuated, and by pools of his own vomit and stomach bile that erupted every time the worst symptoms kicked him in the gut, Nik squeezed his eyes shut against the dim but searing glow of tallow candles burning on an end table across the room. It was tempting to ask for total darkness, as Torben tried to clean each mess as soon as it appeared and endured his stench and moaning, but the man was being generous enough. The least Nik could do was allow his benefactor some light.

He remembered other times when he had fought through this, or had begun to fight, but typically the onset of doxing sent him running to the nearest contact for some manner of relief. He did not want relief this time. For however long he could remain strong, Nik wanted to remember this hell in the hopes that it would remind him to stay off the shart and never go through this again.

He wanted to be clean.

He wanted to be whole.

The Ursa's scarred hand reached beneath the piano to retrieve the latest collection of soiled cloths. Reflexively, Nik flinched and jerked away, chastising himself silently for a reaction he was unable to control. The paranoia of addiction and withdrawal would remain with him until he got clean. He could not help it.

Thankfully, Torben understood. Without Torben, Nik would have nowhere else to go to get through this.

A double knock on the door sounded like explosions between his ears and made Nik shrink back in his shelter until he was pressed against the walls amidst the blankets where he would not easily be seen. It was not exactly hiding, since the smell of bile and the knocking of his shaking knees and elbows against the floor announced his location, but it made him feel safer as Torben shuffled with a growl to the door. So few knew where he lived and he could not imagine a stranger randomly arriving at his fourth-floor brownstone door for any accidental reason.

His privacy had been invaded too much recently. Nik was a welcome guest. Anyone else was not so welcome.

"Moeller…it's Segara."

Inhaled breath held, Torben hesitated, debating the pros and cons of opening the door to the tracker. The initial impulse to ignore the knock warred with the realization that Vance's presence could have something to do with their recent act of subterfuge, but until Nik rasped, "It's okay," as if he thought Torben was waiting for permission, the Ursa had been inclined to pretend he was not home.

Not that the tracker would have believed that.

Muttering beneath his breath, he opened the door.

"Thanks," Vance mumbled as he crossed the threshold to be greeted by the sound of retching beneath the piano. He threw Torben a bemused glance as he squatted to identify the source of the sound and sighed when he recognized the disheveled young man huddled miserably there.

"Hey…"

How Nik managed to speak, how he knew the visitor was friendly when his eyes were squeezed shut and his jaw clenched in pain was a question Vance did not pursue. Nor did he have to ask what was wrong. The air was full of the effects of withdrawal, effects Vance knew well. It was not necessary to ask if Nik was okay. Nik was not going to be okay until the worst of this process was behind him. Nor was he likely to be able to answer any other question Vance felt prompted to ask.

He stretched as he stood to face Torben. His refusal to ask unnecessary questions or make judgments made Torben feel better about his decision to let the mage into his home.

"I need something…and I'm hoping you can get it for me."

Torben scowled but shrugged. "What?"

"That new drug…the one made with anthro…"

"No."

"Juice?" Nik crept on his belly far enough that his face was visible without anyone needing to crouch to see him. "What the eff do you want that for?" He knew the mage drank, the bitterness of alcohol followed Vance most of the time. But Nik had never thought the tracker was also a user.

"I need to track its source…I saw it once before when I…"

"Shart almost killed me."

Vance nodded. "I know. It was your syringe that showed me the way. Wherever it comes from, I believe it's connected to the stolen medishipment…"

"Stolen?" Sweat beaded across Nik's brow as he fought against the shaking that began to consume him again, and he barely managed to draw a blanket around his trembling shoulders. When it slipped from his shaky fingers, Vance helped tuck it around him while Torben wiped up the most recent splattering of bile and water.

Thankfully Nik had not eaten recently, and what he had last eaten had been expelled long ago. The conversation was set aside as he accepted comfort against the tracker's shoulder and Torben, less annoyed by Vance's interruption for the help he was offering, set another pot of tea to boiling.

Eventually, the tremors subsided enough to allow Nik to speak. He pushed away from the physical contact that now made his skin prickle and crawl, and wiped his hand across his face.

"Those weren't mediplies," he muttered, that hand now wiping across his mouth after an aborted attempt by his stomach to expel contents it no longer carried. "I don't know what it was…but it wasn't mediplies."

"How do you…?" It did not matter how Nik knew. Vance imagined that a lot of the day to day business in the Fortress occurred where the addict could hear it, with most never considering that he might glean and store that material for later use. Most likely doubted Nik even cared. The mage grunted. "Doesn't matter. Wherever the shart comes from…Roland was held there…and I need to find it…"

"Suicide," snorted the Ursa, offering him the cup of herbal tea that Nik refused.

"Maybe," Vance agreed as he accepted the cup. "But I promised to take Jia there…to find her friend. If there's any connection between the…juice…Roland's abduction and murder…"

Nik shook his head and then grimaces as his upper body swayed. "Juice wasn't why…"

"Wasn't why what? What do you know, Nik?"

Torben's growl was ignored, as was his curt retort, "You don't have to tell him…"

"Which friend?" Nik countered. "Where is she? Jia? You going to see her?" He did not know what part the tracker had played in getting Roland's body to his daughter, to Roland's family, but if the mage had made a promise to Jia, he would likely have to see her to keep it.

And Nik wanted to know she was safe.

"Someone named Liam." Nik's face grew sad and Vance continued. "I intend to go back tonight…if…" he looked at Torben, "I get what I need to track the route."

Nik sniffed and wiped his nose on the blanket. "I like Liam. He's real." Though Vance did not know what was meant by real, he had already deduced that his quarry was a man of value…at least to Jia. If Nik thought Liam was important too, then finding him increased in priority.

"Then you need to…" Another convulsion pushed through Nik with another attempt by his stomach to eject non-existent contents, and then he looked at Torben and croaked, "Give it to him."

"I'm not going with…"

"Didn't say that…just…give him the books…the papers…so he can get them to her…"

"It's not safe."

"It's what Roland wanted, Torby, for her to have it, and everything…it's time. None better. We wait any longer and…just give it to him."

Vance had no idea what the pair was discussing, but he listened and fought against his instinctive impulse to touch them both, to fill in the gaps of knowledge his ears were not providing.

"It isn't here." Before Nik's scowl and expression of astonished displeasure erupted into words, Torben, obviously comfortable with the younger man's nickname and just as obviously eager to satisfy him, set down his empty cup with a growl. "But I can get it."

He did not know the nature of the items Nik had entrusted him with, did not know what information they contained or why they were important, but he had taken the admonition to protect them at all costs seriously, as if the request had come from co-Laedan Marrock himself. If Marrock wanted them protected, then they would be.

But Marrock was no longer there to direct dispensation and Nik was probably right. They belonged in his daughter's hands. Torben chose to trust that the tracker would get them where they belonged.

"About thirty minutes." He trudged to the door, pulled on his heavy coat and drew his knitted cap down over his ears.

"Still need juice," Vance reminded him, his original purpose in coming here not forgotten, despite this new twist to the story. "I swear…I'm not taking it. I just need a little to…"

"Only if you watch him…and you," Torben grunted with a finger pointed at Nik, "sleep."

"I'll try." Nik was exhausted enough from his body's battle that, as long as his confused internal systems allowed it, he thought he could sleep for a week.

Though Vance frowned, still wanting the opportunity to question Nik about whatever it was the chief thought he should know, he agreed that Nik needed rest. And if agreeing to Torben's conditions meant he got what he had come for, he could wait a little longer for those answers. He took a few credits out of his pocket, credits the chief had given him in case he needed them in the line of duty, and put them in the Ursa's hand.

"Use these."

Torben examined the coins as if he expected them to be marked in some way that could be used against him later, and then pushed them into his coat pocket. He would not need them, but he was not going to reject them either.

"Might take longer…but I'll be back." He helped Nik settle on the ratty sofa rather than on the cold, hard floor beneath the piano, gave Vance a look that suggested he would know if the mage kept Nik awake, and then went out into the night.

To resist the conversation he wanted to have, Vance went to the window and parted the thin hemp curtains to watch Torben amble in the direction of the Plant. It made sense that whatever he was hiding for Nik, it would be hidden at the place the Ursa spent the majority of his time. Though he tried to listen to the apartment, tried to hear that past conversation through the peeling paint on the walls, the movement of the drapes as the wind pushed through the failing seals, in the traces of old wax and stale tea, there was only silence, the only traces of conversation he could detect being ones Torben had with Nik. None of those, however, were the one Vance sought. Most likely that exchange of information and items for protection had taken place elsewhere, somewhere public enough not to attract attention yet private enough for the men to feel safe in their conversation. Somewhere that would not draw attention back to this apartment nor to Torben's place of employment or the Fortress.

Vance expected such care and caution from Roland. He had not expected it from Nik. Whatever the young man's part in these events, Vance felt growing respect for Nik and a growing appreciation for what he was capable of accomplishing without anyone being wiser…all while strung out on some shart or other.

The night's promised rain finally came, intermingling with snow, the drops splattering lazily against the often-patched glass and quickly melting the accompanying flakes. Finally, after what felt longer than he thought it should take, the big man's hunched figure cut slowly through the darkness, cap drawn down further, his collar turned up to protect himself from the cold and moisture. When he disappeared from Vance's view behind a nearby building, the mage let the curtain fall and turned to face the door. Nik, having taken the admonition to sleep to heart, had not shifted position during the Ursa's absence and only cracked his lids open when the click of the key in the door lock ruptured the silence. He jolted upright, threw a glance at Vance as if making sure he was still there, and since the mage showed no alarm when the door opened, Nik decided the arrival must be a friendly one.

He exhaled in relief when Torben entered and closed the door behind him, a tattered canvas satchel in one hand and a small drawstring pouch of waxed hemp cloth in the other. He handed the satchel to Nik, and though hesitant, did eventually offer the contents of his other hand to Vance.

"Not giving you a needle," he mumbled as he pulled off his hat, shook the moisture from it, and then did the same with his coat. When he hung it on the hook on the wall, the water dripping from it into a long, rusty metal tray created a tink…tink…tink…sound in the room.

Fist closing around the pouch, ignoring the traces of the bagger's identity that pushed into his head, Vance stuffed it into his inner coat pocket and murmured, "Don't need one." Maybe later he would pursue the bagger, if the contents of the bag did not lead him where he wanted to go.

Or maybe he would pursue that bagger later, and all others, willing to sell this shart on the street.

"And I brought you this." The second small pouch, produced from his pocket and placed in Vance's hand rattled a little as he took it. "Thought you might want it back."

Though Vance eyed him curiously, he did not take the time to look inside. There was more pressing business at hand.

Nik rubbed his palm over the satchel, toyed with the buckles that held it closed, until with a determined grunt he unfastened both and removed the contents, a loose collection of handwritten pages stuffed into a hempcard folder, an ancient-looking book with a stained cover, and a wide rolled paper, printed with color ink, a relic from the days before the Undoing when the boroughs were a single city, when the wheeled relics still rolled through cluttered streets and decaying buildings still stood strong and proud.

"This…this is for Jia. This is why…everything." He slid the contents across the short table in front of the sofa towards Vance. "I don't know their significance…not really…but it's something my father wants…and something Roland wanted to keep away from him. If anyone knows what it means…Jia will."

Kneeling at the end of the table, Vance unrolled the map and studied it, his fingertips prickling with Roland's residual energy left on the paper. He had seen enough hand-drawn maps of LaGuardia's districts to know where the boundaries of civilization lay, where the Zone began, where the Wilds were, the area Hallister claimed as the limits of Kennedy borough and HOPE, and the borders that separated them all from whatever lay beyond. Most could not read such maps any longer, most could not read, but Vance, as did many of the Protectors, had the advantage of enough education to enable them to do their jobs. Those with higher levels of learning progressed further.

Some thought it unfair, some tried to overcompensate with physical strength, but the usefulness of being able to read the remaining signs and fill out reports was a simple, undeniable benefit.

On the far left of the map, near the bottom corner, a circle of darkening red ink surrounded words that made the hairs at the nape of Vance's neck stand on end.

"Fort Hamilton."

Nik shrugged. "For implies weapons," he murmured, stating the obvious. "I don't know what my father intends…but I can guess."

Pre-Undoing weapons meant guns, possibly lots of them. The Laedans had sought to keep guns out of the public's hands in order to lessen the already violent tendencies fear instilled. With very little available ammunition, guns had, over time, become relics, treasures for collectors more than weapons. Working guns could be found, however, in the hands of the Protectorate and the Laedan Guard, who possessed the capability to manufacture crude ammunition, and had the Laedans' permission to use them when necessary.

If a large collection existed, it was surely wise to confiscate them before the general population got hold of them…if they had not already done so. But if securing them from public availability was the Laedan's intention, why the need for secrecy? And why the need for Marrock to keep these documents out of his co-Laedan's hands?

The question suggested that confiscating the weapons was not Channon's intention, but it did not specify what his intentions might be. It only hinted at things that, as Vance read Marrock's desperation in rolling the map, tucking it into the satchel with the book and notes, might be enough for a man to kill for.

"Jia knows about this?" There had been a mention of missing documents…both by Jia and by Lowell…but neither had specified what those documents were. Lowell seemed determined to cling to secrets. Jia seemed less certain of details and Vance had not asked.

Nik shrugged again. “Dunno what Roland told her. But if he told anyone anything…”

His successor would be the most likely choice. Vance nodded and put everything back into the satchel. There was no time to read it, either the words on it or the impressions they carried. If the notes were Marrock’s private musings, it was not the mage’s place to read them. If there was any clue within about Marrock’s abduction and eventual murder, Vance trusted that Jia would tell him. How else was he to continue on the path towards truth?

The place where Roland had been held, the anthro blood processing facility, would be a good start but not the end of the case. Before Vance could go further, he needed to help bring Liam home.

“I’ll make sure she gets it,” he promised. “Thanks. Both of you.”

“Tell her...” Nik grabbed Vance’s wrist, avoiding skin to skin contact this time. “Tell her I’m sorry…if any of this is my fault…for not telling her. Tell her I hope Liam comes home.” Addiction had clouded his judgment, yes, had fueled his paranoia and apathy, eroded his courage, but he was determined to walk that path no longer. He did not want to be that man anymore. Liam deserved better, Jia deserved better. Jonni deserved better…and now Jonni was dead. Nik was determined that his brother’s death would not be in vain and that Jia would not die too.

“I will.”

“Torby, you should go with…”

“No.” Both Torben and Vance spoke in unison.

“You need me here,” Torben continued, “and I have work…”

Vance clasped Nik’s shoulder. “He’s right. You’ve got some ways to go to be clear of this…and he should stay with you. Plus, if anyone knows what we’ve got here…” Gingerly he patted the satchel he had slung over his shoulder. “Having Torben to watch your back is probably the smart thing to do.”

Nik scowled, looked back and forth between them, then sighed with frustration. No one in the Fortress knew of his friendship with the sposer, no one knew about his efforts to break free of his addictions. If there was anything he could learn from inside the Fortress, from the family, by putting on the façade of an addict, Torben would make the best outside contact to the mage that Nik could have.

It was regrettable that the solitary Ursa had been dragged into the unraveling political tide, but circumstances knitted into place by the Laedans, by Quentin, and by who knew how many others, was dictating the future for them all.

They could either accept the chaos or fight against it. Torben was not the sort of man to roll over and be crushed by unfavorable winds. He was the sort of man to stand and fight back.

The Tracker-Mage seemed likewise willing to do so.

It gave Nik the courage to do the same, to stand in their fight.

"I'll be in touch," Vance promised, intending that it too would be a promise kept.

Chapter 20

The stranger made no sound, his eruption from a dimly lit passage leading into the Beneath coming with such unexpected abruptness that Vance had little time to react before the dark-clad figure snatched at the satchel strap with sufficient force to yank the mage off his feet, spin him sideways, and jerk him hard enough that he hit the tall metal pole bent and twisted sideways at the edge of the street. The strap was strong and secure, it did not snap beneath the force of the tug, but as the buckles were unfastened, Vance walking with his hand inside the satchel against the contents to read the images and impressions they offered, the pull tipped the bag and spilled book, loose pages, and the map across the ground. Lashing out with his injured hand, driving his attacker staggering backward, gave Vance enough opportunity to scoop up the book and pages. It also sent a jolt of pain up his arm, and when his assailant came at him again, his foot striking squarely in the mage's chest, Vance tumbled down the embankment towards the rivulet of rushing rainwater collected in the culvert. His plunge was stopped by the rusted metal dinosaur that someone in days past had pushed there as if to build a dam against the occasionally strong current.

The moment before his head struck the bulk and knocked him unconscious, Vance saw the shadowy figure scoop up the rolled map with one hand and let off a single shot with the pistol-sized crossbow carried in the other. A shot that only made noise when the bolt caught

Vance in the shoulder, embedding there rather than pushing through. His cry, a result of both the bolt's bite and the impact with the vehicle frame, ended in darkness and the softness of pattering rain.

*

"Niki?"

Hoping to find his brother awake, as Nik most often was unless he was wrapped in the stupor of addiction, Donn pushed the door open and peered into the bedroom. The only light within came from one of the many torches on the Fortress' perimeter walls and it illuminated the fresh crack that spidered across the glass, put there, it appeared, by the branches of the wind-whipped tree outside. Nik's bed was unslept in, the linens unruffled, and the room showed little trace of anyone having been here except the broken oil lamp on the floor and a few articles of clothing left in a path from closet to desk…the sort of trail Nik left when deciding what to wear on a day when one addiction or another affected his senses and made him irrationally dissatisfied with color, texture, or appearance. On the desk lay a sheet of parchment and a quill pen, but though there was dried ink on the nib, there were no words on the paper and no discarded pages to suggest difficulty in conveying thoughts.

Whatever he had intended to set into words had never made it out of his drug-addled brain.

Donn grunted as he dragged his finger across the virgin page. Why was Nik not here when he needed him? Not that his twin could offer wise or cohesive advice, although sometimes Nik surprised him with the depth of his words. But he could listen, or appear in his inebriated stupor to be listening, when Donn wanted to talk, to hear his own voice and thoughts without their father's judgmental nonsense clouding the way. Nik never judged him. Never seemed to judge anyone.

Most of the time, Donn suspected Nik did not hear a thing he said.

There were innumerable places in the Fortress where Nik could be. Donn knew many of those places, either because Nik had shown him or he had stumbled across his twin there accidentally. But there were just as many other hiding places Donn was sure he had never found. Not being in his bedroom at this too-late hour did not mean that Nik had escaped the Fortress seeking the embrace of some numbing substance that could cleanse his brother's death from memory for a few blissful hours.

But the odds were, because of that late hour, that into the borough was precisely where Nik had gone.

Just once, Donn wished he too had the ability to escape his worries for longer than the number of minutes it took to bed his wife. That was certainly an escape, but it did not last long enough to make him forget. Just once he would like to forget too.

But Channon duty would not permit it.

Not for Donn at least. Only Nik was permitted forgetfulness, and that was because Nik did not care. Not about what other people thought, not about LaGuardia, not about duty, not about their father's approval.

Of the last two, Donn cared too much. Forgetting was never an option.

*

The scents in the air, wet concrete, and metal, distant baking bread, the tang of ozone left after the crack of thunder that roused him, pulled Vance to consciousness in the pre-dawn hours, a time when the sun had not yet kissed the clouds with gold and pink and only a few of the windows in the buildings above him at street level contained the light of the waking world. His head throbbed in time with the ache in his injured hand, and nearly numb shoulder, on which he lay on the sloped embankment against the automotive skeleton which had stopped his descent. He felt little else until he moved.

That moment of screaming pain reminded him of what had happened to deposit him here.

He had not lain here long, he mused, as he scrambled about looking for the treasures he had been entrusted with. It had been long enough, however, in the dwindling rain and cold, for the cover of the books and folder to gather a damp sheen and for the edges of the papers to begin to warp. He swore beneath his breath and quickly stuffed them back into the bag, this time securing the buckles with his stiff, cold fingers. The pouch of powered plasm was safe at the bottom of the satchel. Though the papers were damaged, he hoped they were still readable enough to prove valuable, to prove worth what it had taken to protect them, what it would take to get them to her. The map, however, was lost, and though he had not been unconscious for long, it was long enough for his assailant to escape easy detection. Given time, Vance knew he could find the fellow, but time was something he did not have. He could make it into the Wilds before sunrise if he followed the channel he was in, and from there make it to the Pack's location before dusk, if his injuries did not hinder him.

Did the thief know what they took? Why had they not taken the rest of the satchel's contents while Vance was unable to prevent it? Why had the mage been left alive?

And who, he wondered as he forced himself to his feet and used the vehicle's rusted body to ease his way to the flat bottom of the culvert running with water, had taken it?

He paused to look back towards Torben's brownstone. If his attacker had followed him from there, those two men might be in danger. A brief debate followed before he groaned and began to trudge east through the water. Might was not strong enough to go on right now. If anyone was foolish enough to invade the Ursa's territory, intending to cause trouble, he knew Torben was capable of defending himself and Nik. And no one, no matter who they worked for, would intentionally kill another Channon heir.

Especially Quentin.

If anyone tried, by the time Vance reached them, it would be too late to change anything.

He would learn those details later, after this phase of his work was complete and he had the answers he needed to return to the borough.

Vance paused to inspect the bolt in his bleeding shoulder, a bolt with an unbreakable metal shaft that could be neither easily pushed through nor pulled out with his wounded hand. He would need to travel with it embedded in his shoulder and pray that no infection set in, nothing was irreversibly torn, and that not enough blood was lost to keep him from reaching the Pack.

Jia could help him. Jia and her brother. And he, in turn, intended to continue helping them, however he was able.

≈*≈

"Fenway? What are you doing here?"

Aman Fenway had been her father's adjunct, trusted adviser, and protector, for as far back as Oasis' memory stretched. She could think of very few times when the icy-eyed, wiry man was not at her father's side, save during personal family occasions or when Geary had sent him off on some special duty. More than once she had wondered exactly what the relationship was between the two men, but she had never asked. Fenway rarely spoke to her, or she to him, even when she had grown old enough for her father to groom her to someday take his place. Fenway had simply continued to silently watch over her as he did her father, making her feel certain that he would protect her with his life if necessary, though not, she imagined, at Geary's expense.

While he had been sent on secretive assignments in the past, to do things Geary trusted no one else to do, she was still surprised to see him at the doorway of her antechamber, his high-necked black sweater, black trousers, and black leather short coat damp from the rain though it had not been raining since she had awakened nearly two hours earlier. Maybe it was not rain but something else, she mused, as she stood to greet him.

Standing was not necessary, but she had never felt the indulgent need to remain seated like royalty when greeting someone.

"An errand," the man said, his gravelly voice a little thinner than she recalled hearing before. Or maybe his voice had always sounded that way and her lack of conversation with him was the only reason he sounded unusual. "For your father."

"An errand here?" Her father had recently departed the Fortress, with Fenway; there seemed no reason for him to send his aide back.

"Out there." His gaze flicked towards the window, but as having an errand on the sea was more illogical than his coming to see her, she guessed he meant an errand beyond the Fortress walls, somewhere in LaGuardia. His tone was evasive and he refused to meet her gaze. He was keeping something from her, but as it was likely a matter of business with her father, Oasis did not press for details.

"I presume you've come to me for a reason? A message from my father?" Something Geary had forgotten to say, perhaps, that he could entrust to no one else.

"I bring you this." From his inside coat pocket, he removed a crumpled, slightly water-damaged scroll, pressed nearly flat from the time spent against his chest. "You know what to do with it."

She began to open it, but his hand on her wrist stopped her. "Not here. Not now." There were voices in the corridor, people meant not to know Fenway was here, she assumed, judging by the slight shifting of his feet and the tension in his shoulders, arms, and jaw.

"Very well." She tucked the scroll inside her dressing robe and tightened the cloth belt to keep it in place. She wore the robe out of habit, for warmth in the drafty Fortress halls, and the scroll's size was barely noticeable. The sooner she could deposit it somewhere safer, however, the better. "Shall I see you out? Is there anything more?"

Shaking his head, Fenway's bow was slight, a gesture of acquiescence she could not recall him making to her before. "Not necessary." His glance trailed down to where the rolled paper was hidden, as if he was having second thoughts about giving it to her, but then he squared his shoulders and added, "I take my leave."

"Of course." A dismissive wave sent him from the room and, she guessed, from the Fortress. Warm slippers were pulled onto her feet before she left the chamber for the one room she believed would be most secure and private for this purpose.

The room where she had found Yiva considering a plunge to her death in the sea.

Unused, the room was unheated, colder than the corridor outside. With effort, she had gotten the external door closed and convinced staff members to seal it against drafts and rain…and so that Yiva would not be able to open it again. The woman could break the glass to get to the unsteady, unstable balcony if she chose, but doing so would draw attention that Oasis imagined Yiva did not want.

The only furnishings here were a wobbly, lopsided desk Oasis had brought from elsewhere and a wide, bench-like seat on which she had placed a collection of pillows and blankets for use when she retreated here to read. There was an oil lamp with a lighter beside it, and in time she intended other furnishings. With the door closed and the lamp and dim light of the morning sun behind the clouds to brighten the room, she spread the scroll across the desk, holding the edges down with the lamp, the lighter, and her hands to keep it from curling closed so that she could examine what she believed her father had sent.

A map of the boroughs. He had given her such academic gifts before, books with images from around the world, images from a lost age. Books with images defining the borders of kingdoms, books that spoke of kings and queens and régimes and wars that had been. Her father's father, or someone before him, had drawn a map of Kennedy borough, marking the borders of their claimed territory in order to avoid conflict with LaGuardia to the north and the militant forces of HOPE to the east. Over the decades, that map had been updated as the Hallisters' policies and the small fleet of usable sea vessels they had developed allowed for the expansion of Kennedy's territory. The borough had engulfed HOPE's on all sides but the east, stretched along a significant portion of the western coast as far as they dared to travel and extend their reach, and had wrapped around Gateway Bay in an effort to protect the vulnerable Kennedy Fortress from the outsiders who sporadically tried to sail in and set roots.

Kennedy possessed more territory than LaGuardia, but LaGuardia, supported by the strength of Marrock-Channon public policy and works, contained more manpower. Behind the combination of the Marrocks and Channons, LaGuardia had a consolidation of power and vision that Geary was determined to use to his advantage.

If he could underhandedly assume control of LaGuardia through the elimination of the Channons and Marrocks, or through marriage with one of those families, how much stronger the Hallisters, and Kennedy Borough, would become.

Her eyes traveled over the page that contained all of Kennedy, all of HOPE, all of LaGuardia, the Zone, and unfamiliar territory east and west, without knowing what she expected to find.

There. There it was.

Fort Hamilton.

The map, and the circled words on the bottom left edge of the water-damaged page, formed the crux of Lowell's plan for a similar push for power consolidation. It was a map Oasis knew her father had been seeking too, part of the reason her marriage to Jonni had been arranged. Fenway had to know her father's plan, about Geary's interest in the mythical fort. Given his loyalty to the man, she assumed this to be a copy of the original, a message meant to tell her that the map was found, a message intending to request her manipulation of Lowell into giving up the quest for the fort or, if that was not possible, setting him up for failure in the finding, or reaching.

She traced her finger over the words and frowned. Lowell was not the only one who wanted this map. Donn did as well. And Thom. Playing each against the other, while appeasing her father, would be a challenging game. It seemed her loyalties should be to her husband, or perhaps to her first love whom she had gone through so much planning in order to be near. Or even to her father, who had groomed her and sent her here to further the Hallister family's name, fortune, and future.

But it was Lowell she felt most compelled to give the map too, the man she felt most confident of manipulating for her own purposes, her own gains…her own security and success.

There was no need to decide today, she thought as she let the paper roll into its long-held shape. The Channons were still in mourning and Thom, to her discomfort, was accused of murder. Not legally accused yet, but with a mage sent to find the truth, it was only a matter of days, maybe weeks, before the trail led back to Thom. Oasis would need to decide how to untangle her acquaintance with him if she wished to, needed to decide which of the men in her life offered the most advantage and security towards the future she envisioned.

Or maybe she would do it on her own. If she could raise an army, go in search of Fort Hamilton's rumored treasure herself, she would do so, bypassing the need for any of those men. But in LaGuardia she was still a stranger, a newcomer, and in Kennedy, she was too much under her father's shadow. Relying on Frances Lord and HOPE was not an option. For now, circumstances forced her to rely on manipulating others, something she was comfortable doing, and inclined to do as soon as she decided which path was wisest to follow.

The page barely finished curling, the friction hiss of paper on paper still in the air when the door opened. She jumped, crumpling the center of the roll in her clenched hand with a feeling of panic, only to release a long breath of relief at the familiar woman's face. It was the look on that face, however, red-rimmed teary eyes, lips swollen from over-forceful ardor and twitching with an effort not to weep that prompted Oasis to action.

The scroll was stuffed hastily inside her robe against her breast as she rushed across the room to Yiva's aid. Unable to imagine Lowell causing such a reaction from the woman he barely seemed to notice, the older woman's distress was left to but a single cause.

Did this explain why Donn had not come to their bed last night?

"I will fix this, Yiva, I swear," she whispered, embracing the blonde who stiffly succumbed without conceding the warmth of it.

In a cracked, broken voice, without lifting her face from where it was pressed into Oasis' shoulder, Yiva asked, "How?" She had sought a way to fix the situation with her son for years and had yet to devise a way that would not result in a painful, humiliating outcome for every Channon in LaGuardia.

"I don't know…but I will think of something."

The answer, the weapon, might be the one nestled against her breast. She just needed to decide how and when, to wield it to her, and Yiva's advantage. Husband or not, treaty or not, there were some things that were more important. Like an alliance with the only other woman of power in LaGuardia.

"I'll think of something," she repeated. "I promise."

Chapter 21

Chief Ernest had half intended to do as his Tracker suggested, go to the Fortress, talk to Yiva, find out what she was afraid of and how it might connect to the deaths of Roland and her son. But his concern for her safety, fear that he might put her in harm's way if he singled her out to talk to, if he made a visit to the Fortress just to see her, as well as a host of minor interruptions around the office that morning proved enough to delay him. The mid-morning eruption of a fire two blocks from the Protectorate, a fire similar in cause and manner to the warehouse fire Segara had found, gave Ernest a more honest excuse to avoid a meeting. In a borough of limited resources, a building fire was a hazard that everyone tended to, a hazard that neighbors from blocks around struggled to put out before it spread and devoured their homes, no matter how shabby those homes might be.

Fortunately, the snow-rain from the night before and the cold weather made the exterior of the brick building too wet to burn well, thus the fire was contained to the interior, and the wooden doors, contained long enough to burn itself out with very little attention necessary by the neighbors or the Protectorate.

Inside, when it was safe enough to enter for investigation, the remains of dozens of empty metal boxes were stacked at the center of the room, and with them, the twisted remains of three bodies. Charred and unrecognizable but still susceptible to the grubber virus if the individuals had been Normal. Unable to tell now, the three were carefully transported to the Protectorate so the on-duty forepath could examine them before that happened, before they were sposed of, but Ernest doubted they would identify the three, or anything more about them, beyond their gender…and possibly a cause of death if the fire alone had not been the cause. Not without Segara or another mage handy. Not without someone capable of reading beyond disfigured flesh who could piece together a picture of who the three had been and why they had been together in the warehouse while the fire raged.

The rest of the Protectors, however, could identify the point of origin, possibly ascertain how similar this fire was to the other, and they could interview everyone living and working around the warehouse that might offer information. What manner of business had been conducted here? Who claimed this building?

Sooner or later, someone might report missing family. If the three had family, maybe Ernest would find some answers.

By focusing his efforts and attention on the fire and its aftermath, working side by side with his Protectors, it kept Ernest away from the Fortress, away from Yiva, away from endangering anyone with his probing questions. It also prevented him from accidentally expressing feelings he should not have and embarrassing himself, and her.

The fire could not have come at a better time.

Morning dawned with more warmth than recent previous days, and with the adults in the Pack focused on tending their new home and investigating the Queens' campus more thoroughly without the threat Pain's siege had caused, the younger pups were left in the care of Reif, Petr Arden, and fourteen-year-old Randi Morgan, one of the youngsters Addi and Trill had adopted from the foster center three years earlier. With the campus' northern border protected by the Zone and the small enclave of mutani living outside of it, the eastern border previously secured by the Queen's College Pack, and the western edge of their staked territory marked by the greens surrounding the fountain, their new territory felt safe, protected. And with Pain still recovering from his injuries under the watchful eye of the Pack adults, in turn, there was no immediate threat. It was decided there was no reason not to take the younger children and Vanya, cooped up indoors too long now, out of the library to run and play in the wet grass and bushes of the fountain green.

True snow would fall soon enough, making outdoor play more difficult. But today was a good day, and they chose to enjoy it.

Since the adults were within earshot should they be needed, it was a safer place for the children to play than any there had been access to outside of their previous den. The opportunity to practice stalking and finding one another, a place to wrestle not filled with crumbling cement debris, was something all Cana needed. In this place, they neither had to hide from HOPE or the fears of others, nor make the long trek into the Wilds just to play.

Rather than join them, Reif stood to one side and watched, keeping an eye on the perimeters of the green as the eight children, all except Addi and Trill's two-year-old son, raced about with exclamations, mock howls, gleeful laughter. At ease, not anticipating trouble, she laughed with the two young men at her side, Randi and Petr. The three were near enough in age for her to consider them equals, even if she was preparing to initiate into adult responsibility. Randi was her buddy, her partner in crime, and she knew there was hope amongst the older pack members that their relationship would turn into something stronger than friendship.

Petr she was just getting to know.

With two new Cana near her age in the pack, however, Reif was eager to explore options she had not previously had. The future of the Pack was important, but she, like her cousin Jia, felt no compulsion to rush into the future with her options untested.

Selecting a mate was serious business. She did not want to settle down on a whim.

The pungent scent of unwashed, frightened Cana, and a sound, a crack of twigs incongruous with the grassy field on which the pups played, attracted the attention of the guardians. Reif was the first to race into action when an unfamiliar pair of Cana darted out of the brush at the south end of the green and attempted to snatch the child nearest to them, Randi's sister May. May's sharp cry brought her brother at a run and Petr ran with them as the children scattered in all directions to avoid the snatching hands.

The intruders were young, barely adults themselves, bedraggled and dirty, and judging by their pinched faces, thin limbs, and sunken eyes, malnourished, but they were light on their feet, a quickness born of dire need. That need meant little, however, when it came to threats against the Pack.

"Cluster!" Reif shouted to the children moments before she barreled into the strange female who had nearly gotten her hands on May. Thinking the hungry-looking pair intended to make a meal out of potentially easy prey, as some were known to do in the lean times since the Undoing, Reif was grateful that Randy, Petr, and even Eddie formed a line to protect the smaller children who gathered in a hurried huddle behind them.

Reif was outnumbered, young and unfamiliar with this manner of fighting, and the pair she faced was desperate. Sola, large for his ten years of age and of enough bulk to be a tough opponent, but not mature enough yet to enter a fight with more experienced adults, pushed Petr forward and took his place in the defensive line. Petr turned to snap and growl at whoever had pushed him, but the sound Reif made as one of the strangers locked his fangs around her bicep, intending to pull her off of his mate and drag her away as they had attempted to do with May, brought out the change to Cana in Petr's mid-leap into the fray. Unable to grasp what was happening around her, Vanya screamed, the sound shrill enough to be heard, above birds and bugs and wind and the chaos of the fight, across the whole campus.

In their inexperience, however, Reif and Petr were still outmatched, until the increasingly familiar black Fela soared over their heads, snarling, swiping sideways with one clawed paw to send the male tumbling through the tall grass. Those claws ripped through the thin fabric of the Cana's ragged shirt, gouging deep into the flesh of his belly. No one immediately recognized the she-Cana who joined him, whose leap ended with jaws clamped around the unknown female's throat and took her to the ground. The sickening crunch of bone and cartilage brought the injured male to his feet with a roar. Whether he thought the woman dead or was too frightened to stay to find out, he broke for the tree line as fast as his limping gate would allow, leaving the female to her fate. Only the Fela's distraction, as Kato's attention turned to his sister who was still wailing behind May's hand though she was not struggling to break away, allowed the attacker to reach the forest alive.

"Go after him!" cried Candace, the woman wiping blood from her mouth with her forearm as she stood over the dead figure at her feet, her normal form resumed. "I've got this." Reif, who had been knocked back and off-balance to land painfully in a puddle by Candace's arrival, scrambled up to do as the woman commanded. But Candace grabbed her arm and growled, "Him…not you."

Kato, satisfied that the children and Vanya were safe now that other Pack members were pouring onto the green, did not argue. Someone had to make sure the stranger was no longer a threat, that he did not have allies he could lead to the library, that he did not intend to retaliate for the death of his companion. No one else had seen where he had gone, and though the scent of the trail left by the blood of his injury was strong enough to follow if Kato chose to wait longer to pursue, he decided not to delay.

Instead, the Fela ran through the underbrush in search of his prey.

Jia, on her feet but still struggling through the residual dizziness of her head injuries, was the last to reach the green as Addi, his arm around Reif's shoulder, lead the younger woman towards the library. Her arm bled from the savage bite, but she looked otherwise unhurt.

"Is everyone alright? What happened?" The taint of unfamiliar Cana, of blood spilled, was heavy in the air, and there was a body at the far end of the green at Candace's feet, but the fight was over.

"Think they were poaching pups," Reif replied apologetically, stopping at the question despite Addi's effort to urge her on. "They came from there," she pointed to the southern rim of trees where Kato had disappeared, "and tried to grab May."

Not knowing if the strangers' efforts were for food or for a child they could absorb into their pack, Reif could not guess whether the choice of May was opportunistic or because she was near enough to breeding age to be worth the risk of grabbing…while being young enough to be unable to effectively fight back. "I'm sorry I couldn't…"

Hand affectionately on Reif's cheek while she assessed the other children clustered to their parents for reassurance, Jia murmured, "It's not your fault." The campus had been Pack-marked to warn off other Cana, and the day's shifting wind might have meant little warning before the strangers struck. Reif had done what any of the other adults would have done, rounding the children together, fighting to protect them. There was little more she could have done except, perhaps, encouraged them to run for shelter.

But without knowing if there were others nearby, running for shelter might have allowed the children to be picked off one by one.

No, it was better they had remained together.

"I shouldn't have brought them out here…"

"Nonsense," Addi murmured. "We all agreed. On a day like today, this is exactly where they should be."

Neel, feeling left out of the excitement since he, as a Normal in an anthro family, had been unable to do much to help, looked at his mother and said, "I'll take care of this," while pointing at the dead woman whose neck was twisted awkwardly to the side.

"As will Helena and I," offered Brie.

Jia offered her hand to Candace, judging that the three women, recent additions to the Pack, believed themselves to be in a precarious position for having killed the offender without a judgment passed by the Alpha. When Candace hesitantly accepted, Jia pulled her closer to press their foreheads together.

"You protected your son," she murmured, guessing by the position Petr had been in when she entered the green that Petr had done his share of fighting on behalf of his brothers and the other children. Any mother seeing that would have done whatever was necessary to protect her child. Jia's own parents had protected her and Addi the same way. "And you protected the others. Thank you."

Only then, her face and lips still smeared with blood, did Candace relax and smile.

Kato followed the bleeding man through the forest that separated the southwestern corner of the campus from the decayed remnants of civilization, stalking slowly, remaining far enough back to avoid easy detection. He could hear the fellow stumbling, staggering as his strength waned, could hear the rustle of branches and crunch of feet dragging through the leaves and sticks on the forest floor. His prey made no effort to remain quiet, only endeavored to keep as far ahead of his pursuer as his weakening body allowed. Before long those sounds ceased and Kato slowed, choosing to retain stealth and anticipate a possible desperate ambush. There could be others waiting; he could not detect them but that did not mean they were not there.

The increasingly heavy blood trail ended with the stranger, weakened by starvation that complicated his blood loss, slumped between a moss-covered mound of fallen concrete and the gnarled side-angled tree that had taken root and grown at the border where civilization and the Wilds met. His hand was clutched to his stomach where blood and entrails tried to squeeze through, as if he could hold life in and hold out the death that inevitably awaited him. He stared at the Fela with wide eyes, wonder perhaps, or surprise, or merely fear. That was what Kato smelled the strongest. Fear and sweat and blood. Hunger. There was no reason to take further action. As quickly as he was bleeding out, he would be dead within a matter of minutes.

Not even a healer mage could help him now.

This was not the first man Kato had killed. It would not be the last.

In the distance, beneath the sound of the wind pushing between and through collapsing buildings, came the sound of children crying and another, equally young voice, doing his best to silence them. Kato hissed, Fela ears flat to his head, guessing from the way the man's eyes filled with panic as they darted towards the nearest intact building, that it had been his destination. He had been a fool to lead an enemy to his lair, but maybe he had believed he could protect those children if he could reach them in time.

By the pleading in his dimming eyes, he feared Kato would devour or at least kill them.

Shedding Fela for Normal, Kato left the fallen man without looking back. There was nothing he could do to save him and he had no interest in turning the man into a meal. Instead, picking his way over sharp shards of glass, metal, and stone in his bare feet, he followed the direction of the crying, the sound now replaced by stifled soft sobs and whimpers as the young voices tried to avoid detection. He had no clothing, only what he might have stolen from the dying man, but as that act seemed crass and callous, he would be nude to anyone living in this stretch of road. It could not be helped.

It was one of the hazards of shifting, one of those means by which anthro could be identified.

By now, after the mourning hunt, anyone surrounding the Queens' campus, knew there was a Cana pack present.

They did not need to know, could not know, that there was a Fela among them too.

The structure he entered had once been a home, the carpeted stairs leading to the second level intact but weakening beneath the assault of age and the elements pushing between the rafters, around the rotting window frames, and through the long unguarded door. The floor of the entry creaked beneath him, bringing a chorus of shushing sounds above him. Above was where Kato would have hidden Vanya if he had been forced to leave her alone to scavenge or hunt. So long as upper levels were stable, they were always safer in his opinion than the more easily accessible ground floors.

What he found at the end of his search, after a hasty inspection of the first two rooms at the top of the stairs, where the story above had buckled and a variety of flora grew in the dirt blowing in through broken windows, was a huddle of six children, four girls…the youngest two appearing to be twins, and two boys, the oldest of whom met the unwanted guest with a rounded beveled length of wood that was once a leg from the collapsed, soiled, moth-eaten bed they had turned into a burrow for warmth and crude, protective shelter. None of them, dirty and thin with hunger, appeared older than ten, and even the oldest appeared small for his age, stunted, perhaps, by malnutrition and possibly the illness that had pock-marked his sunken cheeks. Only the twins appeared to be related, their red hair and identical faces proof of their kinship to the dead man outside. He had been a redhead too. The others, with their variants of eye color, skin tone, and hair shades had, Kato judged, all been orphaned or poached.

Just as the adults had tried to do with May.

A quick sniff of the air marked each one as Cana.

"You're not safe here. Come."

The oldest boy, his curly blonde hair a mop that hung in his eyes and framed his face like a dirty mane, hunkered with his club ready to swing, his fear translating into the yellowing of his eyes and the small points of fangs showing at the corners of his mouth.

"We don't know you. We're not going anywhere."

As he often did with Vanya, Kato crouched to the boy's level. "How long have you been here? Since you've eaten? Had water?"

"Two sleeps."

The small black-haired girl, with the startling black eyes and coppery skin, might have been nearly the age of their guardian or might have been much younger; her husky voice made it difficult to tell. She wiped the noses of the twins without specifying which question she had answered. Her gaze left Kato only long enough to make sure that her swipes did not poke the toddlers in the eyes.

"You heard the howls. You know there is a pack here. The two you were with…they tried to take a girl. They were…" He paused when the boy's lip curled in a snarl. "They're not coming back. You need food and water. Unless you're gonna scav, you'll be dead too if you stay here."

The blonde met the gaze of the black-eyed girl, and though he doubted the twins understood, they both began to cry. From the expressions on the rest of their faces, whatever their ages, they were old enough to understand death, old enough to know that they stood little chance of surviving on their own. Wild predators, cannibals, grubbers, HOPE, were but a few of the threats that could doom them.

He wondered how many others among them had already died to give them a firsthand experience of death.

"Where are your families?"

Their answers were blank stares. Whatever their lives had been before, they had been together long enough that this was the only family they knew.

He frowned, sighed, and took a waddling step backward, still crouched at their level. "Come with me then, if you want to live. We have food…water…warm shelter…other children to play with. I promise you will be safe until we can find your families."

The odds of finding where they had been taken from were small, particularly if they could not recall any details of their lives before their abduction. Kato did not know if Flushing Pack had the resources to accept more pups, but he could not reasonably leave them here to die of starvation, cold, disease, or an attack by anyone with fewer scruples than he had and he could not imagine Jia or the others turning little ones away.

He stood, grabbed a filthy sheet to fashion it into a toga-like garment so he would not have to cross the Wilds nude, and backed into the doorway where he waited for the children to make their decision. He could force them, but that would do nothing more than frighten them. They were frightened enough already. Patience was needed to win them. They could not know if the stranger spoke the truth, if the ones they called Ma and Pa were dead, but the oldest two, at least, knew that their guardians had been seeking others to add to the family. And they were old enough to be lured by the promise of warm meals they had not had in too long. But the middle children did not move until the black-eyed girl got up with one of the twins on her hip. The other girl joined her, picking up the other twin, and gradually the youngest boy followed. They began to shuffle towards Kato, who now waited at the top of the stairs, but before they reached the door they were stopped by the growl and glare from their defensive brother.

It was a warning not to accept the offer that likely came with some negative strings attached, but it was also clear in his wavering gaze that he too longed for the luxuries the older man offered. The oldest children, the obvious alphas of their child-pack by virtue of their age and experience, growled and snarled at one another in a Cana argument Kato did not understand. He could guess, however, and whatever the argument was, the boy eventually gave in, lowered his club but did not drop it, and followed the rest down the stairs.

Kato led them into the street, the lure of food and warmth guiding them although it would be a lengthy walk in their condition. He expected that they would stop many times to rest, to complain, to throw small tantrums in a pique of frustration the way Vanya often had. He would patiently have to remind them often what awaited them at the other end of their walk, and carrying the younger ones was a price he was going to have to pay to get them there.

☙*❧

Donn's demand sent prickles down the Chief's spine for reasons he could not put his fingers on. It was not the first time a Channon had come to the Protectorate seeking assistance in locating their renegade addict. In the past that Channon had most often been Jonni, the only one, Ernest often mused, who seemed consistently concerned with the middle son's whereabouts and life. As with past occurrences, the request came only after Nik had been missing for longer than a day, would most likely result in finding the young man in a dive or alley, passed out in a stupor, lolling in his high, covered in filth or the bodies of others who had gathered to enjoy their addictions together. If Nik was someone other than the Laedan's son, such a search would have been considered by most to be a waste of Protectorate resources.

What did one more junkie matter?

Without Jonni to look for Nik, however, and with Lowell likely enmeshed in borough business, Ernest guest the duty of finding Nik had fallen to Donn, either at his father's insistence or of his own volition. The threatening knife edge to Donn's voice, sharper and more cutting than Lowell's or Jonni's had ever been, served as a warning that, if Nik was not found, or if he was not found in good health…at least alive…there would be consequences.

Ernest did not like to be threatened. By anyone. Especially not someone he still considered to be a boy. He debated, though he had just returned to the Protectorate sooty and sweaty from the warehouse fire scene, going out again to storm the fortress and demand that the Laedan rein in his bully of a son.

The realization that doing so might have negative repercussions, for the Protectorate, for Yiva, was like a sucker punch that kept Ernest from such an impulsive action. Little details from the Channon wedding reception began to come back, Donn's too-close proximity to his mother, that vaguely threatening shadow of an expression he had just given Ernest the same given to Yiva…as it had been numerous times to numerous others in the last few years of the Chief's experience with the mayor of District 3. Though he had seen that expression before, Ernest had never been on the receiving end of it. He had been threatened by criminals and suspects and even by the occasional victim during his tenure, but it was not the sort of thing he expected from the Laedan's son who had come seeking help. Nor was it the sort of thing any mother should endure from their child.

Was Donn the source of Yiva's fears? It made no logical sense, and surely it would be something Lowell was aware of if such threats were occurring beneath his nose.

He could not go to the Fortress with his suspicions and questions. But he could send a subordinate with a summons to the Protectorate, under the guise of having questions about Jonni's death and not having the time to go to the Fortress himself. It was rare to summon anyone to the Protectorate, but these days Ernest was a busy man, especially with this newest duty charged to him. He would summon Yiva, talk to her in the privacy of his office…just as soon as he found Nik.

Again.

He hoped, as he downed a strong drink and peeled off his filthy shirt, determined to at least get clean before he set out on duty once more, that whatever the middle Channon's location, whatever his condition, it was not connected to the subterfuge surrounding Roland Marrock's corpse.

Donn slid the gold bar halfway across the beer and smoke-stained greasy table, keeping it on the hemp napkin he had set down as protection from the sticky surface. The man in the low set, wide-brimmed hat across from him reached for the offering, his hand grayish and covered with warty bumps, but Donn gripped it tighter and refused to let go.

"After you find him," he growled.

The other fellow was nearly twice Donn's girth and at least a head taller, with more years on him then Donn had lived. But the recommendations of the rogue tracker's prowess, a man who worked outside the Protectorate and would do anything to get a job done, no matter how distasteful, had brought the two together in this dimly lit dive which stank too strongly of piss and vomit for Donn to stomach. He did not know the places Nik frequented the way Jonni had, seeing such places as beneath him. He had helped Jonni get Nik home a few times, but he refused to enter such places if he could avoid doing so.

He had only come here because it was where he had been told he could find Tracker Nepo. Better to find the man himself, likely a mutani given his size and grizzled complexion, then to put out a message and have the man come to the Fortress to find him. Better to find him in one of the places he frequented than to raise questions from his father that Donn did not want to answer.

"When it's done," he snapped, reiterating again the terms of the contract he was making with the unusual looking man.

"When which is done?" growled Nepo. "I don't work free. Half up front…"

"You work for what I say…unless you want me to put you out of business."

"I'd like to see you try."

Nepo's lavender eyes narrowed and his thick arms crossed his broad, hairy chest, daring Donn to contradict or challenge him again. If anyone else had threatened him the way this Channon had, there would be a severed limb on the floor next to the table, ripped from its socket for refusing to pay.

But Donn had a reputation too, both for making good on threats and for handsomely rewarding those who did his bidding. Gold was no longer a currency, but its scarcity, especially a full bar of it, made it an adequate payment for the two jobs the mayor of District 3 wanted taken care of. It would be payment enough for at least five such jobs. If Nepo accepted, he knew he might be placing himself at this man's disposal. It was a risk, but Nepo was not afraid of risks any more than he was afraid of Donn shutting down his business.

Nepo was not afraid of anything.

And if his work met Donn's approval, there might be more gold bars to come.

"So I find your brother, get him home. Easy enough." Nepo knew the baggers, the sources, knew the places addicts went to buy, where they congregated to use, where someone was likely to dump an odose or an offender so that no one would ask questions later. "Want me to bring him back if he's a grub."

"He's not a…"

Nepo shrugged. "Have to ask. Never know what I'll find."

Donn brought a perfumed hanker to his nose as a pair of oily shell-like ghosts sloughed past him, leaning on each other for support in their inebriated stupors. He glowered as they passed until their stench no longer produced the impulse to gag, and then he grunted, "If he's…you hold him until I get there. I'll want to see for myself."

Not because he had a morbid need to see his brother as a mindless thing…something many called Nik already due to his numerous addictions and near-constant state of high. If it came to a report of his brother turning, Donn was only going to believe it if he saw the proof himself. He wanted no one, especially someone he was offering substantial payment to, to attempt to scam him with the easy out of declaring Nik dead or turned when he might still be alive somewhere.

"And the other?"

"Anything you find…I don't care how small…you bring it to me. I want to know who he is…what he stands to gain…what his plans are. I don't care what you have to do to dig into his history…his motives. I want it all."

Nepo eyed the gold bar. "It might take more than…" he began.

Again Donn growled. "I'll be the judge of that." Depending on what the tracker found, it might well be worth more than a single bar of gold.

His father might not have reason to investigate, but Donn intended to find out just who Thomas Quentin was…and what he wanted with LaGuardia's Laedan.

Chapter 22

It was difficult not to show how worried she was when Kato's absence dragged on. One hour. Two. He had been sent after a single wounded man, a mortally wounded man according to Candace, and there had been no sounds of a fight, no scent of additional blood, from the periphery of the fountain green where Jia had set Ayla and Candace to patrol, in case others came seeking the dead and the dying.

In case Kato's absence brought further danger to the Pack.

After Jia's third check-in with the pair, however, and no sign of either trouble or the Fela, Candace offered to go after him, scout into the forest far enough to be certain there was nothing amiss. Sheepish about her too visible concern, Jia thanked her and remained at the watch with Ayla that the older woman was not alone.

Not that Jia did not trust her. Two were better than one and she wanted to be there, to be the first to know what Candace found.

It was not long after when a shift in the wind brought with it the familiar scents of packmates and several others as well.

Several who, as Jia moved forward to greet them when they came out of the trees, attentive in case those unfamiliar Cana scents were a threat, turned out to be a collection of pups.

The children were wide-eyed and weary-looking, thin and dirty, clutching each other's hands as the twins restlessly clung to the necks of the adults who carried them. Kato shrugged when he met Jia's gaze.

"He was protecting them," the Fela said with a shrug. Ayla came forward to take one of the red-haired twins from him but the girl clung tighter and started to cry. He shrugged again. "Don't think there were others...adults that is...or children. Couldn't just leave them behind. They'd starve."

"Looks like you poor things already were," Ayla crooned with a very grandmotherly tone that surprisingly set the blonde boy, who still carried his bedpost club, more at ease then either Kato or Candace had done. "What's your names?"

He looked quickly at the black-eyed girl with him, drew back his slender shoulders, and said, "Jack...and that's Mara...Alice and Ann...and Tori and Bruce."

Kato arched one brow. They were more words, beyond threats, then he had been able to get out of the boy. He wondered if it was because he was Fela, and the children had not been sure they could trust him...though he doubted they knew what he was...or if Ayla's matronly manner reminded Jack of some long-forgotten snippet of family memory.

Or since they seemed comfortable with Candace as well, the woman obviously a mother figure, maybe it was his being a man that was frightening. Maybe the man who had been their caregiver had been less than kind.

Or some other had been a threat to their little pack.

Whichever was the case, the children would be more at ease if they had someone to relate to. He thought seeing the other children would do the trick. He had not imagined it would be someone else.

"Well, Jack," said Jia with a welcoming smile as she squatted before them. Already closer to them in stature, they had, thus far, shown none of the previous reluctance with her either. "Do you want something to eat?"

Every small head bobbed eagerly.

Though not sure enough of a meal had been prepared for so many additional mouths, there was meat still from the mourning kill, and it was always adult practice within the Pack to be certain the children were fed. Jia would gladly give up her share to make sure of it.

“Then go with Ayla…and Candace,” she nodded at the woman, already a mother, who carried one red-haired girl and had the doe-eyed blonde named Tori wrapped around her leg. Jia was not concerned about their being adults enough to care for the newcomers. Her only concerns were the need to establish more food growth, a bigger collection of chickens and goats, and whether anyone would come seeking the pups.

The possibility that Kato could be accused of poaching was a very real one to consider.

Mara took Alice from Kato’s arms and the other women led the children towards their library den with gentle hands and soothing voices, Ayla pointing out various things of interest along the way and attempting to draw Jack out of his shell. When they were beyond earshot, Jia dropped her voice and asked, “What of the other?”

“He died,” Kato said with another shrug, not offended that she would question him. It was her job to be cautious. “I didn’t smell other adults in their den; there was no sign of anyone. Looked like they stashed the children where I found them while they were scavving and poaching.” If there had been other children, he believed Jack and Mara would have said so. “Pretty sure all except Alice and Ann were poached …unless the other adults in their pack were killed or…”

Taken. That word went without saying. Killed was bad enough. Taken implied horrors that neither Jia nor Kato could fully imagine.

“Then it’s good you brought them to us. Thank you.” More mouths to feed would be a challenge. But if the children remained with the Pack, if they survived, it meant a bigger, stronger Flushing Pack in the future. And that could only be a good thing.

Safety in numbers. Jia smiled and tilted her head, a gesture to return to the library.

Kato, relieved to know he had done well by the Pack, smiled back.

~*~

“We weren’t expecting you, Grand Mas.” Laedan Hallister offered his hand as was anticipated but he expressed no surprise or offense when HOPE's leader refused to take it. The Grand Mas was a finicky, prickly man, some days overly friendly and bright, other days intense, brooding and barely tolerable. Lord had seemed cordial enough when they crossed paths in LaGuardia's Fortress, but the political nature of the wedding and then the grimness of burying the dead, the in-flux nature of LaGuardia's present and future, had called for a pretense of gentility regardless of the older man's mood or feelings. Grand Mas Lord was a political beast above all else, capable of pretense and masks when the need arose, eager to discard them when they were no longer necessary.

Here, there was no need for artifice. He had come to Kennedy on business, not for a cordial, private social call, so the niceties of a man to man greeting were the farthest things from his mind. It was as if, Hallister mused not for the first time, Grand Mas Lord was two separate men. He was not sure which version he preferred, but at least he was accustomed to dealing with the man's peculiarities.

Lord had only been at the facility one time, on the day its' set up was completed. That had been a day for scrutiny, to give approval for the launch of a project, a plan, a proposal put in place long ago.

Hallister judged this to be a day of inspection as well, after Nik Channon's recent brush with death. If the plasm could be traced here, no one…not Torrance, not Lord, not Hallister, wanted the unnecessary attention and scrutiny.

"Did you come to see me or the facility?"

Lord waved a hand dismissively without answering. "It is still safe, isn't it? The product? The sources? Untraceable?"

Scowling, Hallister rolled his hemp cig between his fingers. "Each source is registered as a willing donor for payment…to their families of course. I assure you, we're clean. Not just the papers, but the facility. Everything's as sterile as possible to avoid contamination, stored in the necessary conditions to keep it that way."

When Lord huffed, the Laedan pointed out the office window with the cig in his hand and continued, "What happens to it out there, that's not our responsibility. We don't control the plasm once it's sold. We have no way to monitor it once it's on the street. Why?"

"No…of course you don't." Lord circled the desk and stopped at the window, the view across the yard, its long-stationary shipping containers washed as gray as the pavement, the metal link fence, the sky. It was a bleak sight. God, he hated gray. He much preferred the lush greens of HOPE's manicured lawns and shrubbery.

He supposed he owed the man something, some sort of answer. HOPE depended on the agreement struck with Hallister when the man had been a much younger Laedan, the influx of credits and resources the deal provided and the removal of people from the streets who had been an unsightly plague since their appearance after the Undoing. HOPE needed the free labor force, it was true, and anthro and mutani were good for that. But some were not fit for labor. Some were fit only for the blood, the research, they could provide to facilities such as this.

"The LaGuardia Protectorate may be on to you."

"On to me?" Hallister's scowl deepened. This was not his project alone. Lord's words troubled him.

"On to this," corrected Lord, gesturing as if to the whole facility and to the movement of product being conducted outside the window in the yard. "After Nik Channon's odose…"

Hallister growled, eyes narrow. "I had nothing to do with…"

Clicking his tongue as though scolding a child or an animal, silencing the Laedan's outburst, Lord continued, "Of course you didn't. But do you think Channon's going to draw that distinction once his mage tracks the source of his son's near-death experience to the business you…"

"We," corrected Hallister more directly.

Lord inhaled a breath, appeared about to retort, and then exhaled slowly. "Yes…of course."

His repetition of 'of course' began to grate on Hallister's nerves.

"We don't want the loss, the disruption, any more than necessary, of course…" Lord did not notice the bristling of Hallister's shoulders and the twitch at the corner of the taller man's eyes when those words were said again. "The expedition is almost prepared; we need the…"

"You're going ahead with it then?"

Brow quirked and the corner of his mouth twisted into a smirk, Lord replied, "We've never chosen not to…we need that cache if we are going to eradicate the mutani, the anthro…"

"Seems we're doing a good job of that," Hallister snorted. "Eradicate them and this, all of it, shuts down. Your workforce vanishes."

"Nonsense," the Grand Mas laughed, the sound more condescending to Hallister's ears than amused. "They'll continue to be born…even if we kill every one of them living right now. It's in our genetics, you know…every one of us. It just takes the right spark to trigger it…or the wrong one." He chuckled again. "And we certainly can't have that cache in their hands, can we? Do you know what would happen? Every one of us would be…"

After a shake of his head, Lord finished. "No…once HOPE has that cache in safekeeping, out of Channon's hand…out of the public's hands…we cull the unfit adults…and every child born after can be monitored, recorded…steered accordingly."

"Minus my cut in payment?" Hallister prompted, regretting the question as soon as it was asked for the response he anticipated.

"Of course." Lord smiled, a snake-like expression that, when he licked his lips, set the Laedan's teeth on edge.

This was not right. Geary knew it in his bones. Something was off. Something needed to change. And it would…as soon as he determined what the Grand Mas was up to.

From the western edge of the campus, the buildings that marked the perimeter of the Flushing Pack's new territory on the western side of the fountain green, Vance whistled, a weak, bird-call sound just human enough to tell the Pack that he was there without being so human that it might draw others he did not have the strength to confront. He was easy prey now, wounded as he was. He had shed his coat with considerable effort the first time he paused within the Wild's shelter, and tucked it through the satchel's strap against his body.

Having brought neither food nor water, he eventually paused at a fast-moving stream to drink, to catch his breath, and there he ended up asleep for longer than he intended. The uncharacteristic warmth of the skin around the arrow's point of entry indicated the possibility of infection, or at least serious irritation of the wound, and as he forced himself to go on, one dragging foot in front of the other, his vision faded in and out from black to fuzzy dim grey. Only determination and his skill as a tracker allowed him to follow the path he, Jia, Kato, and Torben had taken a few days prior. If not for that detectable trail, he would have wandered through the Wilds until he collapsed.

The front and back of his dark grey shirt were stained an even darker color, crimson though that could only be determined by the bolt still protruding there, and the stain on Vance's hand where he kept it pressed to the front of his shoulder during much of his walk. It meant using his injured hand to swipe branches from his path and occasionally steady himself, adding more jolts of pain to the underlying throbbing in his shoulder. By the time he staggered to a stop and announced his arrival, the sound of his own heartbeat drowned out everything else.

He was surprised he was still standing.

How long had he been gone? Three days? Four? Two? He had lost track of time and as he waited for someone to answer, someone to beckon him to a fire's warmth and a chance to sleep away the pain, he worried about what might have changed here during his absence.

But he had come back as promised, with a bonus he had not expected to fall into his hands.

"Tracker." The woman Ilba, one of those who had sided with the outcast Pain but had, it seemed, been welcomed provisionally into the Pack, emerged from the shadows on one side, along with Orliss on another. They recognized him as an ally, if still an outsider, but in his obviously ill health, he was not a threat to them or to the Pack, so long as he was not followed.

They sniffed the air. He seemed to be alone.

"Jia…I need to see…"

"You need a doctor," muttered Orliss. After an exchange of glances with Ilba, he shouldered the mage's weight while she backtracked his trail to be certain there were no surprises following him. The last time he had come, he had brought the unfamiliar Ursa. This time, they wanted to be certain there was no one else.

It felt like hours that they trudged the remaining distance, Vance's feet barely lifting to walk on his own. Once in the warmth of the library, barely aware of the stares he drew, he was coherent enough to recognize a gaggle of unfamiliar children gathered around Ayla, Candace, and Vanya, accepting inspection to make sure they were healthy and clean. He also noted the heavy scent of roast goat, a rarity when there was no need for feasting, and assumed the meal was for the benefit of the emaciated children.

They looked like they needed it.

He was in no condition to ask questions, no condition to respond to the challenging gaze the Fela threw at him, a look that turned icier and more hostile when Jia, coming down from the second level of the library, ran to Vance and caught him before he collapsed when he pulled away from Orliss' grasp to stand on his own.

"I need to…" Vance began.

"You need to get this looked at." Over her shoulder, looking towards the second level where she had been, she called, "Addi…we need you."

"You have to know…"

"Hush."

With Orliss's help, she settled Vance next to the fire and fetched him a cup of water. His hand was shaky, however, and so she held it for him to drink as her brother joined them.

"What…?" started Addi, ripping away the already ruined shirt to examine the point of entry, the point where the arrow tip should protrude through the back of Vance's shoulder but did not, and the construction of the bolt in order to gauge the best course of removal.

"I was…"

Casting her twin a scolding glance for his aborted question that had prompted Vance to speak again, Jia muttered, "Tell us later." As with her father, when they found him weak and uninjured, there was a host of questions she wanted to ask, needed to ask. But unlike their hiding place in the Bunker that night, they were safe here in the library, surrounded by watchful Pack, with no grubber herd or Laedan Guard or HOPE operatives looking for them.

And Vance, to her knowledge, had not been abducted or missing. Injured, yes, but as a Protector, having crossed the Wilds, that injury could have any number of causes, none of which might have any bearing on the Pack. Her survival, the Pack's survival, did not necessarily depend on Mage Segara.

Only Liam's might, and finding Liam was the reason the tracker was here, the reason he needed to recover.

"Don't have anything that will cut through this…but if we push it all the way through, we might be able to get the head off…not gonna lie though…this is gonna hurt."

Vance scowled and muttered, "Yeah…I know."

"Wait here." Addi scrambled up and returned moments later with his medikit and one of the bottles of alcohol Vance had left with the Pack days before. He also brought a small roll of tanned hide, probably rabbit, squirrel or cat. Vance did not have the anthro sense of smell to tell. He snatched the bottle from Addi when it was offered, but the unsteadiness of his good hand again prompted Jia to help him drink.

This was not the time to go macho and refuse the numbing effects of a drink. Vance knew pain, and he was not stupid enough to suffer through what was coming fully coherent.

"Maz…Deuce…" Addi waved the two strongest men over, Orliss having returned to his post on watch, and they came without question. QiangXu, who had taken to spending much of his time with the Cana pack, joined them and took a position that would allow him to assist the medic with his efforts. "Hold him."

Vance did not struggle as they took secure holds on his arms, did not resist Jia's hands clutching his. So much skin to skin contact was bombarding his mental defenses, but it masked the physical pain when Addi poured some of the alcohol over the front and rear of his shoulder. He hated that much contact, hated having so many thoughts and emotions tangling with his own, but in this instance, it proved worth the discomfort, for when the bolt was shoved a few inches further in, allowing the head to emerge through the back of his shoulder, he jerked, twitched, and his eyes rolled back in his head. The arms holding him kept him mostly still, and he managed, barely, to cling to consciousness.

"Stay with us, Mage."

He did not see anyone's lips move, could not identify the voice through the pounding of blood in his ears, but he dutifully nodded and let his head drop forward against Jia's shoulder.

From somewhere in the room he felt a flare of jealousy. Kato. It had to be. There was no one else it would be. But what did it matter? Vance was in no condition to fight the Fela or resist anything that happened around him. He did not think, given his circumstance, that Kato had the nerve to lash out at him when Jia was there.

And if he was jealous of the injury, the pain, that warranted so much attention, he could have it.

Every nerve in his shoulder burned and screamed, the dual effects of the alcohol on the metal bolt now leaching into the muscle and the movement of the bolt within his body as Addi and QiangXu worked to separate the stone had from the metal shaft. The chemist produced a compound that dissolved the binding agent and eventually the arrowhead dropped into the Ursa's hand. More alcohol was poured over the shaft's end to sterilize it, and on the count of three, although Addi only made it to two before acting, the doctor yanked the bolt shaft back through the front of the mage's shoulder.

It did not hurt as much as he expected, not as much as the second pouring of alcohol over the opened wound front and back, not as much as Addi's probing inspection for internal damage, and not as much, when Addi was satisfied with the internal condition, as the pinching of some bit of heated needle that pierced his skin at the sites of the external wounds. The leather in his mouth absorbed the bite and the feeble expressions of pain, but it was not enough to keep him from finally succumbing to unconsciousness.

His body had endured enough.

The other treatments, the salving and bandaging of the stitched wounds, the care of his hand, did not wake him. Exhaustion, pain, and the mental struggle against the thoughts of others blissfully kept him unaware as the Pack went about its evening routine without him.

Only Jia stayed with him. Of that, however, he was also unaware.

☙*❧

The intricately carved wooden headboard of the wide, plush bed was silent now, the creaking long stilled in the late-night darkness of the room in which only a single candle burned on the wall-length dresser opposite him. The flame's likeness danced in the mirrored glass, but it was neither the flame nor his own shirtless reflection as he leaned back that Geary was watching with satisfaction. Instead, his gaze followed the movement of Gayle Torrance's dark skin as she padded barefoot about the room, currently nude but in the process of finding and donning her silken red night robe and slippers. He had given her that robe and slipper set, an expensive gift that had taken considerable effort to acquire, and on the nights he was here with her, in her room, she made a point of wearing it for him.

He liked her in red.

He liked her in nothing.

He liked that she welcomed him, into her bed, into her life, with so few strings attached…save that they kept their relationship hidden from the prying eyes of the outside.

It should not matter. He was Laedan of Kennedy Borough. No one would care what he did, who he slept with, and if they did object, well, it was none of their concern. But Gayle thought they would care, the other doctors with whom she worked, men and women who had clawed for their positions and who might, she believed, retaliate if they thought her position as lead project scientist and doctor had been gained because she was sleeping with the Laedan.

The fact that she was a damn good eff had nothing to do with her project position. Truth was, she was as good at her job as she was in bed. Better even. Geary could think of no one better suited for the work she did.

"We need to relocate the facility."

Gayle, cinching the braided tie around her waist, scowled. "Relocate? Why? When?"

The second question barely mattered. This was the first of three working lab facilities since the plasm project had begun. The need for secrecy, the need to raise as few questions as possible from the people of Kennedy and members of HOPE meant the ever-present possibility of shifting to a new location whenever Geary thought it wisest. She knew he already had potential locations scouted for when such a move became necessary. Gayle did not need to know the political reasons behind his decision, did not need to know what suspicions or rumors or unfortunate chains of events precipitated the choice.

She only needed to know if her life, and the lives of her staff, were in danger.

The stock's safety was less of a concern.

The unanticipated visit from the Grand Mas, which she was aware had transpired, had set the wheels of Geary's mind turning. They had whirled all day, prompting him to a series of actions he might later regret…or that would, he hoped, prove to be the wisest choices he could make. He was betting on the second. The future of Kennedy Borough depended on it. "I've got a location…we should start with the equipment…the staff rooms and facilities, tonight. The faster…the sooner it is done, the better."

With wagons on hand and others at the Laedan's disposal from other sources, the equipment, except for the host of body pods, could be cleared in twelve hours or less. There were spare pods, spare beds in storage elsewhere for transitional use until those here were taken down and moved. Transporting everything else would take twelve hours or more, as care had to be taken not to break the host of sensitive equipment and machines, meaning a temporary halt in production, a loss in time and revenue.

But Geary would have taken those losses, those calculations, into account before announcing this move. Gayle did not need to advise him on that.

"And the stock?"

The stock would be more difficult to transport. The first move had entailed a dozen men and women, a small number easily shifted from one place to another. The second move of nearly double that number had been carried out in two shifts, a non-emergency move that they had taken time to accomplish. With even more stock now, and the urgency with which Gayle sensed Geary wanted this move carried out, transporting them was not going to be an easy thing to arrange.

"Take a dozen or so of the freshest…disconnect the rest."

The icy edge to his voice, a note of plotting that Gayle was familiar with after so many years of acquaintance, made her sit on the bed beside him, facing him, her expression grave.

"Letting them go? Is that…should we…?"

She had no problem with them dying. It was the loss of their resources that she regretted.

"Some will have to be disposed of, of course…some will expire when disconnected from the apparatus I presume?"

"Yes." The apparatus kept nutrients and fluids in their bodies, kept them breathing and sedated to allow them to live through the extended blood extractions. But it was not the same as eating, as living, and some had undoubtedly weakened enough, organs atrophied to the point that, once the artificial system was disconnected, their bodies would be unable to function on their own. Others, those in rotation the longest, were days away from their final extractions anyhow. There was no use in leaving their emaciated bodies for anyone…whomever Geary suspected might be en route to the facility, to find.

"Do it then."

"The assistant?"

Geary shrugged. "Leave him." He continued, cutting off the question Gayle was about to ask with the press of his fingers to her lips. "He doesn't know anything…where he is…who you and the others are…who operates the lab. Someone will have to look after the others until they are found." Or they would all die of starvation. Geary was not concerned either way. "Leave the decoy files I'll give you where they can be found and don't fret. You and the others…everything will be out before there's any danger. Trust me."

Leaning forward to kiss him, Gayle did not need to say that she did. They had known each other too long for those words to be necessary, long enough to know that lounging here in this room with him was a luxury she did not have tonight. Nor did he, most likely. He would do his part to see that the operation was once again made secure, and she would do hers.

Orchestrate the move and get everyone out by the time the next night fell, if they were lucky. Even this room would be left behind, but come tomorrow at midnight, or the following morning at the latest, most of the evidence here would have been erased. Whatever her temporary assistant thought he knew would never be proved.

Chapter 23

"You're still here."

The words sounded hollow, distant and small, not the way his voice usually sounded to his ears, and the pasty, bitter taste of alcohol remained in the crevices of his mouth that his tongue had not filled. The aromas of tea, eggs, and corn mash gruel had pulled him to waking, but it was the glow of the sun's fingers through the nearest window, stroking across his sticky eyelids, that forced Vance to confront the early morning world. Others were waking as well. Maz's children were bounding up and down the stairs with several unfamiliar faces while Xen and Brie tended the fire and prepared breakfast for the Pack. Orliss and Ilba, who must have resumed the night's duty as sentries after bringing the mage to the library were entering through the front door after Uncle and Ele took their place.

There was no sign of Deuce, and though Vance remembered the former Omega being briefly present the night before, he imagined the big man still spent little time with the others.

Habits born during years as an outcast would not vanish overnight. He was probably more at ease on the outside. Just as Vance was.

And while Jia sat where he vaguely remembered her being in his last moments of coherency, at his side, watching over him, Kato was there as well, crouched at his feet, staring at the mage as if expecting him to be a threat, to make a move to keep Jia away from him.

If his head, his hand, and his shoulder did not hurt so much, Vance would have laughed at the absurdity of it.

"Someone's had to keep an eye on you…make sure you live," she replied with a small smile and glance into his eyes. It was not long enough of a look to rouse Kato's ire, but it was long enough to note the weariness and pain etched on the tracker's face.

"I'm not dying." Suffering yes, but it was going to take more than pain to kill him.

She filled a cup with steaming liquid, the source of pungent spiciness, of herbs and ivy tea, and held it to his mouth. "Drink this…it will help with the pain."

Wanting words with Vance, not secret words but not a conversation Kato needed to be privy to, and finding the Fela's persistent stare to be both unnerving and irritating, she kindly asked, "Will you tell Addi he's awake?" Her brother would want to inspect the mage's wounds, change the bandages, make sure the man was not suffering any unnecessary ill effects.

Kato growled, understanding why the request was made and not appreciating being sent away in favor of the Protector, and stood slowly, throwing a warning glance at Vance before stalking away. He needed to check on his sister anyhow, who had disappeared between two shelves of picture books with a few of the older children several minutes before.

Waiting until the Fela's back was turned and he was out of immediate earshot, Jia rolled her eyes and whispered, "I'm sorry about that. He was there all night…"

"Like you…that's why he was there."

"I wasn't expecting you to wake up and attack us," she snorted.

Vance shrugged with his good shoulder, enjoying the warmth of the tea spreading from his belly throughout his body. Not alcohol, but it felt good all the same. "He's jealous."

"Jealous?"

She sounded confused, disbelieving, and surprised all at once. Vance shrugged again. He was not going to spell it out for her. If the young woman did not already see it, the interest of two very different men, it was not Vance's job to bring it to her attention.

"And you? How are you?" He glanced towards her two previous head injuries to clarify what he was asking.

Rubbing the side of her head, she shrugged too. "Better. The dizziness is gone. We…buried him near the fountain…where I think he'd want to be…and Pain is in line for now." Someone in the Pack monitored the new Omega's movements at all times, though he had yet to go far from the haven he had created in the bushes near the library door as he nursed his battle wounds. She felt confident he would not act against her again, not until he was at full health at least, but she admitted feeling safer knowing where he was. She wondered often if this was the way her father had felt about Deuce after learning the truth about him and Theba, and wondered if, like Roland, the suspicions would settle into something less urgent, if she would ever be able to forgive what Pain had twice done to her.

She wondered too if Pain would seek that forgiveness, if Deuce had ever done so, if Pain would continue to challenge her until he was put down, or if he would skulk away, a lone wolf seeking either a new pack or content to live a solitary life.

"And Deuce?"

"I dunno…I mean…" She knew what the tracker was asking without clarification and was not surprised by the question but she did not know how to answer. He was a mage, after all. Knowing things was what they did. But they did not know everything. "The knowledge doesn't change anything. He is who he has always been, and whatever my blood, Roland was my father. I'm still a Marrock. The others accept me…" She looked around the vast room at those she could see and hear. "I don't want to disappoint them."

"You won't." She was strong and capable, if stubborn and inexperienced and a little unsure of herself. There was very little, beyond the obstinate new Omega, to stop her so long as the outside world did not interfere.

It was her position in the Flushing Pack, her duty to them, that spelled the lack of a future between her and Vance. He knew it, even if she did not. If she was not Alpha, perhaps such an arrangement would have been possible. Kato might be able to fit into her life, an anthro by blood though not Cana, but a mage never would.

Truth was, Vance knew he would never really fit anywhere.

"Nik's okay," he started again, changing the subject. "Was doxing when I left him with Torben…maybe Jonni's death scared him clean."

The corners of Jia's mouth twitched with the onslaught of conflicting emotions. "If anything good can come of that…" her words trembled in her throat, "he would want that for Niki." She looked away, her brother's approach excuse enough to hide the tears that pooled in her eyes.

Vance nodded once, both in response to her unspoken sentiments and to the medic who settled on his knees beside them.

Kato was not with him.

Remembering the ultimate cause of the pain in his shoulder and one of the primary reasons for his return to the Pack, Vance looked around him as Addi worked and was relieved to see that his coat and satchel had served him as a pillow as he slept. It did not appear that anyone had rummaged through either, only rolled the coat and shoved both into place beneath his head. When he reached for them, he hissed with the stretching exertion that pulled at the stitches in his shoulder.

"Hold still." Addi wiped off the old salve from both wounds and made a fresh application. "These should heal in a few weeks…as long as we keep infection out and you take it easy." He could have cauterized the wounds, but that came with an extra risk of infection inside and out, and he did not have enough antibiotics for any sort of extended treatment. "Inside may take longer…those muscles need to heal too, so you'll have to be careful not to overexert yourself. Even when they do, you'll probably still suffer stiffness in that shoulder for the rest of your life."

"Great." He did not blame Addi or anyone else. It had been his own lack of attention that had left him open to the blindsiding ambush. Between his shoulder and his hand, if he continued at this pace, he would be unfit for duty by the time this mission was over. "But that's not happening…not yet."

He tugged the satchel onto his lap and pulled the contents from it as the rest of the Pack began to gather for the morning meal in response to Xen's summons. Kato came back as well, taking up a position at Jia's other side with a determined effort not to look at the injured tracker. Vance handed Jia the book and then the leather folder of loose pages with their water-damaged edges. "Think you've been looking for these. I haven't read them…but I'm pretty sure this tells you what you wanted to know…about what your father knew."

Breath hitching, Jia accepted the unfamiliar objects with excited, trembling hands as Vance added, "I'm sorry about the damage; someone jumped me, tried to steal them. They fell into the street. I saved those…and I think they're mostly okay…but whoever he was, he got the map."

"Map?"

Uncle's question trailed off on an anxious note, the answer already revealed in the question. The recent Pack difficulties, and their troubles in LaGuardia, revolved around Roland's claims of a map and ledger containing dangerous information, a plot he judged to be detrimental to LaGuardia's future. Jia's belief in her father's claim, and his subsequent abduction, each contributed further to a fracturing of the Pack. It appeared, as she opened the book to the marker Roland had left in it, that her belief in her father had been well-founded.

Did that also mean that the hunt and his capture, and successive death, were interconnected as she claimed?

Had Jia, and this mage, been right all along?"

"What is Fort Hamilton?" Those two words on the page the book opened to, the corner folded down and a strip of hemp ribbon wedged into place, jumped out at her as Addi peered over his sister's shoulder.

"It's said there was a great force of men there once," replied Ayla. When the others looked at her, she shrugged. "My father used to talk about the days of the Undoing…when the armies took to the streets to keep peace…to help restore order…"

"Armies," Xan muttered, "implies weapons."

"Guns."

Maz's word left that group silent as Jia flipped through several more pages. It would take too long to read the entire thing, to try to decipher the parts that had been eroded by water, and time, she felt, was running out.

For Liam, if not for them.

"Can you imagine what someone could do with so many guns?" whispered Trill.

Uncle snorted. "Imagine what the Channons will do with them."

"Or Quentin," Addi corrected before his sister could do so. The odds of the Channons involvement in the events surrounding their father had increased, but he knew Jia did not want to believe that their father's best friend had conspired in his death over a cache of guns.

Addi did not want to believe it either.

Perhaps neither Jonni nor Nik was involved. Perhaps not Lowell, but both knew that killing to protect such information was something Donn was quite likely to do. More likely, perhaps, than Quentin.

Tearing her eyes from the page, Jia looked at Vance. "But they have the map now…do you know who…?"

"It was dark…not yet dawn…and he wore black. There was no physical contact, but from his size, his strength…it had to be a man. After he…" He gingerly touched the edges of the bandage on the front of his shoulder. "He left me for dead without the rest of this. I could have tracked him, but thought it more important to get this to you before someone else got their hands on it."

"Agreed…it was better." Knowing whose hands the map had fallen into would have been useful, but it seemed to her that, if the map thief had been a Channon agent, or had been working for Quentin, he would have taken the rest of the documents and killed the mage to cover his tracks. It seemed more likely the theft had been one of those random acts of opportunity the boroughs were known for, scavs stealing things from others that they hoped, in turn, to sell.

There were markets for just about everything.

The thief likely had not even known what he had until later, until he had time to study it. It had appeared valuable at the moment taken, and so it was.

A creak on the ledge above, at the top of the stairs, announced Deuce's arrival though the Pack had already felt his proximity. His words, however, were unexpected. "I say we get there first…make damn sure no one else gets those guns."

"We don't have the…" started Xan.

"QiangXu can provide us with explosives," Wist offered eagerly, the promised excitement of finding a fort full of weapons, confiscating and destroying all of those guns, maybe pocketing a few for the sake of historical value, made him bounce where he sat.

Though keeping such dangers out of the hands of those who might want to use them against anthros, mutani, and anyone who did not submit or agree to the wielders' code, seemed like a wise choice, it would not be an easy job for the entire pack, especially with so many pups in the fold, so Trill interjected, "We don't know where it…"

"I've seen the map," murmured Vance. "Before it was taken. I saw it…I can find it…and I think Torben knows…"

"Torben? Is that how you got this?" asked Kato, suspicious of the unfamiliar Ursa still, especially now that he was connected to this map and books.

Wincing at the pain in his shoulder, Vance raked his black hair out of his face. "He hid it for Nik…who hid it for Roland."

Not a single Marrock or Channon or member of the Flushing Pack would have considered that the answers they sought might rest with the junkie Channon. It seemed the least likely place for Roland to have turned for secrecy.

"Nik wanted you to have it…when it was safe…thought it was time," mumbled Vance.

Deuce, now at the fire though maintaining an awkward distance, said, "Roland wants those guns…if they're there…out of Channon hands. Why else would they fall out? Why else get those papers out of the Fortress…hide them where no one would…?"

"What do you know?" Addi challenged. The man had, in a way, robbed him of a sister, and left him with conflicting feelings.

But Deuce refused to be baited. "I know they fought the last time they spoke. I know from Roland's behavior that he did not feel safe…that he did not feel the Pack was safe."

"And we did discuss relocating the Pack…for security," Maz added, reminding them of previous Pack discussions that revealed just how long Roland had carried that burden of uncertainty and fear.

Uncle nodded. "Skittish…secretive…wary." Uncle, along with Maz and Pain, had been Roland's contemporaries and closest friends. But their Alpha had not shared his secrets and fears with any of them. Some had been planted in the heart and mind of his daughter. The rest had been entrusted to an addict.

How he had ever imagined Jia would get those details from Nik was impossible to know.

"It will take time to prepare," Jia finally said, grateful that Vance and Kato were not making this debate any more difficult than it had to be and were not pushing for any particular outcome. One way or another, she suspected the mage would locate Fort Hamilton, either alone or with the Pack's support, to keep those weapons, if they existed, out of the wrong hands. And Kato, while wanting those weapons to remain far away from him and his sister, and being willing to do his part in locating or destroying them, was also just as willing to keep himself and Vanya as far away from their threat as possible. He was a vicious fighter when necessary, but he was not the sort of man to look for trouble when it was easier to avoid it.

"Logistics…supplies…security for the Pack," she continued, "but first…we need to bring Liam home."

Some might have considered Liam's survival a closed subject, as recent events had eclipsed his abduction and prevented any action on his behalf. They knew that the more time that passed, the higher the chances were that he would no longer be found…dead or alive.

The reminder that their Alpha had not forgotten him, that she was still determined to bring one of their own home if she could, was reassurance to many that they had chosen their leader wisely.

Xen gave a grateful, apologetic smile. The possibility of never seeing her brother again, her only living family now that HOPE had taken both her mother and her aunt, had pushed her to temporarily cut ties with the pack. She was thankful that the Alpha she had doubted had neither forgotten nor given up, was thankful that her behavior had not contributed to Jia choosing to abandon Liam to his fate.

"You can get us there?"

Vance turned his good hand over to clasp her smaller one, ignoring the prickle that came from both the contact and from the lifting of hairs across Kato's arms when the Fela growled.

Assuming he still had the keycard and that the pouch of plasm he possessed had been manufactured in the same facility as the dose that had nearly killed Nik, the facility where Roland had been held captive, Vance nodded. "I've got what I need to get us there…but I can't tell you what we'll find when we reach it. Numbers…what type of protections might be in place…what we might find inside…whether he'll still be…"

"You're not going anywhere for at least a day," grunted Addi. He would prefer it to be longer, but if his sister had some plan in mind, a day would have to do.

"It'll take us at least that long to make preparations, get equipment," Jia agreed. The rescue, if they could pull it off, would be a good test of the Pack's strength, would give them some idea whether they could hope to work together to find, and take, Fort Hamilton on their own, if the place still stood and had not already been ransacked by scavs. If they had any chance of succeeding in such an undertaking, she would be more confident of their odds if she had Liam beside her.

"I'll talk to QiangXu…and tonight we'll discuss this more."

Chapter 24

Liam had barely gotten comfortable beneath the minimal warmth his single, threadbare blanket offered when the lab and warehouse lights blinked on to full intensity. It was not the usual slow-brightening of the automatic dimmer, and since the warehouse was typically kept at a lower lighting level, likely to conserve generator power, he knew at once there was to be some change in routine that he was not going to like. The duty of cleaning his charges had taken longer than usual that day due to both some change in their intravenous feeding that had caused an increase of thin, watery waste from their weakening bodies, as well as the introduction of some stronger cleaning solution that needed additional water to wash off. It left the stocks' skin mottled, almost burned in appearance, but the staff assured Liam it needed to be done, and so he obeyed.

Fortunately, very few of those in stasis reacted to the cleaning. If it hurt them, Liam could not tell. But it stung his hands, leaving them red and tender, so he knew it was not likely as beneficial for his charges as the staff claimed.

He tried once, unsuccessfully, to argue that something was wrong, that they were being poisoned or improperly fed, that the cleaner was harming them, but the technician on duty struck him across the face and demanded that he shut up and do his job.

With the threat of the furnace looming, though unspoken, Liam kept further thoughts to himself. But still, he worried, particularly since there was an unusual amount of foot traffic outside the lab and a more frequent than usual clatter of wheels in the world outside.

His worries were magnified by the influx of people into the lab now, men and women who carefully wrapped every piece of fragile equipment and instrument, emptied drawers and cupboards, packed it all into hempcrates and carried it into the corridor where Liam lost sight of them. By the time Doctor Torrance appeared, the woman sweeping into the storage room with business-like arrogance, the lab was empty of everything except those cupboards, shelves, the sink, and the wires and tubing that hung from the ceiling.

Whatever equipment was installed above the ceiling panels was apparently not to be moved.

"What's happening? Where are we going?"

Liam did not expect an answer beyond the anxious pounding of his heart. If they were moved, this facility abandoned, there would be little hope of Roland finding him. Liam was as good as dead. As a dead man then, there was no harm in pressing for an answer, in demanding some degree of truth. Let them kill him. If he was dead already, what would that matter?

"What's going on?"

Doctor Torrance ignored him as she focused on the handwritten chart she carried, a listing of each individual in stasis. She called out sixteen numbers, the most recent arrivals, and those technicians with her scurried to detach the pods from the tracks and tubing above their heads. They were placed on gurneys and wheeled from the room in the direction all of the equipment was being taken. She continued to ignore the skinny blonde man who followed her until at last, satisfied with those she had chosen, she tucked the clipboard beneath her arm and said to him. "Take them all down."

For a few breathless seconds, Liam only stared as if she had spoken in a foreign language. "You can't…" he stammered. "You can't burn them! They're alive!"

He was sure the others were being transported to another facility.

He was equally sure that the rest of these poor souls were about to be incinerated as non-productive waste.

The doctor's expression silenced his tirade and they stood silently, gazes locked. Liam did not know what she was thinking, what she was contemplating doing to him for his insolence. He did not think she knew his thoughts either, though he wished she did, wished he could reach her and change her mind about the horrors committed in this place in the name of what…science? Research? Genocide?

Eventually, she shrugged and muttered, "Or don't. Leave them there. Suit yourself. I don't care."

That was just it, Liam thought, watching dumbfounded as she left him alone, following those she had chosen to be saved, turning off the lights as she went out.

Not only the lights. The circulation fans as well. The feeding and hydration tubes no longer dripped. The ventilators that allowed each victim to breathe, even those too weak now to breathe on their own, were silent. The electric hum coursing through the wires grew fainter as the minutes passed. Somewhere beyond the external walls, the growl of wheels on the cracked, hard-packed surface of aging asphalt began again; the sound drew closer, passed the wall of this room that once contained doors, and then eased away behind the others until they could no longer be heard either. The last buzz of the electrical systems went with it.

They were alone.

Abandoned.

Left to die.

Shocked, stunned, Liam held his breath, listened to his pounding heart…and stared into the devastation of silent, total darkness.

❧*❧

The unanticipated bruising grip at her elbow warned Oasis too late that Donn was there, too late for Thom to intervene when her husband spun her around as the Laedan's aide had already stalked away in a huff from the accusations he thought he heard in her question.

"I told you…" Donn barked, the fist connecting with the side of her head the punctuation to his uncompleted sentence. The blow landed near enough to her ear that it brought a sharp sting of pain and a loud ringing that drown out any words he might have said next.

But she knew what they would have been, and as he had never struck her before, had never inflicted pain outside of their bedroom and the sexual games they engaged in, it stunned her into momentary silence as he yanked her along by that elbow into the nearest corridor where they were less likely to be interrupted.

She wondered if anyone had seen what he had done.

"You told me to manipulate the answers out of…" she began with a sniffle she tried to mask. She would not cry. She would not.

"I told you not to eff him…"

"I'm not! I haven't…I wouldn't…" Cupping the side of her head where the pain in her ear refused to subside, she turned her head enough to make hearing him easier while also, she hoped, hiding those traitorous tears before they fell.

Never mind that she and Thom had a history. That had been before, before he had come to LaGuardia, before her marriage. Years before. It was long behind her now. Behind them. And though part of a young girl's dream had been that their joint, if separate, foray into LaGuardia, away from her father, would afford them the chance to be together, many things had changed since then. She had changed. She was wise enough now to know that dream was unattainable.

A means to an end. Nothing more.

"I saw…"

"What? You saw me trying to gain his trust!" she exclaimed, exasperated. "I was asking if he'd seen Nik, if he knew where he is…"

The mention of his twin brought a shadowy scowl over Donn's face and a tightening, pinching grip on her arm. She managed to yank free but knew his fingers left bruises and that his nails drew blood.

"What about Nik?"

"I don't know! I asked if he had seen him…but he walked away without giving me an answer…and you didn't give me the chance to pursue it." Walked away, she now suspected, because he had seen Donn's approach and had perhaps felt threatened by it. Threatened enough to protect himself and leave Oasis to fend against her husband's temper.

That action, in itself, was telling.

Oasis continued, rubbing her aching elbow instead of the side of her head. "If Nik knows anything…if Thom thinks he does…like you said…then maybe he…"

Donn's growl was feral and as dangerous as any anthros. If Nik knew anything about Jonni's death, if Thom thought he did, if Nik was seen as a threat…how likely was it that Thom would try to hurt or kill Nik as he may have done to Jonni and Marrock? Maybe he had done so already. Surprised he had not considered that sooner in his search for his absent twin, Donn took several angry strides in the direction Thom had gone.

He stopped short, however, the sudden thought that he was being played causing him to turn back, clear the distance between them with frightening swiftness, and connect one full fisted blow into her belly that made her double over and drop to her knees on the tile floor.

"If you ever touch him again…if I ever see him touch you…" he hissed, catching her face in his hand and yanking it up so that she had no choice but to look at him. "You are my wife. I won't share you. Don't ever think I will."

And with one shove that knocked her head and shoulder against the wall with a crack, he charged after Quentin, not intending for the man to be as fortunate as Oasis had been.

There was no reason for anyone to have followed him home, no way for anyone to know, or guess, that the Ursa armed with a woven hemp sack of supplies meant to create the night's soothing, healing soup, was harboring the middle Channon son…or anyone else. Segara had not known, and Torben knew that, short of having the information tortured out of him, the mage was not going to give away Nik or Torben's whereabouts. And nothing Torben had done recently had been far outside of his normal routine…except for the days off he had taken from work to cross the Wilds, and then the single day spent at home nursing Nik through the worst of the doxing.

Torben was never sick. He worked even when he felt under the weather. Only an occasional emergency home repair led him to miss work. Otherwise, he worked full shifts, sometimes more than one in a row, every day of the week, since the deaths of his wife and child.

What else did he have to live for?

Maybe the days off had been enough to rouse someone's suspicion, but he trusted the other sposers to not question his absence, except out of worry. Someone would have come to check on him before they dared to report him, or before daring to contact the Protectorate out of concern or fear. Doing so would have gone against the sposer's code. It was not the way things were done.

Perhaps he had missed a fight he had scheduled…as fight organizers could be sticklers for any absence or betrayal that cost them money on bets. Though he searched his memory, Torben knew he had not scheduled any fight recently, he rarely did as he preferred to show up at a fight when the mood struck him.

And he was not a man prone to lapses of memory.

Nothing else, however, explained the brute of a man with warty, grayish skin who broke down the door of his brownstone suite with a single kick and barged in as if it was his home to enter.

"Channon…I'm taking you home."

Nik jerked up off the sofa where he had been lounging, half asleep, feet propped on the table, with an expression of surprise and fear.

"Not taking him anywhere."

Torben, his eyes shifting to pale amber, growled and swung, his big fist catching the stranger on the side of the neck hard enough that he was flung across the room. The stranger hit the rickety sofa with its mostly flattened cushions of faded blue fabric, barreled over the back of it, and rolled across the floor with enough force that his movement was only stopped by the wall, barely missing Nik in his flight.

One of the other Channons, Nik's father or brother most likely, must have hired the brute. Nik assumed it to be true as he dove out of the path of the flung man and scurried to the most distant corner of the room he could reach, keeping Torben's taller, broader body between them. His decision to use the Ursa as a shield, however, was immediately regretted when the stranger, on his feet after a blow that might have snapped the spine of nearly anyone else, produced a shocker from a loop on his belt.

A Protector? Did that mean, Nik thought, scanning hastily around for anything he could use as a weapon, that their subterfuge with Marrock's body had been uncovered? That the Chief, the forepath Guire, or Mage Segara, had talked…either willingly or under torture?

His father was a manipulative bully of a man…but torture?

No, torture was more Donn's forte. So Donn had sent this brute to find Nik…to bring him home? It seemed likely, but how he could have connected Nik to sposer Moeller, how he could have found him here, was a confusing dilemma best solved another day.

Nik dodged back and forth, trying to stay behind Torben, still looking for an adequate weapon as the Ursa and the stranger took turns swinging at one another and ducking out of each other's way. Twice the shocker met the Ursa's thick arms, but all the jolt of electricity did…enough to take down any normal man…was bring thick, greying brown fur across Torben's skin and face, bring fangs into his mouth, and fill the room with the stench of sizzling skin and fur. Eventually, the useless shocker was dropped and the pair locked in a wrestling hold, one trying to avoid claws and jaws, the other trying to avoid the wide-bladed serrated hunting knife the other wielded once the shocker was dropped in its favor.

Torben had the advantage of strength, of size, of prize-fighter experience, but he was hindered by his need to protect the man behind him. There was no opportunity in that fight to consider that the man might be here only to escort Nik back to the Fortress, back to his family. A man with honorable intentions would not have burst into the home of another, breaking the door off its jamb, on the offensive.

A man only did things like that if he intended harm.

The prospect that Torben was the one he wished to hurt, after his announcement of taking Nik home, never entered the Ursa's thoughts.

The raking of the blade across Torben's side brought out the full change, the rending of fabric so that it fell away from his body like a snake shedding its skin. His roar in that final shift drove the attacker back enough that Nik was able to dart in, snatch up the discarded shocker, roll beneath the Ursa's arm, and come up to strike the stranger in the groin, sending the stinging jolt of power through his body and dropping him to his knees in a fit of convulsions.

Nik only dropped the shocker when the floor shook behind him beneath the weight of the bear collapsing too, shattering the low wooden table upon which he landed.

"Torby!"

He scrambled to Torben's side, the other convulsing man forgotten as Nik pulled his friend's head onto his lap and bent nearer to study the gash on the man's hairy side. The cut was not as deep as he feared, the change of form having forced some of the torn hide to heal, but his too rigid posture, his body stiffed as though immobilized by heavy restraints, suggested something was wrong.

Something too much like what Nik had seen happen to Roland.

"No you don't," he cried, beginning to scramble to his feet to fetch water, alcohol, towels, anything he could find to clean the wound of whatever agent was poisoning his friend through that cut.

"Nik…"

The Ursa's paw-like hand held Nik's fast, the guttural growl and the big man's gaze turning Nik's attention back to their uninvited guest. The stranger, bleeding from gashes left by long claws and still glassy-eyed from the shocker's effect, was trying to push to his knees, as if to get to his feet for another attack. Without thinking, Nik charged, a leg from the broken table in his hand, and with one crack against the stranger's head, dropped the man to the floor once more.

This time he did not move.

Dragging him by his ankles, Nik pulled him across the room to the nearest window. Not a strong man, it took great effort to force the long-unused window open and then to heave the hulking fellow from the floor. "Time for you to go."

The morality of the act did not cross his mind. A stranger, hand of the Laedan or not, had attacked him, attacked his friend. His friend, of which he had so few, might be dying because of it, and that was all that mattered to Nik. With a grunt of exertion and a solid push, the body tumbled out the window, hitting tree limbs, strung up laundry, and fabricated hemp and wood porch shades on the way down.

Nik did not hear any of it.

By the time he knelt, Torben's nude body was human once more, the cut to his flesh now a jagged red line with purple veining that supported Nik's fears that the sposer had been poisoned.

"Let me…"

"Nothing you can do…just…help me up…"

It was a struggle to right the sofa and drag Torben onto it as the groggy man was limp and disoriented and of little help in the effort.

"I'm not going to let you die because of me."

"I'm not dying." Torben could not be certain of that, but his senses felt to be returning a little more with each breath, the change back to human aiding in the healing. It did not clean the toxins from his blood, but because whatever was pumping through him was not causing any pain, was not affecting his heart's rhythm or his ability to breathe, he believed it to be some incapacitating agent rather than a lethal one. The constitution that kept him from intoxication and illness would, he believed, save him from whatever coursed through his system.

Ripping his shirt off over his head, Nik used it to dab sweat from Torben's face and then to clean away the blood on the skin where the gash had been. "They did this because of me…"

"They…"

"You heard him. He wanted to take me home. My Fa…Donn…I don't know." Certainly not his mother. None of this was his mother's doing. She no longer had the fortitude to arrange something like this…if she ever had. "I'm sure they must think I'm dead in an alley…or have been abducted by the Fela they think…shart, maybe they think you're in on it all."

He sighed, went to the kitchen, and returned with a cup of lukewarm tea he had made for himself some time ago before he had fallen asleep, before Torben had come home.

He had to step over the dropped bag of food, spilled across the floor, and looked at it dispassionately.

"Maybe he's right…I should go home."

He did not want to. Here he felt clean, felt safe. Here he felt no need to use, no need to hide, no need to pretend and play games in order to survive.

But remaining in Torben's home was hiding, of a different sort, and if he stayed longer, someone else was bound to come for him. Someone worse than the man he had pushed through the window. If that fellow, whoever he was, had found Nik here, it was only a matter of time before someone else did too.

Maybe Torben was not dying now, though Nik was not convinced he would live, but the sposer might not be so fortunate next time.

"They're gonna keep looking until I'm home."

"Maybe it wasn't them…your family," snorted Torben, downing the tea, relieved to taste the variety of healing ingredients in it he had created for Nik and hoping they would help him recover his strength and senses as well. "Maybe Quentin sent him."

Nik scowled. He had not considered the possibility that Quentin might want him dead. The man he had thrown from the apartment, possibly to his death, might only be the first of many assassins sent. Torben had saved his life, if that was true, but how many more times might he have to do the same if Nik stayed?

The best place for Nik to be, he decided, was home, behind the protective walls of the Fortress. In the wake of Jonni and Roland's death, security there was tighter than it had been throughout the rest of Nik's life. Not even Quentin, he hoped, would be foolish enough to risk bringing an assassin into the Fortress.

He might resort to poison, a forced odose, but not an outside assassin. Out here, everyone associated with Nik was a target, and anyone could be a threat.

On the inside, with a good act of oblivion, perhaps he could lull Quentin into thinking he was no threat.

Inside, Nik could take care of himself. Out here, he was exposed.

"All the more reason for me to go back. I'll be safer there. I can do this, Torby. I have to…but only if you're gonna be okay."

"You go back there, you're gonna need a bodyguard."

Nik laughed, a merry sound colored at the edges with the worry he was trying to subdue. After the paranoia that had initiated his flight from the Fortress, the very real possibility that someone, that Quentin, wanted him dead, was not an easy one to face. "I might be able to get Fa to agree to that…once you're up to strength…but I don't want them connecting us…not now…not yet."

Maybe after another attempt on his life, even if he had to stage one himself, he could argue the need for that sort of protection. Shart, maybe with an act of drug-induced paranoia, he could still proclaim the need for one and perhaps his father would indulge him. But why the sposer? How could he explain that without revealing a longer relationship with the big Ursa?

That would require more consideration and organization.

"Let me think about it…we can't be careless."

He stood up, relieved that the sposer's complexion had lost its yellow pallor, that his eyes showed clarity and that the purple veining around the wound had already diminished. Torben, still scowling, nodded.

"No…we can't be careless," Nik muttered. On that, they agreed.

The decision, the groundwork of a plan, had been made before her chance meeting with Thom that had erupted into the frightening confrontation with Donn. She had not been afraid of her husband before, was not certain she feared him now, but the blood seeping from her ear did worry her. The bruising around it could be hidden with her hair, if she was careful, and the shadow across her stomach did not show beneath the dark blue of the layered blouse she wore. Even her bruised and scratched elbow was masked by her long sleeves. But the damage to her ear affected her hearing and the blow to her stomach resulted in stiff movement as she resolutely faced the first step into the destiny she chose to carve for herself. She was not going to spend her life afraid. She was going to do whatever it took to secure her future…starting with speaking to Lowell.

At this hour, she knew him to be in the family sitting room, not in his office which would have offered more privacy, but rather awaiting dinner with his wife and sons and Oasis. With Nik missing and Donn on the hunt for Thom, Oasis only risked Yiva being with Lowell as he waited for the meal to be served. She would prefer to find him alone, but as she did not expect him to be, she braced herself for launching her plan in the other woman's presence.

Whatever result that might have.

But when Lowell opened the door to her too-tentative knock, some of her steel melted at the thought of breaking the matronly woman's heart. Lowell was alone. It took no act of falsehood to stumble through the doorway and into the arms that seemed prepared to catch her without his being aware of the state she was in.

The catch, one arm positioned across her belly, made her wince and grunt in pain, and the stumbling displaced her hair so that the subdermal shadow left by Donn's fist against her temple was impossible to hide.

"By hell…what has happened?"

"It is nothing," Oasis mumbled, her voice failing despite her effort to keep it even. "I was careless…"

Careless might have caused one injury or the other, but not both. Lowell was no fool. In her words, in her tone, however, Lowell heard the echo of Yiva's voice, when he had confronted her in the past about bruises…but surely Oasis' injuries were not Ernest's doing.

Nor, he realized, had those seen on Yiva been at the Chief's hand.

He opened his mouth to say something as he assisted her to the sofa but she resisted long enough to thrust the item she carried, a long roll of paper, into his hand.

"I think you've been looking for this."

Though distracted by that interruption, he was prepared to set it aside in favor of forcing answers about her injuries that would either subdue his outrage or fuel it. But again, before he could drop the scroll onto the end table or voice the flurry of questions pushing into the back of his throat, she spoke, her eyes wide, eager, and determined.

"It's a map to Fort Hamilton."

Lowell lurched back as if burned, tugged the string that bound the scroll, and yanked the rolled paper open with such force that it nearly tore the page in two. It was indeed a map, as she claimed, and circled in the lower left was the name of the fabled fort, words scrawled in the blank margins of the page in a shorthand only Lowell could read.

Lowell…and Roland if the man had still been alive.

It was his own handwriting.

This was the map he had believed lost. His map. Believed stolen…by his best friend.

And yet Oasis had found it?

"How did you…where…?"

She looked frightened then, as if her answer would bring further injury…as if finding this map had been the cause of her suffering. As if his hand, gripping her shoulder, caused great pain. He inhaled, calming himself, and let her go, instead cupping her chin gently in that previously bruising hand.

"Tell me, Oasis. I will protect you."

She wanted to smile, to offer some small expression of gratitude without revealing any of the elation or confidence she felt. She did believe he would protect her. Of those three in LaGuardia she could play, Lowell was the only one she trusted to any small degree. It was the primary reason she had come to him with the map she could have just as easily given to Donn, or to Thom, sent back to her father or hoarded for herself.

"I found it in his office…in his things…hidden…I didn't know what it was…and when he found me there…"

She shuddered and tucked her hair behind her ear on one side of her head before arranging the hair on the other side to cover the bruising. Both sides of her head hurt, but at least the side where her head had impacted the wall only sported minor swelling under her hair that was not easily detected.

"I didn't think it was forbidden to be there…I'm his wife…and I only wanted to…"

The snarl that pushed beyond curled lips was just the sound she hoped to hear. "I told him to never…" he started, allowing the map to curl back into its roll as the inner chamber door opened and Yiva entered the room. He stopped speaking to stare at his wife, a guilty startle that prompted him to mentally scramble for words of excuse or apology. But Yiva's frightened rabbit expression as she stared, not at him, but at Oasis, cut Lowell's words off again as that cold suspicion from moments before began to grow within the seemingly bottomless pit of his stomach.

Not Ernest.

Donnovan?

That should have been the most preposterous thought in the world if not for the evidence on the side of Oasis' face and the confession she had just made.

Donnovan. Oasis. But surely not Yiva.

But if not Donnovan…who?

"Don't tell him about…" The young woman's eyes flicked down to the rolled page in Lowell's hand. "If he knows I…"

"I won't. Stay with her." He might have been making the demand of Oasis, or of his wife, refusing to give those fleeting questions any more consideration, convincing himself for the moment that he was misreading everything he saw. "He'll answer for this," he muttered as he thrust the rolled map onto the top shelf of his book cabinet and stomped out of the room. "He'll never know you came to me."

His son would answer for a lot of things.

The theft of that map was not the only one.

Alone together, Yiva continued to stare, but after a brief raising of her head and a momentary meeting of their gazes, Oasis was unable to look at her. There had been nothing to see, Lowell's hand beneath her chin, and nothing to hear except for words about a map and the innocent invasion of Donn's office. But it was the implied violent reaction to that invasion of privacy, and the way Oasis winced when she turned away, that spoke the truth, and whatever else Yiva might have overheard from beyond the door, when she sat beside Oasis on the sofa, it was obvious in her eyes that Yiva knew the truth. She knew, Oasis was certain, because she had been at the receiving end of those hurtful hands too often herself.

"You shouldn't let him..." Yiva started weakly.

"No one lets him do anything...he does what he wants." Oasis rubbed her elbow and pretended to study the flowers on the table.

"You can stop him." She pushed back the younger woman's chestnut brown hair and tucked it gently behind her ear, visually inspecting the damage at the side of her head without touching it.

"How?" If there was a way, why had Yiva not used it to her own advantage before?

Biting her lip, swallowing the bitter inner turmoil bubbling in the back of her throat that burned as it slipped into her belly, Yiva whispered, "Tell him you're pregnant."

If she had thought she could have used that ruse to fend off her son, Yiva would have done it long ago. But she was beyond the age of easy conception, had not conceived again since the premature ending of the pregnancy that might have given Donn and Nik a younger sibling, and Yiva doubted her son would have given much consideration to the safety of his father's unborn child. If he had thought it was his own, he probably would have gone out of his way to make sure such a child was never born. For his own child, however, with his wife, Yiva was willing to believe Donn could be swayed to more gentle treatment of the woman.

"I would be lying..."

"Would you?" They had been married but a matter of weeks, and intimate surely during that time. It would be too early to be certain of a pregnancy, but long enough since their wedding night that such a claim would not be impossible. "He won't know that...there's always a chance...and there are ways to fake proof...ways to fake a miscarry later...if you're not..." As often as pregnancies ended in shed blood and the loss of unborn life since the Undoing, a lost baby would not be unusual. And as rare as pregnancies were, as much as Donnovan wanted to carry on the Channon legacy, protecting an unborn child by showing gentleness and kindness to his wife would be expected.

Pregnant women, since the Undoing, were akin to gods.

"Why would you…he'll…" Oasis began, her lip trembling in earnest now because she knew too well what Yiva would be giving up by suggesting this. To Oasis' knowledge, her husband had not gone to his mother since the day of their marriage, had not tormented or harmed her once. But without his willing wife to satisfy his appetites, both women knew what the outcome would be, what Donn would do. "I can't do that…I can't let him…"

Yiva clasped the young woman's hands in hers. "You can. You will. You must." Her eyes fluttered closed as she sighed. There was only one way to prevent the inevitable. Yiva did not know if she had the courage to do what must be done, but she was being given no choice. Oasis did not deserve the suffering Yiva had endured.

It had to end. If her husband would not end it, if he did not make Donnovan answer for his crimes as he said he would, then there was only one other man who could.

And Yiva was the only one who could make that happen.

"It will be okay. I'll protect you," she whispered, pressing her forehead to Oasis'. "I will protect us both."

Chapter 25

The heap in which he lay, soft with filth and rot, roused him with the stench of decaying vegetables and an assortment of debris that made his stomach churn and twist. He rolled to the side in time to avoid vomiting on himself, the movement stirring more revolting smells that forced him to his feet in the hopes of escaping them. His body was bruised and scraped from where branches and wooden latticework had broken his fall, and the gashes on his exposed skin were deep and bled still, announcing that he had not lain in that decay long enough for his blood to congeal and scab. His head throbbed, the pain of it screaming in time to his labored heartbeat, but he was breathing, alive. He did not remember falling, but he did remember the blow to the head and the young man who had landed it.

If he had not been paid a significant sum to get that troublesome fellow home, the payment that awaited him when that happened, Nepo would have opted for killing him.

No one, not even a Laedan's son, got away with an assault like that. Why had he not just come along quietly as Nepo asked?

But, he wagered, as he glanced up at the now-closed window through which he believed he had fallen, his prey was likely no longer there. What the sposer wanted with the Channon boy, what sort of ransom he hoped to manipulate for himself or what disgusting uses he had thought to make of the boy, were beyond him. Maybe later, once his payment was collected, Nepo would turn this miscreant over to the Protectorate for abduction and immoral crimes.

Or for being anthro.

There were no laws against such things unless between an adult and a child, however, and Nik was no child. Those particular laws did not apply…so long as both men were willing. But there were natural laws that forbade any such doings with anthro, and for a Channon, those natural laws applied ten-fold.

The Ursa would get his for whatever his intentions had been…or simply because he was anthro.

If the Protectors would not see to it, Nepo would.

"I told you never to hurt her again!"

Lowell found his son in the Fortress lobby, grabbed him by the arm, and threw him against the nearest wall with a fury Donnovan had never experienced before. In his current frame of mind, furious with the man he could not find, afraid that some harm had befallen his twin, his father's anger only added fuel to his own. There was no one in the gallery at this hour, except for the men guarding the door who were locking it so that they too could have dinner.

With the outside gates barred and guarded, and the inside doors locked, it was unlikely anyone was going to get in who should not. Unless one of the Fortress residents or staff members was the threat, everyone was safe for the night.

Donn did not have to ask what his father meant. If Oasis had joined the family dinner table, as he imagined she would, the bruise on the side of her face might be obvious. His own fault. While he did not think her weak enough to snivel to his father like a child, he also did not think her weak enough to hide like a frightened mouse the way his mother did.

Lowell would have demanded the truth regardless.

He should have warned her to keep her mouth shut.

After what Lowell had previously seen, however, she might not have needed to say anything for the Laedan to guess at the truth, to conclude it on his own.

"She's my wife!"

"You bring disgrace and dishonor to the name of Channon…"

"She's an unfaithful bitch!"

Lowell's mouth snapped shut as he glowered at his son. Unfaithfulness in marriage would have set him off too if he had seen any sign of it in Yiva in the days when they were striving to produce children to bear the Channon name. "Who?" he barked, the burning need to know demanding an answer that he should not have a right to. His son could not be talking about him. Donn would have confronted him, son to father, man to man, if that was the case. Maybe he did not know…only suspected infidelity…or perhaps there was someone else.

In which case, she had also been unfaithful to Lowell.

A ridiculous notion, since he had no claim on her, but the jealous beast that lifted its head and roared in his breast demanded an answer.

"Doesn't matter, that's between her and me. But if I ever…"

"If she ever…if you ever…you will remember you are a Channon and you will behave accordingly," Lowell warned. Their name meant something in the public eye, placing them at a higher standard than the common people. Whatever she had done, Lowell would not see her struck again. "If you have a grievance, if you have proof, bring it to me, as your Laedan. I will decide her sentence. You will not hit her again unless you want the world to know your…our…business."

Again Donn snorted, the sound undercut by the growl that said his father had no right to interfere. But Lowell was Laedan, as he said, the face the public saw, and in keeping that name respectable in the eyes of those they ruled, the man had every right.

He did not, however, have to like or agree with it.

But as a Channon, he did not, he felt, have to obey.

"And if you ever…" Lowell leaned closer until his face was inches from his son's, Donn unable to escape from where he was pinned against the wall, "steal from me again, I will strip you of your rights as mayor, expel you from this house, and leave you with nothing…"

"Leave everything to Quentin? Nik?" This time Donn's snort was one of derision and disgust as he tried to determine exactly what theft his father was accusing him of.

"Once he's doxed…" Lowell ignored the mention of his aide. Quentin was invaluable, was a lot of things, but he was not a Channon by blood and Lowell could not in good faith bequeath him what was pledged to his sons by the right of genealogical succession.

"Nik can't find his head most days and he's probably dead now…"

Eyes narrowed further so that very little of the blue and black was visible between slitted lids, Lowell hissed, "What do you mean?"

"Haven't seen him lately, have you? Since Jonni…"

"Don't you dare say his name."

"So we're forbidden to talk about my brother now? You gonna say the same thing about Niki when he doesn't come home…or comes home in a bag? You gonna cut me out too for being such a…"

The sound in Donn's throat made Lowell angry, but his words did even more. "Disappointment," Lowell grunted with a toss of his head, finishing Donn's sentence. It might not be the word Donn intended; it was one Lowell had never thought he would say about any of his sons, and to think it applicable for the son that was the most like him in many ways was a bitter pill.

It was the ways Donn was not like him that troubled Lowell most.

Intending to seek out Nik, now that he had been made aware that his middle son was missing, Lowell stepped away. Wisely, Donn made no effort to move or lash out despite the burning desire to do so.

"We will finish this later. No one…my sons included…steals from me and gets away with it. When I return, you will tell me…"

"Nothing to tell." Donn's tone and mien were icy and hard. "But maybe you should ask Thom." He did not know what his father knew, or suspected, or how. Whatever theft he was being accused of, even if it was the one he had orchestrated, Donn had nothing to say, nothing to reveal. He had acted for his own good, for the betterment of LaGuardia, something he did not believe his father had the balls for any longer.

"Oh yes," Lowell growled, "There is. There is plenty…and you are going to tell me all of it." Right after he found Nik…and had words with Thomas Quentin.

Donn held his breath to avoid saying anything that would further antagonize his father or raise additional suspicion. Most of what the man had said was meaningless, harmless, but the chance of being stripped of what authority and power he possessed was a threat Donn heeded. The cache of weapons he had stolen was an adequate start towards cementing his own strength, overthrowing the Laedan, and taking his place as LaGuardia's leader. But without knowing if there were other such stashes scattered throughout LaGuardia, what other resources his father might have hidden, Donn did not think he had enough leverage yet to win a confrontation.

What he needed were the weapons at Fort Hamilton. What he needed was to find them first and keep them out of his father's hands.

What he also needed, he thought with a bitter growl when Quentin's athletic frame crossed the gallery, headed for the stairs and likely, Donn thought, dinner with the Channons, with whom he seemed entirely too familiar, was to be rid of that man for good.

Thom was not family, and Donn was tired of treating him as such.

"Quentin!"

His roar of outrage echoed in the multi-leveled gallery, where not long ago he had gained a wife before the whole of Queens' elite. He charged like a running bull, spurred by the red flag of increasing hatred for the man who seemed determined to ruin him, his family, his life. Maybe Oasis had told the truth and she had no interest in Thom Quentin. Maybe she had kept her behavior within the parameters Donn had spelled out. Donn had known of Quentin's interest in her before sending her to spy for him, but seeing glances across tables and rooms was one thing. Watching it when the two stood near one another was less acceptable than Donn had expected.

Maybe he felt something for Oasis after all. Maybe she was something more to him than a piece of property.

There was little time for Quentin to acknowledge the roar and react before Donn's arms caught him around the middle, his head butted into Thom's ribs with enough force to crack them, and drive him over a wrought metal table to the stone floor.

Donn wasted no energy on words, made no effort to express the multitude of reasons behind the assault. Quentin's attention to Oasis, lies about Marrock that had started a cascading chain of events they could no longer control, his manipulation of Lowell, his audacious quest for power that rightfully belonged to Donn and his brothers…his brother now. The very real possibility that he had killed, or had at least been a party to, Jonni's death and might have orchestrated Nik's too.

And especially, he thought with raging bitterness, the confidence broken with his father. Donn had not told anyone other than Grand Mas Lord about the weapons shipment he had hijacked. He trusted the Grand Mas to keep his secret. If anyone else had told Lowell, the words had to have come from Quentin.

Or Quentin had told Lowell the truth himself.

For all of those sins, and a myriad of others Donn imagined he was not yet privy to, Quentin had to pay.

They rolled across the floor, failing to break free of the other's grasp and failing to do each other any significant harm. Only when Donn got a foot wedged between their bodies did it enable him to kick hard enough to shove Quentin backward, an act that greeted his ears with another crack of ribs.

One more blow like that, Donn thought irrationally, and ribs would puncture lungs…and Quentin would die the same way Jonni had, drowning in his own blood.

That same thought brought unbidden, uncontrolled gold into Quentin's eyes, proof to Donn of everything Nik had tried to tell him. He roared again, this time determined that this confirmation would be the end of Quentin and his manipulative quest for power at the Channon table. All he needed to do was goad the man into becoming whatever manner of beast he was inside.

Quentin, not certain what had instigated Donn's wrath but knowing it could have been anything, or nothing, saw this fight as an opportunity to further manipulate Lowell in his favor. Donn was too unstable to be trusted with the reins of power, and Nik was too unbalanced from substance abuse. With Jonni gone, there was only one other option for LaGuardia…at least until the day Oasis bore a child. Lowell had to appoint Quentin as one of his mayors…and in time as his successor.

But as he lashed out with a strength not natural for any Normal man, flinging Donn into the nearest pillar, he realized he could not attain that goal if he killed this assailant as he had done the other. If it came to it, he could argue Jonni's death as the accident it was, but his proximity to a second Channon death, even in self-defense, would cast a shadow he would never be able to dispel.

He was unaware of the gold in his eyes.

He had to end this fight as diplomatically as possible, with necessary force if not words, but not with death. For he had no doubt, judging by the rage in Donn's eyes as the blonde charged again, feigned right out of Quentin's grasp, and elbowed him brutally in the side before tripping him and knocking him to the floor, that Donn would kill him if given the opportunity.

Several blows, bruises, bites and fractured bones later, Quentin was losing both the belief that this could be ended tactfully and the desire for it to be so. If one of them was going to die tonight, it was not going to be him.

The only way to fight against Quentin's anthro strength was to fight dirty, and Donn was the master of dirty. Even the small knife kept in his boot, there for protection should he ever find himself under assault in LaGuardia's street, was used against the unarmed man. This was the closest thing to an assault Donn had ever experienced, and as Quentin's death was justifiable in his eyes, he did not care if drawing the blade and leaving several gashes on the man's arms, legs, torso, and face was not fighting fair.

This was not about being fair. This was about justice. This was about satisfaction. This was about revenge.

"Mas Channon…Mas Quentin…please…"

They had been initially alone, they both believed it, though neither had checked to see if it had been true. But neither had any inkling how long the horrified little man in the uniform of Fortress staff had been in the lobby, how much he had seen or heard. His unexpected voice, mousy and small as it was, was enough to distract Quentin from the fight and make him back away from it, bloody and bruised and aching in ways and places he had never experienced before. It gave Donn an opening, a brief window long enough to sink the short blade into Quentin's hip. He had aimed higher, but Quentin's forearm and fist came down across Donn's back, diverting the blow to somewhere less lethal and knocking Donn face down to the ground.

The blade twisted as Quentin pulled away, and in the time it took Donn to regain his senses and push to his knees, Thom had limped beyond his easy reach. If Donn had the strength and clear-headedness, the breath and the focus, he would have charged again, tackling him and finishing what he had started with the knife left embedded between Quentin's ribs.

But such an act, an attack against a surrendering opponent, would make him look to be the aggressor, a murderer, and with a witness to see it, who may already have seen more than he should have, it might not go in Donn's favor when the matter came up before his father and the borough juds.

The prudent thing to do was let Quentin go…for now.

"What did you see?" Donn barked at the trembling fellow who wisely remained out of Donn's reach but was near enough to realize that he was in danger if Donn decided to lunge at him too.

"I…"

"He…" the word was heated, bitter, brutal and brittle all at once, punctuated by the outstretched arm and pointing finger that referred to the retreating man's back, "attacked me."

"I…" the man started again, gaze darting back and forth between them and once towards the staircase that had been his destination when he had stumbled into the madness he had just witnessed.

What he might have seen, might know, was not obvious. Donn only cared that the man reported the incident the way Donn saw it.

"Say anything different and your entire family…everyone you love…will suffer in the most excruciating ways imaginable."

Donn did not know if the man had a family. He was of an age to have a wife and children, but if not he at least had parents, siblings, and friends. People Donn could use as leverage, as pawns he was not opposed to playing.

"If anyone," he stressed again, "asks, he started this. Understand?"

The little man nodded his head with jerky, fearful movements and babbled, "Yes, mas," with a puffing squeak of a voice about to crack.

"Go on then." Donn waved his hand and the man scurried away, his original mission forgotten or no longer important.

From the wet stain on the floor, it was likely he intended to find a clean pair of trousers.

The thought of the fear he had instilled made Donn chuckle in spite of his body's pain.

☙*❧

The darkness of the empty, crumbling backstreets which Nik was intimately familiar with did not bother him. He had been in these streets so often that he was a known, familiar face to those who came this way. And the dark had never been frightening.

As a small boy, Nik remembered many late nights, to his parents' exasperation, spent perched on an open window ledge, watching the clouds, imagining what the stars he read about must look like behind them, listening to the wind, the rain, the throbbing of the sea, the screech of the night birds, the cries of dogs, cats, wolves and more, a nightly symphony lost with the rising of the sun and the waking of the rest of the world, bringing with it the intrusion of voices. How many times had Jia sat there with him, with or without Addi, Liam, Jonni or Donn, making up childish stories, plotting a future that none of them would ever come to see?

Too much had changed since those innocent days to go back to the dreams of what might have been. Too much based on secrets, threats, deceptions, jealousies, and quests for power born of a maturing view of the world and their insecurity in it.

Nik had insecurities. He knew who he was. What he was. He might not know what he wanted out of life anymore, but he knew what he did not want.

He did not want anyone else to die. He did not want one of his best friends to be banished for a twist of genetics she had not asked for. He did not want her to be afraid for her life, to be afraid to come home. He did not want his father to get his hands on a cache of weapons. He did not want Donn to be a sadistic bastard.

He did not want Jonni to be dead.

He wanted justice for the dead and his friends to be safe, and it was those desires that brought him back through the Fortress with a mock, exaggerated stagger, the gate opened for him at this obscene hour, in spite of the peril to his life that might await him inside.

If he was going to die, better inside than out.

If others around him could be strong, so could he.

A small man, one of the Fortress staff judging by his uniform though Nik did not recognize him, scurried past, a felt hat clutched and twisted in his hands as though being wrung of moisture as he slipped through the closing gates into the borough streets. Donn's snarled words followed the fellow, threatening his job, his pay, those dearest to him, his life, for whatever act of displeasure he had committed. Nik had seen similar fear often enough on the faces of Fortress staff forced to endure his father's wrath, though such threats had been muted and capable of reversal by the now-dead co-Laedan.

With no one left to temper Lowell's outbursts, the chances of him following through on threats increased. Such threats coming from Donn had only Lowell to subvert them. There was no way to know if the Laedan would side with the employee or with his son.

Well maybe I can help that much, Nik mused as he crossed the courtyard and entered the lobby past the pair of door attendants stationed for the night shift to protect the Channons and their staff from the renegade Fela who had yet to be apprehended.

Donn was no longer in the lobby.

So he and Jia had not yet been found. It was easy to assume that by the presence of the guards. Good for them. Nik had helped them as much as he could, now it was his obligation to help that poor frightened fellow until the next step could be taken.

Whatever the cause of the man's fear, Nik believed he could soothe it. Donn would listen to him, surely.

But first, still weak and shaky from doxing, the remains of that horror still lingering around the edges of his body's needs and his brain's desires, Nik needed to sleep…in his own bed, between his own sheets, with his own freshly laundered pillow. The guards would announce his return to his father and mother when they awoke. That would allow him plenty of time to decide on the necessary face to present to the others if he was going to stay alive and get to the bottom of the Fortress' horrors.

The puddle on the floor was noted and ignored.

The debates waged throughout the day as the logistics surrounding her intentions to find and rescue Liam and seek justice from her father's abductors fought to take shape. Jia listened to every argument from every pack member, cases for and against who should and should not accompany the Tracker Mage into the unknown. There were considerations to be made for the indeterminate number of adversaries they might face when they discovered the place Segara intended to lead them to, the unidentified defenses the facility might have, the possibilities there were of running into anthro hunters, Laedan Guards, or HOPE agents.

And there was the safety and care of the Pack to ensure. Though Kato announced both of the Cana who had attempted to poach their pups were dead, and the children found and brought back with him swore that they had seen no other adults, that there were none in their little pack to be a threat, there was still a chance that those adults were out there. It was also possible that the original families of these children were looking for them and that they could track the pups here during Jia's absence.

If she was not here to speak for them, there was a chance that another Alpha might attempt to overpower the Pack as Pain had done. In the event of conflict, in the event that Pain rose up once again or conspired with strangers against the Flushing Pack…or if any other threat arose, Jia had to be certain that enough strong adults remained to defend the children and each other.

Addi's resolve that Liam might need a doctor was also a factor to consider, given the condition Roland had been in when they found him. Removing the only trained medic from the Pack was a concern. Thankfully, Ele had experience treating wounds, setting bones, stitching up the injured, overseeing the dying; many in the Zone relied on the hard-faced man for care. There was also an available mutani midwife to aid them who, like QiangXu, had a lifetime's experience in mixing medicines, poultices, packs, and salves.

If Addi came with her, Jia felt the Pack would be in competent medical hands so long as Ele was here. Addi had as much right to avenge their father's death as she had., and if she was going to face an unknown threat, she felt better doing so with her twin at her side.

So long as Pain chose not to defy her again, she believed the Pack would be safe where they were. With the entire resources of the Zone behind them, with their solid relationship with QiangXu and his long-standing treaty with the mutani who lived outside of the Zone, the Flushing Pack was the safest it had ever been.

Kato trusted his sister's welfare to those who had gone out of their way to protect her before more than he trusted Jia in the mage's company. He demanded to go with her; he did not voice his reasons, but Jia knew them, and after their last foray into LaGuardia, where he had helped save her life, it was easy to admit she wanted him beside her just as much as she wanted Addi and Segara there.

The tracker held the key to finding Liam. Addi held the key to their survival. Kato held the key to keeping her level-headed. A fair trade and all equally necessary.

Xen's choice to accompany the expedition, despite her husband's protests, was not only logical but, Jia believed, crucial. Cana instincts would lead Xen to her brother, once they were near enough to him, if the mage's senses failed or some unfortunate end befell him. And putting herself at the Alpha's disposal, swearing to follow her lead in the field, was an ideal way for the young woman to get back in Jia's good graces, prove herself to the Pack.

Roland had been taken in an effort to protect Xen and Liam's aunt. Xen would be damned if she would allow a similar fate to befall Jia in an attempt to save her brother…and she wanted to be there when Liam was found, to see him alive and whole again with her own eyes before something happened to him on the return home as it had to Roland.

Full of youthful zeal and lust for adventure, Wist offered his speed and agility to the effort. He had spent many hours under QiangXu's tutelage, and when the Ursa chemist presented an offering of explosive powder, something that required but a spark to ignite, it was Wist's familiarity with the compound that made him a logical choice to join them. And the discussion of the potential need to enter the neutral sector, to possibly cross into HOPE's territory if that was where Vance's lead took them, offered up Helena as their final team member. The three Cana women Jia had brought into the Pack knew the neutral sector and had all crossed HOPE's borders with the intention of rescuing the members of their own lost pack. That effort had failed, but if there was the chance that any of those they had lost could be found where Jia was going, they wanted one of their own to join her.

Flighty, skittish Brie was better suited to aide in the care of the extended collection of pups, and Candace, with her own children to consider, would be most useful here with the Pack as well. Trill and Ayla could not be expected to supervise all of the pups, even with Reif's help.

So Helena it was.

"I should go with you."

Deuce's voice, low and colored with hints of obvious stress, sounded worried. After snapping her satchel closed, each member of the team carrying only the basics of survival for what they hoped would be a short time away…as well as extra mediplies and food to offer to Liam and any other survivors they found, she looked into the man's eyes in a way she never had before.

They had not had the opportunity for conversation since the revelation of their blood relationship had been revealed and she wished there was time to do so before leaving. Had he always been this protective of her? Was their kinship the cause that had driven him to follow her and Addi every time they separated from the Pack, that had prompted him to risk his life in moments when most omegas would have done otherwise? Having shadowed her most of her life with no one to tell him to do otherwise, how difficult was it for him to be instructed to remain behind.

"Maz is acting alpha…and Orliss his second…" she murmured, "but if Pain…"

Her voice trailed off and Deuce lowered his gaze. Pain was still recovering from injuries more serious than Jia's, would likely be so for another week or two, but if she was absent longer than anticipated, long enough for Pain to grow strong again…if he moved against the Pack, or if he dared his injuries and tried to retaliate before he was healthy, she did not trust Maz to put down the man who had been his partner since the death of his wife. It was unfair to ask that of Maz, and so Jia's best option was to leave the one man who she knew would do what was best for the Pack without reservation. Deuce had done the same for years, beneath an Alpha who had detested him. Protecting the Pack, for the Alpha he loved and respected…his own child if his story was accurate…was an unquestionable honor and duty.

Orliss would be here too. And Ele and Uncle and the rest. But Deuce was the one she trusted the most with this duty. It was no small thing she asked of him. He knew it; he took pride in it.

But he did not like her leaving without him on a mission of unquestionable danger.

The others going with her were bidding friends and family farewell and beginning to gather where Vance waited by the library door, cutting himself off from the emotions of others by staring into the moisture-heavy clouds and focusing on some detail deep in the darkness that only he could sense.

Or maybe he stared at nothing and only wanted not to feel like the isolated outsider he was in the midst of the Cana he was bound to.

If she did not need him so badly to find Liam, she might have asked him to stay behind, give himself time to recover and heal from injuries of his own. The thought of doing this without him, however, was unbearable.

She did not need to look into his eyes to know he felt the same.

"We should go."

That was Kato's voice sidling up behind her on the cat-silent steps Fela were known for. She could not always rely on her ears to know he was there. It was her other senses, eyes and nose, that told her when he was near, when he was content or unsettled or angry. Sometimes only his heartbeat and his breathing and the scent of Fela alerted her.

His footsteps, his movements, rarely did.

His appearance in her line of sight, directly blocking her view of Vance in the doorway, was not coincidental or accidental and was nearly enough to elicit an eye roll.

Squeezing her hand, Deuce pressed them both to his bowed head in a gesture of submission, servitude, and affection. "Go. I will do as you ask…if you come back to us safely. We will be here."

"I'll be back.. And if you need to, get everyone into the Zone."

"Yes."

She met Xan's eyes across the fire. The hour was late, later than she had intended to be away, but the pups were still awake, each watching the adults about to step into the unknown in search of one of their own. It was good for them to know that their Alpha cared about them, that she would never leave any of them behind. They, like the adults, like Xan, feared for the lives of those about to depart.

"And I will bring everyone home safe. Liam included."

It was a foolish promise to make, but it was one, as she picked up her satchel, hung it over her shoulder, and fell into step beside Kato and met Vance's gaze as she left the warmth of the library, that she had every intention of keeping.

Chapter 26

The window in his room was broken, a branch from the tree outside caught in the dismembered crevices of glass, bringing with it a remembrance of what he had believed to be gunfire, the sound which had sent Nik into the night to Torben's door. He felt foolish now, that the dox-induced paranoia had led him to think he was somehow worth the expense of a rare bullet when there were easier ways, cheaper ways, to accomplish his death if that was someone's goal. A hammer, some nails, and a hemp towel left where it had fallen after his last bath would serve to block out most of the chilling wind until the window could be properly fixed.

It did not occur to him, as he pounded the first two spikes into the plaster wall, that the noise would attract the attention of anyone at this hour of the night. Donn had switched rooms, after all, to a larger suite befitting a man and his wife, and with Jonni gone, there was only Quentin who might be disturbed.

Nik gave the man no thought…until he paused to rub his thumb absently over the jagged edge of broken glass. A single knock and the door opened, and Nik, in his surprise and the lingering edges of his fright, spun to see who had come to kill him.

He had forgotten to lock the door. He expected it to be Quentin.

Never mind that a killer was unlikely to knock before entering.

The sting across his thumb and the smear of red it left on the glass were barely noticed.

“Thought you were dead too!” Donn exclaimed, barging across the room to clutch his twin against him.

“Why…because you wanted me to be?” The accusation might prompt an admission from his brother, if that thug had been sent for him, or it would lend confirmation to Nik’s belief that Torben had been assaulted protecting him from someone Quentin had sent. That was the truth Nik expected to hear.

He had to ask.

Stepping back to study his twin’s pinched, shadowed face, Donn frowned and asked, “Wanted you to be…Niki, you idiot…why would you think that? Why would I want you dead?”

Nik plopped himself into the nearest chair, legs spread before him in exaggerated relaxation, bleeding thumb shoved into his mouth. “Well, someone did…does. He was huge, Donni. Biggest shartin’ man I ever saw…eyes glowin’ purple. I swear…like those vine flowers…” His head cocked towards the window, towards the cultivated lattice growth of morning glories that had grown there all of his life.

The words were mumbled around his thumb, giving them the slurred quality that was often present during one of his highs, and he kept his eyes as wide as he could to exaggerate the rush of some substance or other. There was a note in his voice that suggested his tale could be a hallucinogenic fabrication, a product of drugs, alcohol, and his own fertile imagination.

“Purple? Niki…he was looking for you.” Donn chortled, relieved to know he had hired a man capable of doing the job he was hired for.

“I know,” Nik exclaimed, cutting him off. “He tried to beat up…he tried to kill me…so I threw him out a window and ran home.”

Squatting in front of his brother, the movement painful as his nerves responded to the evidence of his recent fight, Donn took hold of Nik’s wrist and brought his finger down to examine the cut. It was difficult to imagine Nik having the strength to throw a man the size and girth of Nepo out a window, so it was that much easier to assume that some, or most, of his twin’s words were drugged-exaggerations.

“He was there to bring you home…before you odosed again…or someone…” Donn shook his head. “Doesn’t look so bad. Could wrap it, but a little pressure ought to stop the bleeding.”

Only in that position, Donn’s face lower than Nik’s and thus catching the light of the oil lamp on the nearby end table more clearly, did Nik notice the bruises and cuts, the swollen flesh and split skin that gave evidence of a recent fight. It could have been any random fellow in the street, as Donn was known to pick fights with strangers when he was out of sorts, angry or frustrated. It could have been the small fellow Nik had passed as he entered the Fortress, although the man had not seemed injured to Nik. It could have been a fight with their father. Nik traced the swelling along the deep red and purple of Donn’s cheekbone and frowned.

Refusing to answer the questions likely to follow such notice, unless he was lucky enough for Nik’s addictions to sidetrack him, Donn muttered, “You were right, Niki. I saw it. His eyes…like you said. When you went missing…I thought he might have…that he had…so I needed someone to find you…bring you home safe.”

It was not often that a note of desperation bubbled in Donn’s voice. Normally cocky, self-assured, dominant and brutal, it was unusual for him to express concern for anyone other than himself. But Nik had been right. He knew he had been. Quentin did want to kill him. Donn knew it too and wanted to protect him.

He did not believe the purple-eyed stranger had intended to let him live. The way he had attacked Torben suggested that murder was his only interest. Maybe, Nik mused, Quentin had gotten to him too.

Or maybe his brother was lying. It would not be the first time.

“So what ya gonna do? About him?” He meant both the hunter and Quentin, maybe even their father…for surely Lowell would believe such news from Donn where he had not believed it from Nik. The Laedan needed to know the truth; Quentin needed to go.

“Dunno…I’ll make a plan…I’ll think of something.” With Nik’s face between his hands and their foreheads pressed together, he said in a strained voice. “Trust me, Niki. No one’s gonna hurt you. I’ll never let anyone do that.”

No one, Nik thought with a nod, except you. He believed his brother loved him…but he also believed that Donn was a man who would never allow something as tiresome as love and familial bonds to keep him from success.

*

The dead were accumulating in a distant corner of the dark room, soon to outnumber the living, Liam wagered, as he pulled another lifeless lump away from those who were clustered for warmth and mutual comfort. He had stopped counting both groups, not wanting to know how many were lost, how many remained, how many more he stood to lose if he did not devise a way out of this place before they froze or died of thirst or starvation.

Once the sounds of their captors were gone, he snuck into the lab and then into the corridors wanting to be certain what his senses told him was accurate. No-one stopped him, the lab doors unlocked. Not one meditool, one tube, one generator or cooling unit remained. No beds, no tables, no chairs or gurneys, no towels or baskets of dirty laundry could be found. In one cabinet, in a hastily emptied room, he found three overlooked blankets, and in the kitchen, he found a single large unopened bag of ground cornmeal and a slab of thick, salted bacon. With little water except for what remained in the tipped over collection barrels, however, and with the furnaces now grown cold, full of partially burned bodies improperly stuff into them as if to hastily dispose of evidence, there was no hope of cooking his meager finds. A folder had been left on the laboratory counter, but Liam could not read it in the dark and so left it for later perusal.

Whatever it said, it was probably not going to help them.

There were no windows to break on the ground level for escape, and most of the interior doors were open, leaving rooms for his perusal. Those interior doors that were locked he did not have the strength to break. The exterior doors were sealed, and though he rammed repeatedly against them until his shoulders were bruised and aching, they appeared to be barred from the outside.

Maybe with the aid of some of the others, when they awoke from their drug-induced slumber, their combined strength would be enough to break through. Or they could break through the internal doors that he thought blocked off stairs to an upper level and perhaps there they would find windows they could jump through. Alone, Liam was helpless to do anything more than watch each of them die.

Odds were, if they got out, it was unlikely to be by breaking out from the inside. He doubted they were left for a different transport.

They were left to perish.

By the time he returned to his charges, the first few were awake, disoriented and weak from the long disuse of muscles and internal organs. With the group huddled against the inner lab wall, he spread the blankets to cover the shoulders of those on the outer edge, an effort to keep their collective body warmth in their midst, each life benefitting the other. As each awoke, they were offered a handful of cornmeal, a morsel of bacon, and a few swallows of water from the bowl Liam brought. He did his best to explain where they were, what had happened to them, why they were here, but as he had no idea where this building was located, and what had been done with the stolen blood, he felt his efforts to reassure them were ineffectual.

How could he promise a rescue he could not know would come?

He tried, from the stories of the others brokenly related as they regained awareness and voices, to pinpoint a location, to find a pattern that might offer clues. But there were victims from LaGuardia, as he was, victims from Kennedy, victims from the Wilds, from the neutral sector, and even one from the Zone who had made the mistake of leaving it only to be quickly cornered and brought to this place. Such a widespread gleaning meant they could be consolidated anywhere. Only the fact that a few reported having been in work camps deep within HOPE territory provided any sort of detail, and it was not a promising one. For HOPE prisoners to have been transferred here had to mean they must be within HOPE's secure boundaries, for it seemed improbable that HOPE would have sent their prisoners anywhere else.

So HOPE was behind his abduction. Behind Roland's capture.

Rubbing the back of his head where he remembered the blow that felled him and left him vulnerable to capture, Liam scowled. He remembered those captors, and not one had worn HOPE insignia. Dressed and masked entirely in black, they had borne no distinctive marks. Mercenaries, perhaps, hired by HOPE to hunt anthro for this bleeding, an attempt to avoid public outrage by distancing the HOPE establishment from a hunt that could have had any number of non-anthro casualties.

The events that had led to that hunt, and those preceding Roland's abduction and the death of Liam's mother and aunt, suggested something more complex than HOPE's anti-anthrozooidic agenda.

Plasm, someone said. A drug made from the blood of anthro.

That, to Liam, seemed insane. As insane as them being trapped and left to die in an abandoned building.

Stuck in this place, he was not going to find answers.

Unless they could escape, answers were not going to matter.

"Hey…" Someone nudged him. "I think he's…"

A woman pointed. The one spoken of slumped against the wall, staring with unblinking eyes into nothing.

Liam groaned. Another lost. Weakness was picking them off, but at least the deaths were further apart now. Before long, however, that pattern was destined to reverse.

Yiva stayed with her throughout the night, refusing to leave Oasis to Donn's mercy should he return with further fury behind his fists because of whatever Lowell decided to do. There, in the private Channon sitting room, however, no one came, not Donn, not Lowell, not even a member of the staff when the distant sound of the heating generator shifting on and the slight brightening outside of the windows, announced the coming of morning. Any meal that had been served had long ago been cleared away, and soon, breakfast would replace it. On the sofa where she had curled, Yiva did not stir, did not make a sound, other than to reach in her sleep for the blanket that slid from her shoulders to hang precariously on the floor. When Oasis adjusted it, covering her and tucking it beneath the older woman's chin, Yiva muttered something and turned her face away.

She looked innocent, less world-weary and frightened in her slumber. Oasis wondered how she looked when she slept.

Though she had dozed sporadically during the night, Oasis had been unable to sleep fitfully, waiting as she had been for Lowell's return with reassurance, or for Donn to burst in, his father's blood on his hands, to kill her too. It seemed an absurd possibility that her husband could do such a thing, but over the brief course of their marriage, particularly during the last twenty-four hours, Oasis had wondered more and more if the possibility existed behind Donnovan's brittle blue eyes.

Now that it was morning, wondering if Donn had retired to their chambers, if she could speak sensibly to him if the night's rage had passed, she picked up her slippers, adjusted the blanket over Yiva once more, and crept on bare feet through the corridors to her rooms. It was a relief to find that Donn was not there, did not appear to have been there all night, but the relief did not last long or root deep. If he had come, and she had not been there, there would be retribution.

Of that, she had no doubt.

She changed her clothes, selecting with care a blouse that would cover the bruises, and again attempted to style her hair in a fashion that would hide the damage to the side of her head. The ringing in her ear had not diminished and she realized last night, as she and Yiva talked, that she needed to keep her head turned in order to hear properly. It was a troublesome inconvenience, one she was going to have a difficult time masking, but she was determined to do her best, to not bring any strain or shame upon the name of Channon she now bore. And after pausing with her hand on her belly, reminding herself of the other promise she had made, she reentered the corridor, shoulders drawn back with dignity and grace despite the strain that put on her bruised abdomen, and decided to seek out her husband.

She took a few steps down the hall, in the direction of Donn's private office where she had been forbidden to go, where she expected him to be since he had not been in their bedroom and had not come looking for her, but was stopped by a strangled sound of pain behind a partially open door. It was open just a crack, as if the effort to close it had failed and left it ajar, or the person behind it had not wanted to announce themselves with the clicking the latch would make, but the noises within, the clink of metal against metal, the sloshing of water, and another groan were unmistakable.

She should not go inside. If she did, if Donn found her there, last night's brutal episode would seem like a mild game. But curiosity prompted her to push the door open further. The hinges did not squeak, the edged did not rub on the floor or the frame as some doors in the Fortress did, but still, the man inside looked at her, having heard her breathing, perhaps, or her heartbeat.

Maybe the change in light from the corridor announced her arrival.

He could not hide the discolored splotches across his chest that announced broken ribs, nor hide the cuts and gashes on his arms, neck, torso, and face. His hand in a metal bowl of water, clutching the cloth with which he was washing away blood, rested now, the echo of his signet ring against the side silent. On the floor at his feet, torn, bloody clothes lay jumbled, and the strips of gauze he intended to wrap around his body to protect his ribs hung over the seat of the nearest chair.

But just as he could not hide his injuries, nor the labored achiness of his movements, Oasis could not hide hers from him, even though they were covered with clothes and hair. Thom scowled, shuffled his feet as if he would come to her, but he instead resumed what he had been doing, refusing to look at her.

"You should not be here."

"Neither should you." She meant what she said. After what Donn had done to her…and to Thom because of her, with suspicion hanging over him for the deaths of Jonni and Roland, his continued residence in the Fortress was begging for an unpleasant, ill-fated end. She might not feel for him as she once had, but she did not want to see him dead.

He fumbled with the wrappings, winced and choked on his pain as he tried to catch them, and then struggled to pick them up from the floor. Oasis entered to do it for him, leaving the door wide open so that anyone passing would see that there was nothing inappropriate happening in the room. Thom grunted, tried to swat her hands away and take the wrappings, but she muttered, "Stop it. Hush," and proceeded to wrap the strips to pad his fractured ribs.

Her nearness gave him a better view of the bruises on her cheek, jaw, and ear. "He did that." It was a question, although it was one he had not intended to ask aloud, but it came out as an acknowledgment of the sort of man Donn Channon was. Recalling their brief exchange last night, he guessed that Donn had seen him leaning near to Oasis' ear to utter what had been a warning to stay away if she was going to seek him out every time Donn had a suspicion or a question. The gesture had been misinterpreted, and now, seeing what Channon had done to his bride, Thom had a change of heart.

Maybe her coming to him was not at her husband's bidding after all…else there would be no reason for him to lash out at Oasis and then at Thom after seeing them together.

Maybe, he mused with a quick glance into her eyes, her concern, her questions, were sincere and meant out of worry for him.

He regretted the harshness with which he had treated her.

"And he did this." There was no doubt about it, not after the way Donn had charged away from her in search of Thom. If this had been Lowell's doing for any reason, Oasis doubted Thom would be here.

He would be dead.

"You should go…before something worse…"

"There's no proof of anything they think I might have done. No one knows anything but you." He studied her fondly, pondering whether she would betray him, and though he nearly touched her cheek with gentle fingers, his hand fell before contact was made.

After what Donn had done, the woman he had known in Kennedy would not endure it. If she betrayed anyone, it would be Donn.

"Donn does not need proof. He only needs suspicion…and he has that already." Unlike Lowell, Donn did not need tangible evidence to act. He acted on blind rage and suspicious instinct. Why else would he easily believe the Marrocks to be anthro, when Lowell had continued to resist that possibility, despite any suspicion, until the end?

"I'm not going to run away like a beaten dog," Thom snarled. "I'm not going to substantiate their misgivings by…"

"Not even if I could tell you how to get to Fort Hamilton?"

Tirade cut short, he caught her wrist and glowered at her. "What do you know about Fort Hamilton?" Perhaps Donn had made mention of that place, or she had overheard him talking, seen some document or book he had carelessly left open. Thom had never spoken of that place with her, so her knowing his interest in it was suspect.

Or maybe she had guessed it would be the sort of information he would be interested in.

"I've seen Lowell's map…"

"That map was stolen by…"

"He has it." Thom was suspicious, but he also sounded betrayed and worried and she wondered why. "I can't get it for you…but I've seen it…and though I can't make a detailed one…I can draw a rough map for you…if you will leave here and be safe."

She did not know what resources Thom had, but she knew him. He had been in LaGuardia long enough to make friends, make contacts, accumulate supporters and formulate plans, plans that hinged on that map the same way Lowell's did. Lowell had the map, had the greater resources, but also had greater responsibilities that tied him to the Fortress. If the two matched forces out there, in the ruined borough streets, the odds were against Thom's success. She would regret his death, if it came to that, but it would be one less complication for her to overcome. And if he succeeded over Lowell, over Donn, it would be her assistance that would enable it, her giving him the map he needed that opened the doorway for him. Her hand in his success and her perceived support would win her security.

If she could convince Thom to take this step, the way she knew Lowell would soon, there was only one more move on the game board to make. A trickier one, but one she was determined to see through to the end if she was to make sure that she and Yiva and Lowell's positions in LaGuardia were safe and secure.

Manipulating Donn, while remaining in his good graces, would not be easy.

"Then draw it for me."

She chuckled and stepped away from him now that the bindings were tight enough. "Not here…not now." She tilted her head towards the open door. "I'll leave it for you…in your box…if you promise you'll get away from here before they learn the truth."

Thom snorted again. No one would learn the truth. With Nik gone and only Oasis having an inkling of what the truth really was, he felt safe enough to remain in the Fortress.

Whatever Donn thought he had seen during their fight could be attributed to a trick of the lighting.

Should he face Donn again, however, his safety would be at risk.

"I'll consider it."

Oasis shrugged. She could not make him do anything he did not want to do. She could only open this door and give him direction to pass through it.

Maybe he should take her warnings, this fight with Donn and the possibility that Lowell could, at any time, connect Donn's rambling about yellow eyes to those Nik had made, more seriously than he had.

Or maybe Thom was worrying for nothing.

☙*❧

The nag he had stolen balked at the sound of every barking dog, every shouting voice, and every loud noise they passed, so that Nepo regretted his choice of steeds within the first few streets he traveled. But the sway-backed brown mare, likely a cart puller rather than a riding horse, was the first such animal he found, and with the aches and injuries left from the fight and the fall from the Ursa's apartment, if he was to make it south in a reasonable amount of time, he had to find some form of transportation other than his feet. The horse might not get him there faster than his normal walking pace, but at least it would get him there and he could rest and recover in the meantime. Without it, he would have to wait until he recovered from his injuries.

Waiting was futile if he wanted to be paid sooner rather than later.

He knew the Channon kid had returned to the Fortress none the worse for his adventures. Maybe Nepo had not delivered him, maybe he would have to answer for roughing up the sposer he believed had been holding Nik against his will with ulterior motives, but all he had to do was show himself to Nik to prove that he was the one who had prompted the young man to run for the safety of home. A little spin on the story and Nepo felt confident Donn would pay him as promised.

One way or the other, Donn would pay him.

The other duty was more complicated and required a trip into the southern borough where he had not traveled in a long time. If the sole clue Channon had given him was true, Kennedy was the place to start in search of answers.

It would be damn amusing to see Hallister's face one more time.

Chapter 27

The night-long sojourn south through the quiet streets was uneventful save for the sightings of a lone Fela on a hunt, a trio of scavs going about their business beneath the cover of darkness, and an unfamiliar Ursa perched atop a building watching the streets she could monitor from above. As this was the path they had taken on their journey to the library, streets they had traveled to enter the Wilds, streets they had hunted, where Roland had often passed, they were familiar enough to avoid most pitfalls of collapsed structures and other blockages that might slow their progress. Jia stopped the group as they neared the intersection where she and Kato had first met, where she and her pack had stood their ground against pursuers who intended to subject them to the horrors Roland had experienced, or worse, and those that Liam must surely be facing if he lived.

Jia clung to hope that he did. She refused to consider any outcome other than his survival and rescue. She needed her best friend at her side where he had been all of their lives. She needed him to be okay.

Her concern at the intersection, as the Cana and Fela conducted a sweep of the surrounding buildings and Vance, lacking the ability to shift, strode cautiously into the center, the gun Ernest had provided him drawn should he need it, his Protector blade in his other hand, was that the encounter here had prompted hunters to patrol the area. Whoever they had been, HOPE, Laedan Guard, street rabble or guerillas, they had taken their dead from this remote, unincorporated region and might have left a patrol stationed here to catch them, should the Pack's path home lead them back.

That the mage promised the area was empty of threats, that he squatted at the center of the intersection, fingers splayed on the buckling, cracked pavement with his head bowed but cocked to one side as if listening for something, smelling for something intangible, should have been reassuring. She trusted him more than she should, perhaps, given the short time of their acquaintance, but she did not trust anyone enough to put the lives of all of those with her at risk.

Even if he risked his own life by exposing himself in that unprotected intersection with his weapons holstered now, in the end, she could only rely on her own decisions and senses. Should anything go wrong, she had only herself to blame.

The opportunity for extended investigation allowed a few minutes of rest, allowed a drink from fresh rainwater pooled in abandoned, manmade depressions around the area, to settle nerves that grew more on edge the further from the library they traveled. No one spoke, the direction to circle the intersection was given with silent gestures and looks that were easily understood, but now that they had shifted back to their Normal forms, they dressed and came together at the place where Vance still squatted in the street.

Travel in Cana and Fela true form, or even hybrid would be faster. Out of deference to their tracker-guide, however, they elected to walk as Normals.

"Anything?"

Vance glanced at Jia, the aura of Cana strong about her after the recent shift, reminding him of a time not so long ago when he had first met her, when he had found her presence, especially that part of her, to be both daunting and alluring. Odd, he thought, that he felt at ease in her company now, the necessary pressures of this mission forcing a trust he rarely extended to others. Even knowing she could tear him to pieces if she chose no longer filled him with trepidation.

This was the closest he had worked with anthro. He was satisfied to learn they were not as fearsome as popular mythos claimed.

At least, he mused as he took her hand in his good hand and used it as leverage to stand, those of the Flushing Pack were not. Not to him. Not anymore.

"It's been clear for days."

There had been traffic through here, travelers, scavs, but no one to trouble or hinder them. Whoever the hunters had been, they had collected their dead and returned to wherever they called home.

Kato, the last to rejoin the group, still in full Fela form, circled them, ears flat, lips curled in a snarl, less inclined to be polite and tolerating in this guise than in his Normal form. Vance refused to acknowledge the threat, keeping his attention instead on the road in the direction they traveled. Only when he released Jia's hand, steady on his feet now, to push his hair out of his face, wincing at the pain in his shoulder in the process, and Jia absently placed her hand on the Fela's side, did the snarl subside and Kato's feline ears prick forward.

"Which way now?" asked Xen, readjusting her pack and drawing her knife from her belt. Unlike the others, she had kept her weapon in hand the entire journey thus far, her gaze continuously shifting towards the mage she did not fully trust. She might have come to accept Jia as Alpha, had promised to follow and obey her on this mission, but those feelings of confidence did not extend to the tracker-mage Jia was willing to entrust the Pack's future, and Liam's, to.

"The Bunker."

Jia and Addi exchanged a look at Vance's suggestion and Addi nodded. The Bunker had been the last place Addi had seen their father alive, and if Roland's trail backward, to the place of his incarceration, could be traced, it would be easier for the mage to begin doing so from there. He did not know how tracker magic worked, but he had seen Vance touch objects and people and produce an insight or impression or clue from that contact. Returning to the place where Roland had lain, where he had fallen in the street when they found each other again, was a logical thing to do.

It would also be an adequate place to shelter and rest for the coming daylight hours, with food still stashed there that Addi had been unable to stuff in his packs, and water available from where it fell from the roof after every rain. They had been clear of precipitation thus far, and the chill in the air suggested the possibility of snow rather than rain. The heaviness of the air suggested they might not remain so lucky, but perhaps it would fall while they slept and by evening the air might be clear of falling moisture again.

Besides, judging from the injuries Roland had sported, wherever he had come from could not be that far from the shelter of the Bunker. That too made it the ideal first destination.

"Into the borough?" Helena asked with concern. They had not said that was where the Bunker was, but she could guess that from their shared looks. She had never been in LaGuardia, but she had heard the talk amongst the Flushing Pack, knew the difficulties they had faced there, how forces in the borough had cost them their Alpha, how they had been hunted, chased from their den, made unwelcome in the borough they once called home.

"Briefly…but the Bunker is safe. It's ours, more secure for today then crossing south into unknown…"

"Not unknown to me."

Willing to hear other options if they were viable ones, loath to dismiss ideas that might bring her closer to Liam, Jia asked, "Do you know a place? Somewhere to rest without risk of attack or discovery?"

As she spoke, Kato slipped away from the group.

Several moments of reluctant silence later, Helena shook her head. "There was…our den…but…" But after the way her pack had been hunted, she could not say it was a safe location any longer. She was familiar with the neutral sector, and with the unincorporated streets due west of it, even with some of Kennedy's northernmost streets, but in wild regions without structured law, it was impossible to know what other Cana might have laid claim to any of the havens she had once known. In the time she had been away, in the time since the Flushing Pack's absence from southern LaGuardia and the new marriage alliance between Channons and Hallisters, there was also no certain way of knowing what changes might have been wrought in the streets that had once served as a neutral border between boroughs.

Somewhere familiar in security, at least familiar to some of them, would be best, and by the time Kato returned, dressed, his wild mane of hair tied back from his face and neck and his pack hanging from one shoulder, those with Jia had relented to her decision.

It was a decision Vance accepted with a nod, grateful that his suggestion was appropriate. That place where Roland's blood stained the crumbling pavement would provide an ideal window, combined with the plasm in his bag, to the path that awaited them. Returning to LaGuardia with Jia felt like going back to the beginning.

It was where they needed to start.

Every Fortress staff member was awakened during the course of the night, in whatever order Lowell was able to find them or thought to question them, and though they resented the disturbance, they dutifully answered the Laedan's anxious, demanding questions. The day Nik had last spoken to him, three days ago…four…was the last anyone could definitively claim to have seen the now oldest Channon son, when the young man had barged through the front gates into LaGuardia's streets with a harried look on his face. Though he had seemed distraught in his flight, those at gate duty, those he passed who were the last to see him, thought nothing more of the moment beyond the acknowledgment of a known addict leaving in an apparent search for indulgence. Despite Lowell's desire to remain furious, how could he when it might have been his refusal to listen to Nik's concerns and fears that had prompted yet another quest for chemical acceptance.

In the end, weren't his son's addictions on his father's shoulders?

That none had witnessed his return was more worrisome than his departure, but with so many of the Laedan Guards still combing the streets for Jia and the Fela said to have murdered Roland and Jonni, there was little Lowell could do to contribute. He had no idea where Nik went outside of the Fortress. He had no idea who he knew, who he considered friends, what he did other than imbibe and indulge his blood's hunger.

He made sure that those Guards not currently on watch, not currently seeking the murderer, knew to keep their eyes open for his son, that they would instruct the rest of their ranks to do the same, but beyond that, his hands felt tied behind his back.

He could not search LaGuardia himself. He had no inkling where a search should begin. If Roland were here, he would know. Or Jonni.

But neither was able to do so any longer.

Perhaps Donn might know, but after that volatile conflict between them the night before, Donn had remained out of Lowell's path. The questions Donn had raised, the implications he planted about Oasis, about Quentin, had lodged like thorns in Lowell's breast, festering.

Lowell could not find either of them. Both Donn and Thom were in the Fortress, Lowell was sure of it, but in his circles of the complex, it was easy to pass without any effort to actually avoid one another.

It was just as easy to miss that his wayward child had returned home during the course of the night spent looking for him. When dawn brought the news from another staff member that Nik was sprawled, snoring, in his own bed, found there when she went to gather the previous day and night's dirty clothing, Lowell breathed a heavy-hearted sigh of relief. That relief was not complete, however, until he saw the back of Nik's blonde head on his pillows for himself, until he watched the gentle rise and steady fall of the young man's ribs for several minutes to assure himself that his son lived. Drunken, drug-induced stupor or no, Nik was home. He was alive.

It was one less thing to worry about. His other son, however, Oasis, and Thom Quentin, were matters he would confront after breakfast and a stiff, rousing, sobering drink.

He was sure he would need that drink to get through his day.

The bodies of the grubbers in the street had been removed long ago, as Vance had imagined they would be. The people living nearest the bunker would have either burned the bodies themselves or would have alerted the nearest Protectorate office, or the nearest sposers, so that the dead could be dealt with in an expedient manner. The dead, be they grubbers or not, attracted additional grubbers, attracted rats and flies and other scavengers, creating unsafe, unhealthy conditions in an already unsafe, unhealthy world. The grubbers would have been removed to a plant for processing as quickly upon discovery as could be arranged. Their absence, and the absence of the sound of them shuffling inside the bunker or other nearby buildings, was no surprise.

What was a surprise was finding an unfamiliar cluster of Fela hunkered in the structure the Flushing Pack had carefully marked as theirs. The invasion of their Bunker made the Marrock twins growl as they, and those with them, fanned out to watch the most immediate entranceways in the hopes of drawing out, and chasing away, the trespassers. The group was small, five individuals Jia could detect, young and frightened, but their fright was not her concern. They knew they were in marked territory and yet had chosen to squat there.

She wanted them out.

The sun was rising. Her companions were as weary as she was. They needed the Bunker's shelter, strangers be damned. She called her group back to her when they were satisfied that five was all there were, and in a decided show of force and solidarity, they approached the mangled gate of the once barricaded entry together.

A young male stepped into the street to meet them, their scent on the morning air announcing their presence to those inside. His shoulders were drawn back in a stance of defiance, but he was barely older than Wist, barely past the age of maturity, though that did not detract from his bravado. His skin was browned, either naturally or from too much exposure to the weak, cloud-hidden sun, his brown hair streaked with pale blonde, his eyes a bright, royal blue that stood out in stark contrast to his regal features.

"Leave us," he shouted, his sure-footed stance that of a man prepared to face conflict. "This isn't your place. We claim this as sanctuary."

A claim of sanctuary meant someone among them was injured. Jia sniffed the air again, but from where she stood, there were too many morning smells to pick out what sort of trouble the Fela were in. With a hand gesture directing the others to remain behind her, though she knew Vance was prepared to pull Protector's rank to evict the strangers if necessary, she took several careful steps forward, directly into the flow of the early dawn breeze that would carry her scent, the Marrock scent, to the young man they faced. He would match her scent to the markings within the Barracks. He would know who she was.

"Are you sure of that?"

The question was spoken in a friendly, diplomatic tone, as she had no interest in conflict or confrontation given what lay ahead for herself and those with her. She, Kato, and Vance were recuperating from a variety of injuries and needed to save their strength as much as possible for any battles to come. This matter was but an inconvenience that could be handled without violence if the intruding Fela were willing to listen to reason.

But the stranger's reaction to the perceived derision was a growl. "You weren't here…it's ours now."

"You thank that is how Cana territory works?" Obviously young, he likely had little experience with Cana and their territorial ways. Or perhaps ownership worked differently amongst anthro where he was from. Behind him, three equally young faces, all female, peered through the grate behind the automotive skeleton Deuce had pushed into place when they had been here last.

The Fela Jia had met before rarely congregated together A family, she guessed, perhaps a rare pride of which her father had sometimes spoken. As Fela rather than Cana, there was no actual seizure of Pack territory, unless they refused to give Jia and those with her the right of way, only an empty shelter found when the cluster of Fela was in need.

There was no reason they could not share the vast space for the length of a day.

She was further determined to negotiate now that she saw the four young siblings. Sharing the shelter was acceptable…if she could convince them of the same.

Defensively, the boy growled again, fear bleeding around the edges of his bluster. With one other deeper inside the building, one who did not come forward, he knew his family was outmatched but he was determined to fight for this shelter rather than move to another. The thought of sharing it seemed not to have crossed his mind. If not for the supplies stashed within, and the need to get Vance to the last place Roland had lain, Jia might have considered another shelter too.

But they needed this one.

"Let me," Addi whispered, his hand on her elbow distracting her from the Fela's challenging growl and aggressive step forward. The boy seemed reluctant, however, to move far from the narrow entrance that would take him back to the girls and whoever was inside, if the Cana chose to attack.

Jia nodded at her brother.

Addi took a step closer to greet him, the least threatening looking member of their group, his hands open innocently.

"The other with you? Is injured, yes?"

Jia had detected the scent of Fela blood in the air by now, stale but fresh enough to be recent. It could have been from any number of nearby sources, given the current of the breeze, including a reopening of Kato's wounds, but Kato, his interest peaked by the largest group of Fela he had ever encountered, showed no indication of being in pain. Jia decided to trust her brother.

Maybe he was right.

"I'm a doctor, see?" He slowly pulled a roll of gauze from his bag, hesitating when the Fela snarled and growled as if expecting a weapon to be taken out. The young man crouched, body tensed and coiled to leap, and the women behind him growled in warning too.

A quick glance from the boy outside silenced them.

He studied the object in Addi's hand but did not yet speak.

"May I?" asked Kato, for once not pushing into action when he might have already taken this matter into his own hands. He was even less familiar with other Fela then Jia, solitary as he was, limited in close relationships to Vanya, their mother, and now the Flushing Pack. But he was Fela, and that, perhaps, might be enough to prompt the younger man to trust him.

Again Jia nodded. Letting one Fela reach out to another was worth a try, since nothing else was working and they were wasting time.

"We're here to rest for the day…on our hunt to find blood scavs."

The young Fela looked back at the women who muttered amongst themselves with notes of panic in their voices. Kato, not making direct eye contact with the man in his low bodied, casual approach, uttered a single, feline sound, almost a rumbling purr, before he continued. "We need to rest here…want to help you…and then be on our way. There's no reason we can't share this place…is there? We'll be safer, stronger, together. Let Addi help…let us pass…" His head tilted in deference to the Alpha Cana on whose behalf he spoke, aware that she might interpret his words as giving away the Bunker though it was not his intention, "and then we'll leave you to it come nightfall."

He did not know the importance of the Bunker to Jia or the Pack, beyond it being claimed territory, but he wagered that rescuing Liam was worth the loss of the building, particularly if they had no intention of living within LaGuardia's borders again. If his guess was wrong, he would hear about it later, while the companions took their rest.

"Beren…let them in."

The distant voice was weak, small and reedy, but carried enough weight with the youngster that though he bristled, the one called Beren stepped aside in reluctant obedience. Addi was the first through the curled back grate, medical bag in hand, with both Xen and Wist close behind to protect their medic should the invitation be a trap. Helena followed as Beren and Kato stood face to face, slightly off-sided, as though sizing each other up in a cautious but non-threatening manner. Jia would have preferred to be the last through the door, but from the posture of the Fela, she determined at this moment that last was not her place and so, after ushering Vance in before her, trusting he would pick up threats as quickly as she would, she entered the Bunker.

In the distance, a pair of roosters crowed nearly in tandem.

Against the frame of the car where grubbers had kept Addi pinned as he waited for Jia, Kato and the mage to join him the last time he was here, an older woman with the same light streaked hair as the four younger ones slumped weakly, her belly packed with every form of absorbent material the pride had been able to find. It was not enough, however, to stop the bleeding, and when Addi knelt next to her, drawing back the packing to examine the damage after her permissive nod, he frowned.

A grubber's bite, he deduced, and while anthro were believed to be immune to the transforming effect of the grubber disease, they were not immune to the infection often present in the bite of one of those decaying, rotting things. The mottled skin surrounding the putrid yellow edges of the bite was a sure sign of sepsis, and given the location of the wound, with the outer flesh torn away to expose the more delicate tissue and organs beneath, there was nothing Addi could do to save the woman's life.

There was always a chance, when the bite was to a limb, that amputation and a liberal dousing of alcohol might keep the infection from spreading if carried out swiftly after the attack. A bite to the torso, however, meant it was only a matter of time before the vital organs succumbed to the viral onslaught and shut down. Judging by the appearance of the wound, shc had suffered with it for at least a day.

This woman, no anthro herself judging by the scent of her blood, already knew her fate. Her concern, when she looked past Addi to her children, was for their safety when confronting what she was destined to become…and what would become of them afterward.

"What happened?" Addi murmured, drawing out the flask of alcohol he carried, filling the tall cap and pressing it to her lips.

So long as her infected blood did not come in contact with the cap, there would be no danger to anyone else drinking from it. Alcohol was one of the few things that seemed to counteract the grubber's poison.

"Running from hunters…" she rasped, grimacing with the alcohol burn, but as it distracted her from the wracking pain throughout her body, it was a welcome burn. She sounded sleepy, disoriented, and Addi guessed it was a matter of hours or less before she succumbed to her injury. "Escaped…into…Beneath…"

"Were there for days," mumbled one of the young women sadly.

"Might not have been days," corrected one of the others in the tone of an older sibling correcting an exaggerating younger one.

Beren shrugged. "Long enough. They got Fa…but we…" he shrugged again as if he did not care, as if he was stronger than he sounded. "Tried to get past some Unders…and it was there…the legless grubber…floating in the muck. Got her up here…"

But it was a battle against a death they could not win despite the fight they had previously survived. Since their clothing was dry, it had been some time, a day, perhaps more, since their escape from Beneath and coming up into this place via the same entry point the grubbers had flooded from before to trap Addi in this same rusted vehicle.

The third girl, the oldest, her belly swollen as if with child, asked, "Do you have anything to eat? It's been a long time…" She was embarrassed to ask, but the Fela group did not look well equipped.

Helena squatted, set her bag between her feet, and was the first to offer the food she carried for them to distribute amongst themselves. If what Addi and Jia said was true, there was food hidden in this place she could use to replace hers. These four were not Cana, but they were people, and having been where this family was not long ago, on the run, hungry and desperate to survive, she sympathized with their misfortune and the loss of their family.

"You said hunters?" It was the first time Vance had spoken since meeting the Fela, as this was a matter between anthro that he did not want to intrude upon. Hunters, however, were a concern for all of them, and wherever these people had entered the Below, if there were hunters there, it might be near enough to the destination he and his companions sought to be noteworthy.

At least he preferred to know who he might be up against.

"HOPE." The dying woman lapsed into silence, her eyes closed though her chest continued to rise and fall in a quick, shallow rhythm.

Vance scowled as he and his companions exchanged looks. HOPE's involvement was an expected possibility. Who else would have the resources to capture so many anthro, extract and process their blood to create a dangerous drug, and then distribute it widely through the boroughs? If they were forced to travel in HOPE's territory, what chance did they have of success?

"Where were you? Before?"

Staring at the man who, without his Protector coat announcing his status and with no trace of anthro in his scent, was just a Normal somehow caught up with this Cana group…in the same way the lone Fela among them was, the same way his mother was, Beren hesitated before replying, his skin prickling in a warning that Vance sensed. Beren might not know what Vance was, that a tracker was in their midst, but he detected a possible threat and approached Vance accordingly, sniffing the air as he circled, seeking some clue as to what that dangerous difference might be.

Each moment without answers sent prickles up and down the Fela's skin as his anxiety grew, and Vance resisted the temptation to look to Jia or anyone else for help. Refusing to give in to the fears he had initially experienced in the Alpha Cana's company, remembering how well, overall, that meeting had gone, he fought to keep his breathing calm and waited for answers.

When he thought Beren might spring at Vance, clamp his jaws around the back of his neck, Kato was there, a shield that Beren, in his youthful inexperience, still knew better than to challenge.

"The mage is with us."

The three young women growled in anxious discomfort and drew together, shoulder to shoulder, to protect one another. Beren drew backward in a crouching posture that would have shown ears flattened to his head if he were in Fela or hybrid form.

Their mother neither moved nor woke.

Mage meant one of two things, healer or tracker. Visually, it was not possible to tell which, thus making it difficult to determine how much of a threat he was. Mages were rare, healers rarer still, but that rarity did not automatically mean Vance was a tracker. Jia, not wanting to chance a dangerous decision, stepped into an identical protective position next to Kato to defend Vance, catching his uninjured hand in hers and holding it tight. "We need him to find the ones who are taking anthro…who've taken a friend…who steal our blood and turn it into…"

"They make plasm from Cana," Beren snipped defensively, unwilling to consider that his father had been taken for this same purpose. "Not from Fela…not from…mages."

Vance cleared his throat. "Primarily, yes. But it can be taken from any anthro. Cana happen to be the most abundant." And the easiest to find, as they moved in groups and thus did not blend into society as readily as solitary Fela and Ursa could. Beren's family had either stood out as a pride in some way to the hunters who had sought them, or else they had been outed by neighbors.

"They took my best friend…and we are going to find him," repeated Jia, "get him back."

"How can you…?"

"With Mage Segara…"

"With this," Vance said simultaneously, producing the small pouch of yellow powder from his satchel. No one could see what was in it, but they could smell the taint of copper, of old blood.

"Is that…?"

The question from whichever sister voiced it sounded aghast and offended that the mage dared to bring that substance into their midst.

"It could be one of our…"

"Someone died for that…"

Vance closed his fist around the pouch when Wist tried to snatch it from him. "And a lot more will die if we don't find where this came from…if we don't try to stop it…"

"You're only seven," grunted Beren "You'll never…"

"We will," Jia said, emphasizing her words, "get my friend back. We will shut down the facility where he's being held."

How many other facilities there were, where they were, how they could be thwarted, was a formidable step to consider later.

Vance shrugged, moving away from their protection to the place where Roland had rested, had bled, where he might have died that night without the aid of his son. "Even if there are more than one, even if we don't stop them all ourselves…we can expose them, what they're doing…to the Laedans, to the public."

Yes, he thought bitterly, sitting cross-legged on the still dark red stain Roland had left, there would always be those daring enough to seek some sort of answer, medicinal or recreational or fantastical, in the blood of anthrozooids. Normals had been utilizing the skin, the bones the meat, the organs, the blood, of anthro and mutani in search of their own betterment since the Undoing brought the three sub-races into being, just as mankind had once used parts of any number of beasts for their health, for decoration, for impossibly mythological purposes and possibilities for which they were never intended.

But it was his hope that the underlying fears of most, who worried that such exposure might somehow turn them into something else, would be enough to halt the sale and trade of this insidious drug. If he could be a small part of the solution in ending production of this substance, Vance would have done something worth dying for.

Drawing his Protector's blade, the sharpest instrument he had, he then unwrapped the bandaging of his injured hand. Jia scowled.

"What are you doing?"

"When you came to the Protectorate…when we started off to find your father…this," he took the pouch, "was in my blood. Not a lot; I'd held Nik Channon's broken syringe and gotten some in that way…but it was enough to show what I needed to…"

"You're expecting it will show the way…that it was made in the same lab?" Addi scowled too.

"Can't be many of them; the power…the equipment needed to manufacture…it must take a lot of resources. And if it matches what I remember…what I read here…" His eyes fluttered closed as he pressed the fingertips of his injured hand to the blood-shadowed concrete and was quiet for many moments, knowing he was now revealed as a tracker rather than a healer. "If it matches," he whispered, "I'll know the way."

"And if it doesn't?" murmured Helena.

"We'll…you'll…" Vance nodded at Jia, "decide what to do then."

He dragged the tip of the blade across his thumb, producing a thin line of red that dripped onto his trousers. The bag of powder had already been drawn open.

"You'll be okay? This won't…harm you?"

Vance shrugged. "I don't know. Only done this once…" and that was accidental. He was lucky he had not died or odosed. "But there's no other way…no better way. After I put my hand back to the floor…"

he glanced where his hand had been, where he had touched Roland's blood. "And I'll still have this."

From his pocket, with his other hand, he produced the one item he had carried with him since the night they found Roland alive.

The keycard.

If he was fortunate, when they found where they needed to be, that card would allow them the access they needed to get Liam free.

At least it might serve as an additional map to their destination.

"Isn't that enough?"

"The more I have…the more I see…the clearer the path. Just don't let me die," he chuckled darkly, "if you can help it."

"Vance…"

It was too late for words. He had already thrust his bleeding thumb into the pouch of yellow powder. There was a jolt that knocked him back as the drug took hold and the images, the whirling, throbbing, pulsing crimson sensations engulfed him again. They were familiar this time, the deafening thunder of the multitude of heartbeats struggling to cling to lives stolen to produce the contents of this pouch. The whirring, spinning that separated elements, peeling some away, left others to tingle and burn as they raced through every blood path in his body, into his heart, into his lungs, into his brain. Splashes of color, reds and yellows, blues and purples, colors that wound around his organs to tighten and suck away the things a man needed to live.

"He's odosing!" Not knowing how being a mage worked, beyond what little Jia had witnessed thus far, the rigid convulsing of his body as he dropped back against the hard floor looked to be a bad thing, a dangerous thing. Addi shoved his pack beneath the man's head to keep him from repeatedly hitting against the ground and checked the pulse points at the side of Vance's neck and inner wrist.

He shook his head in answer to Jia's exclamation.

"I don't think so. His pulse is elevated, but not dangerously so. He's breathing fast…but again, not too fast. And he is breathing. Besides…" He closed the pouch of powder, tucked it away for safekeeping while considering if it was too soon to destroy it or if Vance might need it again, and removed the knife from Vance's reach.

He wiped the rest of the blood and yellow dust from the mage's thumb, trusting that what was in his bloodstream already was enough. "He could not have gotten much that way…not like he'd injected or ingested it. Not enough there to…"

Unless the plasm was laced with some other substance, something strong, pure, and deadly. But Addi did not have the equipment to analyze the pouch's content or Vance's blood. He had to trust that his assessment was accurate, had to believe the mage knew what he was doing and was in no danger.

Without Vance, they might never find Liam and Jia would never forgive herself.

"I'll watch him," Addi promised, squeezing his sister's hand. Given the condition of both patients in the Bunker, he could easily watch both. He could treat Vance's hand and shoulder while they waited and do his best to make his patients comfortable. "We're here until nightfall…might as well eat…rest…"

"What if he's not…?" Unable to finish her question, Jia sat cross-legged beside the mage, brushing his hair from his sweating forehead, nestling her satchel between her legs and clutching it tightly, the other hand resting light upon Vance's chest.

"Let's not invite trouble where there isn't any," murmured Kato, bending to kiss the top of her head the way he did with Vanya when she was restless and troubled. "He'll be okay." Whatever his feelings were about Segara, he knew the tracker was crucial to their success.

Face uptilted, Jia nuzzled Kato's chin, needing his support as much as she did Addi's. But her hand did not leave the rise and fall of Vance's chest. So much, it seemed, he was risking for her when she had done nothing to deserve it.

When he awoke, if he awoke, after the long hours of daylight ahead of them, she intended to find out why.

Chapter 28

She had never been to the Protectorate alone. Indeed, Yiva had not gone anywhere outside of LaGuardia's Fortress alone since the day of her marriage. Even in the days before that, as the sheltered only child of the prominent Trover family, she had been pampered and well protected, always in the company of servants and the girl brought in at an early age to be her constant friend and companion.

It had been unfortunate for the girl's family, for the girl, and for Yiva, that she was discovered to be Ursa some six years later.

Yiva had no idea what had become of the girl; she only knew she had spent the rest of her childhood alone except for the children of her family's servants. Always guarded, always attended and provided for, but alone nonetheless.

It had been a great boon for her and her family when Lowell's interest was made known, and an even greater fortune for them when the accepted proposal of marriage resulted in one of the longest marriages in her family's history.

The Trovers were granted land for additional hemp production, all of which passed into Channon hands when her parents died, but they had lived a life of additional luxury for all of their final days.

Yiva felt she had done something good for her family by agreeing to that marriage.

And how blessed she was, despite the loss of four children never born, to have produced three healthy Channon heirs.

She spoke to no one about the loss of her eldest boy. Her pain was a private thing, locked deep in her heart as so many other things had been since her childhood friend was taken away. Her worry for Nik came out often to her middle son, small comments and gestures made now and then intended to give him something, anything, that he could cling to as a line to pull him out of his life of addiction. She did not have the strength to do more, not any longer, and since she, like her husband, believed Nik's suffering to be the parents' doing, how could she ever hope to undo it?

He had been such a delightful child…and then the most difficult. Not his fault. Not hers either. Her fault had been in guessing at the truth and refusing to accept it, agreeing instead to treatment after treatment Lowell suggested, treatments meant to help Nik sleep like a normal child. It had either been that or risk having Lowell reject their son for the truth and send him away to the Zone where she would never see him again.

All because he would not sleep.

Nik was not like those others. What was a little sleep deprivation and insomnia compared to visible, physical defects that marked mutani as different…unwanted…not like everyone else?

And Donn?

She sighed, staring at the tall, double doors in front of her. Though born of her blood and her body, he had stopped being her son. She did not care if she never saw him again.

In the secret places of her heart, she wished it was Donn beneath the garden tree and not Jonni.

How cold was it for a mother to wish her child dead and gone?

That apathy and loathing had led her here today, the end of her rope finally reached. Perhaps she could not protect herself, but she could try to protect Oasis.

But Chief Ernest was no fool, and admitting anything so personal to the family was opening herself up for revelations she had fought to hide for years, from Lowell and from herself. If she did this, the consequences for her husband were almost as equally horrifying to consider. What if he hurt her? Killed her? Or worse, what if he sent her away? Where would she go? How would she survive? Without family, knowing so few outside of the Fortress except for her husband's allies who would never look at her the same, how would she endure outside of the only life she knew?

It had taken her most of the day to build up the courage to come this far. The dinner hour was not so far away now, and her relief at knowing Nik was home, safe according to the servant who had informed her of the news, prompted Yiva to want to share a meal with the only decent, civilized child she had left. He was troubled, yes, but he was a good boy. She wanted him to know that, if he remembered nothing else about her after this day was done.

Now she had nearly talked herself out of speaking, but a pair of on-duty Protectors emerged from the building, saw her standing alone on the Protectorate steps, and held the door open with friendly smiles.

"Hello, Laedani. Please." One of them motioned her through the open door with a bow, a convivial gesture that eased her nerves enough that she could lift heavy feet up the remaining stairs. They did not ask why she was here, nor if she was alone. No one stood with her, so that was obvious. A Channon in the Protectorate was surely business, and whatever business it was, it was none of theirs.

"The Chief…is he…?"

"In his office…to the left. You can't miss him."

Head bowed to hide a nervous smile of gratitude, she murmured, "Thank you," and followed their directions into the building.

They were right. Though she had never been here, had never been in one of these old Pre-Undoing buildings that still stood in this part of the borough and still functioned in much the way they had before, it took only a brief look around to find what she sought. Ancient, rough desks and worn, mismatched tile floors stretched straight ahead from the wide central room, right down a dim corridor, and left towards a small room isolated from the rest by windowed walls and an open door that was impossible to miss. The figure behind the desk, his sparse hair askew, bustled side to side as he stuffed files into one cabinet, replaced them on his desk with others, and then took out a bottle of pale amber liquid to place it beside a well-used glass. His was a familiar face, comforting, welcome, and seeing him filled her with unexpected strength and resolve.

He was not as tall as Lowell. He was thickly built, with extra weight around the middle and a face marred by years of strain, drink, and fatigue, but he was a handsome man and she found it peculiar to think of him that way after all of the years she had known him.

Whatever Lowell's reactions would be to what she was about to do, however he might feel about her after, Yiva believed she had an ally in Ernest. He would help and protect her, as promised, if he could.

"Here to see Chief?"

The woman's voice at her side startled her, but Yiva nodded and followed the fresh-faced girl in the Protector's uniform across the remaining steps separating her from Ernest.

"Chief…I got those numbers you wanted…and there's someone here to see you."

"Thank you, Higgins." He looked up, having just barely settled in his off-balance chair, and was quickly on his feet again, his hand momentarily outstretched in greeting only to drop to his side as if thinking twice about touching her. "Please, come in. Sit if you wish." He accepted the collection of folders and documents from Higgins and added, "Please…close the door...see that no one disturbs us." It might be seen as improper to be alone with the Laedan's wife, but she would be here on business, would undoubtedly want privacy, and since they could be seen through the office windows, spies could be certain nothing improper would transpire.

Hands clutched in her lap, Yiva waited for the click of the latch to signify that they were as alone as they could be, but she was hyper-aware of the windows that gave the others a view of her being here. They might not hear her, but they would see. What if that was enough to damn her in Lowell's eyes?

They had already seen her, however, come through the door, enter the office. The rest was irrelevant.

"Want a drink?" She looked like she needed one. He knew he did.

Yiva shook her head no but held out her hand for the glass he had already poured, a clean one taken from somewhere inside of his desk.

He seemed uncertain where he should be, she thought, as he came from behind the desk, returned there, and then came back again to lean against the edge of the wide, cluttered surface. Though he eyed the empty space on the sofa next to her, he refused to sit.

She was unexpectedly disappointed he did not.

After swallowing the too strong liquor that made her choke and cough with its roughness and waving off his apology when he realized he should have served her something better and more to her tastes, she clutched the glass between her hands and stared at the dregs of amber clinging to the bottom.

"He's hurting her. I want him to stop…I want you to stop him…before she…before someone else dies."

"Dies?" Barely able to hear her, not wanting her to speak louder about the horror she suggested in case anyone passed near enough to listen, he set his glass on the corner of the desk and sat beside her, careful not to allow physical contact. "Who are we talking about?"

The only other woman in the Fortress of consequence to him and the majority of LaGuardia at least was Oasis Hallister-Channon. His mind raced through the possibilities of who Yiva was referring to, who might be hurting the young woman, but despite the sickening feeling knotting around the alcohol in his belly, his mind refused to make the conclusive leap that seemed too easy to make.

"She deserves better than this…she deserves what Jonni should have…not him…he's not fit…not for anyone…"

That was answer enough.

Donnovan.

And from the reddening of Yiva's cheeks and throat that were not caused by the rush of alcohol in her blood, from the trembling grip on the glass in her hand, from all of the clues he had collected since the day of the Hallister-Channon marriage, Ernest knew there was another victim as well. Though he did not know the details, he did not need to. His fear for her was confirmed.

But how in the hell was he supposed to prove it? How could he solve a problem of this magnitude?

If the Laedan knew and had done nothing, accusations coming from the Protectorate Chief were going to be ill-received. If Lowell did not know, his reactions would be little different, with the exception of a factor of disbelief that most parents felt when such truths about their children were revealed. Such an intervention from the Chief might result in greater danger for both women, but to do nothing felt like a sticky, cold ball of unyielding dough caught in the back of his throat, cutting off efforts to swallow, his efforts to breathe.

"Will she…would she admit this? To me? To Lowell? Would you?"

"I can't do that!" The razor high edge of her tone was a knife cut across his throat. It dislodged the lump but did little to offer relief.

"The Laedan's not likely to believe me if I go to him without evidence…and Donnovan will deny everything without that same evidence. I need you…I need you both…to…"

"I can't…you don't understand. I…can't." The glass slipped from her hand, cracking as it hit the floor and she leaped to her feet. Fear and embarrassment collided in her eyes, splitting tears from the bonds that held them back. "I shouldn't have come here…this was a mistake…I'm sorry…forget I…"

"Yiva." Ernest caught her hand, cold and shaking, with such force against her pull that he was surprised she could stand. He held her there, still and secure, only the angle of her arm visible to others through the glass to reveal any contact between them, to expose her upset. Ernest believed his people knew him, would not think he was doing anything more than offering comfort.

But there was always a first time.

"I want to help. I swear. I will help you. I will do anything, everything, I can for you, for her. If either of you needs a place to go, shelter or protection, I'll get you that too. I swear it. But the only way to do this that will work is to take it to Lowell…all three of us together…before Donnovan learns what we're doing. If you want me to do this…if you're both willing…say the word and I will be there."

It might cost him. His retirement. What remained of his career. His life. But what was the point of all of his years of service if he was not willing to muster up the courage to do what was right when it counted? How could he turn his back on two women in need, living in fear of a powerful man? On this woman?

She said nothing, no agreement, no refusal, no plea or expression of gratitude for his offer. She pulled free of his hand, perhaps the gentlest gesture of compassion she had experienced in years, and hurried out of his office, out of the Protectorate, as fast as she could, the hard soles of her slippers clicking on the tile and then on the cement steps as she disappeared into LaGuardia's streets.

He knew where she was going. She was going home.

Back to him.

Perhaps he should go with her, offer an escort.

But perhaps she had an escort already, waiting dutifully outside. Ernest's offer would look suspect without a damn good explanation.

Besides, she did not want his company.

Ernest felt that he had failed her, betrayed her.

But what else, he wondered with a groan, was he supposed to do?

☙*❧

"Fa?"

Nik had not left his room since the night before, sleeping later than usual and nursing the last of the dox tremors with the tea mixture Torben had sent with him. His room smelled like an herbalist's storefront, but since Lowell would be unable to distinguish the smells of curative tea from any other substance Nik had smoked or burned in the past, he doubted his father would realize his middle son was more clear-headed then he had been since he was a very young boy.

The itchy dryness that reddened his eyes only supported the appearance of yet another drug binge.

Lowell did his best not to frown as he studied the room through squinted eyes. There was no drug haze to squint through, only the steaminess of water boiled on the makeshift hot-plate Nik kept on a table near the window, but Lowell squinted, a reflex common every time he opened Nik's bedroom door. It took moments to realize it was steam, not smoke, filling the air, coating the glass and the walls with a damp sheen of condensation, and though his expression relaxed in relief, he wondered what manner of new drug there was that would be consumed in tea rather than through the veins or lungs.

Maybe it was wisest he did not ask.

"Glad to see you home…we were worried…"

Were you, Nik wanted to ask. Instead, he rubbed a towel through his damp hair, having apparently just bathed judging by the steaming bowl of murky, soapy water on the desk and the cloth hanging over the edge of it, further cause for the foggy haze in the room. "Yeah. I'm back. I always come back."

"I hope so, Nik…by the stars, I hope so." Lowell did not often admit how true that hope was for him, how deep his fears of his son's death were. Now more than ever, after losing one son he thought he would never lose. Saying those words were the closest he could get to admitting how much he loved Nik. "What happened to the window?"

Taken aback by the emotion in the man's voice, Nik shrugged. "Branch…that last storm."

Lowell nodded. There appeared to be a leaf stuck in one of the cracks. Plausible enough. There had been reports of other minor damage around the Fortress after that night, and several trees had been uprooted throughout the borough. It felt better to believe that than to think Nik had broken it in some stuporous fit.

"Did you want something?" His father so rarely came to his private room that seeing him raised uncomfortable alarms in Nik's head. Why he should be afraid of his father, he could not say. Maybe the fear was a residual effect of the doxing.

"No…I heard you were home…I had to see for myself." He had seen Nik asleep in bed earlier, but asleep had not been good enough. Lowell wanted to look into Nik's eyes and see that this particular son was not yet lost.

Small as Lowell's voice was, there was honest relief in it, sincere concern, and Nik swallowed, the decision made. It was the best time to say this, the only time his father might be compelled to believe him.

"You remember what I said? About Quentin? About his…?"

Tension rippled across Lowell's shoulders and face. Nik's breath caught. "I remember." If the claim had been uttered in a drug stupor, Nik should have forgotten it. That he had not was significant.

"Ask Donn. He knows now. He saw it too," Nik murmured, forcing enough slur into his voice and words that his father might write them off as hallucination rather than lash out at him if they proved to be words he did not want to hear.

"Saw what?"

"Yellow eyes. Quentin's eyes." A swallow, his hands twisting the damp towel in his anxiety, and then he finished. "Cat eyes. Anthro eyes. Donn saw them too. Ask him."

"Donnovan is not here," Lowell spat, turning towards the door with a bitterness of expression towards his other son's name that made Nik blink in surprise. He wondered what he had missed while he was gone. What his brother had done. "Dinner will be soon. Your mother expects you. Be there."

"Yes, sir."

Lowell stalked from the room, not noting the first unslurred words of obedience Nik had uttered in years.

~*~

The Felas' mother had given up her breath during the day while everyone slept. There was nowhere suitable to bury her, no way to summon the Protectorate or a sposer without revealing their hideaway and raising questions none wanted to answer. It had taken words between Kato and the Fela siblings, a tale about how he had been forced to put down his own mother when the turn came, to convince Beren of the necessity of being the one to do the same to their mother. Expecting his sisters to do it was not fair. Allowing these strangers to do it would be something he would regret for the rest of his life.

It had to be him.

This was not his mother anymore. Only a shell. The thing that would emerge to devour them was no more his mother than Kato was.

The fact that his story was largely untrue, that he had been forced to flee from his mother and the grubbers that consumed her in order to protect his sister, was a fact Kato hid from Beren and everyone else.

They could not flee from this place so easily, the way Kato had fled his home. They were hunted and they had nowhere else to go. No plan, no supplies, little chance or hope for survival.

As the hours dragged towards the next setting of the sun, the mage still had not awakened.

It seemed too long to Jia, too long for him to lay in unmoving sleep as she watched Kato and Beren drag the dead woman's body into the street for the sposers to find. Watched them break her arms and legs so that, should she turn, she would be unable to walk or crawl, watched them drive a length of rebar through her skull to be sure she did not. It was a common practice for the dead who could not be immediately processed. No one living in the buildings nearby would think anything amiss with the sudden appearance of a corpse in the street. They would, however, question so many anthro in a building thought to be empty if they found them there. The cold was setting in, seeping into their bones, and as evening approached, snow began to fall, a light dusting that melted as soon as it hit the ground.

Come nightfall, and the falling of the ambient temperature of air and ground, it would start to stick.

But they had nothing with which to build a fire, and would not dare to build one if they could.

The fear of hunters was too fresh in each of them to take the risk.

Thankfully, there were no tracks in snow to lead back to the Bunker once Kato and Beren returned.

By the time Vance opened his eyes, their deep brown emerging with a start as he lurched upright…and swayed beneath the wave of dizziness that rushed over him, the sun had nearly set. His shoulder injuries had been cleaned and treated again as he slept, he could tell by the stiffness of the fresh bandages against his skin. The scent of nearby cook fires, roasting meat and stewing vegetables, greeted him, offering little comfort as his stomach growled. The others had already eaten from the supplies brought or scavenged within the Bunker and he was surprised when Xen offered him the remaining chunk of pork and a potato from their stash.

Despite his stomach's demand for food, however, it was an offer Vance needed to decline. The swaying in his head, as if his body rested on a boat on the sea, was a potent reminder that he would lose anything he put into his stomach, especially the alcohol his raw nerves craved.

He would save it, he thought, wrapping it in a bit of cloth and tucking it into a pocket of his satchel. Maybe later, he would eat.

"We should go…" he started.

Addi scowled and felt the mage's forehead, his wound, for signs of fever or infection. "You're not…"

"I can do this…I can find the way…I know…" Vance mumbled, accepting Jia's offered hand and trying to use it as leverage to stand.

She frowned and steadied him as he began to drop. She had left him long enough to sleep and keep watch at the window when Kato and Beren took his mother's body outside; she was grateful he had not stirred sooner. "You can't go anywhere, not like this."

"Just give me a few minutes." Clutching to her arm, he pushed up off his knees slowly, steadied himself, and then clasped onto Addi on his other side when he was upright in the hopes of stopping the world from spinning. He winced and closed his eyes.

"Your shoulder? Hand?" asked Addi. Given his injuries, both sources of pain seemed likely.

"My head." It was not pain exactly, but rather the brightness of the path he needed to follow, something more felt than seen, something he needed to pursue while it was fresh and hot.

"I can give you something; you should sleep."

"No. I'm okay. I'm not going to get any rest with this in my head."

Jia squeezed his hand, her excitement palpable, only to immediately release it when he stiffened and she realized what she had done to his injured hand…and the strength of emotion she probably passed through the physical contact. "You know the way? Tell us."

He shook his head, eyes still closed to lessen the spinning of the world around him. "I can't. It's not directions like that…it's a trail…a path…like the scent of an animal when you hunt." He looked into her eyes, willing her to understand. He could no more direct her then she would have been able to guide someone in following prey. The only way to know where the path led was to follow it. It had to be him.

"You can barely stand," groused Wist. Being slowed down by the unsteady man was no better an option, in his opinion, then waiting in this cold, uncomfortable building.

"I can do this." He was a mage. A tracker. A Protector. He was, as his mother had often called him, a damned stubborn Segara. He would do this if it killed him…if he had to crawl the entire way.

"We're coming too."

Jia faced Beren who, prepared for a fight, shook his head stubbornly and continued, "There's nothing for us here…nothing to go back to. Nowhere to go. We can't wait for Fa who might not…but we can help you find them; maybe find him too. You need bodies…hands…claws and fangs." He grinned, but his expression was not as confident as he hoped. "Let us help."

"It could be dangerous."

The oldest of the Fela sisters nodded grimly. "So is staying here. If Fa's out there…if he's alive…we should try to find him…just like you finding your friend."

If Jia said no, she believed they would still follow, putting themselves in harm's way without direction from someone older, more experienced, someone who might have more knowledge than they did. Just as she had gone in search of her own father, Jia could not accept denying these four the right to find theirs.

"Do you think you can do this…with…?" Her gaze traveled down to the woman's swollen belly.

"I can," the woman said stubbornly. "I will." She made no mention of the father of her child, no mention of whether he was alive, if he had been taken as well, or if he was already out of her life, but Jia believed the woman's stubbornness was born of the desire to find him too. It was enough.

"If you come…you do as I say, okay?" she asked. "I don't want anyone hurt or killed because someone refuses to listen." The admonition was not only for the unfamiliar Fela, and she hoped those with her understood that. Right now, she had no specific plan, no better plan than to follow wherever Vance led. They had to find the end before any plan could be made. But it was a step, and when the time came to formulate another step, she wanted to be as sure that these youngsters would follow her guidance as she was those Pack members traveling with her.

All of their heads bobbed. “We will,” Beren promised, though his gaze shifted to Kato for affirmation, confirmation, and support.

Their pride was without a leader. They were looking, both Kato and Jia realized, for someone to fill that position, someone to teach and guide them. He said nothing as he began to round up the packs and satchels scattered around the bunker. He thought of Vanya, of his own future of what it was he wanted out of life.

Truthfully, he was not certain of the answer, although Vanya had already made her choice. Not so long ago, the answer had been to travel west until he could travel no more, until he found a better, safer place for Vanya to live and thrive. With the Flushing Pack, he had found that. For himself, however, he was not sure what he wanted. Perhaps he had already found what he had sought and was not ready to admit it.

Maybe it was time, when this was over and Liam was found, to move again.

“You ready, mage?” he grunted.

Still leaning against Jia, a position he was not willing to give up unless someone else stepped in to support him, Vance nodded, “I’m ready.”

Jia nodded. “Let’s do this…let’s find Liam…and get him home.”

Chapter 29

With the support of his company, his eyes mostly useless in the gloom as he followed the minute clues his inner senses revealed rather than the regular visual images of dark borough streets and crumbling infrastructure, Vance directed the group through the southern streets of LaGuardia towards the several block stretch owned by neither borough, controlled by no Laedans, no Protectorate, and only marginally by HOPE's influence. Passage was known to be difficult through that devastated swath of Queens, devastated because without the boroughs' backing there was little effort made to make repairs or clean up debris. Unowned, without any efforts made to incorporate it, it belonged only to those who dared to struggle to make the region home. Here they were ungoverned. Here there was only the law of survival. There was nothing friendly about most of those living here; it was every individual, every family, for themselves, but at this hour, few paid the group any heed save for a pair of dogs who snapped and snarled at them from behind a makeshift fence.

Not wanting to draw attention to themselves, Vance threw them the morsel of meat he had saved for eating and the dogs turned to fighting over it instead of paying attention to the passing group.

Jia fretted, as did the others, about their direction, pointed as they were towards Kennedy's heavily patrolled border. She had never been there. Most of those with her had never been there. There had never been any need. LaGuardia had given the Flushing Pack everything they wanted…except for long-lasting security.

If Kennedy's border was anything like LaGuardia's, it was going to be a challenge to pass. Getting out of a borough was rarely a problem. Only getting in could be, unless one knew the unguarded passage points. They could take back alleys and side streets, but those were likely to be blocked with traps and mines.

If Vance had ever been into Kennedy, he did not say so.

The Fela siblings showed the least trepidation about crossing through the neutral sector, as they and their mother and father had once called these ungoverned streets home. It explained why they showed less respect for the ownership of the Bunker than others might have. Here one fought for what they wanted, territory markers be damned. When they emerged into LaGuardia from Below, they probably had been unaware they had crossed any border.

They were not at ease with the mage directing them, and more than once they tried to steer the group into different streets, through collapsed buildings and empty alleys they claimed to be safe.

But Jia did not dare take the risk. Regardless of the obstacles they encountered, any that slowed forward progress however temporarily, through this unfamiliar territory, following Vance's directions to the letter felt wisest. She did not want to take the chance of veering from his instruction more than necessary if it increased the odds that the tracker might lose his way. Every time they were forced to deviate from the course, he suffered incredible pain.

Beren seemed to believe the tracker was faking that pain in order to have his way. Wist expressed the same opinion because he would rather have found the easiest route rather than the straightest.

Jia, believing his suffering, did not want to cause him any more of it than was necessary.

The group's acceptance of her leadership and their obligation to the duty of finding Liam, bringing him home, kept them in silent formation around her, despite any misgivings they harbored.

This was for one of their own, and no power in the universe would divide them tonight.

Now, crouched behind the long body of a decaying vehicle, its aged metal wheels nearly fused to the tracks beneath that had warped and fallen from the path above their heads, they paused to study their options and make a choice. This stretch of Kennedy's border was marked by these metal rails. Most of the buildings that once existed below the tracks had been cleared, offering few hiding places, and where the rails had collapsed, the metal was shaped and twisted, with sharp barbed wire stretched from one anchor to the next. The barrier was manned by guarded outposts to discourage anyone from crossing.

"There…that way…" Vance pointed, his words still slurred and his vision still dulled though he had grown steadier during the time taken to cross through near-empty streets.

Fearing that someone would see the mage and his raised arm, Kato grabbed Vance's wrist and yanked him back down. The tracker snarled and Addi judiciously positioned himself between the two men to avoid an argument.

"Not now," Jia hissed, scowling at the obstacles in their line of sight. Several blocks to her left, through the neutral sector, were places Candace said they might have passed through with little difficulty, so long as they avoided the traps and mines set for trespassers.

Here they faced guards, uniformed men and women likely either bored with their duties or else too high strung and trigger happy to find day-to-day interaction in the borough advisable, hired and positioned here looking for trouble and an excuse to hurt someone. Without knowing if the guards stationed at the passable entry points had been told to watch for the distinctively marked Fela siblings, without knowing if they might recognize the dangerous nature of what Wist carried, the legitimate route seemed impractical.

But Vance's guidance had brought them this far, to this crossing. If they were to enter Kennedy borough, possibly cross the borders into HOPE's territory which they knew was not so far away, if they were going to follow his lead precisely, Jia would accept the protection she felt came with it.

"Straight ahead…I can feel it."

"We can't barge across a street with those guards…" snorted Wist.

"But we can go under it."

Heads turned curiously towards Beren.

"There's an entrance to Below; it runs straight. They guard it, sometimes use it to travel, but there are only ever a few protecting the way, two or three at most. They'll have shockers, sleep darts, but if we get past, we can get across and go anywhere without being noticed."

"People get lost there," warned Xen. How many times had her parents warned her and Liam never to enter the Below, when they, as children, thought those shadows made a good place to hide and shirk their duties? How often had she, in turn, told the younger pups of the dangers in the Below, of grubbers and Unders, of dangerous currents of filth and flood and sea overflow, and the flotsam of civilization that the rains of time had carried into the veins of the boroughs?

Knowing it was not a path to choose lightly, Jia whispered, "Where's the entrance?"

Beren pointed to the right of their position, but there was nothing to see but more cement and steel pillars, more sharp wire, more partially elevated tracks and the crumbling buildings lining the border.

"Vance?"

It was not that his opinion mattered more than anyone else's. If the tracker could guide them through the Below, it might be a better option to consider than confronting patrolling Kennedy guards.

"I can get us through," Beren sulked. "I've been there before."

Maybe he could, but Jia felt more inclined to trust the tracker's experienced instincts than those of a stranger who might have passed that way once or twice in his young life…and had gotten lost down there to enter LaGuardia with a grubber-bitten mother in tow.

The mage nodded, knowing what she asked without the need for words. However far away that ingress to the Below was, reaching it would take them away from where they intended to go. From where they stood, the bright point at the end of his vision's quest was four or five miles away at most. It was a guess, impossible to determine the actual distance in this unfamiliar territory, but he knew the undulating red pulsing path, like blood being pumped through an artery, was true. The focal point of the whirring and spinning that occasionally swept him off his feet was there, the end of the thread. The unpleasant, dizzying effect was not going to end until he reached the eye of the plasm storm he had thrown himself into.

If they entered the random turns of Below, there was no telling how long of a delay that path might cost them, no telling if he would be able to see the path clearly from that dank place or if he would be able to follow it if he could.

But there was another way. A way Jia was not going to like but which was, he believed, their best hope for success.

"If Beren can…"

"Of course I can…"

One of Beren's sister cuffed him on the side of the head for interrupting and he growled, a sound loud enough to attract the attention of the nearest border guard. Everyone behind the fallen rail car fell silent, and though the guard returned to his pacing in short order, apparently deciding the sound was nothing more than the heavy wind roaring through the open windows, cracks, and crevices in the buildings lining the far side of the border, the group was reticent to resume their debate where they were. Jia led them back to the corner of the nearest building where they could speak in the shelter of the shadows with less possibility of being heard.

Thankfully the snow had stopped falling, and what there had been had long ago melted away.

The backward pull against the internal current of his chosen track made Vance grimace and rub the bridge of his nose but he brushed off Addi's offered care. This was a pain he was used to, made worse by the drug circulating in his body, but familiar all the same. It offset the renewed ache in his shoulder that he was struggling to ignore.

"If the way is clear," he continued once they were safe, "I can get us through, once we get past anyone protecting the entrance…"

"And if it doesn't?" asked Helena. "If you lose the…you'll be lost down there…the rest of us too."

"We won't be lost," Beren again protested.

"Not if there's an anchor up here."

"An anchor?" asked Addi, not liking the sound of any division of their team and its resources.

Still rubbing his temples, Vance nodded. He had used anchors before, people and objects intended to lead him back to places so that he did not lose his way. It was a skill he had honed as a child, using it to follow his father during a day's work or to find his way home to his mother when his adventures took him too far away into unfamiliar streets. He had never tried to use it to travel through the Below, had never tried to use it to get in and then get back out again on the same route. And he hated using people as anchors as it created a vulnerable, intimate link that toyed uncomfortably with his mage senses. But he believed it could be done. If he was to get through the watery maze and back up to dry land somewhere near enough to their intended destination, it might be worth the effort to try.

"Someone would have to go across…straight across…straight ahead. It will help guide me to the surface…bring me back to the line we must follow…if the other paths fail down there."

Xen snorted. "No one's getting across that." She pointed towards the border guards. "They'll never let us…"

"I can. Me and Addi…"

"Jia…"

She shook her head at her brother's protest. "We're Marrocks; they'll let us through if we claim diplomatic commission. It's too soon; they shouldn't know about Father, and even if they do…his children on commission to entreaty Laedan Hallister…especially me…" She had been groomed to take Roland's place in LaGuardia as co-Laedan after all. Whether anyone thought it would be her…or thought it would be Addi…if they knew Roland was lost, they would know that a new Marrock would take his place.

"Provided they believe us…"

"Of course they will." She had made a contingency plan for crossing the Kennedy border in case they needed it, though she had hoped they would not. "We cross here…normally…and the rest of you follow Beren to the Below…and follow Vance through it."

She could feel and hear the reservations of her company, the resistance to this plan, but getting so many across the border here would be suspect and nearly impossible without conflict. Looking for another way across would take too long. She did not think they could reach their destination and stage a rescue tonight, but the closer they got before the sun rose, the better she would feel.

"Vance…what do I need to do to be…" It had to be her. Having Addi be the mage's anchor never crossed her mind.

It was not a planned action. The dread of the discomfort he would endure as he deviated from the more direct path, in addition to an underlying fear of letting her cross the border without protection, the fear that he might not be able to make it through the Below, that he might be directing others to their deaths should they be lost in the sludge-filled tunnels and the border guards opened fire, made him turn, catch her face between his hand, and plant his lips on hers. It was only for a moment, a sacred moment for him in its purity and power, but it was enough that, when he drew back against a feline growl and amber of Kato's eyes, Vance could feel the anchoring connection there, strong enough that he would be able to follow her for days if it became necessary to do so to return to her again.

As intense as the sensation of her mouth was, the tying of thoughts and breath, nearly blinding in its newness, to the underlying plasm path he had chosen to follow, Vance was reminded again why he avoided the physical and emotional entanglement of relationships.

"Find a safe location; wait for me when you're across…I'll find you." He turned abruptly, ignoring attempted comments or reactions from anyone else, and muttered to the rest, "Let's go."

Again Kato growled, a feral warning, and Vance felt certain the Fela was going to shift and spring on him now that his back was turned and tear him apart with fangs and claws.

Instead, rather than demand to accompany Jia and Addi across the expanse before them…which was what Kato wanted…he paused long enough in that growl to kiss Jia himself, making certain it was a longer kiss than the tracker had left, before stalking into step behind Vance and the others as if to erase the mage's kiss from her memory.

The concern that he might have disrupted whatever anchoring Vance intended in that kiss never crossed Kato's mind.

Addi rolled his eyes, grabbed his sister's hand, and muttered, "Come on." Stunned by unexpected kisses, only his pulling her into motion allowed Jia to move.

She took only a few steps however before she stopped to watch the others go. She had no idea how far they would have to travel to reach the entrance to the Below, and she wanted to be certain they made it there without incident. She also wanted to keep both men in her sights as long as possible. Her mouth tingled, her heart hammered in her ears as it did after an exhilarating hunt, and the heat and flush of desire burned through her blood. She knew that feeling, even if she had never pursued it…only now she did not know which man, if either, was the cause of it. Perhaps both.

She had to force herself to breathe, to think, to believe that the tracker and the Fela would not kill each other as soon as they were out of her sight. She had to force herself to believe that both were competent enough to follow the plan until they had Liam, alive or dead, home again. That belief, her responsibility to the Pack, and Addi's hand pulling hers…an anchor of his own…were all that kept her from pursuing them in the desperate hope of keeping them safe.

Surprised that Kato had not lashed out at him, not having been looking at the Fela when he kissed Jia too, Vance chose to ignore Kato now that they were moving, choosing instead to keep alert to their surroundings as they skirted debris and warped rail pillars to reach the entrance to Below that Beren had spoken of. As the younger Fela had indicated, there were three guards there, weaving an intricate pattern of watch so that one was always on the right of the opening, another always on the left, and the third pacing between them. Those on the side remained still until the one pacing between them had crossed the space back and forth five times and then he would take a side post and the next person would walk the path. A strategy, Vance presumed, to keep each of them from becoming bored and complacent in an extended stationary watch. He imagined the pattern was meant to be confusing to anyone watching it…but it was not to him.

There were knives at their sides, and the sort of simple gun he knew was used to fire a sedating agent at an attacker or escapee. Many LaGuardia Protectors carried the same. On their right hips, each carried a shocker as well, as Beren had said they would. But the three were outnumbered, and Vance doubted, from their bored expressions and ongoing trivial dialogue, that they were expecting trouble.

They were barely paying attention to their assignment.

An armed trio in uniform was likely enough to ward off occasional passersby or random individual adventurous enough to consider delving into the Below. Most, however, knew the dangers there and would never consider the route to be worth risking their lives.

What then, Vance wondered, were these three protecting?

“Divide and conquer?” whispered Beren.

“No need,” Helena replied. The four Fela were barely more than cubs, unlikely to be experienced fighters. “We’ve got this.” She caught the gazes of Xen and Wist, the other Cana in the group, and as one they shed their packs and their clothes. “Bring those…or else,” she said with a smirk. Then she and the Cana formed a three-pronged attack, leaping with a yip, claiming their hybrid forms, as if they had fought and hunted together all of their lives.

It was an inborn Cana instinct to hunt as a pack, something the normally solitary Fela did not undertake. Whether it was different for a pride or not, this was not the time for debate. It was time to act. And act they did.

Jia nodded at Addi, the yipping distracting her from her dazed, lingering stare and from the taste of those kisses, forcing her to focus on the task at hand. The rest were on the move. Though she could no longer see them, she trusted they had found the opening to the Below.

It was time for the twins to move as well.

In the frigid, locked warehouse of what had been a blood handling lab, sheltered from the evening wind but none the warmer for it, Liam lifted his head. The sound was faint, carried on the roaring gale that pushed through fissures in the ceiling that the structure's heating system no longer combatted, but it was enough to send a prickle up the nape of his neck and make him straighten as if to hear better.

"What is it?" asked the nearest woman, the strain of chattering in her voice making it difficult to hear or comprehend her words.

"I don't..."

Liam sniffed the air but scented nothing but the staleness of death accumulating around them, and though he cocked his head to the other side, the sound he believed he had heard did not come again. He sighed and pulled the closest bodies nearer to increase their chances for warmth. If they changed, took advantage of fur instead of human nudity, they might stand a chance. As weak as most of them were, he did not think many would be capable of a transformation.

The cold was winning. How much longer, he mused, until there were none of them left?

Unless his senses were deceiving him, however, he believed he had heard it. The initiating yip of a Cana hunt.

Did he dare risk the possibility that there were guards on the exterior perimeter, keeping watch in case they tried to escape, keeping watch until they were dead?

Did he dare howl?

Gun in one hand, a shocker in the other, Vance started forward as the powerful, solid bodies of the Cana forms clashed with their targets, dropping each of the guards before there was an opportunity to charge their shockers or draw their tranq guns to meet the attack. The snarls, the snaps, the shouts of surprise and pain, left three uniformed forms in various contorted positions and left the Fela youngsters in awe as they picked up dropped clothing and bags and followed in Vance and Kato's wake. No one emerged from the maw of the Below, no one came from any of the nearest structures. If the guards at the crossing heard the noise, it would take time for them to reach the tunnel, time enough for Vance and the others to disappear into the darkness.

If there were other dangers nearby, it appeared that none had been alerted by the skirmish.

The Cana ducked just far enough into the tunnel, to the top of the worn stairs where the paleness of light allowed them to hurriedly dress when the Fela reached them with their belongings. Vance did not take time to study the downed guards, though he did take the shocker, knife and dart gun from the individual he passed closest too.

Kato and Beren followed his cue and did likewise, stripping the others of their weaponry too. Dead, the trio would not need them any longer. Alive…well, there was no wisdom in leaving them armed to pursue and attack the intruders later.

Vance snapped the shocker into the locked position so that its popping, hissing, sparking glow lit up the tunnel as far as the bottom of the stairs. With luck, it had enough charge to get them through the passages and back to the surface near their intended destination.

They had two more shockers in their inventory if they needed them, and sleep darts to use against Unders if they encountered any. The mage doubted they would be overpowered.

At the bottom of their descent, in an unavoidable pool of foul-smelling slop, Vance stopped to lean against the rusted metal rail that still ran the length of the tunnel. He took an open-mouthed breath, hoping to avoid the smell as he focused beyond the clawing pain between his temples, and regretted it at once as the air settled on his tongue and left a bitter taste in addition to the coppery tang that had been with him since he awoke from his plasm hit over an hour ago.

He coughed and spat to remove the flavor.

Beside him, Kato chortled.

Vance lowered the shocker so the glow did not reveal his frown.

"That way."

He turned left, where the tunnel ran in the direction in which Jia's life force burned, in the direction that would take him back to the path they were meant to follow.

He hoped.

"But there's a way up just over…" protested Beren.

It was Vance's turn to growl, but he otherwise ignored the interruption and started along the ledge to the left. The tunnel center looked to be knee-deep with water, and he would rather not risk floating grubbers or other unseen hazards by wading through it. Nor, it seemed, did any of the Fela want that, as they clung more tightly to the wall than he did.

He was certain this was the way to go. Perhaps not the most direct route, but direct enough. Besides, whatever those three officers had been guarding was here. It seemed wise to discover what that was…before they all lived to regret not doing so.

"Jia Marrock," she said diplomatically, one hand offered to the guards who met them as they approached the center of the crossing point. The command to halt and the drawn weapons had created the desired effect, causing the twins to stop as asked.

That they showed no nervousness or reservation at the approach of the border patrol agents, that they smiled and the young woman offered her hand in a friendly, businesslike manner, suggested they were not the usual sort who attempted to cross the Kennedy border at this spot rather than one of the primary roads crossing the neutral sector. She imagined it was most often those fleeing for their lives who came through here, or else someone hoping to smuggle goods or other people through a less heavily monitored checkpoint.

This pair of travelers appeared to have nothing to hide.

"We've been commissioned by our father, Roland, to an audience with Laedan Hallister."

"How do we know you're who you…?"

"May I?" Since they would not take her at her word, Jia slipped her satchel off her shoulder and paused before opening the front pocket, giving the guards a chance to stop her should they think she was about to draw a hidden weapon. She had a knife on her hip, as many who crossed the hostile neutral sector did. She would be a fool to be completely unarmed, even if on a diplomatic mission.

Especially if on a diplomatic mission for LaGuardia's Laedans.

But hidden weapons invited suspicions, so her efforts to initiate trust and minimize those suspicions were noted and appreciated.

"I have this." The paper roll, the size of a page taken from some book in the library, was sealed with a smidge of candle wax and imprinted with a stylized letter M. It was a sigil Addi had seen before, one he knew belonged to their father although he could not recall seeing it used. But he paid less attention to governmental affairs than Jia had, so he did not feel surprised by her knowledge or use of it.

What he did know, however, was that his father was dead and thus unable to produce any sort of message for Laedan Hallister. Whatever was written on this page, it was either some undelivered document he had left in his office, that Jia had retrieved, or else she had fabricated this herself. If the message was of her own creation, it was possible the impression in the wax was as well, the entire offering a ruse relying on the likelihood that these men would know little beyond a basic understanding of the alphabet and their own signatures, and thus would be unable to read the scroll's contents, let alone recognize the signature of one of LaGuardia's Laedans.

Her gamble paid off, the document official-looking enough to the guards' untrained eyes that they accepted it with waving hands and wishes for safe travels as they allowed the Marrock siblings to cross into Kennedy Borough unhindered.

Mind made up, the risk seeming to be one worth taking if they were going to die anyhow, Liam accepted the Cana change, threw back his head, and howled.

Addi held his breath. Two steps. Six. Waiting for their ruse to fail, waiting for the guards to change their minds and either stop them, call them back, or shoot them in the back with or without warning.

But neither fate met them. What did greet them, when they made it safely into the street opposite the checkpoint, rounded a corner, and paused out of sight of the guards to calm their thundering hearts, was a single, mournful howl.

Jia clutched Addi's hand tight enough to make him grunt in pain but he understood why. Though the sound reverberated through the unfamiliar streets, echoing off of buildings that masked its location, pushing against the strong gale blowing from behind their backs, it was no wolf howl.

It was Cana.

And though they were too near to the border guards to risk a reply, Jia and Addi both met the sound with the deepest rush of joy they had felt in days.

Liam was alive.

Chapter 30

The ledge on either side of the tunnel remained narrow, once a walking path perhaps but now strewn with debris left by rising water, passing Unders, and lost souls who had come and been unable to find their way out again. The encroaching narrowness seemed to discourage Unders from passing any longer, as none were seen and any dead that had been here had, it seemed, been dragged from the ledge into the murky water by the rats living in the borough's dank underbelly. The stationary, stagnant water was well below the ledge and free of visible grubbers or things moving beneath the surface except for the occasional swimming rat. Age-old art, stylized words and symbols bereft of meaning since the Undoing robbed the world of those who had drawn them, marred the walls like the ancient languages left in photos of caves and pyramids from far off lands that none passing this way would ever see. The damp tainted the images with mildew and a thin, iridescent oozing slime in many places, but unlike similar art on the sides of buildings on the surface, this had yet to succumb to the decay of collapsing stone. At least not in this tunnel.

Vision strained by the combination of dim lighting and the crackling, conflicting paths in his head, the reception of both that were muted by their distance beneath the ground, Vance was forced to relinquish the lead position of their queue to Kato. They only turned once, into a tunnel that faced them in the southerly direction they needed to travel. It felt to have been hours, their sluggish pace on that slippery ledge slowing their progress, but as they followed Kato's steps and Vance's instructions forward, Beren assured them there were other exits here.

They just had to find one.

"Wait."

Vance's hand on Kato's arm stopped him and the others paused to listen, expecting to hear the sound of grubbers or Unders ahead, or pick up on a sight or scent they had yet to notice but that the tracker somehow did.

It annoyed Kato that Vance should notice anything that his anthro senses did not, and he growled softly at the hindrance.

He saw no diverging paths within range of the shocker's light, but perhaps Vance sensed one and wanted to change direction.

"They've been here recently."

"Who?"

Vance shook his head, uncertain who they were, and placed his good hand flat against the slick surface of the tunnel wall, slowly sliding down until he was crouched with his other hand on the floor. The surface of the ledge was covered in fine grit that none of them had paid particular attention to, despite the fact that the crunching sound of it had grown louder and more persistent as if the amount of sandy substance had increased over the distance of the last ten steps. The only reason Vance could imagine it being there was as a deliberate effort to reduce the slipperiness of the surface, brought here intentionally for that purpose or else on the soles of frequent shoes traveling back and forth from outside.

That meant there must be an exit nearby.

He motioned for the shocker that he had handed to Kato when the Fela had taken the lead. It still burned, though the light was beginning to flicker and fade as the charge reached depletion. Xen took it from Kato and edged closer to put it into the mage's hands.

The light revealed nothing in the water, only bits of broken chairs lodged into the sludge, pine cones and branches and a bloated, decaying cat bobbing on the agitated surface. The gentle swaying of the water, ripples generated by a distance source, drew his attention left to the very edge of the light's reach.

"There…what's that?"

Not sensing the presence of anyone else, Kato decided it was safe enough to move closer alone, and started to do so in a low, cautious crouch. "Let's find out."

The group inched forward after him, with only Xen remaining with Vance as the tracker got to his feet.

What they found was no illusion of light on the water's surface or refracted from the walls around them. There were several wooden objects blocking the water's flow, small damaged boats and carts, broken timbers, chunks of stone and cement and asphalt, and other large pieces of debris creating a dam-like structure that brought the water's surface on the far side nearly to the lip of the ledge, a structure through which the water, over time, had found fissures to enable it to trickle and dribble through to a lower level on the side from where they had come. Metal spikes, three that they could count within the perimeter of the light's glow, had been driven into the cement for an unknown purpose, creating cracks that destabilized the ledge though it was not any sort of immediate threat.

But it was a door on the opposite wall, with the eroded remains of unreadable text and a symbol like a fork of lightning which drew their focus. It appeared that the door had once been fully metal, but had been eroded, or perhaps cut away in places, over time, and had been repaired with wooden slats and straps of newer iron at the top, the middle, and the bottom, the door kept closed by crude rusted links of chain affixed to an eyebolt sunk into the wall.

"Grubs?" whispered Helena. It was the most likely reason for anyone to have gone to the trouble of barring a door in a place like this. Her limited experience with the Below was of a place littered with grubbers, and as they had not yet encountered any, it was possible that someone had made an effort to lure them somewhere for containment until the Protectorate, the sposers, or someone brave and authoritative, could deal with them.

But behind the door was silence, and the foul odor of decay that typically accompanied grubbers was absent as it had been in the rest of the tunnel thus far. If there were grubbers, they were incapacitated and had been for so long that their stench had dissipated.

Nor did it seem like someone would have trapped Unders here, for those same reasons. There were no sounds of breathing, of life, and no stink of the dead.

"I'd guess it's locked to dissuade looting," murmured Vance, testing the sturdiness of the makeshift dam that separated them from the door. It seemed reasonable that the debris was here not to form a dam but to create a bridge to make crossing easier, and he was curious, despite the pull of the path in his head towards the surface, towards Jia in order to end the excruciating pain in his skull and body, to know what someone had gone to so much trouble to hide.

If Hallister Guards manned at least one entrance to this place, perhaps this is what they were protecting.

The debris bridge tottered and shifted beneath him and he waved at the others, muttering, "Stay back," as he balanced his way across.

The waterlogged wood was soft, approaching the day when it would collapse and float down the tunnel in the gush of water it would release, but it held for him this day. How many bodies it might convey across the chasm before it fell, however, was a test for another time.

"Careful," whispered one of the Fela sisters.

Vance nodded and continued across with a grim expression.

On the other side, he studied the door as closely as his blurry vision allowed. Where once there had been a knob, there was now only a bored hole, not large enough to see through without a light source on the other side. The hole was large enough, however, to slide the shocker through, and when it disappeared into the room behind, erasing what little light they had in the tunnel, Wist growled, "Shart…why'd you…?"

Kato's hand clasped over the young man's mouth. While he might despise the mage's interest in Jia, he begrudgingly grew more respectful and appreciative of Vance's skills as time passed. He resented losing their light source, but they had other shockers, and if

Vance could force that door open, they would have the original one back. If there was something of use behind that door, food or a stash of contraband, or any sort of threat, it was best they knew about it.

Leaning against the door as Vance peeped through the hole revealed only a collection of flat, wide, metal boxes, dark green in color, latched and hinged shut. His leaning also revealed a softening of the rotted planks and the looseness of the rusted hinges and eyebolt the chain knotted through. Using his knife as pulling leverage at the bolt, and pushing against the planks with his undamaged shoulder, Vance stumbled and swore as the door gave way and deposited him on the other side with the dropped shocker.

"What is it?"

"What did you find?'

"Come on…we should go…"

Ignoring the nervous comments, Vance popped the latches on one of the boxes and slowly opened it, wary of what he might find inside. Nestled within careful partitions, lined with padding so that the objects did not touch one another, were eleven oblong objects, evenly ridged and capped with a small round ring, a handle, and a pin that locked both in place. The twelfth slot was empty, one of the objects removed, and as Vance removed another, he struggled to close out all of his other senses in order to read any clues this fist-sized orb and its box could show him. He remembered well, from his earliest days as Protector, when he and a few of coworkers had been summoned to a home where a group of playing children had found a similar item, a similar box. The first child, unfortunate soul that he had been, had believed the item to be a toy, and in front of his parents, the Protectors, and a gaggle of onlookers, removed the metal pin, shifted the orb in his hand…and left nothing in the street except the bloody, fiery, smoky debris of an explosion and a car-sized crater in the road where the child had stood.

No toy. These were weapons, a stash which, if ignited, would collapse the tunnel around them and bring whatever was on the surface down to fill in the crater that remained. From his estimated count, there were at least twenty-six of these defensive metal boxes, and if each box contained a dozen orbs, it was enough explosive power to arm nearly every Protector in LaGuardia. Or Kennedy.

But why would anyone want to? Why hide them here? To keep them out of the common mans' hands, or as a stash for future use?

Had Hallister, or someone else in Kennedy Borough already found Fort Hamilton?

Scowling, Vance closed the box and opened another. This one was full. He doubted this was Fort Hamilton, or even the fabled Fort's supply of weaponry. There was not enough of it here. The wise thing to do, in his opinion, would have been to spread any such find thin, make it more difficult for thieves to ransack. And maybe that had been done. Maybe this was but a small portion of a much larger collection.

But he did not believe these had come from the Fort.

If Hallister had found the Fort, the whole of Queens would know.

"Kato…need some help here."

Surprised by the request, the light on his feet Fela joined the mage on the opposite ledge, but unlike Vance, he did not recognize what he saw. The objects were metal, not food, and did not look like any sort of tool or toy he had ever come across.

"What are they?"

"An advantage."

Uncertain if the small explosives were safe to transport outside of their boxes, loading any of them into their satchels, pouches, and pockets did not seem wise. The spheres were light, the box of twelve weighing less than a large rabbit, but the boxes would be awkward to carry and would hinder quiet movement through the streets. Taking one box with them, however, might afford them an answer to their rescue attempt when it came, or offer a way to distract or destroy potential enemies.

With his injured hand and shoulder, however, carrying the box would not fall to Vance.

"We take a box and get out of here."

Now that he knew where the stash was, perhaps they could return later for the rest.

Removing them from Laedan Hallister's arsenal, if that was indeed who they belonged to, seemed a wise choice. As wise, he believed, as keeping the contents of the mythological Fort Hamilton out of the hands of Lowell and Donn Channon.

"We wait here."

They had traveled in as straight a line as they could along the route Vance had indicated, through unlit streets of shabby structures turned into private residences established after the Undoing. The southeasterly trajectory took them deeper into Kennedy Borough, but not so deep, the twins believed, that they were at risk of encountering more of Hallister's guards. The Kennedy Fortress was many miles away, and now that they were no longer near the border, Laedan Guards or random Protectorate patrols at this hour of the night seemed unlikely. Three or four blocks ahead, the typical array of decaying city edifices ended at the perimeter of an open area that they were too far away from to identify. If that was where they were heading, or if their destination was somewhere beyond it, then waiting in this corner lot filled with abandoned skeletal vehicles for Vance to catch up to them, to lead them, waiting for the support in numbers of Kato and the others, seemed their best decision.

They had followed Liam's howl this far. They waited here.

Even though waiting was the most difficult thing Jia could do.

Addi would have preferred a roof over his head and four walls to shield them from the wind, but he understood.

They needed to be in the open, where their companions could find them, where they could be vigilant for threats from every direction, where they were safe and yet exposed. The hulks of old cars and trucks would have to be shelter enough.

It might still be pure luck if their companions found them. There was no way to know how those in the Below were faring.

They did not hear that howl again.

Chapter 31

He had felt so many things surrounding his mother throughout the course of his life, good things, bad things, confusing things. But they all boiled down to a single desire, a single need…to manipulate and control the one person he believed needed to be on his side regardless of his failings and shortcomings as an individual, as a leader, as a man. Her favoritism of Nik, perceived as evident from the first when the middle Channon had, as a child, begun to exhibit the annoying trait of rarely sleeping…or at least not sleeping when his parents felt he should. That problem had always distracted her from the younger twin, and so the child quickly, subconsciously, begun to seek and develop ways to demand his share of her attention.

Be it destroying the aquarium of snails, frogs, and pond fish Nik had been given, to a faked drowning in the bay where the Channons had sometimes spent their seasonal summer days when the boys were still small and Lowell's faith in Roland had been unshakable. From the phase of overeating the wild berries which grew along the Fortress walls…to the point of making himself ill…or the installing of a noose in the sturdy branches outside of her bedroom window where she would be sure to see it in the morning when she woke. Donnovan's plea for her attention, his efforts to manipulate her into giving it to him, had succeeded from the first and with each success, he demanded more, and it seemed she had no will, desire, or ability to refuse him.

When the day came, when feeling friendless and alone as the older Jonni went off on some adventure with the Marrock children and Nik found favor at their father's side for a tour of some local business that Donn found boring, it made it that much easier for Donnovan to seek to bury that loneliness in his mother.

With a propensity to bully those who might have been his friends, he always got what he wanted from them too, but he knew his success had nothing to do with being liked. He wanted to be liked. He wanted the attention of the young women who came to call with their families but who fawned over Jonni…the eldest, the heir…or laughed with the easy-going, fun-loving Nik…or engaged in intellectual conversations with the studious Addi Marrock. Try as he did, Donnovan could not make the girls enjoy his company, as he was neither easy-going, studious, or suave. But he could make them endure it, and when finally, in his frustration on that day, he found his mother alone in her sewing room, it had been a too easy impulse to take what he wanted from her instead. He was taller than her by then. Heavier. Stronger.

She could not stop him, could not resist as he bent her to his will. And when his body's virgin physical needs were spent and she lay sobbing, curled on the floor heavy with the scent of sex and fear, Donnovan discovered a feeling of power he had never felt before.

And in all of the years since that day, he had never felt that sense of power with anyone else.

Not even his wife.

Donn needed Yiva to complete him, to give him purpose and strength.

Without her, he felt like nothing. He felt nothing. Without her, he was nothing.

Her departure from the Fortress earlier was noteworthy, as he could not recall his mother ever going anywhere in the borough without her husband at her side. Typically, if she wanted something not available within the walls of home, she sent a staff member to fetch it for her, be it food, fabric, a commodity or remedy, or the occasional companionship of one of the other women of standing who lived within a short distance of the Fortress. Donnovan was curious enough to follow her meanderings through the streets, noting who she paused to talk to, what she stopped to look at, the treats she purchased from window vendors.

A taste of freedom then, perhaps an escape from the memories of her eldest son which permeated the Fortress like lingering smoke.

Such an escape was excusable, understandable, and part of Donnovan would have liked to be there at her side, enjoying that same escape from the pain of loss. He and Jonni had been more rivals then brothers, but still, Donnovan had loved him.

When Yiva stopped before the Protectorate doors, however, staring up at them for too long for her stopping there to seem casual and coincidental, Donnovan's curiosity turned to suspicion.

He hoped she knew some detail about Quentin that sharing with the Protectors would mean being rid of his father's parasitic right-hand. Beneath that hope, however, his suspicion rooted and grew.

At that hour of the evening, Jonni was still dead, and unless she knew otherwise, Nik was still missing. With the rumors circulating through the Fortress about a fight between Donn and Quentin, a fight dutifully reported as having been initiated by Quentin, it was possible Yiva had come here seeking justice for one or more of the wrongs done to her sons.

If one of those were true, however, why not summon the Chief to the Fortress to meet with her the way Lowell normally did? Why the furtive skulking through the city to the Protectorate, alone, without even one of the Laedan guards?

Was she hiding from her husband? From Quentin? Or her son?

Had she ended up on these steps purely by chance?

Or was something going on between her and the Chief that Donnovan should know about? A relationship not proper for the wife of the Laedan? A liaison she should not have with anyone but him?

Or was it Nik?

Of course it was Nik. It was always Nik.

Her subsequent flight from the Protectorate some minutes later, her obvious upset and the haste in her steps burned him with worry and jealousy and he followed, intending to see that she reached the

Fortress unharmed and there have it out with her about her purpose for this excursion into the borough. But her frequent pauses as she walked, to wipe her eyes, adjust her skirts, smooth her hair, gradually pushed Nik and his jealousy towards his brother out of his mind and convinced Donn that there had been some impropriety with the Chief, or someone else in the Protectorate. As his anger intensified, her erratic path proved to him that she knew she was being followed…

…or that she hoped to throw off anyone who might have seen her in the borough, at the Protectorate…just in case she was later asked where she had been.

Donnovan would not stand for it. He had to know the truth.

His father had to know the truth.

By the time he caught her, overtaking her in the streets that he was barely more familiar with than she was, he snatched at her arm and dragged her into the nearest unlit alley, intending to know the facts of her betrayal before he let her go, before he took everything he knew to his father and made sure she never left the Fortress alone again.

She gave a short scream, the sound barely a yelp before his hand clapped over her mouth, not knowing at first who had grabbed her. As loud as the musical chatter and conversation were that spilled into the street from the adjoining dive, the cry was masked, unnoticed.

Useless.

Donnovan pulled her the length of the alley through the hemp paper garbage, rotted food, and waste collected there and threw her against the rusting wall of chain link stretched between the buildings on either side of them. It created a clattering, and when her blonde hair caught in the twisted link as he spun her to face him, and she tried to pull free in additional panic now that she saw who had caught her, she cried out again at the pain it caused and the overwhelming terror of her predicament.

His hand across her mouth, however, forced her silent.

"How dare you betray me with him of all people!"

Wide-eyed, she began to hyperventilate, unable to suck in enough air through her flared nostrils, the panic of being discovered out here, the possibility that he knew what she had done…or tried to do…on behalf of his wife erasing all rational thought from her mind.

She shook her head, unable to speak with his hand over her face.

"Why were you there? What did you do?"

His hand moved enough to make speech possible, but her voice behind it was muffled and barely intelligible as she panted, "I didn't tell anyone…I swear…I would never…you know I wouldn't…"

"Tell anyone what?"

That he had been the instigator of the fight with Quentin? Preposterous. There was no way for her to know that, and there was nothing else to know. He had done a lot of dubious things in his life, many less than moral, and even illegal things, on behalf of the mayoral power he wielded…things he believed best for his District and for LaGuardia as a whole. But she would not know of any of those either. Yiva did not have a head for politics and never concerned herself with them. Any of those things she might think she knew would be denied by her husband on behalf of the consolidated power in the borough. There was not one shred of proof of anything he had ever done that she could have taken to the Chief, and everything he had said and done with his wife was covered entirely by the rules and privilege of marriage. There was nothing she could use against Donnovan…

…except for the relationship with her son.

His already dark features turned crimson with fury, his bloodshot eyes bulging and fists tightening around her arm, over her mouth, with a bruising strength that made her scream again…a sound which prompted him to jerk her away from the fence and throw her down amidst the alley filth.

She was filth.

She would never…she loved him. He needed her. She knew that. She needed him too. Of course she did. No one loved her the way he did…as much as he did…

Whore.

There were no words to voice the confusion, the outrage, the horror, the agony of betrayal slicing through him, cutting his soul from his body, his soul from his mind. His mother…his protector…his rock…his lover…turned against him? How could she do such a thing? To him? To the one who loved her more than he loved anyone else?

She struggled to be free, but he was astride her now, and when she tried to scream again, he struck her face with enough force that her head bounced against the dirty pavement, turning her voice into a series of incoherent sobbing and cries. He took her then, striking her about the face, the neck, the shoulders and breasts as he spent all of his broken-hearted outrage on the one who had borne him, who had given him everything he ever wanted and needed, and who had now ripped all of that away.

It was her fault. Chief Ernest's fault, yes…Lowell's fault. And Nik's fault. Always Nik's fault.

But mostly it was hers.

When he stood at last, wiping his bloodied fists against his stained trousers before fumbling to fasten them, he did not look at the twisted, disfigured thing she had become. She was no longer what he wanted her to be. She was nothing. He composed himself, swiping the betraying dampness from his cheeks and raking a hand through his blonde hair without realizing the streaks of crimson he was leaving there, and then stalked away without looking back.

Whatever had become of her, she deserved it. She had killed him…her own son. No mother deserved to live after that. No one did.

Dead inside, shoulders drawn back, his expression cold and blank, Donnovan pushed the last conscious thoughts away. What exited the shadows of that alley was but a wraith of the man who had entered it.

The tranquilizing darts came in useful as Kato, carrying the box of hope Vance had discovered, led them out of the Below via an exit where another three guards, dressed identically to the guards they had found before, kept watch with the same pattern of position. The night's wind, again heavy with moisture though it had not resumed falling, blew directly into the tunnel, carrying the scent of the three, and their bored, gossiping chatter, to the collection of Cana, Fela, and mage, announcing they were there. It was strong enough to mask the scents and sounds of those inside the tunnel, masking their presence, giving the three Fela sisters the opportunity to shoot the sleepers at the guards. When all three bald men dropped, the group waited long enough to be confident that no one else was there, that no one had seen the guards' uncharacteristic behavior. Judging it to be safe now, they came to the surface, most breathing with relief to be in the open air again and out of the stifling, musty stench of Below.

Wist swiped one of the guards' hats and set it upon his head as the men were dragged inside the tunnel opening to hide them. Beren, meanwhile, claimed the rifle another of the three had dropped, the only true gun any of the guards had carried.

A rifle was a rare commodity. Vance wondered again as he leaned against the tunnel opening as the others dragged the guards out of sight and confiscated their dart guns, shockers and knives, as he readjusted to the plasm path in his blood and mind's eye, if Hallister had found Fort Hamilton.

There had been other sources of such weapons since the Undoing, of course. Private stashes, Protectorate offices, security facilities. Maybe the Hallisters had simply been better at locating, seizing, and distributing those things then the Channons and Marrocks had been.

Maybe, as was often said throughout LaGuardia, the Marrocks of old had been better at confiscating and destroying any weapons found to get them off of the streets and out of the hands of the people they governed. Maybe the Hallisters had preferred to keep those things rather than destroy them.

Maybe that was the real reason Lowell Channon wanted to find Fort Hamilton…and the real reason Roland was dead. Without Roland, Channon would have an easier time building up an arsenal to mirror what Vance suspected Kennedy Borough had.

While the rest of his party caught their breaths, rested and assessed their location, the tracker closed his eyes and rubbed his temples. Tangled with the fading, but still strong, crimson threads that pulled him across Kennedy in search of the endpoint he hoped would blot out the plasm's effects in his blood, was the black and amber pulse that told him Jia and her brother were nearby. Not within sight, but near enough that he could almost smell her if he tried. Another hour at least had passed with them beneath the ground but it seemed Jia was safe.

They needed to move, needed to find their destination before the sun rose, before the vision in his blood faded too much and he lost the way. But he needed to find her first, needed to prove she had gotten this far uninjured. He needed to rejoin their group into a cohesive whole and he needed to touch her, to break the link that held them.

He could not allow that link to continue. Enough time had passed that he was mortified by that kiss, by his own behavior. He could not leave the link open much longer. The strain of it would surely kill him…or at least drive him mad, if he did not sever it and apologize for what he should not have done.

"Which way?" Kato sniffed the air, but the strength of the gusting wind brought with it so many mixed signals that sorting them was going to take too long unless he shifted. Nothing suggested any Cana nearby, not Jia or Addi or anyone likely to be a threat.

At this hour, most ought to be asleep, unless they were scavs or replacement guards on the way to relieve these three of duty.

It was that possibility, and the possibility of some early Protectorate patrol passing, that prompted Kato to speak. He needed to be sure Jia was safe too. It had been too long without any sign or contact with her.

Vance pointed to his left, to the east of where they stood. "There. They are there…close…"

"Close is good," agreed Xen. Close to the Alpha meant closer to finding Liam, her primary concern now that she had escaped the stagnation of the Below.

Assuming that Vance would again need assistance to walk as his continuing weak appearance suggested, now that he no longer had the tunnel wall to lean on for support, Helena and Beren, the strap of the rifle slung over his shoulder, moved into place to support the mage's weight. But he waved them away, determined, now that the discomfort of the plasm link was lessening the more time passed and the nearer they got to its source, to cover the final distance on his own. The focal point was strong, the whirling pull stronger, and his proximity to it made it easier to follow and less unpleasant to concentrate on.

His steps were still shaky and more sluggish than he liked, but now it was more akin to the effect of a day's weariness or a night's drunken indulgence.

Weariness he was accustomed to. Drunkenness too.

Half a block away, when they came in sight of the corner lot, once used for parking or for the sale of autos, Addi and Jia saw the group's approach before Vance and the others saw them. Jia crept, crab-like, to where they might see her and gave a short, birdsong whistle.

Vance was not the only member of the rescue crew to breathe a sigh of relief.

"Together," said the older man, the jagged scar on his face that ran from his cheek up into his receding hairline crinkling as he spoke. "If more of us…if they're there…maybe they'll hear us…"

"And maybe," someone else groaned in weary, chattering fear, "whoever they are, they'll come and kill us."

It was a risk. Liam knew it. But he believed the second speaker, a Fela if his senses were accurate, spoke out of fear of other Cana. No one had come before, to his solitary howl, for good or for ill. Maybe they were too far away. Or maybe no one was coming. But if anyone was guarding them, they had not come in response to his howl, and he doubted they would come if another was attempted.

If fortune favored them, if anyone, Cana, Fela, Ursa or otherwise, heard the men and women trapped here, they might be inclined to come to the rescue. It made the risk to shift, to howl, worth the effort.

In anthro form, at least they would have the advantage of fur to keep warm.

As cold as they were, more bodies dragged into the heap at the end of the room, was the risk really so bad if they were dead already?

Four Cana in unison. The Fela, and others in the group, refused to shift. Four Cana huddled in a human-like group embrace, put their muzzles together and bayed at the unseen moon.

Heads turned. Aided by the head-on wind, the tracker heard it too, a distress cry of a sound. A mournful, frightened, Cana call of anguish.

Around him, the members of the Flushing pack shifted to hybrid as one, clothing rending to accommodate the different musculature of the man-beasts.

As Vance reached for her, touched her to break their connection, the Flushing Pack howled as one.

We are here, Vance heard in that howl, the sound cutting into his head, into his heart, into his core as the words were sung to the night.

We are here.

Wait for us.

We are coming.

Vance fell to his knees, head in his hands, fighting back a scream.

We are coming.

Wait for us.

Chapter 32

Blood seeped from his nose, from his ears, the smell of copper and the rumbling rush of it pulsing through his veins on top of the plasm phantoms haunting him barely enough to mute the Cana howl that entwined itself around him and rubbed against his mage senses like beach sand inside his clothes. He had heard Cana howl before, but never at this proximity, and his body, his senses, had never reacted this way. Vance could only attribute the reaction to either the remnants of the powdered anthro plasm in his system…or else to the link he had created to Jia that was only meant to facilitate the reunification of the group after their separation. Arms wrapped around his head, head between his knees, he did his best to block out the sound as he waited for it to cease.

The Fela siblings clung together, huddled against the melancholy force of the sound, and Kato took several steps back to put distance between himself and the Cana. He told himself it was intended to be a respectful distance, nothing more, but the roughness of the sound was unlike what he had heard the night Roland had been laid to rest, or the night the Pack had located the Queens College Library. This sound hurt, emotionally, physically, and he knew he was not the only one relieved when it ended. He was glad, with his glance at the Fela siblings, and the mage, that he was not the only one suffering and not the only one left at ease when the night grew silent again.

Jia's exuberance, her impulse to run towards the sound of Cana in distress was undercut by first Kato's uncomfortable expression and then the sight of the tracker curled into a fetal position on the ground. The blood around his ears alarmed her, and when she helped him to sit up, revealing more blood beneath his nose, on his hands and arms where their use as a shield put his nose and ears in contact with both…and the blood on the ground where it had dripped when his head was between his knees, made her blanch. In her Cana state, the scent of fresh blood and the still echoing cries of her friend's fear made her eager for a hunt, but she was also eager to undo whatever harm had been done to the mage she had relied on to get this far.

Trying to adjust her shirt to be a decent covering now that it no longer fit properly with her shift back to Normal, she murmured, "Vance?" He winced when she grasped his wounded shoulder and she let her hand slide down to his knee. Had she done this, she wondered? Was this the reaction of an anthro's blood in the body of a Normal…or a mage? Was this the effect it had on Nik and other users? Was this a result of whatever anchoring he had used to help him find her?

Was the tracker dying?"

He shook his head, her hand on his knee bearing her thoughts to him as loudly and clearly as if there had been skin to skin contact. The effect of the exchange made him shudder and grimace, a bitter negative sensation he had never thought to feel with her which left him with a morose sense of isolation. He covered her hand with his wrapped one, ignoring the throbbing where the end of his finger had been, and with an effort of will severed the anchor that tethered him to her. His suffering was his own fault for establishing that anchor, after all, brief though it had been.

He should have known better. He did know better.

A tracker mage's life was, by necessity and the nature of the tactile gift they had been given, a solitary one.

Not a gift, he again confessed to himself. A gift was something one wanted. Something one asked for. And year after year, one failed friendship, one failed relationship, after another, he was reminded again and again just how unwanted this ability could be.

Before he could withdraw from her hand or request she did not touch him again, Kato pulled her to her feet as Addi, behind her, spoke.

"We've got to do this now…before someone comes." Whether anyone recognized the howls as Cana rather than wolf, it was the sort of sound that drew hunters, or at least uneasy residents, to a scene in the hopes of a kill or capture.

And if, as Vance suspected, HOPE was to be found at the end of their quest, being discovered was the last thing any of them wanted.

Vance nodded. Moving, doing what they had come to do, was the best thing. He used Wist's arm to pry himself to his feet, wiping the blood from his upper lip as he did so. But that bleeding, the consequences of that howl on his head, on his senses, had erased all traces of the path within. His blood felt empty, his veins hollow. He felt blind.

"I should stay."

"We need you," started Xen. Whatever her misgivings about the mage had been, mistrusting of his kind as any anthro would be, Vance had brought them this close to her brother…and her brother was still alive. Jia too had kept her promise even after the way Xen had briefly betrayed her. The power of the whipping wind forced its way between and through buildings, making it difficult to tell which direction the howls had come from, but they were close. Without the tracker, it might take too long to find Liam. Without the tracker, by the time they found him, it might be too late. They might not reach Liam at all.

They had come too far to give up.

"The trail's cold; I can't…" He shook his head. He had no anthro senses, no anthro strengths. There was little more he could do except put distance between him and Jia.

Grasping his wrists, however, holding him firmly as she stared into his dark eyes and ignoring whatever discomfort her touch caused him, Jia refused to believe what he was saying. "The trail may be cold…but you know the way. You've already seen it…and you have the keycard. You can recreate it…you can find the way. You can remember. Please, Vance…we need you."

I need you.

He almost pulled away from her, refusing to believe her unspoken words, refusing to believe they had come from her, choosing to believe instead that his own desperation had fabricated them. In the throes of his self-reproach and self-pity, he did not want to be needed by anyone. He wanted to go home, back to LaGuardia, back to his sofa. He wanted a drink, wanted to return to the mundane existence he had slogged through for years before the morning Laedan Channon had asked him to find a stolen shipment of medıplies.

But he could not go back, and frankly, he knew, he could not turn his back on what he had begun. He was not that sort of man. He had a job to do…two of them. Find that supply shipment, whatever and wherever it was, which could have ended up at the same location where Roland had been held. Find and bring Roland and Liam home. His duty to Roland was over, completed when the man had been put to earth. But his duty to Liam remained. Both duties meant reaching the center of the now silently still vortex. Both meant forging ahead.

And Jia was right. He was not called the best Tracker in LaGuardia for nothing. He had seen the way, had been following it for hours. He had only to trace the residue in his memory, the clues on the keycard, the hints on the wind that the Cana may or may not be able to find, and he would get there.

He would find the end.

If HOPE was there, his status as Protector, as Mage, as a man on a mission from Laedan Channon, might be the only thing that could get any of them out of this alive.

"They heard us."

Excitement had revived the weak and weary cluster of perhaps two dozen men and women who had, until that moment, been resigned to a frozen, starving fate.

"Will they come?"

"For all of us?"

"They'll be here," Liam promised, his heart pounding as he led those capable of movement to the wall he was sure had once been a set of warehouse doors. He had not heard Roland's voice, but he had heard others just as familiar. They were close…Jia was close…and though he had no inkling of the obstacles they might face to reach him in his prison, in getting them out, he was certain Jia would try.

His best friend was too stubborn to do anything else.

"Stay right here…listen for them," he instructed the others clustered around him, their ears pressed to the wall eagerly. "If you hear anything out there, beat on the wall…"

"Where are you…?" someone started with a note of distress.

The emaciated faces stared at him out of the darkness, only anthro senses allowing him to see them there. They were almost beyond caring for their fate but did not want him to leave them to it…whatever it would be. They did not want the one who had cared for them, who had given each one food and water, had taken away the dead, made sure they were as warm as they could be in this place, to abandon them.

Liam frowned but relented without protest. His intent to go to the nearest door, to draw their rescuers there if he could, would be just as futile. All of those doors were barred from the outside, probably locked, and not easily opened. Banging on those doors to announce their location, to let others know they were here and alive, could be as easily accomplished from here.

Reuniting with Jia, with whomever else had come from the Pack for him, would happen soon enough. Appointed Alpha of the dying, Liam would remain where he was until they no longer needed him.

Together, their fists beat on the wall. They paused to listen, ears pressed to the plaster surface, a surface that absorbed some of their efforts. Still nothing. Not yet.

But Liam was not discouraged. They were coming.

He started pounding again.

☙*❧

It did not look right and was, Oasis knew, not accurate when it came to either the distances between the points it portrayed or the likely obstacles to be found between LaGuardia's Fortress and the location that so many now sought.

But it was near enough in likeness, with enough important places marked, to give Thom a chance, near enough to prompt him to leave the Fortress and LaGuardia she hoped. She did not want him here, in harm's way, in her way, and getting him out into the open was, she imagined, the easiest way to accomplish both ends at once.

The sheet was folded and pressed between the pages of an innocent-looking ancient tome about places of entertainment once available in Queens…movie houses and parks, sports arenas and musical venues, bars and eateries. A harmless tome that no one was likely to question. Then, ignoring the Fortress employees she passed, she went to the message room, to the array of open wall boxes where correspondences could be left for anyone in the Fortress by others inside or outside, and placed the book in Thomas Quentin's box.

She had not seen him again. She did not want to. She did not know if he had already left the Fortress, if he hid somewhere within it still, or if perhaps Lowell or Donnovan had already disposed of him.

But she left what she had promised for him, as she said she would, before the deadline she had promised to have it there. She would give him a reasonable amount of time to retrieve it and make use of it.

If he did not, if it was still there in a few days, she would remove it and destroy the map.

She could not be linked to the map, to Thom, in any way. She had to protect herself.

If Quentin was too foolish to make use of the key she offered, well, that was his unfortunate business, not hers. She would not leave herself exposed any longer than she had to.

Chapter 33

The sprawling complex of low buildings, most a single story in height, was surrounded by layered rows of razor wire and unmanned watchtowers. It appeared deserted. No glow of lights shown from the few windows in the only second story area the structure possessed, nor around the edges of the only ground level doors they could see. At this hour of pre-dawn, however, that lack of light was not proof it was empty, it only supported the emptiness suggested by the lack of gate attendants or guards in the towers. No one walked the grounds. The stacks designed to vent smoke and steam from the heating system were inactive and there was a noticeable lack of sound that would have been produced by such systems. Whatever the nature of this facility, a medilab, a hospital, a warehouse or production unit, it was possible they ceased working at night, shut everything down to reduce the expense of running it. Perhaps they did not have enough personnel to run twenty-four-hour shifts.

That did not, however, excuse the lack of guards or patrolmen.

Unless the facility's owners thought they were immune to assault, theft or invasion.

Nor would it explain why the gates they could see from behind the crumbling wall where they had taken position had been left open without a single person to protect or service them. It was as if the owners, the caretakers, had simply left, leaving the metal storage containers, and whatever remained inside, behind.

"Gotta be a trap," hissed Beren. He could not argue about the rightness of the place, as he did not have the mage's senses, but there was undoubtedly someone here, announced by the periodic banging on the walls at the northern end of the building.

"How could it be…they couldn't have known we were coming," countered Helena. Other than the members of the Flushing Pack, and those residing around the Queen's College Library, no one had known they were looking for Liam or had any notion where they might end up in their search for him.

No one could have known they would end up here.

"He knew," Wist muttered, staring at the back of the tracker's head. "Maybe all of this shart about a path…using the plasm as a map to find…"

Vance did not have to see the annoyed glare to know it was there.

Jia growled without looking at either of them, her focus on the fenced yard and the wall from where the occasional banging originated. "He didn't know," she muttered.

No one dared to contradict her.

"If I had to guess…" Vance shuffled in a duck-like waddle several feet sideways to escape the refractions of negative emotion as well as to get a better view and assess the location with his practiced Protector's experience. Everyone's adrenaline was high, their fears and worries elevated; all of those heightened emotions made it difficult to assess what his senses were showing him.

This place could have been a palace on par with the Fortress if it were better protected.

He stopped at the street's edge, the street that led to the main gate, and risked creeping into the middle of the cleared roadway to press his good hand to the rutted, broken remnants of pavement. Jia followed as far as the edge of the building, watching him, wondering what he had left unsaid as she watched for threats and blocked any of those with her from taking the same risk the tracker was taking.

He was right. Many wagons had recently passed here, pulled by strong horses and oxen, heavy wagons full of people and goods who had continued back along the western road as far as he could see, the road they had recently followed to get here. Those wagons were part of the reason this portion of the trail seemed fresh to him. If they had arrived sooner, a day earlier at least, they would have crossed paths with those wagons, and though he thought he could backtrack along the wagon's route and discover where they were going, what they were doing, who the owners were, that was not his mission tonight.

Maybe after Liam was safe, assuming he was in the building before them as Jia and the others believed, Vance would follow this new evidence trail. If the stolen mediplies shipment had traveled this way, then it was surely still his duty to find it.

But one duty at a time, and the survivors…since there sounded to be several individuals inside the building, were the priority. The trail west was not going to evaporate yet.

The banging began again, and when Jia waved for him to return to the group, Vance reluctantly obeyed.

"Well?" asked Xen impatiently.

"I'd guess the news of Roland's death got back to them…and they decided to relocate before a formal inquiry brought investigators."

Jia nodded, grim-faced. So her father had been here. Without windows, with so few doors, she wondered how he had escaped…and how he had made it across the Kennedy border, across the neutral sector, and across LaGuardia's border, without being more injured then he had been. How he made it to the Bunker alive.

"It'll be suicide to go through those gates and…" started Beren.

Helena frowned at him. "There's no one here except…"

No one except whoever was pounding again on the walls, the sound once more disrupting the silence. There were others in buildings around the perimeter, citizens of Kennedy, men and women unlikely connected to this place beyond being potential employees of it, residents who probably had little idea of the work being done by HOPE…or someone else…in their midst. People likely growing irritated by a banging that was surely disturbing their sleep. Kato knew if he could sense them, the other anthro could too. They might be threats if they were not sleeping, the way he should be, if they chose not to ignore the sound and instead decided to investigate its source.

"Going through is exactly what we do," Kato grunted. "But then what?"

Shaking his bag to remind them with the clatter within of the explosive content QiangXu had provided, Wist grinned and offered, "We blow the doors off."

Addi shook his head. "That would attract too much attention."

"Anything we do is going to attract attention," Xen pointed out.

"And we don't know that the doors are even locked," argued Helena. "They left the gates open after all…"

"Obviously a trap," Beren repeated.

"Maybe," Jia agreed, taking all of the comments into account. "If the doors aren't locked...there would be no need for the knocking. But if not through the gate, what options do we have?" Why find somewhere to cut through the fence with the tools they had brought, pass through elsewhere, when this way was open before them?

"I'll go." There was no other option as far as Vance was concerned. Still in the shadows, he drew his Protector's coat out of his bag and struggled to get it on. He had not worn it before so as not to attract attention to a LaGuardia Protector in the Wilds, in the neutral sector, or in Kennedy's streets. Now his professional status might be the key they needed to get inside. If anyone was anticipating an official inquest, who better than a LaGuardia Protectorate Tracker-Mage?

He would either be shot on sight the way Sal had been, or he would be greeted and brought inside for a tour of what he suspected was a largely empty building.

Empty of objects, however, did not mean empty to the senses of a tracker. Whatever had happened inside, whoever had been there, Vance would know.

"While I've got their attention, the rest of you can get in and get the others out."

It did not seem the wisest of plans to Jia, Vance going inside alone, but it had merit. Anything they attempted would come with risk attached. They had known there would be risk before setting out on this path. This far in, this close to their objective, avoiding risk was not only impossible, but it would also mean failure.

"Helena…you and the girls cover our backs here." The Fela siblings had the least amount of experience in the group, and if anyone could get them to safety, could get back to Queens College, could draw attention away from Jia and the others and lead a chase through Kennedy's streets, it would be the fleet-footed Helena…the survivor…the one most familiar, or so she claimed, with Kennedy.

And if there was trouble, the four would serve as a warning to those going inside.

The rest, those she trusted to fight, she wanted at her side. If there came a conflict, it was going to happen inside of those seemingly empty walls. Jia wanted to be certain that they, and Liam, had the best chance for survival she could give them.

Nods were exchanged, embraces shared between the Fela siblings, and then Vance, after taking one of the explosive orbs from the box, strode into the street, across the empty swath that formed an outer perimeter around the razor wire boundary, and without any nervous hesitation or uncertainty, passed through the gates, his good hand in his pocket fingering that weapon, his other casually at his side.

He had shown the others how to use those orbs, instructed them the best he could, as they snuck through the streets in the dark to the place they now hid. The others had agreed they would not use them unless they had to, a precaution he demanded because he did not want to be responsible if someone blew themselves up the way that unfortunate child had done years ago.

Now each person took one and pocketed it too. Kato shoved the metal box into his pack after taking other objects out for redistribution in the others' bags.

Vance hoped the devices worked. He also hoped the decision to dispense them and explain their use would not be his biggest regret.

But he made it across the yard without incident, raising no alarms, drawing no weapons fire, bringing no one running from the building or from those on the outside of the fence, no one from the forty-foot metal boxes that might have been storage or housing or workshops. No one from the towers. Feeling the eyes of the anthro group following him as he reached the exterior wall on which those inside were banging, he paused to knock back three times though he did not speak to announce his intentions. If those within heard him, as he assumed they must, he hoped they understood that help had arrived.

He made it to the only doors on the side of the building facing the group, wide double doors through which he was confident the departing wagons had been loaded.

The ruts in the mud, dry save for the traces the recent dusting of snow had left, proved how often used this path was.

Lifting the long metal bar that ran from one side of the sheet metal doors to the other would be difficult, and loud, with one good hand and one good shoulder…both on opposite sides of his body. And the old fashioned padlock that held the latch closed was going to require something more than the keycard or his long knife or shocker to open.

He needed the others.

Though he stood in the shadows against the dark grey siding of the building, with only the dimness of moonlight behind the clouds to see by, he knew his audience of Fela and Cana were watching. Without a sound, he waved them to him…

…and waited with bated breath.

*

"Back away from the wall."

"Why?"

Liam could not say. It was not Jia's scent on the other side of the wall, but someone was there, someone who offered a hunch in that three-time knock. It was a signal surely, though one without a specific meaning. It was a hunch he would rather follow and be wrong then a hunch he chose to ignore until someone was injured or killed.

"The doors are locked…barred. Unless they have keys…it's going to take breaking through…"

The heads around him bobbed in understanding.

"Help me with the others."

Those who could helped those who were weaker, moving them into the center of the room where they would hopefully be beyond the reach of any breaking in effort about to be made. Eyes turned warily to the walls, the lab door, the air duct, and the ceiling above, no one knowing where help was destined to come from. If someone, on their side or against them, was going to break in, the survivors wanted to be prepared to shelter and protect one another.

Not even Liam was certain that that external knocking was working in their favor.

Pistol in hand, Vance kept watch as Wist and Beren hoisted the long iron rod from the tongs that held it across the double door and set it on the ground. The tracks above their heads and the ones in the cement at their feet, in which the metal wheels along the upper and lower edges of the door rested, were worn smooth, shiny in places, suggesting frequent use, but none of them carried any easy means or expertise to pick the lock, and none of them were strong enough to break its rusty metal loop.

Beren's effort to fire the shotgun at the lock, ill-advised and unexpected as it was, proved that the gun was unloaded, a foolhardy thing for the men guarding the Below to have done. Given a shortage of bullets, perhaps the weapon had been carried as a gamble, in the hopes that the sight of it would be enough to frighten off miscreants and trespassers. Beren, in his annoyance, growled and rammed the butt of the weapon against the rusted lock, filling the night with the rumbling reverberation of the sheet metal doors.

Addi's uttered, "Are you crazy?" was greeted by the lock falling away as the group as one spun or crouched in preparation for a fight if anyone came charging as a result of the sound.

Hoping that the noise would be mistaken for thunder, the same as the clatter of those small wheels in their worn tracks, Kato grasped the edge of one door and heaved with enough effort to open it just far enough for each member to squeeze inside one at a time. Opening the door only a little would, he hoped, reduce the amount of sound. Better than pushing the door back all the way. He hoped that the additional noise was not going to matter.

If anyone had heard the sounds, if anyone arrived to investigate the sources, how far the door was open, the lock broken and the barring pole on the ground were evidence enough of a break-in.

Jia and her compliment were greeted by a vast room heavy with the odor of burnt flesh and decay, smells Vance was the first to recognize from visits made to one sposer facility or another…to collect bodies or deliver them or to inspect the effects of the dead who had been taken in for dispensation. It seemed from their matching scowls, that Jia and Addi recognized those smells and this place as well. The processing of the dead created fertilizers, generated power…and from the looks of the bodies shoved too many at a time into the open furnace door, also to hide evidence.

All three were confident about the uses of this room.

Powering this place. Ridding themselves of the dead.

Of evidence.

So many at once.

Addi crossed to the furnace to peer at the dead. Those not yet burned, not yet beyond recognition, most dead for days if he had to guess, all shared one thing in common beyond emaciation.

"Anthro," he murmured.

Cana, to be exact, but that was not to say that all of these bodies were Cana. What others could be beneath, what the ones were who were already charred and twisted, was impossible to tell.

They could pull the partially burned corpses from the furnace for further examination, they could take the time to restart the furnace and finish the sposing, but what would be the point? They were dead. Nothing would change that. The dead were not currently their concern.

They were here for the living.

More alert now, they crossed the room, angling for the door that opened into a three-branched corridor. Despite their caution, no one came, either from the corridors or from outside. The arrival of an external threat still seemed likely, but as Helena had yet to give them a warning, Jia chose to believe they were safe.

At the head of the group, she glanced up and down the corridor, and into the path straight ahead of them. No lights burned, every other door she could see without the use of a light source was open, and Liam's scent, recent enough to be fresh, flowed in every direction. He must have been investigating, or else had been forced to walk these corridors for unknown reasons. They could not tell where he was now, however, but she guessed he was with the group that had since ceased pounding on the building's walls.

That meant, most likely, left.

"Xen…go that way."

Xen's protesting frown meant that she too had the same thought about her brother's whereabouts within this complex and that she preferred to go to him, to be the one to find him. But though the scents of others passing here were fading, not fresh enough to be within the last few hours, they could not take the chance that there were threats hiding elsewhere in the facility.

They would have to divide their resources. The corridor to the right looked to be the shortest and seemed to end at a closed door. Xen could scout it and rejoin the others quickly. She was being trusted, tested, to do as the Alpha required, trusted to see to their group's safety.

They were the only reasons she relented to the order. She would see her brother soon enough.

"Wist…Beren…guard our backs here."

"But…" started Wist.

"I want…" chimed Beren.

Vance shoved his pistol into Wist's hands, though he doubted the young man had any notion of how to use it. "Anyone you don't know comes through those," he gestured to the external doubled doors where they had entered at the other side of this room, "you point and pull the trigger. It's already primed."

There was not enough time for a shooting lesson, to show him how to prep it for a second shot, and there were only three bullets in the gun. If fortune was with them, Wist was not going to need it.

"And you've got the sleep guns…and the rifle," added Kato.

Beren scowled. "But it has no…"

"Anyone coming through there isn't going to know that," Jia reminded him. "Vance…Addi…take that way. Kato…with me."

"But if Liam's…"

Jia enfolded her brother in a brief embrace. "If he's living, he will survive a few more minutes," she promised, clinging to that belief. He had to survive that long. The chemical smells emanating from the hall she had directed her brother and the mage into were likely from sources the trained doctor and Protector would have a better chance of identifying then she would. "If there's trouble…you know the signal."

Three of them did. The three Cana from the Flushing Pack who had learned such signals under Roland's leadership, the three sent in separate directions. A wise Alpha precaution. Xen nodded again, understanding growing, and started off in her assigned direction. Each of those three, she, Addi, and Jia, knew the signals and could alert the others, summon the others, warn them.

If any such alarm was needed here, at their point of entry into the complex, they knew the commotion made by guns, the shouts the two youngest men would make, would be heard and understood without the pair needing special signals.

Behind the wall at the edge of the Kennedy Borough Street, three tawny Fela and one black Cana spread out to maintain a better visible assessment of possible threats. They listened to the silence stretch and settle again after the explosive sounds of vibrating metal and the rolling door had ended. In the buildings around them, people awoke, may have peeped through dark windows, but no one emerged.

The night remained quiet.

*

After another day of dodging Fortress staff and each of the Channons he knew was out for his blood, he was forced to face the most painful decision he might ever have to make. He had contacts, people he had bribed, people he had done favors for and who owed him in return, relationships he had cultivated, people who would shield him on the outside should anyone come looking for him as he suspected they inevitably would. And he had a small host of mercenaries he had been able to pay to come to his aid when the time came. He still believed this twist in fortune was reversible, that he would return to the Laedan's good graces, once that rogue Fela was arrested and he could prove, through false testimony and torture, that the other was to blame for the deaths of Jonni and Roland. And once Nik turned back to the clutches of abuse, no one was going to believe anything he said about Thom being Fela.

They could demand a blood test. It had been done. But they were not infallible and Thom believed he could work his way out of that predicament.

If a mage was brought in, however, it would make disguising evidence more difficult.

For now, he reluctantly realized, before sneaking in the dead of night down to the message desk, that his chances of survival and success would be better on the outside. Until he could prove himself innocent, a victim of slander by the sadistic venom spewed by Donnovan and Nik, he was safer elsewhere.

He could turn all of this around on Donnovan. For his own sake. For Oasis.

And he would.

But not if he remained inside the Fortress playing hideseek with his employer.

It was a peculiar book she had left for him, a tome of entertainments he had never shown any use for or interest in, but it was a book taken from someone's collection that no one would miss, that no one would notice or care about should they find it on him. He did not need the book itself. All he wanted was the folded rectangle hemp page tucked inside, which he opened now and spread on the message center counter to study in the pale light of the night candle in the sconce on the wall.

The real thing would have been better. This hand-drawn map, little better than any child could have done, showed no streets, few landmarks, and no hint of what obstacles might be in his path. But as no one alive in LaGuardia, to his knowledge, had traveled the roads beyond the western borders, there was no way for anyone to know, even if they possessed a real map, what obstacles lay in store either.

The Undoing had changed many things. Nature and mankind's efforts to eke out survival had done the rest. Anyone seeking a landmark could only gauge the basic direction of a place, and possibly the distance, and hope they were correct.

Donn was not prepared for such a quest. And Jonni's death, and the necessities of restructuring the borough's government because of it, would take time for Lowell to manage. Thom knew that. If he gathered his resources quickly, however many he could pay to travel with him with the few credits, jewels, bits of gold and favors he had saved and managed to stuff into his duffle tonight, he could be on his way to Fort Hamilton before anyone else.

With an early enough start, he could reach it first.

He could win.

He smiled smugly and stuffed the book and its folded map into his bag and cinched it closed.

In its place, in the cabinet slot where the book had been, he left a simple braided band of copper and silver strands. She would find it and know what it meant.

She would understand.

Chapter 34

A kitchen that yielded nothing to eat and empty rooms heavy with the scents of night sweat, unwashed bodies, and sex, offered proof that others had lived here until recently. There were no furnishings, no bedding, to contain those smells, but it lingered in the peeling paint on the walls and in the uncirculated air. There had not been many here, Xen determined, as she tracked the scents of perhaps two to three dozen men and women crisscrossing the corridors, trailing in and out of the rooms. Enough to do the work, to maintain the equipment and the building, to guard the staff, the stock and the supplies, but nothing more. None of the scents were familiar except Liam's where he had entered rooms long enough to make the same scenting investigation she was making before moving on.

His scent was fairly fresh. He had not been here so long ago.

Spilled soil on the floor in a room with glass ceiling panels and a mulch box of rotting foodstuffs revealed a room once used for gardening, for raising the food the people here ate. The barrels along one wall, with narrow tubes running from ceiling spouts used to fill them, had been tipped sideways and were now mostly dry. Any water collected for use by the residents had drained away through the round grates in the floor, the holes beneath the grates wide enough for a man to pass into if they were desperate enough.

But the grates were heavy, not easily moved by one Normal person, and stuck into place as if they had not been moved in a long while. When she listened to the sounds beneath her, all she could hear was the continual drip, drip, that suggested water coming in from somewhere. Somewhere else. Not this room.

There was no sewage stench so this was not a collector for waste.

This was intended for reusable water only. Water for cooking, for cleaning, for drinking or bathing. Water to be saved…but there were no people, no anthro, there.

The underfloor passages might be worth exploring later. Now there were more pressing matters at hand.

Nothing of interest, empty rooms without furnishings or physical traces of inhabitation except for a freezer unit encased on three sides by the wall, a unit too large and bulky and heavy to move easily. It was perhaps the only reason such an item, still cold enough inside with ice clinging to the interior walls, to prove that there had been power to it not long ago, had not been taken away. Such a commodity was expensive. Valuable.

Maybe the building's owners intended to come back for it once the thaw completed and their relocation efforts were finished.

Whatever it had stored, it was empty now, and without Vance's gifted touch, there was no way Jia could know if it had held food, or if it had protected documents in the dry portions of the unit, or if it had housed the blood stolen from numerous unfortunate anthro.

"Jia…look…"

The heavy hemp paper folder Kato slid along the surface of the built-in counter was open as if someone had been investigating its contents. A scattering of other pages, some blank, some with columns of numbers, what looked to be names, and a few hand-drawn diagrams that reminded her of those in the texts Addi had studied as he trained to be a doctor, were spread on the counter nearby. She did not have the expertise or understanding to decipher their code, nor the light to see them clearly, but the symbol on the outside of the folder, pressed into the thick paper as if scorched by a brand, was something with which many, Laedan, prominent, or common alike, were familiar, even if they could not read.

HOPE.

A peek at the other sheets revealed more names and numbers, or designations of numbers on charts, and more diagrams that would take time to study, decipher, and understand. But it was proof that Vance was correct, that HOPE was behind the abduction of anthro, behind the poisoning of the population with a drug rooted in anthro blood.

But was it enough proof, she mused, as she stuffed the loose pages into the folder and then slid the folder into her satchel, to tear the organization down?

"This was the lab."

The chemical stench was strong here, chemicals used to process blood, to clean instruments and hands, to wipe traces of humanity from the floor, the walls, the cabinet doors and surfaces. Any equipment that had been here was gone, except units in the ceiling that they could not reach, but Vance knew the room's use the moment he touched the latch, slid the stolen keycard through the electrically disabled lock just to see what would happen, and pushed the partially ajar door open.

He traced his fingers over every surface, absorbing the muted deaths of frail people who had not been aware they were dying, the numbness of those individuals responsible for those deaths in the course of doing whatever jobs they were compensated to do, the apathy of the ones in charge. Laedan Hallister had been here at some time, the echoes of his voice too faint to detect the words but it was still a tone and cadence the mage recognized. Vance did not know why the man had been here…but he had been.

And beneath that, stronger to his senses, was the horror of two men who had done their best, in their assisting capacity, to ease the suffering of those they could not set free. Roland had been here. Roland had served here.

Men and women had died here.

Addi did not need the tracker's senses to know it too.

Nor did he need them to identify the cluster visible through the large plate viewing window, one very similar to that which separated the Fortress infirmary from the corridor beyond it. Once the door was open between the lab and that too cold, sterile, otherwise empty room, the scent was all anthro, and overwhelmingly Cana.

"Liam? Liam…are you here?"

Addi whistled, a three-note burst, as he rushed through the door without thought that someone could be guarding those poor souls.

Vance tried to catch his arm but missed.

Someone surged up from the mass of bodies, thin and unsteady. Reflexively, assuming an attack though he had missed catching Addi's arm, Vance threw his body between the group and the doctor, shoving him back against the wall.

"Addison?"

*

She trailed behind him for a time, though she did not care what he was doing, what his choices were. If he wanted to leave, let him leave. It was better for her, for everyone, if he did. But she wanted to see it for herself. Wanted to be certain it happened.

There was no way she could have gone with him. She had no desire to and was relieved that he had not asked her. Still, part of her was curious, part of her wanted some sort of proof of whether he cared or not. She wanted to see with her own eyes so she would believe, finally, that he would abandon her in an act of self-preservation.

Just the way he had left her in her father's house many years ago.

"Liam!"

Addi's whistle and cry brought Jia running at a speed that surprised her, her need to see that her best friend as alive driving her. She pushed past her brother and Vance, rushing to embrace the thin blonde. Her need to touch him, scent him, to prove his reality was cut abruptly short by a high pitched Fela yowl from outside the complex, a sound followed shortly by the distant shouts of men ordering other men and a smattering of gunfire they had not expected to hear. The frightened, naked gaggle in the center of the room cried out in terror but there was nowhere for them to run and they were too weak to fight back if it was a fight they were facing.

"We'll never make it out the way we came," shouted Xen as she burst into the large room, dragging Beren and Wist with her. There was no point in leaving them at the door inadequately equipped against the deadlier weapons bearing down on their position. Anyone outside would see where they had entered, if they had not already, and they had not yet found any other usable exits. The two young men would be needlessly slaughtered if they stayed where they were.

From this room, there was no getting past those on their way in.

They were forced to make their stand here.

"Wist…the powder."

It was a long shot, Vance knew, but if those attacking from without were targeting their original point of entry, funneling in there, they might not be near the wall on the northern edge of the building where the captives had been pounding. That sound had been thin and hollow to him, a vibrating echo of a sound that suggested to the tracker the same assessment Liam had previously made.

There had been a door there. The material was less dense, more easily gotten through, if QiangXu's contribution to their cause was worth the time he had taken to make it.

Those outside would not be expecting what Vance had in mind…and with luck at least some of those in the room would be able to get beyond the wire fence to freedom.

☙*❧

"Where are you going at this hour?"

Lowell's bitter voice, strained and gravelly, was the last he expected to hear in the middle of the night, and it stopped Quentin in his tracks before he could open the Fortress doors. He had the appropriate credential keys. Coming and going was his right, a privilege afforded by the position he held, a position granted by the man glowering like a savage thing from the corridor opening through which he emerged. He swayed on his feet, drunk in the depression burying him after the loss of one son and wallowing still in the fury planted within by another, and his sadness at the loss of his friend.

It was a privilege the Laedan had granted, but it was also one he could take away.

"I have bus…" Quentin began, confident he could subdue the man he had spent years learning how to circumvent and manipulate. The right words, the right tone. He could sway Lowell to almost anything.

Lowell stalked closer, his steps more staggering then steady, his mien set. "Bullshit with the business. It's three in the morning."

"Is it?" Quentin blinked in feigned surprise and took a step to the side, out of the man's path, as if towards one of the nearby bench seats. "There was…Nik has been…"

"You don't need a duffle for…"

He set the duffle down, to open it, prove its contents. Or most of them. "He needs clothes; he's a mess…I'm not going to bring him…"

"Stop lying to me!"

The Laedan was too close, and when Quentin, refusing to show fear, picked up the unopened bag again and moved as if still intent on reaching the door, he said calmly, "I swear, Lowell, I'm not…"

"Nik's asleep in his bed…been home for a day at least. You don't care about my boys. You never have."

Stammering, caught off guard by the news of Nik's return which he should have investigated and verified sooner, Quentin shrugged. "Maybe the message is old…it was in my box…of course I…"

Such a message, such news, was not the sort to have been left in the message center, not if it was a message seeking prompt action as any request to bring Nik home would have been. Quentin realized the error of the words as soon as he said them, as soon as Lowell's next hammering words spewed forth.

"You care only about yourself! If you care about them at all, it's about how you can get rid of…"

"There's no need to…"

"No? Then you're going to stop denying that you killed my…"

"I haven't…"

"You killed my best friend!"

The swing of Lowell's fist, inexact and unsteady as he was, caught Quentin off guard and knocked him back against the bench. Only a hand catching the nearest support column kept him from falling.

"I want you out of this…and don't come back…"

The front doors of the Fortress opened, interrupting Lowell's efforts at a full-fledged assault. The glint on the glass and the shuffling sound of leather boots on the tile announcing the arrival of one gate attendant and the bedraggled, beaten-down morose appearance of the stoop-shouldered Protectorate Chief.

"Laedan…"

Ernest's voice cracked. There was no way to say what he had come to say…and no need to, when the swaying, unsteady Laedan turned to face him and caught sight of the two Protectors behind the chief and the gruesome sight they carried on a stretcher between them.

Lowell reached for the hand that dangled over the stretcher's edge, stumbled, and collapsed with a strangled, echoing cry.

QiangXu's powder was hastily spread along the base of the wall as those with dart guns and firearms and explosive orbs faced the lab doors to ward off what would soon be an unavoidable attack. It was a haphazard spread, but one Vance was banking on serving his purpose. When Wist rejoined the group at a run, the mage pulled the fist-sized orb from his pocket and drew out the metal pin.

"Stay back…cover your faces and heads…when I say run…"

The handle was released and the object thrown as hard as he could at the distant northern wall.

He ducked, back turned, moments before the impact came. The blast shook the night, sucked the oxygen from the air to add fuel to the eruption of fire. Dust and rock, metal and plaster, smoke and flame, and the wall separating them from the outside world was no more.

"Go!"

End Part 2

About the Author

With fantasy and sci-fi as her passions, Tamara has written multiple novels to date, including the first four books of the Kestrel Harper Saga, the first installment of The Scarecrow Trials, and the stand-alone novel Suspicion's Gate. Bleed the Earth is the second book in the Blood Wild Chronicles.

When not indulging in her love of words, Tamara relaxes in the company of her pack of Papillions, her horde of cats, and an ever-growing collection of films.

Learn more about Tamara's work at www.agdhani.com

CPSIA information can be obtained
at www.ICGtesting.com
Printed in the USA
LVHW010833200720
661094LV00030B/1045

9 781733 670845